# ANOTHER FORM OF
# DEMOCRACY

# ANOTHER FORM OF
# DEMOCRACY

# MIKE HILL

authorHOUSE®

AuthorHouse™
1663 Liberty Drive
Bloomington, IN 47403
www.authorhouse.com
Phone: 1-800-839-8640

Published by AuthorHouse    08/15/2012

ISBN: 978-1-4678-8402-0 (sc)
ISBN: 978-1-4678-8405-1 (e)

# CHAPTER 1

The ringing of the alarm clock brought him to partial awareness, making him remember the last nightcaps he had shared with Chris, his deputy and friend of 30 years. Well past midnight before he had been able to tumble into bed and, now, five hours later, he was forced to scrape himself together and climb out of it. He was not helped in this by the fact that his wife, Susan, was softly snoring, oblivious to the superhuman efforts her husband was engaged in, in getting out of bed. Finally, with a resigned sigh, Richard Grant, chief constable, pulled himself upright and, slipping into his loafers, wended his way to the bathroom, stopping only to glance through a gap in the curtains at the breaking dawn.

'Rain, bloody rain and its only Monday', he said to himself, walking into the bathroom, and flinching as the electric light struck his drink affected eyes. Glancing into the mirror, he saw his naked reflection. Fifty eight years old, six feet tall with fair hair, which was sleep mussed at the moment, he had piercing blue eyes which were more 'patriotic' after the late evening drink session, the whites being shot through with red.

His body was still in good shape, although his regular gym classes had been allowed to slide a little and he could discern a slight thickening at the waist. Normally clean shaven, he was sporting a twenty four hour stubble and reached into the cabinet for his shaving tackle.

'God, you were beautiful, but where has it all gone? Thank goodness for clothes.' With that earth shattering thought, he stepped into the shower and started to lather his body with one of the many shower gels his wife liked to buy for him. 'I either stink or she must think I'm a poofter,' he thought, not for the first time, looking at the multi coloured bottles filling the shower tray.

Richard, who had been a police officer all his working life, thought back over the last three years. From assistant commissioner in the Metropolitan Police Force he had been promoted chief constable to this large county

1

force, changing from a cramped apartment in Central London to this glorious detached home on the outskirts of the town. Standing in its own grounds, surrounded by lovely gardens tended by his wife and a local jobbing gardner, he had finally started to come to peace with himself, after a life time of very active policing. His wife loved the house, the town, the people and the fact that she was only a relatively short train ride from the London shops. He had waited a long time for this, but now he realised he could afford to look forward to a final few years in command and then retirement.

His son, David, was now working as a research chemist with a well known American drug company and his daughter, Elisabeth, was in her final year at London University. A warm, close and loving family, a job he loved, what else could a man ask for?

Turning the water jet to cold, he gasped as the last of the alcoholic cobwebs were washed away and his genitals tried to escape into the warmth of his upper body. Wrapping himself into the bathrobe he had 'borrowed' during his holiday on the Indian ocean island of Mauritius, he promised himself for the thousandth time that he would retire to that island and return the bathrobe. 'Oh, Flick and Flack and the grapefruit plantation, the coral seas, the fishing the . . . . and oh stop it and come back to reality.' His wife, if she was awake, would chastise him for talking to himself, but he would simply reply that he was obliged to every time he wished to talk to someone intelligent.

Picking up the shaving cream, he started to lather his cheeks.

Five minutes later, dressed in a neat blue suit, silk tie (purchased by his wife on one of her London shopping trips) and highly polished black shoes, he wandered into the kitchen. Taking two slices of wholemeal bread, he dropped them into the toaster and switched on the kettle for the morning tea. 'Good morning, darling' startled him from his reverie and, turning he saw the woman in his life, his wife of 29 years. 'Just tea for me, I'll eat later after my shower' she said.

Looking at his wife, Richard saw a middle aged woman with a very well preserved figure, tousled blonde hair, held in a loose pony tail. Of medium height, she was dressed in a pink housecoat and fluffy slippers, and to Richard she looked absolutely beautiful.

'Love you' said Richard, smiling at his wife.

She replied 'Sure, how much?' arching an eyebrow seductively and pursing her lips.

'More than yesterday, but a lot less than tomorrow,' came the reply

This was a ritual that had stood the test of time as many Police officer's marriages ended in divorce, in the main due to the enormous demands made upon them by the vagaries of their job.

'I don't know when I will be home tonight' Richard said, pushing a piece of toast into his mouth, 'but the TWAT is coming today.'

He picked up his mug of hot tea as his wife replied, 'I do wish you would refrain from the use of such language in the house,' scowling at him ferociously.

Richard with a huge smile on his face said, 'It's the name he goes by and boy does it suit him.'

Thomas William Arthur Thompson, was one of her Majestys' Inspectors of Constabulary, one of the many freemasons who now unfortunately litter the upper ranks of the Police Service. Richard, who had been offered the chance to join with them, was one of the few senior serving policemen who had constantly refused to join, arguing rightly that his oath as a Police officer was to serve everyone, whereas the masons first priority was to serve fellow masons. However, successive Home Secretaries seemed to find them useful for passing on their own whims, often to the detriment of the police service, and Richard had noticed of late that more and more of his good, junior officers, were resigning to work in other fields.

Richard had known Thompson for several years, having met him on some of the various college and Senior Command courses and thoroughly disliked him. He had noticed that he offered no imput whatsoever during practical policing exercises, preferring to state loudly that he was an administrative officer and therefore uninterested in the sharp end of policing. He could have added that owing to the fact that he was never involved in controversy, his fulgurant rise in the service was assured, owing to the fact that the majority of local and national political figures preferred a docile 'yes' man to the 'loose cannons' such as Richard.

'Can't win them all my dear,' he said with a smile, 'but I must admit I find it very frustrating.

Unfortunately he is coming at a time when we are heavily engaged in a National operation against an organised body of criminals.' He picked up his cup and sipped his tea, glancing at the kitchen clock whilst doing so.

Susan, who had been listening intently to every word he said, noticed his glance. She saw that it was nearly time for him to leave for the office, but did not want him going off to work, worrying about the forthcoming inspection. Settling her teacup in its saucer, she smiled and said, 'You could retire and write your memoires. You are nearing sixty years of age and not getting any younger.'

'What would you offer me if I retired now? Unlimited gardening, repainting the house or just going on daily shopping trips with you.'

Susan reached across the table, looking up into her husbands face and as he smiled she took his hand in both of hers. 'I love you and want us to spend years and years together doing things we want to do, when we want to do them. There have been so many times when your job has interfered with our personal lives, holidays ruined, the children unable to enjoy both their parents, unlike their friends, and worse of all, the waiting for you to come home, never knowing the reason for your absence or the danger you could be in.'

'You know I am indestructible' said Richard, laughing. 'Away with you wench and your worrying.'

'Oh Richard, you know that I worry about you and I hate to see you getting depressed and upset because of your job. No one appreciates the things you do and everyone criticises when things go wrong,' replied Susan, pushing back a strand of hair which had fallen across her face.

Richard, knowing she was right, squeezed her hand and looking into her eyes said, 'I would agree with you, but I feel that I can still help to pass on the message. Not everyone, happily is like Thompson, but we are getting fewer. It is necessary that we try to impress on the powers that be to commit themselves to putting more men back on the beat. It is the only way to combat the rising increase in crime and disorder.'

Susan, who had heard his views many times said nothing, knowing that he would continue his speech on the future of the police service as he saw it. 'There must be more men on the streets, on their feet, in direct contact with Joe Public. We used to chat with the old ladies and the shopkeepers and they would give us those little bits of information so important in combatting crime.'

'Times have changed darling, and we must all change with it,' replied Susan.

'Perhaps times have changed, but people have not changed. Ninety per cent of crime and one hundred percent of public disorder is local and could be fought more easily if we had the men on the streets. In my young days we knew who was at it and could act accordingly.

Today, we spend millions on technology and computers and to what avail? Once in a blue moon we can say that modern technology aided this or that arrest, but nothing beats the presence on the streets of a good competent bobby.'

'My eternal optimist' said Susan affectionately. 'You know I love you and will help all I can, but I must admit that I will be over the moon when you announce your retirement.'

Richard selected another piece of toast, debating with himself whether to just butter it or to add a coating of chunky marmalade of which he was particularly fond. After several seconds of reflection, he added the marmalade and said 'The next time I find myself up against the wall or unable to give the help and assistance to my men, I shall put in for retirement straight away'.

Mimicking a violinist, his wife said, 'If I had ten bob for everytime I heard those words, I would be a very rich woman. But don't you worry, rich or poor I won't leave you. You have me until the death.'

'Is that a threat or a promise?' replied Richard, laughing softly to himself.

'Take your pick, I'll stick with your decision,' replied Susan, with a grin.

Their joint laughter was interrupted by the sound of a car horn. 'Your carriage, my liege,' said Susan, dropping him a mock curtsey, whilst referring to his official car with driver which was drawing up on the driveway outside their detached home, a house which had also been supplied by the Police Authority.

'Don't forget' said Richard by ways of a parting shot, 'if I retire we will have to buy our own house.'

'Gladly, gladly kind Sir. Can I start looking today?'

With a smile, Richard kissed his wife's cheek and then walked to the parked Jaguar, thanking his driver who was standing with the rear door open. Once installed on the comfortable rear seat, Richard picked up his complementary copy of the Telegraph and started to read. The driver slipped the car into automatic drive and, with barely a whisper, the car started down the drive on the nine mile journey to Police headquarters.

Normally, Richard enjoyed the drive, but this morning his thoughts were on the forthcoming inspection of his Force. Everything had been done that could be done, or so he hoped, but he knew that the 'august personnage' he would have to deal with later was a real pain and could do irreparable damage if not handled with kid gloves.

Physically, Thompson stood six feet tall, two stones overweight, with his stomach disguised by the expertly tailored uniform he loved to wear. 'Makes him think he's a real mans copper' thought Richard, 'but it would take a lot more than a bespoke uniform to complete the transformation.'

Thinking to himself, he realised that Thompson had served in at least six different Police Forces, moving each time on promotion. Perhaps he was moved on because he was useless, the old adage being that if you cannot make him function to your expectations, then promote him and pass the problem onto someone else. In the case of Thompson, however, he had risen to the dizzying heights of Inspector of Constabulary and was now in a position where he could do irreparable damage to whole Police forces and certainly to individual officers who crossed him.

With this sobering thought, Richard leaned back on the seat and closed his eyes. He started by reflecting on the passage of time, of his lowly beginnings in the North as a cadet and after as a serving bobby, until as Superintendent he had transferred to the Metropolitan Police, taking over in serious crimes. Then had followed a period of secondment to Interpol in Lyon, France, where he had instigated various liaisons throughout the policing world, making several good contacts and friends in Forces all over the globe. Finally, he had the chance to head this County force and he had accepted the challenge and never regretted it—even today he would not change places with anyone.

His reverie was interrupted by his arrival at headquarters and, after thanking his driver, he strode into his office shouting to his secretary, Barbara, to organise coffe and a meeting with his deputies, in that order. Five minutes later, he was seated at the conference table in his office, with his deputy chief and friend of thirty years, Chris Wooler, facing him, he being flanked by the two assistant chief constables.

After the coffee had been served Richard addressed the group. 'Gentlemen, I cannot stress enough the importance of this visit and inspection. The Inspector has a job to do and unfortunately this one loves to nit pick and criticise. He loves to think of himself as one of the boys but be careful. If he can inflict damage on us then he will do, as you are aware that we, in company with the majority of Forces throughout the Country, are faced with a programme of austerity and the likes of our friend are there to enforce it. So, be careful. He loves to push his rank and to browbeat, but I have confidence in you all to put in a good display.'

Chris Wooler, after reflection, then said, 'He has already looked into admin. and I personally showed him round the information room and lock up. As expected, there were not many questions asked and what were asked were easily answered. I have a feeling that he may have saved the best until last, and that will be up to you Sir, to field the questions as you see fit.'

'Thank you, my friend for the vote of confidence. I only hope I can keep my personal feelings under control and my hands to myself,' replied Richard with a smile.

'Any questions?' was met by silence, so Richard continued, 'Chris will be available all day to deal with any problem that may arise. OK by you Chris?'

'No problem, Sir' replied Chris.

With that, Richard said, by means of a parting shot, 'You all know the nickname of our illustrious visitor, but please try to refrain from using it.' With smiles all round, the meeting came to a close, the deputies returning to their other duties.

Once alone, Richard picked up the telephone and dialled his Chief Superintendent of the Criminal Investigation Department. On hearing a growled 'Hello' that signalled the presence of his long serving and even longer suffering chief of detectives, he said 'How did it go this morning Bill?'

'To start with I've been up all night nursemaiding these youngsters and after a a six hour wait in bollock freezing conditions, we managed to get Danny Priest and his brother Billy. They were caught bang to rights unloading some automatic rifles and ammuntion from that break in at the ordnance depot down South; you remember it was about a month ago. They're not saying anything at the moment, but as they were caught in the act, I am not particularly bothered. What does bother me however, is the fact that there is no trace of the five hundred kilos of plastic explosive which went missing at the same time.'

'I can count on you old man' said Richard, 'to solve the problem and I can only say how much I would have liked to have been with you when you nailed the Priests. What about the elder brother? Was he not there?' asked Richard, concerned about loose ends.

'When we revealed ourselves, their car shot off and we assume Eric Priest was driving. The car was found thirty miles away, completely burned out. We're having it examined, but I don't hold out much hope for anything helpful.'

'Well, as I said old man, well done,' replied Richard, very pleased with the news.

'Just you go steady on the old man bit,' said Bill most disrespectfully, 'you are two years older than me. As for wishing you were with us last night, all I can say is that you are a lying bastard as you were undoubtedly lying in bed with that beautiful wife of yours, with a belly full of hot bum, (this latter a reflection on the sleeping position known as 'spoons'). Smiling to himself, Richard replaced the receiver well pleased with the news of the arrests and recovery of the stolen firearms.

He spent a few seconds reflecting on Bill, William Bowler, a brilliant, long serving detective whose reputation would live on long after he had retired. 'He'll be going soon' thought Richard, 'and then what shall we do?' Experienced detectives with thirty years of dedicated service to the Force, he thought, were rarer than rocking horse shit, and Richard knew he would never find another like Bill.

'Could always try to persuade him to do a bit longer', thought Richard, but deep down he knew that Bill would go when he could, and who could blame him? 'Certainly not me' Richard said to himself, thinking back all those years when, as young detectives, full of enthusiasm and get up and go, they had worked all hours, without any overtime payments, in order to finalise an investigaion with an arrest and, hopefully, a conviction.

'Today, no one gives a shit, all overtime is paid so there is not much to be had, and successive Home Secretaries tear their hair out, exhorting chief constables to perform miracles with few resources and fewer inexperienced police officers. There just is no one today who can teach them how to do the job. Anyone can read a book, but investigating officers are born and then trained to be good investigating officers—the problem being the lack of good trainers. On top of which, it won't get any better' was his last sobering thought on the subject.

His reminiscing was interrupted by the telephone. On answering, he heard Barbara say,

'Your visitor is on his way up,' pleasing Richard to know that the jungle telegraph still functioned.

# CHAPTER 2

That same morning, whilst Richard Grant was eating his breakfast, Mansour Ahmad was holding a meeting in a non-descript terraced house in East London. Ahmad, a thirty four year old Pakistani, naturalised English since he was thirteen years of age, was a good looking, well muscled individual. He was a local business man with interests in a restaurant and a London based amusement arcade. He had been elected a local councillor after the last borough elections, and invested himself heavily in the local political scene in South West London.

Apart from these activities, he was also the London and South of England representative of the Al Qaida, terrorist organisation. Within the organisation he was known as 'Zanzibar' and all those present at the meeting that morning, knew him only by his pseudonym.

The house, which was owned by the local council, was sparsely furnished and offered very few creature comforts. Seated in the ground floor sitting room were three Pakistanis, an Afghan, Ahmad's brother, Hassan, and an Englishman named Eric Priest.

The three Pakistanis had been selected by Mansour Ahmad with the help and assistance of his superiors, both in England and Pakistan. Mohamed Ranzon, known as Ali, Mohsin Akhbar known as Mustapha and Adil Khan, nicknamed 'Jimmy' were all from the Peshawar region.

Umar Razad, the Afghan, had been highly recommended by the Taliban as a good and loyal soldier. All were single in the twenty five to thirty age range and all were unknown to the Police in England.

Mansour Ahmad, who was seated across from his brother and Eric Priest, was in a foul mood.

'So what happened,' said Mansour, addressing Eric Priest, 'There should have beeen no problems.'

Eric, looking thoroughly uncomfortable in the presence of men who he knew to be unstable to say the least, glared at Mansour, but made no reply. 'What I can't understand', continued Mansour, 'is the fact that I personally paid off the local bobby and the road traffic police were eating in my restaurant. So, I know that there should have been no local police nearby'.

Eric Priest looked around the group and saw no help in any of the expressionless faces surrounding him. Glaring at Mansour, he said in a belligerent tone, 'I drove to the tip with Danny and there was no one except Billy, who had gone ahead to prepare the cellar in that old house on the tip.'

Mansour continued to look at Eric and said 'Yes, well go on'.

Eric replied, 'Before we started to unload the guns we had a swift look around. There was no one, but no one. I stayed in the car whilst Danny and Billy unloaded the guns. Danny had just taken out the last two rifles and slammed the boot lid shut. 'Two minutes our kid and we're away,' he said, going towards the cellar for the last time. He had just started down the steps of the cellar when all hell broke loose. Fucking coppers everywhere, coming up out of the ground, flashing their flashlights and screaming like animals. I gunned the motor and was gone—I couldn't do nothing for my brothers.'

'What happened to the car?' asked Mansour.

'I drove into the country and burned it. Then I came here to see you.'

No one spoke, each apparently lost in his own thoughts. Hassan Ahmad broke the silence; asking Eric if he had been followed to that mornings rendezvous. 'What do you take me for?' said Eric, 'a beginner? I was doing crime whilst you were still in fucking nappies.'

'How could the police have known?' questioned Mansour. 'There were only us in the know.'

'Are you calling me a grass?' said Eric, 'because if you are I'll do your fucking head in you poxy cunt. We took all the risks, whilst you fuckers just watched television.'

'Then how can you explain the presence of the Police?' said Mansour. 'And how can you explain how you got away if the police were so efficient?'

'I don't know', replied Eric, by now looking thoroughly uncomfortable, 'but I know it wasn't me.'

'I would love to believe you' said Mansour, 'but I just cannot understand how the police knew. Who were these police? Something special or what?'

'I don't know' said Eric, 'the only one I recognised was that fat bastard Bill Bowler from the regional crime squad.' He looked around the table trying to find support from a friendly face, but all he saw was hatred and suspicion. 'How could they have known?' continued Eric, 'and now my brothers are locked up and I'm shitting myself, because they are forced to come knocking on my door. I can't stand going down for a term again, it's too hard at my age.'

Silence fell and Mansour looked at the other members of the group. Each looked him in the eye with the exception of Eric, who looked as though he was about to burst into tears.

'Someone has a big mouth' said Mansour.

Eric shouted, 'Well it's not me, I wouldn't grass on my own brothers. It must be one of you bleeders or why not even you, Zanzibar. Everyone knows you fucking arabs can't be trusted. You wait. I'll go and see Danny 'cos he'll know what to do.'

With that he sat and glared at Mansour who, without dropping his own eyes, made a prearranged hand signal to his brother, Hassan. Quick as a flash, Hassan seized Eric's hair, pulling his head backward and exposing his throat. Before Eric could react, a razor sharp blade was drawn across his throat, severing his vocal cards and carotid artery.

A thick jet of blood shot across the table, hitting Mansour Ahmad full in the chest. The already lifeless body of Eric slid down to the floor.

The silence following this act of violence was broken by Mansour who said, 'Get that piece of shit out of my sight. He won't betray anyone else and certainly not our cause. Allah is great and soon all Europe will know and fear us. 'Mustapha' said Mansour, 'go with Ali and get rid of the body. Ali knows where to go. We'll clean up here and I will contact you each individually this evening. The loss of the guns will set us back, but we still have the explosives and we must show these western decadents that there is only one way, and that is the Islamic way as shown by our Prophet, Mohammed. Allah is great and we are made great for we are his servants and we alone know the pathway to eternal glory.'

Ali and Mustapha left the room and went to a small door leading to the cellar. They descended the stairs and found a roll of heavy industrial plastic and an old, moth eaten carpet. They carried these items back into the room, where the others were already engaged in washing down the blood soaked table and floor. The body of Eric Priest was unmoved and so Ali and Mustapha unrolled the plastic and laid the body in the centre of the plastic sheet. After carefully folding the plastic over the body, they wrapped the plastic covered body in the roll of carpeting. This task completed, Ali said 'Come brother, we will commit our friend to the deep.'

They picked up the carpet wrapped body and carried it out into a rear yard where there was parked an old Ford Transit van. Placing the body in the back of the van, Ali took the wheel and set off for the Thames at Teddington Lock, in the western suburbs of London.

They drove in silence, each lost in his own thoughts with Ali concentrating on his driving.

Traffic was light and on reaching Ferry Road, he parked the van. The two of them carried the carpet wrapped body some two hundred yards to where a small cabin cruiser was moored against a jetty.

'This is Zanzibars' boat' said Ali. 'It needs a coat of paint but the motor works all right.'

Ensuring that they were not observed, they placed the body in the well of the boat. Ali went in to the cabin and after several minutes the motor started. Returning to Mustapha, he cast off from the jetty and steered the boat into mid channel, down river and away from the lock.

'Look in the cabin, Mustapha, there are some heavy weights and chains. We will strip the body, weigh it down and throw it over the side. The water is very deep at this point and also tidal, so if the body doesn't settle it will be carried out to sea.'

'Why strip the body? We could just throw it overboard as it is.'

Ali looked at him and said, 'Zanzibar insists. He says that the clothes could help the body to float back to the surface, or, in the case of the body being found, the clothes could help with identification.'

With the boat idling in the middle of the river, the two terrorists unwrapped and stripped the body, before wrapping it in lengths of weighted chains. Satisfied that the chains were attached securely and, making sure they were not observed, they quickly lifted and dropped the body over the side, where it slowly disappeared from view beneath the murky surface.

Returning to the tiller, Ali swung the boat around and, against the current, steered the boat back to its moorings. The whole operation had taken less then an hour.

Once the boat was securely moored, Ali picked up the bloodstained clothing and placed it in a plastic bag. 'This must be burned, Zanzibars orders.'

'Then give it to me' said Mustapha, 'for there is a big solid fuel boiler in the cellar at home and once committed to the flames, there will be no trace of what happened today.'

'That's good of you' said Ali, 'for I have no such means of disposal. Are you certain that it will cause no problems?'

'Sure I'm sure' said Mustapha, 'just leave it to me.' So saying he picked up the plastic bag and together they returned to the Transit van.

'I'll drop you near to your home, Mustapha, so that you can get rid of those clothes.'

'Anywhere on the Old Kent Road will do, my friend. I have nothing planned for the rest of the day.'

'No problem, but unlike you I have another little job to do so I will drop you where you wish and then I'll be on my way.

# CHAPTER 3

At nine o'clock precisely, the Chief Constables door was thrust open and in strode the Inspector of Constabulary, Mr. Thompson, known colloquially as the 'Twat'. 'One normally stands when I enter a room' bellowed Thompson, glowering at Richard, who remained nonplussed behind his desk.

Looking up, he said to Thompson, 'One normally knocks before opening my door. It is known as acting politely, which is something I hope we can do together this morning.'

Thompson glared at Richard, slamming his briefcase onto Richard's paper strewn desk and shouted, 'Politeness. I am your superior officer and you had better not forget that if you have any hope of receiving a good report after my visit.'

Richard remained very calm, although he was sorely tempted to forgo his own advice to his junior officers, and simply punch Thompson in the face. However he calmly replied, 'Superior never, senior perhaps.'

'Don't split hairs with me. You do not seem to realise the power I hold over you and any future you may have in the Police Service. I am charged by my superiors to come here today and with, or without your help, formulate a report which will outline the needs of your Force in the coming years. We are not playing college games,' this a referral to the Bramshill College where the Senior Police Command courses were held, 'but are about to discuss the needs and necessities of frontline policing in the future.'

Richard smiled to himself, thinking back to the conversation he had had with his wife that morning. Arranging his features into what he hoped was a serious, concerned expression, he replied, 'An excellent opening speech. However, I think I must point out at this stage of the proceedings, that apart from the fact that we are both members of the same Police organisation, the similarities between us ends there. I have known you for several years now and can honestly say that I do not like you any more now than I did the day of our first meeting.' With that, he gathered together the papers which had been disarranged by Thompson's brief case, placed his hands firmly on the desk and waited for Thompsons next remark.

'You want it that way, so be it,'said Thompson, seating himself and arranging his uniform, so that his over extended stomach was mostly concealed by the skilful cut of his jacket. 'At the end of the day you will regret your rashness in upsetting me. I was selected to investigate this Force and investigate it I will. I have already seen several examples of your officers on my way here today, and I can say here and now that I was not inspired, no, not inspired at all.'

Resisting a smile, Richard tried to imagine what could inspire this fat toad, who was preening himself, waiting for a reply. Richard stared at Thompson, who immediately broke eye contact. 'I will not be threatened nor browbeaten by you. You ask your questions and I will answer them to the best of my ability because, in spite of your inferences, the future of this Force is far more important to me, than it will ever be to you.'

Opening his briefcase, Thompson took out a folder marked 'Confidential' and started to read from a sheet of neatly typed questions. 'I see here, that arrests for drug trafficking and other associated drug offences are very few and far between. You must surely be aware of the importance placed upon this subject by Her Majesty's Government and yet you seem to blatantly ignore it. Could we start by asking you why this is?'

'I could start by asking you about your own involvement in drug offences and arrests, but this would be unfair' said Richard, noting that Thompsons already high colour was reaching new proportions, 'as I already know that the answer is none. However, my answer is simple and is drawn from years of experience. Why waste time, effort and money on something for which there is no cure. Have you not drawn any conclusions from the problems of the Prohibition in the States during the thirties? Al Capone and all that. The problem was solved when alcohol was legalised.'

Thompson stared at Richard, astounded. 'Are you seriously suggesting that we legalise drugs? You are mad. Even the Prime Minister is voicing concern over the growing problems that hard drugs are causing and the vast fortunes that are being made by the traffickers. Your comments should raise more than a few eyebrows when my report goes in.'

Richard said nothing, waiting for Thompson to regain his composure. Finally he said, 'What makes drug trafficking so lucrative? The answer is the vast profits that are made by those dealing in the trade. The drugs themselves come from plants, which, if my information is correct are very easy to cultivate and all that is required is the necessary knowledge to transform those plants into the drugs. Should that transformation work be carried out by recognised drug laboratories, then the drugs could be treated in the same manner as any product for public consumption, that is to say taxes for the Government and extra profits for private enterprise.

'Hallucinating' said Thompson, amazed at these revelations. 'Why not just say that our Government Ministers and their contacts are involved in this disgusting trade?'

'You know Thompson, you may never know how close you could be to the truth. I do not know who the real wheelers and dealers are, but I do know it is not only the likes of Al Pacino's 'Scarface'. When you realise the amount of drugs seized in a year throughout the World is a tiny portion of the whole, then you can begin to understand the organisation behind the drug trafficking. Here look at this.'

Richard reached into a drawer and withdrew a small pile of papers, neatly stapled. 'I do not know if you are au fait with the workings of internet, but one can find some very interesting pieces of information.' Glancing at the papers, Thompson noted the title 'CIA and Contras cocaine trafficking in the U.S'. 'Read that' said Richard. 'It is very instructive. When the Americans needed money to finance the Contras in the mid-eighties, the CIA hit on the wonderful idea of transporting drugs in huge quantities into the States, using official CIA transport. They made millions and millions which was used, or so the story goes, to purchase arms for Nicaraguan rebels. When the rebellion ended, did the trafficking end with it? I do not know, but if I was asked to hazard a guess, I would say no. A gift horse such as that must have provided monies for various organisations, individuals and so forth. Throughout the World huge amounts of money are required for the production, transportation and subsequent distribution of the drugs. In addition, official acceptation is required when one considers the huge quantities which are transported. Legalise the drug business and the vast profits would disappear. Put the drugs in the shops with the flour and the sugar at one pound a pound.

I would not use it, but why make it difficult for the poor devils who do need it? There are millions of people who use drugs and if they were legalised it would be a simple matter to introduce legislation relating to the sale, supply and use. Take away the illicit aspect and youngsters would not bother with it.

'You can watch any film on television and you see people sniffing or injecting drugs, whilst the so called traffickers wallow in the lap of luxury. I am convinced that if drugs were treated in the same way as tobacco products, we would be doing ourselves a great service.'

Taking his wallet from his pocket, Richard withdrew a twenty pound note. 'I will bet you this note that if you instigate a search of all diplomatic bags coming into the Country, not forgetting that a transport plane can be classed as a diplomatic bag, that you will find all manner of forbidden goods, including drugs. Are you on?'

'As I stated earlier, I think you must be mad. Perhaps you've been at the magic mushrooms,' smirked Thompson.

Richard contemplated what to say next. It was apparent that Thompson would never be able to imagine the possibilities that perhaps there was some truth in Richard's reasoning.

Richard himself had no proof whatsoever, but he did have that in built sixth sense that told him he was not far from the truth. Throughout the years, he had been amazed by the ingenuity of the criminal mind and he realised that many police officers could never bring themselves to understand that a criminal could, in many instances be far more cunning and intelligent than those charged with arresting them. Admittedly, most criminals were not of this ilk, but that was what, to Richards mind, made the job so interesting. However, whereas he could possibly admire a spectacular or particularly daring crime, he had nothing but revulsion for those who preached to the public about law and order, whilst quietly filling their pockets from the proceeds of crime. Yes, thought Richard, and there are a lot more than one would imagine, but why explain it to Thompson? The poor sod would never understand.

Instead Richard, after a further moments contemplation, said, 'What about white collar crime?

There are many good and honest people who devote their lives to politics and in trying to help improve the quality of life for their constituents. Unfortunately, there are others who are in it for the money or who are corrupted by the lifestyle they find themselves leading. Recently we have seen those politicians who have been falsifying their expenses. That is criminal, although it would appear that only a few will be prosecuted, which, unfortunately happens to be the case in many instances where politicians are caught with their hands in the cookie jar.'

Richard decided that he had said enough on that subject and waited pariently for Thompson's reaction. Slowly, Thompson smiled and said, 'I can only re-iterate what I have said already and that is that in my mind you are certifiable and certainly not fit to run a Police Force.' He then picked up his file and made a pretence of studying it.

Richard leaned back in his chair, stretched, and then, after placing his two hands firmly on the table, he looked across at Thompson and said, 'We have a drug squad, a small one I must admit, and they together with Customs and sometimes alone, make arrests and seize drugs.

Statistically, I could argue that the reasons for the low arrest record is due to the very efficient drugs prevention schemes we run. I am responsible for the policing in this County and my priorities are cutting down crime and public disorder. Many crimes are committed by persons who need money to buy their drugs and if you legalise the drugs, many of those crimes would not be committed. You do not agree with me on this so lets agree to disagree. What shall we discuss next?'

He then sat back in his chair and waited for Thompson to finish his study of the file which he was still holding. Thompson coughed, placed the file on the desk and picked up his pen before saying, 'Am I to believe then, that you have no intention of increasing the size of your drugs squad, as is suggested by National Policy? The drugs problem can be solved, but only by good, committed police officers who are devoted to the task in hand and backed up by equally keen and devoted senior officers.'

Richard simply said, 'If that is your standpoint, then you personally are ruled out of your own synopsis on the drug problem. Let me point out that drugs have been a problem since the mid sixties when it started with amphetamines. Now fifty years on, where are we? The problem has grown so vast that we are spending an ever increasing percentage of our official funding on this and to what avail. We are wasting our time and money so lets legalise and pass on to other things.

'A waste of time is it? This subject is on everyones lips,' ranted Thompson, causing Richard to laugh inwardly as he pictured crowds of people with cocaine powder on their lips and nostrils.

'Now Richard, don't be goaded' he said to himself, and recomposing his features he said simply,

'You have your list. Fire away, but let me tell you that last night we made important inroads into this terrorist business, with the arrest of two men and, more importantly, the recovery of the stolen rifles and ammunition. That should please your masters.'

'How much has it cost to date, this on going terrorist investigation? Weeks of wasted time and money for a simple arrest of two local thieves and a few guns. I have already spoken to the Home Secretary on this subject and he is in full agreement with me.' Giving Richard time to digest his words, Thompson continued, 'We have decided that this so called terrorist investigation will be taken over by the Metropolitan Police who are far more suited to carrying out this sort of work. You speak of terrorists, those two you arrested last night are not even Arabs, let alone terrorists.'

Richard stared at Thompson, unable to believe his ears. Was the man serious? It was certain that Thompson had no information other than of the arrests of the Priest brothers, but what had he said to the Home Secretary? Further more on what basis had he formulated his plans to transfer this investigation? Finally and at a complete loss of what to say he simply said, 'I cannot believe what I am hearing.'

Seeing his discomfiture, Thompson pressed home his advantage 'Not only will the file be passed to the Met., the Home Secretary has expressed the desire that you be informed of his wishes that you concentrate your efforts on police/public relations and that your officers be made aware of his wishes.' Seeing the effect this was having on Richard, Thompson continued, 'Personally, the sooner we have a National Police Force the better. More control from the Government will soon cool the ardour of the cowboys such as you and the two or three others like you.'

Jumping to his feet, Richard placed both hands on the desk top and leaned across the desk, putting his face directly into the face of Thompson, who instinctively moved backwards, fearing for his safety. 'Don't worry' said Richard, 'I am not going to hit you, although the longing to do so is foremost in my mind. However, I will say that you do not understand what is happening out there. This terrorist investigation has taken six months simply to get a reliable source into contact with the terrorist organisation. We do not know all the actors in this group, but the arrests last night are the first tangibles we have to show that we are moving in the right direction.'

'I do not like to repeat myself,' Thompson said arrogantly, 'but if it is here or the Met. who carry out the investigation, I personally can see no difference. A whole team of men and you have taken six months to arrest two locals. The Met. can deal with this easily enough. The Commissioner is a personal friend and an officer of long experience, otherwise he would not be where he is today. We have already spoken, albeit informally, and he has assured me that his men can cope with another little investigation.'

Richard finally seated himself and put his head in his hands. 'I could weep' he thought.

'What has he done? He just cannot grasp what such an investigation entails. How best to approach him,' seeing disaster looming in the not too distant future. 'The Met. are not qualified to deal with this problem. I cannot go into details, but people's lives would be put into extreme danger if any outside interference is brought into the investigation. There shall be no outside interference in this matter whilst I am Chief Constable of this Force.'.

Laughing out loud, Thompson said, 'That can be soon arranged.'

Resisting the urge to splatter Thompson's fat features across the office wall, Richard felt an icy calm come over him.

Taking a deep breath he said, 'You know as well as I that dismissing me is not that easy. I would also add that any attempt to do so or any attempt to interfere in this enquiry would cause me to immediately blow the enquiry sky high. There is no way that I would knowingly endanger any of my men or informants.'

'We will see' replied Thompson, thoroughly enjoying himself now. 'You will be cut down to size and I will enjoy doing the cutting.'

'Where were you when that Brazilian guy was shot dead?' said Richard suddenly.

Thompson replied, 'What's that got to do with this conversation?'

'Everything,' said Richard, 'because I don't want anything like that happening in my Force.

That poor sod who was shot dead had done nothing wrong and yet he is dead. And why?

Because people who have reached dizzying heights in the Police Service make life threatening decisions over a distance whereas such decisions can only be made by persons present. I may be outspoken but I am a Police Officer of many years standing and those officers pursuing that innocent man should have been the only ones to make the decision to shoot. Naturally, the subsequent enquiries revealed that no one was to blame, as has been the case in other instances over the years where senior police officers have cocked up. You could perhaps enlighten me as to how decisions are reached in such cases?'

Richard could not restrain the smallest of smiles from touching his lips as he watched Thompson's face change to a colour which could only be described as puce. Finally, recovering his composure, Thompson said, 'One statement you made interests me and that is 'whilst I am Chief Constable'. A simple telephone call from me and the end of your career will be decided in the five minutes that follow. I was prepared to give you some leeway, but you have decided to buck me, so be it.' Sitting back in his seat, with a very satisfied smile on his face, he stared at Richard, daring him to reply.

Richard sat silently contemplating the figure in front of him. Suddenly, he reached across the desk and picked up Thompson's file of papers. 'Put that down' cried Thompson, 'that is my personal property and you have no right to take it. I can honestly say that I shall enjoy writing my report on you and your Force. Certainly, for you it will be the end of your career and if I have my way you would be fired without pension.' Sitting back in his chair he regarded Richard, waiting for him to at least apologise or beg him to reconsider.

However, Richard ignored him and continued to read the file he had taken. 'You write here', said Richard, 'that substantial savings must be made. That is quite simple. We can sell off the majority of the car fleet, put the garage work out to tender, close and subsequently sell off the very expensive office and garaging space in the City centre and, with the savings we can employ more men, who will spend their time on their feet looking after Joe Public. How about that for starters?'

'What a neanderthal you are, Grant, those ideas went out with the Ark. The modern Police Force will be technologically superior and far better equipped with vehicles than it is at the moment. In this way calls can be dealt with more efficiently and the officers in cars can cover far more ground, so we will require less of them. Officers hiding away in admin. jobs will be shooed outside and we will replace them with civilians at a far lesser cost than a Police Officer. I have prepared the facts and figures for the Home Secretary, who has already cast an eye over them, congratulating me all the way down the line. Yes, Grant, you are looking at the next Chief Inspector of Constabulary and naturally the knighthood will follow. However, you will most likely not be around by then. You, and one or two others on my list will be gone and I with the aid of my assistants will model the Police Force for the next decade.'

Silence followed. Richard looked at the fat, obnoxious creature in front of him. Finally, he said, 'I instructed my staff, just before your arrival, telling them to be courteous to you. However, after that diatribe, I can no longer restrain my natural impulses. For a twat, twat, you are a twat, not only a twat, but a fucking useless twat. You have spent your life crawling up so many arses that you could be considered a sexual deviant. If my memory serves me correctly, and, if it doesn't this should help,' continued Richard, without raising his voice, taking a file from a drawer in his desk, 'your personal file.'

'That is not possible' screeched Thompson; 'those files are confidential.'

'You continue to make the same errors that you made when we first met all those years ago—that we are all pals together. Forget it. I have forgotten more about policing than you will ever know.

If I remember correctly, and I am sure that I do, you have never been a bobby. You have never arrested anyone, you have never given evidence in a Court of law and I am sure that the only angry man capable of ripping you from limb to limb that you have encountered is myself. I would gladly resign now; my wife would be over the moon, but I cannot in all conscience pack up and leave this service, which I have loved and served for over thirty years, leaving its future in the hands of a bunch of pillocks, you included.'

Pausing for breath, he looked across at Thompson, restraining from shuddering when he realised that the future of the Police Service rested in the hands of him and his Masonic mates.

'You have never had to tell a mother that her five year old child has been killed by a bus and is lying in the mortuary, having been autopsied. What would you do? Use your increased technology to send her an E-mail telling her to go and pick up the bits? When you came here this morning I did not want this converation, but you have forced it onto me, and now you shall hear me out.'

Pausing for breath, Richard looked across at Thompson, noting the naked fury in his eyes.

'You made insinuations about the persons arrested last night, saying they were not terrorists. They are in direct contact with the official Al Qaida representative in Great Britain, who, at this moment in time is in the act of robbing ordnance stores and colliery explosive stores up and down the Country, with one idea in mind—that is to create mayhem that will make the eleventh of September seem like a firework display. This information to a cretin like you is of no use because you would not know what to do with it. I am sure that if you were to take charge, your first act would be to tuck your trousers into your socks as you would undoubtedly shit yourself. This enquiry is being dealt with strictly on a 'need to know' basis and you and your Government cohorts do not need to know. Whilst I am in charge here only those who need to know shall know and no one outside the enquiry and I mean noone, will be told anything. Go back to London, tell them that this investigation is necessary and that all funding requested should be forwarded without any questions being asked.'

Spluttering in the face of this ice cold attack, Thompson said, 'You are threatening me, yes, you are fucking threatening me. Do you realise who you are fucking talking too, you fucking ex-chief fucking constable? Never in all my life has anyone dared to speak to me in such a manner.'

Richard smiled grimly. 'Then there is hope for you yet. You lost your temper and uttered a four letter word several times. There is a use for computers and all other aids to policing, but nothing replaces the bobby on the streets. The public must be reassured and the only way to guarantee that is the physical presence of authority. If you cannot see that and you feel confident that your methods will work, then there is little point in continuing this meeting.'

Thompson, who had risen to his feet, fell back into his chair, seething with rage, yet unable to find the right reply. Finally he said in a low threatening tone, 'You, you cunt, I'll have you and all the other fuckers who think like you. It's me the future of the Police Service, you will see.

I promise you that when I return to London I will give a verbatim report to my Minister, which should seal your fate. Then we will see who is the Twat.' With that he seated himself and started to place his papers into his brief case.

'A verbatim report. How will you manage that? You have made no notes and your memory, I am sure, cannot assimilate all that has been driscussed this morning.' Richard stood, looking down at Thompson and continued, 'If it wasn't so pathetic it could even by funny. You could lecture at the Police College on the art of 'twatting'. I am sure that would go down a scream with your pant wetting friends'.

By this time Thompson was nearly overcome with fury. 'I'll remember enough of this conversation to hang you out to dry, you bastard. You'll be lucky to finish with a pension when I'm through with you.'

'My dear chap, control yourself' said Richard smiling sweetly. 'I would not wish your verbatim report not to be a verbatim report. If you could just wait a couple more minutes I will make a verbatim copy.' Turning towards the drinks cabinet and under the angry glare of Thompson, he opened the cabinet. Thompson, thinking he was about to offer him a conciliatory drink, opened his mouth to refuse when Richard calmly said, 'Just hang in there for a couple of ticks. I'll get Barbara to make you a copy.'

Moving slowly sideways, Thompson stared into the drinks cabinet, seeing only soft drinks, bottled water and a still moving tape recorder, which had recorded the conversation held that morning between himself and Richard. Turning off the recorder, Richard said, 'You see twat, I thought of this, but you did not. If I hear anything other than good reports emanating from you and yours in London, I shall retire immediately and hand this tape to the local radio station in order that the public at large can be appraised of the Police Service of tomorrow.

Within twenty four hours the Beeb would have a copy and then everyone would know what a twat you are. Do you understand me?'

Unable to reply, owing to the fact that his vocal chords appeared to be paralysed by fear and/or rage, Thompson turned and stumbled towards the door, clutching his attache case to his chest.

'You've not heard the last of this', was his parting shot, as he reached for the door handle.

Richard replied, 'Careful old boy, to date we have never had an Inspector of Constabulary pass on due to an apopletic fit, but in your case we could always live in hope.'

After seeing the door close behind Thompson, Richard reached into the bottom right hand drawer of his desk and drew out a bottle of his favourite tipple, 'Black Bottle' whisky. Selecting two glasses from his drinks cabinet, he picked up the internal telephone and rang his deputy and friend, Chris.

'Has the twat gone?' was all he said.

Richard replied, 'Yes, I am virtually assured that we passed with flying colours and should expect a good report in several weeks time. So, come on up and have a drink while we discuss our future strategy.'

Two minutes later the two friends chinked their glasses, but instead of discussing strategy, they listened to the tape recording of that mornings battle. 'Another fine mess you got me into, Stanley', chuckled Chris whilst trying to imitate the inimitable Oliver Hardy.

'Drink up, it's nearly lunchtime and I could eat a horse. However, I would imagine the Twat will be off his food for weeks,' said Richard with a grin.

# CHAPTER 4

Susan Grant, the chiefs' wife accompanied by Chris's wife, Millie, were down in London on their weekly shopping jaunt. This had been a regular date on Thursdays for the last few months, both women enjoying the City shops and their leisurely, and usually, expensive lunch somewhere chic in the West End. They had, as usual, taken the train earlier in the day, and, after a coffee to bolster their spirits, had started in on the shops in Bond Street. Whilst looking in the window of Alexander McQueens, Susan noticed an Asian man, reflected in the shop window, who was standing on the other side of the road.

'Strange', she said to Millie, 'I'm sure I've seen that Asian guy on the train this morning. The same age and size and wearing a leather jacket, yes, I'm sure it is the same person. Perhaps he is following us.'

'What Asian man?' asked Millie, 'I can't see anyone'.

'The one over . . . .', Susan started to say before realising that the man had disappeared. 'Must have been mistaken, but I was sure he was following us.'

'Taking your dreams for reality', smiled Millie, taking her friends arm and pulling her towards Oxford Street. 'Times money as my Chris likes to say, although I must confess I do not understand the expression, as he has very little spare time and not a lot of money either.'

Laughing together, the two friends continued their shopping expedition, whilst keeping a wary eye out for wandering arabs.

Ali could not say honestly if the women had seen him or not. It was the third Thursday in a row he had followed them, noting what they did. To him it seemed a futile exercise, but knowing the strange moods and terrible temper of Zanzibar. He noted all relative times, trains, stations and restaurants. Why was not for him to question. He was a good soldier; he had trained hard in the desert regions of Algeria with the best of Al Qaida, and was known as someone who could be trusted. So he followed and noted, but now, not knowing if he had been spotted or not, he decided to go back to the railway station. The two women had taken the express on the other two occasions that he had followed them and he expected they would do likewise today. Knowing he would spot them on their return, he himself returned to the station, settling into the platform buffet to wait.

# CHAPTER 5

The following morning, Ali left his bedsit and set out for a meeting with Zanzibar. He had received telephoned instructions and was now heading towards the underground. The day was fine, but cool, a good day to be alive, thought Ali. His thoughts moved to Zanzibar. What could he want that had prompted a ten o'clock meeting in, of all places, an amusement arcade in Oxford Street? It was less than twenty four hours ago that he had disposed of the body of Eric Priest, a job he had not appreciated, but he had learned that it was healthier to follow Zanzibars instructions than to question them. Eric was now fish food, safely weighted down by a large anchor and chain under the dirty, oily water of the Thames. Ali had balked at the idea of stripping the body before committing it to the deep, but on reflection he realised that Zanzibar made sense, when he said that air could become trapped in the clothes and possibly, at some future date cause the body to float to the surface. He also pointed out that clothes could help identify a corpse. Finally, he was satisfied when Mustapha told him not to worry and that he personally would destroy all traces of the clothing, which was very heavily bloodstained.

'Could be a good man to back me up' thought Ali. 'Should always have someone trustworthy covering your back in action' and he thought that the quietly spoken Mustapha was just such a person. 'Only hope he destroyed the clothes as we certainly don't want any comebacks from them.' With that sobering thought, he descended into the underground, stopping only to buy a coke from one of the many vending machines.

The train rattled into the station and, whilst waiting for the arriving commuters to descend, Ali looked at the image of himself reflected in the dirty carriage window. Twenty eight years old, Ali realised that he was starting to look fatter. When he had returned from the training camp he had been lean, but now, after the easy suburban life and far too much junk food, he had started to look a little plump. Making a mental note to take more exercise, he entered the carriage and, on finding a seat, slowly finished his coke, whilst once against wondering why this meeting and for what purpose.

Thirty minutes later he walked into the arcade and immediately saw Zanzibar who was talking to another Arab, a small, insignificant man of about fifty years of age. This man was dressed in jeans and a dirty white tee shirt as opposed to Zanzibar who was, as usual very well turned out. Seeing Ali, Mansour broke off his conversation and waved to Ali to join them.

'Meet Wahid, a very good friend. Wahid is the engineer here in the arcade, an expert with the electronics and a key member of our team.' The two shook hands, Ali sensing a concealed inner strength in the others shake.

'What happened yesterday?' asked Mansour, 'Did the women stick to plan?'

'Exactly the same as the last two times,' replied Ali, deciding it better not to mention the fact that perhaps he had been spotted following the women.

'Good, good', replied Mansour. 'Now tell me, you can drive can't you?'

'Yes, I have a driving licence since I am eighteen years of age, but I cannot afford a car,' he replied.

'That is of no concern,' replied Mansour. 'I want you to take my car and go to this address.'

He handed a piece of paper to Ali, who noted that the address was in Basingstoke, a good hours drive from London. 'Take your time, you are expected. You will be met by one of my family favourites who will entrust to you a package. Drive carefully, do not attract attention to yourself and when you have the package come back here. I have plans to make and the package is very important to my plans.'

He handed a set of keys to Ali saying, 'It's the Audi parked in the yard at the rear of the arcade. Drive carefully, do not draw attention to yourself, and take care of my car.'

'With Allah beside me I will experience no problems,' replied Ali, smiling confidently.

Going outside, he quickly found the car, a fairly new model A4. Settling himself into the drivers seat, he adjusted the mirrors, the seat position and, after selecting a pop radio station, he switched on the ignition, being immediately rewarded by the sound of a very healthy engine.

Manoeuvring the car skilfully, he drove out of the rear yard and made his way into Oxford Street, thus beginning the run down to Basingstoke.

Soon he was on the M3, keeping well within the speed limit and with a steady eye on the rear view mirror, he settled back, enjoying the drive through the delightful Hampshire country side. He soon saw the sign for junction six, the Basingstoke turnoff, and, having turned, entered the outskirts of the small market town. Glancing down at the piece of paper bearing the address given by Mansour, he noted that he was nearly there. Indicating, he took a left followed almost immediately by a right and found himself in a neat, tree lined street of semi-detached houses.

Pulling to a stop outside number fourteen, he got out of the car, carefully locking the door.

'No need for that', said a voice, 'here there are only honest people and everyone knows that Audi car. Come in, come in, you are most welcome my brother.' Turning, Ali saw an elderly Pakistani gentleman holding open the garden gate leading to number fourteen. Silver haired and neatly dressed in casual clothing, the stranger said, 'Come, you are most welcome to our humble home, as all of Zanzibar's friends are welcome. Come and meet my wife who is in the process of preparing a lovely lunch. A young man such as you has a good appetite, I would imagine.'

Ali followed the elderly man into the house. A small entrance hall gave onto three doors, two open ones indicating a dining room and a small lounge, and, from behind the closed door came the enticing smell of curry, thus indicating the kitchen. The elderly gentlemen led Ali into the lounge and indicated that he be seated. 'Have you known Zanzibar a long time?' Ali asked as by way of conversation.

'All my life, he is my favourite nephew,' was the reply.

Ali looked around the small lounge, noting the recent decorations and admiring the leather, three piece suite. Standing on a low, glass topped coffee table was a carafe of water, glasses and a bowl of potato chips. 'Take a seat' said the elderly gentleman, 'my wife will join us shortly. You must be ready for some refreshment after the long drive from London.' Smiling to himself, Ali took a seat and a glass of ice cold water.

A few minutes later his host was joined by his wife who announced that lunch would be ready in a few minutes time. As Zanzibar had instructed him to take his time, Ali understood that he was expected to stay for lunch.

Five minutes later, the lady of the house informed the two men that lunch was served and led them into the dining room, where Ali noticed the table had been laid for three people. Seating themselves, the men waited whilst the lady of the house carried into the dining room a steaming casserole dish of sweet smelling curry, followed by a large bowl of fluffy white rice.

Before eating, the host recited a short prayer and after said, 'Please, serve yourself, you must be hungry. Young men are always hungry. I know I was, when I was younger."

Ali did not require a second invitation; the food smelled so good after his normal meals of fast food that he set to with a vigour, which pleased his hostess. 'This is so good' he said, helping himself to a second helping of rice and curry and was pleased when he saw the smile on his hosts' face. 'Do you have children? 'asked Ali, by way of conversation.

'I had two wonderful sons', replied the uncle, 'but unfortunately they were both killed whilst serving the cause in Afghanistan. We miss them both terribly, but take comfort from the thought that they are at this moment seated with Mohamed in the Kingdom to which we all hope to obtain entry some day. Not all are allowed to enter, but that is the will of Allah.'

'I agree' said Ali 'and I am touched by the sacrifice that you have been forced to make', at the same time admiring the simple way in which the old man had explained his sad loss.

'We will avenge them,' Ali continued, 'and all those other heroes who have given their lives to the cause of Allah. We shall not stop until all the infidels are dead or have acclaimed Allah as the one true God.' He was pleased to note that his reply appeared to please the elderly couple, who were smiling at each other.

'I will make some mint tea to steel you for the long ride back to London,' said the old lady, getting to her feet.

'And I shall fetch the parcel requested by my favourite nephew' said her husband. 'Come with me and we will place it in the car together.'

The two men left the house and went towards a garden hut sitting at the bottom of a small, but well kept garden. Opening the door to the hut, the old man indicated a carton, wrapped in brown paper, which was placed on a workbench. Ali moved forward to pick upthe carton as the old man cried out, 'Be careful it is heavy.'

'Not to a young fit man', laughed Ali, but was surprised to find that the parcel weighed at least thirty pounds. Making light of the weight, Ali carried the parcel to the parked Audi and, after opening the boot, placed the parcel carefully inside, slamming the lid closed and locking it with the key.

'Come' said the old man, 'we will now drink our mint tea to fortify you for the long drive back to London.'

Returning to the house, the two men found their hostess had already served the sweet, mint tea and was waiting for them with a plate of homemade biscuits. 'What a change from MacDonalds,' thought Ali, who had thoroughly enjoyed his day. 'In what way can I repay you for a wonderful meal and a wonderful time in your company', he said.

'Simply arrive safely in London with the parcel for our nephew,' replied the uncle.

After finishing his tea and accepting a paper bag containing the remainder of the delicious, homemade biscuits, Ali went out to the car, to start the drive back to London.

Twenty minutes later, he turned onto the M3, this time heading back into London, feeling pleased with himself at being trusted to carry out such a task for his leader and at having been chosen to meet and even dine with members of his family. His reverie was broken by the sound of a screaming siren and, looking into the rear view mirror, he saw a Police Jaguar road patrol car, sitting on his tail and saw that he was the centre of their attention. The patrol car overtook him, signalling for him to pull onto the hard shoulder.

'Are you a racing driver,' the police officer asked Ali, his voice heavy with sarcasm 'One hundred and five miles an hour.'

Ali felt sick. What would Zanzibar say?

'Is this your car?' asked the officer.

'No it belongs to a friend.'

'I hope your friend is not a drug trafficker.'

Ali, laughingly replied, 'No, he isn't.'

'This is no laughing matter,' said the officer, 'for all we know this is a go fast car full of drugs. Come on, out you get and open up the boot.'

Ali felt sick as he suddenly realised he had no idea what was in the parcel sitting snugly in the boot of the car. Before he could reply, the police officers colleague, who had remained in the patrol car, called to his partner, who hurrried across to him. After a brief conversation he returned to Ali and said, 'Who does the car belong to.'

Ali replied, 'I told you. A friend.'

'And this friend, does he have a name?' asked the officer.

What could he do? He couldn't run away, he had to somehow try to brazen his way out of this. Whilst his brain raced trying to think of a reply, the police officer was joined by his colleague, who said, 'That's not his brother.'

The colleague said, 'I know, but I am waiting for him to tell me.'

Ali suddenly realised that the officer had checked on the ownership of the car and so said, 'Wait a minute, the car papers are in the glove box'

'So get them' said the police officer.

Ali opened the glove compartment and took out a sheaf of papers relating to a long term rental agreement which he handed to the officer. The officer opened the rental document and, after reading the details, nudged his colleague, who broke into a grin. 'How well do you know the person who normally drives this car?' asked the first officer.

Ali replied, 'Very well, but I suppose now he will not be pleased with me and I have always looked upon him as my friend.'

'Well this is your lucky day as this gentleman is our friend too. If only all you Pakis were as good as him, there would be no racial problems in this Country. All of us traffic lads know him, he's someone you can really count on. So, on your way and keep your speed down.'

'He will be very angry with me when he finds out I have been stopped,' said Ali.

'Don't worry,' replied the officer, 'we won't tell him as we're regular guys. Just keep your speed down.'

With that the officers walked back to their car, climbed in and drove away.

Ali could not believe his good luck. He got back into the Audi and breathed deeply until the trembling in his arms and legs ceased. Then, after drawing in a deep breath, he restarted the car and set off on the remainder of the journey, his speed never exceeding the legal limit.

As he neared his destination, Ali decided that he would make no mention of having been stopped by the Police. There was no point in making waves when everything was going so well.

Each day he felt closer to Zanzibar, a feeling bordering on love, for he, Ali, had no family or friends and very few contacts outside of their little terrorist cell. Zanzibar must trust him and Ali promised himself, that from now on, he could count on him whatever the circumstances and whatever the occasion.

After parking the car, he walked the short distance to the arcade. Now, in the evening the arcade was busy, the bright lights of the machines flashing gaily, whilst people pushed money into the slots, occasionally being rewarded with a tinkling of coins, following a small win.

Making his way to the back of the arcade, Ali saw that Zanzibar was still in the office, in the company of the engineer.

'Good trip? my friend,' asked Mansour, smilingly. 'Did you bring the parcel?'

'I left it in the car boot, I'll go and fetch it.'

'No, no give the keys to Wahid' said Mansour, indicating the engineer, 'he knows what to do with it.' Ali handed the keys to the engineer, who promptly left the arcade. 'By the way' continued Mansour, 'did you by any chance have a glance at the contents of the parcel?'

'Certainly not,' replied Ali. 'You told me to fetch the parcel not interest myself in its contents.'

Mansour put his arm around Ali's shoulders, drawing him a little closer. Ali could smell the warm, masculine odour emanating from Mansour, an odour intermingled with an expensive body lotion. Never, in all his short life, could Ali remember anyone showing him such affection. Feeling embarassed, Ali made to pull away from the embrace, but Mansour pulled him closer, saying, 'Good, you are a good and trusted friend and with each passing day I feel I can trust you a little more. Soon, there will be much to do as Allah is breathing down my neck, wanting his important work done. You are amongst the few I feel I can really trust. Now, how are you fixed for cash, as you must be hungry? I myself have eaten and knowing the road from Basingstoke there is not much chance of food.'

'It is true,' replied Ali, 'that I do not have much money, but I did eat a wonderful meal with your uncle and his wife. They are such nice people, you are very fortunate to have such a nice family.'

'You will see,' Mansour replied with a smile, 'my family will be your family in time. Our little group is already part of my greater family and those who show true allegiance to the cause will soon become part of my inner family, part of my intimate circle.'

Ali could not believe his ears at these words. He, through circumstances that had forced him to be a 'loner' nearly all his lfe was suddenly about to become a part of an intimate group, a family member. He felt like crying with pleasure and, Mansour, sensing his discomfort gave him a final squeeze and, reaching into his pocket, took out his wallet. He counted out two hundred and fifty pounds. 'Here is some spending money.'

Taking the money, almost with reverence, Ali placed it carefully into his wallet.

'I have grown so used to the fast food here that my stomach is perhaps craving for a nice steak. Do you have any recommendations?'

Laughing heartily, Mansour flung his arm around Ali's shoulders and pulled him towards the front of the arcade, where there was sited a London tourist board information stand.

Mansour quickly found a booklet entitled 'Where to eat at reasonable rates in London' and handed this booklet to Ali.

'You will find something satisfactory I am sure, as this booklet gives you the best restaurants in Central London. I myself have other duties to attend to or I would show you round myself. Now go and enjoy yourself,' said Mansour, already heading back into the arcade.

Feeling proud and wanted after this short conversation and the unexpected intimacy shown to him by Mansour, Ali smiled his thanks, leaving the arcade a new and dedicated believer in Mansour. 'Truly a great person', he said to himself, 'someone I could die for.'

# CHAPTER 6

Saturday morning was the one morning when Richard did not go into the office, unless he was requested to do so. After visiting the bathroom, he noticed that dawn was only just breaking and decided to return to bed. Climbing back into the still warm spot he had earlier vacated, he pulled the bed covers over his shoulders and turned towards his still sleeping wife.

She was sleeping, lying on her right side, with one arm flung over her head and her legs drawn up towards her chest. Her hair was spread around the pillow and Richard snuggled up behind her. Like him she wore no night clothes and as he snuggled a little bit closer, he realised he had been thinking about such an occasion as this, since Bill Bowler had made his comment about a 'belly full of hot bum,' during their last telephone conversation.

He could feel the heat emanting from her body and he allowed his mind and imagination free range. He snuggled even closer and felt his penis start to harden. His left arm crept around his wifes waist and, reaching up, he started to fondle her breast. He felt the nipple start to rise between his fingers and he slowly increased the pressure on this rapidly expanding object.

Moving even closer, he let his hand drop from her breast and let it slowly meander down her belly until his fingertips felt the silky hairs of her pubis. Evidently, she was still asleep, so Richard continued walking his fingers into the warm crevice between her thighs and gently started to massage her clitoris. His erection was now at its zenith and, using his free hand he pushed his erect organ downwards, until its tip was resting in the gap revealed by the position of her bent legs.

He continued massaging her clitoris and pushing gently with his erect penis, when, suddenly his wife started slowly gyrating her hips and a soft moan escaped her lips. Richard could not believe his good luck and continued with his administrations, his wife's actions now becoming somewhat frenzied.

Susan's thighs started to open and Richard worked his hand faster, when, suddenly and without any warning whatsoever, his wife turned, throwing him onto his back. In the same movement, his wife rose above him, straddled him and, with her hand guided his throbbing sex into her warm, most secret place. Then, still with her eyes closed she went to work, grinding down on him with her gyrating hips.

Richard looked up at his wife. She had borne two children, but was still very fit, keeping her body in trim with weekly visits to the gymnasium. She had retained her beauty and, looking up at her he realised just how much he loved her and how much she meant to him. Now, she was breathing faster and faster and he reached up and took hold of her buttocks and started to thrust in time with her gyrating. He could feel the inner muscles of her vagina start to squeeze his penis and he knew he could not control himself much longer. Susan bent at the waist, allowing her breasts to brush his face and he immediately started to suck one of her nipples. 'Don't you dare come you bastard' she panted, and as Richard tried to control himself, she started a juddering motion, completely uncontrolled and Richard, unable to control himself any longer, felt himself come in several long spurts. They continued for several seconds longer then Susan fell forward onto him. He could feel her rapidly beating heart trying to keep pace with his own, and then burst into hearty laughter when his wife said, 'That'll teach you to spoil my beauty sleep.' Wrapping his arms around her he kissed her long and lovingly on her open mouth.

Finally he released her and together they made their way to the bathroom.

Standing together in front of the mirror, Richard said, 'When you come to think of it there's over a hundred years of experience that went into that little performance,' and his wife replied, 'Yes, but are you capable of a repeat in a few minutes?'

'Let's take a shower and we'll see,' said Richard dubilously.

Half an hour later, having showered and dressed, they were seated in the dining room eating hot toast and butter. 'What shall we do today,' asked Susan. 'I need to do a bit of shopping.' 'Fine by me' replied Richard. 'We'll go up to the shops and afterwards I shall take you to the new curry place in Deepsend. After all the exercise this morning we will need to fuel you up.'

'Yes I agree with you' said Susan with a smile. 'It was such a surprise to be woken in such a fashion. The wonderful thing is that after all these years of marriage we can still put on a performance like that.'

'Must be all the practice—oops—, what have I said,' said Richard jokingly.

He was silenced when his wife said 'Just you try it my boyo, and I'll break that truncheon in two'.

'You have a cruel, sadistic streak in you, Mrs. Grant,' said Richard.

However he was pleased when she said, 'Perhaps, but I love you. Now, fetch the car round and I'll get my coat.'

Five minutes later they were sitting in Richards pride and joy, a 1993 model Mercedes 320SL, a gleaming black cabriolet with a powerful six cylinder engine, (the cylinders on line and not 'V' as on the later models) as Richard loved to point out. Owing to the fine sunny day, Richard had lowered the canvas top and, with the wind break net in place behind their heads, they enjoyed the warm weather without the gusting air.

Arriving at the shops, Richard soon found a parking place and, whilst Susan was taking the shopping bags from the boot, Richard pressed on the electric roof button, never failing to be impressed at the swiftness and quietness as the roof rose from its storage place to settle with a solid 'thunk' in the roof support holes. Holding the button, he waited until the side windows had raised themselves, and when in place, released the button and climbed out of the car. He placed the key in the doorlock and, on turning it listened to the different exterior and interior locks clicking into place. 'Nearly twenty years old and like new. The Germans show us what can be done when you leave things alone and not nationalise them as we did here.' thought Richard. Taking a shopping caddy he followed his wife into the local supermarket.

An hour and a half later, with the shopping safely stored in the boot of the car, Richard drew to a halt on the small car park at the side of the New Delhi restaurant. They found themselves seated by the middle aged owner of the restaurant, at a nice corner table, away from the kitchen and the main entrance, but with a commanding view through the large, lace curtained window. Two glasses of smooth port wine in the guise of an aperitif were served, and, after studying the extensive menu, both decided on the menu of the day, the only other decision being the strength of the curry.

At the end of the exceptionally fine meal they ordered coffee and as they were waiting for the coffee to arrive, Susan suddenly grabbed hold of her husbands arm. 'What is it darling? asked Richard, startled by the actions of his wife, 'You are so pale.'

'Shush, it's that man entering the restaurant,' said Susan in way of explanation.

Looking towards the door, Richard saw a young Asian man, casually yet smartly dressed, enter the restaurant and approach the owner. 'Hello Mr. Khan, is Jimmy here?, asked the young man.

'No, Ali, he's gone down into the town. Can I give him a message?' enquired Mr. Khan.

'It's all right.' I'll probably see him later,' replied Ali with a smile with that, he left the restaurant and walked away along the street.

'You looked as though you had seen a ghost. What is it all about?, asked Richard, somewhat bemused by his wife's obvious discomfiture.

Still clinging to her husband's arm, Susan replied, 'When I went down to London with Millie last week, I saw that man on the train. Later, I saw him again or at least I saw his reflection in a shop window and I was sure he was following us. Millie tut-tutted this saying I was imagining things and, to be truthful, when I looked again he had disappeared.'

Richard knew his wife to be a sensible person and not one to be easily upset. 'Simple coincidence, old girl, you heard him ask for the owners son,' said Richard, in the hope of assuaging his wife's fears.

'Probably so, but it seemed so strange to me' replied Susan.

At that moment, the owner approached their table to ascertain if they required his services further. Richard thanked him and requested the bill, which when presented, he found to be extremely reasonable.

Handing his credit card over to the owner in payment, Richard asked, 'That young chap who just came in. Do you know him?'

'Why do you ask?' was the reply.

'My wife travels to London quite often and she is certain that she has seen him on the train,' replied Richard.

'That's hardly surprising' said Mr. Khan, 'he and my son are both studying in London and they always travel by train.'

Laughing, Richard turned to his wife and said, 'There, the mystery is solved. Your admirer is just another commuter.'

Mr. Khan then said, 'He is a good boy Ali. His family lived in the same village as my family in Pakistan. His father was a militant, always demonstrating in order to try to obtain a better standard of life for the village, which did not go well with the government. One day, he disappeared and has never been since. When we decided to emigrate to England, his wife asked if Ali could come with us. Surprisingly, the government allowed him the necessary visas to come to England to study. He lives on his own, but maintains a good contact with us. He is a really nice boy.'

'Thank you for the explanation and also for the meal which was excellent,'said Richard. 'We will undoubtedly visit you again in the not too distant future.'

With that they left the restaurant to start the short drive home.

# CHAPTER 7

The following Monday morning found Richard in his office, trying to catch up on the ever increasing pile of paperwork. A knock on the door aroused him and he was pleased, but surprised to see his Chief detective enter and approach his desk. 'Good morning, Sir, do you have a minute. I have something to discusss.'

Whilst Bill was seating himself, Richard started thinking it was at least twenty five plus years that he and Bill had been colleagues and now good friends. Both were excellent police officers and Bill a very competent detective. 'What's on your mind?' asked Richard. 'I can give you more men but not more money.'

'No nothing so mundane' said Bill. 'I would like to speak to you about the Priest brothers and those guns. I am very worried that we can find no trace of the explosives nor of Eric Priest.'

'What about your informant? asked Richard 'Can't he help?'

'You know, Sir, that we cannot contact him, we have to wait for him to contact us.

He's playing a very dangerous game and so we have to play by his rules. It is very frustrating as the Priests' will be up before the beak in a couple of days and I would like some further information to make sure we keep those bastards locked up. If they were to get bail . . . .'

'I know' said Richard, looking hard at his friend and colleague,'but it's the price we pay for progress. My wife said only this morning that no one cares a shit these days, but unfortunately, we do. Joe Public only bothers when his personal bubble is threatened, and, like everyone else, expects us to fix it. How many times have we put our careers on the line for the sake of Justice? Lucky that the Twat does not know otherwise thee and me would be out on our uppers;'

Laughing, Bill replied, 'There but for the grace of God . . . .'

'Bill, Bill what are you saying? Have you told untruths in order that some poor, over protected, legally aided criminal got his just desserts. I am ashamed of you,' said Richard, 'what a terrible thing to do thus keeping our prisons full.'

'You do not understand,' replied Bill, laughing, 'the last time was that Green bloke who burst into tears when I told him he was staying locked up until his Court appearance.' 'But you said I could have bail, Mr. Bowler if I admitted it,' replied Green. 'Yes, but what you did not understand old love,' said I, 'was that we were playing a game called liars and you lost.' Both men burst into laughter.

'That reminds me of a true story which took place here a few months ago,' said Richard. 'I was sitting in the lock up court . . . .'

'You were what?' asked Bill.' What on earth were you doing in such a place?'

'All be it' replied Richard smiling, 'that is has nothing to do with you how I spend my time, but I was there for someone who was going to be making allegations of something or other. Also, it has nothing to do with my story, so shut up and listen.'

'Yes Sir' said Bill, throwing a mock salute, 'I am all ears.'

'Well it was a case of drunk and disorderly and the arresting officer, a dog handler, was giving evidence. The prosecutor asked what was said and the officer replied that he had made use of an obscene expression, and attempted to hand a piece of paper to the magistrates. 'What is that officer?' asked the beak and he replied 'The obscene expression which the defendant used.' 'What was the expression?' repeated the beak and the officer said, 'It's written on the piece of paper.' 'Come, come officer, we are all men of the world, what did he say?'

'He said, fuck off you fat fucking cunt.' replied the dog handler. 'Thankyou officer, and then what happened? asked the beak. Quick as a flash the dog handler replied 'He kicked my fucking dog!'

Bill burst into laughter, joined by Richard and with tears rolling down their cheeks both men got to their feet and left, heading towards the canteen.

# CHAPTER 8

It was after eight in the evening and Bill Bowler was still in his office when the private phone on his desk rang. On answering, a voice said 'Can we meet?'

Recognising the voice Bill replied, 'Certainly, where and when?'

'Usual place in half an hour.'

'I'll be there', replied Bill, replacing the telephone handset and getting to his feet.

Twenty five minutes later he was seated in the snug of the 'Dog and Pheasant' behind a pint of beer, wondering what news awaited him. The pub was about half full, typical for a mid week in the village, and Bill soon found himself a small table where he could watch the door into the bar. Five minutes later, in strolled a well dressed Asian, of about thirty years of age, medium build and who, on being asked by the licensee what he would like to drink, selected a coca cola. Taking his drink, he went to the far end of the bar, where he studied various photographs of local activities, which were displayed on the walls of the room.

Bill studied the Asian, noting how he seemed to blend easily into the surroundings, whereas he himself always thought he was instantly recognised as Police. Suddenly, the Asian finished his glass and without a word or a backward glance, he left the bar. Bill finished his pint, noting that no one had taken any sort of interest in the Asian and, after saying goodnight to the landlord, he also left the pub.

After starting his car he left the car park and drove away out of the village in the direction of the main road to London. However, after two miles he signalled his intention of turning into a well set back layby, which he did, parking his car behind a nondescript Ford saloon.

'Good to see you, my friend,' said a voice, and the Asian man, who Bill had last seen leaving the pub, materialised by his side.

'And you too, my friend,' replied Bill, getting out of his car and stretching, in the hope of ironing out the kinks in his back which he believed to be a proof of old age creeping up on him. 'Shall we walk?' said Bill, 'it's a nice evening and I've been cooped up too long in my office.'

'Certainly', replied the Asian, and, after locking their cars, they strolled along a pathway leading to a small clearing and picnic area.

'This is what I love about your Country,' said the Asian,' the quiet and the calm of an evening in the countryside.'

'Yes, it does help to try to forget what we have to do day in and day out,' replied Bill and then, changing the subject said, 'What have you got for me?'

'Shall we sit?' said the Asian, indicating the picnic tables and both he and Bill took a seat, facing each other.

The Asian, Mohsin Akbar, a Pakistani army captain and expert on infiltration within the various terrorist groups, also known as Mustapha, waited for Bill to open the conversation. 'I'm very worried' said Bill. 'We can find no trace of the explosives albeit that the guns have been identified as coming from that depot break in, and the Priest brothers are saying nothing. On top of that we can find no trace of the elder Priest brother.'

A silence fell, then Mohsin said, 'The explosives, I have no knowledge of their whereabouts. This organisation, of which I am certain this chappie Zanzibar is one of the leaders, is very compartmentalised and everything is done on a very tight need to know basis. However, as to your Eric Priest, he is feeding the fishes in the Thames since yesterday midday.'

'What,' cried Bill, 'are you certain? Do you know where?' Mohsin calmly and quietly related the facts leading to the death of Priest and his subsequent 'burial' and, on completion, Bill said, 'Well he's no loss to mankind, but we were hoping to find him and sweat him to try to get the information leading to these explosives. Do you think you could do anything which could accelerate the investigation as we are becoming increasingly nervous not knowing where the explosives are and what they are are going to be used for?'

'I'm sorry,' said Mohsin, 'but I'm playing a very dangerous game with this group. The man Zanzibar, is like an electric livewire and he appears to trust no one. When we meet, which is very infrequently, I am contacted by another member of the group. He is younger than I, but seems experienced in the ways of the terrorists. I would not be surprised if he had not trained in the desert region of Algeria as he is confident in his actions and in his dealings within the group. He was with me when Priest was committed to the deep.'

'We must find something somewhere and soon, otherwise we are going to be on the receiving end of a very nasty incident. My chief is very concerned as am I, but I must confess at the moment that I am clueless as to their intentions. All our usual contacts have been seen and nothing, absolutely nothing.' declared Bill, despondently, looking at Mohsin in the hope of seeing some salvation.

'What about the Priests you have in custody? Can you get nowhere there?'

'Wouldn't give you the time of day, and there's absolutely no point in seeing them again, it's just a complete waste of time.'

'They do not know their brother is fishfood do they. That may give them a change of mind.'

Bill smiled grimly. 'They would laugh in my face. They would just take it to be a ruse in order to get them to talk.'

'It is true that in our Country we have a different policy as regards questioning prisoners,' said Mohsin. 'We are less bothered about the niceties of the law and the presumption of innocence, and far more interested in arriving at the truth in the minimum of time. There has been far too much loss of life with these bastards who use a sort of religion as an excuse for their deeds. The truth is that the majority are fanatics and will stop at nothing in order to try to impose their will. The most dangerous aspects are the young, impressionable people, who are quickly taught to believe in eternal life and will willingly go to their deaths as a walking bomb. When everything is considered, they kill as many of their own as they do other civilians, but the reality is that the leaders, in spite of their rhetoric, are mainly in the movement for personal advancement and gain.'

'I agree with everything you say, but that does not help me with the existing problem. Unfortunately, in this Country, the do-gooders and meddlers who are only too ready to scream out against police brutality and the non respect of prisoners rights, are also the ones to shout their criticisms of the police when a bomb goes off with the usual loss of life and horrendous injuries. I can retire in a few months and I think I will.'

'Don't blame you at all, but I think it may be a good idea for you to once again see the Priests. Who knows, perhaps this time they may be persuaded to talk.'

'Little chance of that,' replied Bill, 'but I will give it some thought.'

They both got to their feet and wended their way back to their respective cars. As Bill was opening the door, Mohsin called to him, 'Here, take this. It may help the Priests to open up.' With that he handed a plastice wrapped parcel to Bill and with a laconic wave of his hand, started the engine of his car and drove away. Bill placed the parcel on the passenger seat of his car and drove away, having decided that come what may, he was going to enjoy a decent drink and a meal and try to forget the job for a while.

# CHAPTER 9

That same evening, Ali was sitting in his sparsely furnished bed sit, reading the Koran. Since his stay at the training camp he had tried to read and memorise passages each day, as his Imman had strongly recommended that for the body to be strong it was necessary that the will and resolve was also strong. In common with many of the young men wanting to become soldiers of Allah, Ali was not a brilliant, well educated person, but had, through sheer grit, earned himself a college course, which he attended as often as possible.

His one problem was one of loneliness, as Zanzibar had stressed that it was very dangerous to try to live a normal life, as at any moment he could be called away for an urgent operation and, he could endanger himself and others by being indiscreet in a conversation. The ringing of his telephone aroused him from his reverie and, on answering was surprised to hear the voice of Zanzibar.

'Oh my brother,' said Zanzibar, 'am I disturbing you?'

'No, no not at all' replied Ali nervously, wondering what Zanzibar could want from him at this time of the evening.

'I was feeling hungry,' said Zanzibar, 'and I do not like to dine alone. Would you care to join me?'

Ali could not believe his ears. From feeling low to a high peak of excitement in a split second was something that Ali had never before experienced.

An invitation from the one person he admired and, yes even adored, if the truth was known, filled him with an overwhelming joy. 'Yes, yes please,' stammered Ali, feeling inadequate on the telephone, 'but when and where.'

'Be at the tube station at the end of your road in thirty minutes,' replied Zanaibar, 'and I will be waiting. You know the car.' With that he hung up, leaving Ali staring at the telephone in his hand. An invitation to dine with his hero and in thirty minutes. Struggling to his feet he hurtled into the small shower stall and started to scrub his body.

Twenty five minutes later, dressed in his one suit and well polished shoes, he was standing outside the tube station, nervously dancing from one foot to the other. He saw the Audi arrive, execute a smart 'U' turn and pull up beside him. 'Jump in, we're off to enjoy the delights of the big City' said Zanzibar and with that Ali settled into the passenger seat and, after securing his seat belt, settled back to enjoy the drive.

Their first stop was the amusement arcade where Mansour left Ali in the car whilst he absented himself, returning a few minutes later with a big smile on his face. Tapping his breast pocket he said,'They're having a good night in there so I decided they could pay for dinner.' 'Do you own the arcade?'asked Ali and Mansour, with a sudden change of tone and demeanour said, 'When I want you to know something I will tell you, but until then no questions. What is it they say here?' he said with a smile, 'ask no questions and hear no lies.' Ali made a mental note to never again question Zanzibar on his life style and activities.

Pulling into the kerb on a side street in Soho, Mansour said, 'Come, the night is young, let's have fun.' With that they entered a dimly lit bar with several tables set for dinner, a few diners already being seated. The first thing that Ali noticed was that all the customers were male.

'That table there' said Mansour, indicating a table for two in a corner furthest from the bar, 'should do us admirably.' With that they seated themselves and were immediately approached by a waiter who handed them two large menu cards. 'A small aperitif, perhaps, gentlemen' asked the waiter and Mansour replied, 'We do not drink alcohol but some iced water would be fine.'

The waiter left them to study their menus and Mansour asked, 'Is there anything that particularly appeals to you, apart from myself that is,' and Ali looked at him in surprise at this question.

'Don't be afraid to reply,' said Mansour, smiling, for Ali seemed unsure of himself, 'as I told you before I like you and think we could become friends.'

He laid his right hand on Ali's left hand and gazed into his eyes and Ali did not know what to say or how to react, the emotions coursing through his body at these soft words and the what, yes, caress that he had received from Mansour.

'It was just so unexpected' he replied, 'unexpected but beautiful at the same time.'

'Would you like me to order for us both as I know this establishment intimately and I am sure our tastes in food as in other things are similar. Am I not right?' he asked amusingly.

'Yes, I feel as though I have known you for years and not simply the few months that I have been in London,' replied Ali with a smile.

Soft dance music was being played and Ali noticed that two or three couples were dancing provocatively on the minute dance floor. It was the first time he had seen men dancing together in such a fashion and, strangely enough it excited him. His thoughts were disturbed by the return of the waiter, who left a large carafe of iced water in the centre of the table and then started to write down their order dictated by Mansour.

When the waiter had withdrawn, Mansour poured two glasses of iced water and toasted Ali saying, 'To the start of a wonderful friendship.'

Ali who had become strangely tongue tied managed to stammer 'I hope so, I truly hope so.'

'Would you care to dance,' asked Mansour, rising to his feet whilst offering his hand.

'Yes, why not. I have never danced like that . . . .

'Come' interrupted Mansour, 'I will instruct you in the finer arts of dancing.' With that the two men joined the other couples on the dance floor.

Mansour placed his arms around Ali, who did likewise and the two started to circle slowly. Ali could feel the hard muscled body of Mansour and smelled the manly smell of his body mixed with a light perfume which he found particularly enticing. He then felt Mansour softly massaging his back with both his hands and Ali, to his embarrassment, found himself becoming excited to the extent that he felt the beginning of an erection. 'I knew I had made the right choice,' whispered Mansour who had lowered his head in order to whisper in Ali's ear, and at the same time gave him the smallest of kisses on his cheek.

The waiter once again appeared carrying their order, and the two men returned to their table. Ali was still trying to work out whether he had dreamed the last few minutes or whether they had really happened. 'Come my friend, let's eat for who knows we may need the strength later.' They both started to eat, commenting on the excellence of the cuisine.

At the end of the meal, Mansour said, 'Now that we have eaten and I know that you enjoy dancing, we will go to another address I know where we can relax and get to know each other a lot better.' Signalling to the waiter who hurried across with the bill, Mansour produced a wad of banknotes from his coat pocket, peeling off enough to settle the bill and leave a handsome tip. Wishing the waiter goodnight, the two men left the restaurant and returned to their car. 'You will enjoy this club, my friend,' said Mansour, 'it is specially for young men to enjoy themselves in total comfort and security.' With that he started the car and drove away.

A few minutes later, quite close to Mayfair, he stopped in a quiet side street and with Ali, left the car and approached a well lighted door in a large, detached house. After ringing the bell, they were permitted to enter by a very good looking, well muscled young man, dressed in slacks and a skin hugging tee shirt. Mansour handed him a card, similar to a credit card, which the young man placed in a video scanner set upon a low table.

Noting the details, he smiled, saying 'Welcome friends, the night is young and the company is a mix of young and not so young. Enjoy yourselves and do not forget, anything you may require is usually obtainable.'

Mansour and Ali walked along the thickly carpeted corridor, entering a large room by way of a curtained covered doorway. The room was luxuriously furnished with large canapes, low tables, on which were set incense burners, creating a cosy if somewhat stuffy atmosphere, the walls being covered in what could only be described as erotic paintings of muscular men involved in either physical work or sex. There were about twenty men in the room, most of them sitting although several were slowly moving on the dance floor. A large bar filled the wall the furthest from the entrance, the bar man in appearance and dress seeming to be the twin of the one who had earlier granted entry to Mansour and Ali.

After looking round the room, Mansour touched Ali's shoulder, indicating a vacant table with a half circle canape, thick cushioned, with other cushions scattered on the floor. 'The canape or the floor? Which would you prefer?'

Ali, who had never even imagined that such a place could exist, simply said 'You choose, either is all right by me.'

"Then we shall take the canape,' replied Mansour, sinking into the deep cushions, being joined immediately by Ali.

'What shall we drink?' 'Here they make extremely nice, non-alcoholic cocktails. Would you like to try one?'

'Please, I would like that very much,' whereupon Mansour raised himself and went to the bar, returning a short time later with two gaudily coloured drinks in expensive tulip shaped glasses.

Handing one to Ali, Mansour said, 'To us,' and as they chinked glasses, Mansour held out his free hand and said, 'Here take this.'

Ali looked down into the outstretched hand and saw a small white pill nestled there. 'What is it?' asked Ali, somewhat alarmed.

Mansour, seeing the look of concern on his face said, 'Don't worry, it will help you to relax.'

Nervously, Ali took the pill and before he could put it into his mouth, Mansour had produced another one, saying, 'Look I shall take one also, then we can both be relaxed.' Thus saying, the two men swallowed the 'Ecstasy' tablets and tasted their drinks, washing down the tablets. Then settling back into the deep cushions, they studied the other customers, waiting for the pills to take effect.

# CHAPTER 10

That same evening, Richard was sitting at home, trying to get interested in a new book and half watching the television which was showing some old movie with Fred Astaire, his wife being particularly fond of that style of film. Suddenly, the telephone shrilled. Looking at the clock, Richard muttered, 'Who can that be at this hour?' and went to answer the telephone, saying 'Hello, Richard Grant here' in guise of a welcome to the unknown caller.

'Firstly, let me apologise for ringing so late in the evening,' said a cultured, obviously well educated voice, 'I am Lord Mervyn Hamilton and I would like to see you at your earliest convenience.' Lord Hamilton, the old 'hanging' judge, the scourge of the criminal class, who, in the days of the Assize Courts could silence counsel or witnesses, simply with a withering look. What on earth could he want?

'My Lord', replied Richard, indicating to his wife to turn down the sound of the television, 'this is most unexpected.'

'Firstly, let me apologise to your dear wife for interfering with the film, yes, we are watching the same programme, but I have something very important to discuss with you and the sooner the better.'

'What on earth could you have to discuss with me?' questioned Richard, completely at a loss as to why such an exalted person should wish to discuss anything with him.

'Not on the telephone, dear chap. When can you be next in London?'

'Normally, I will be there on Thursday,' replied Richard, 'as I have a meeting planned, but nothing that cannot be rearranged.'

'In that case' replied Lord Hamilton, 'can we say eleven thirty in my chambers? You do remember where they are, don't you?'

Laughing, Richard replied, 'I would hardly forget that address, myLord.'

'Then till Thursday' came the reply, followed by a click as the communication was cut.

'Who on earth was that?' asked Susan as Richard replaced the telephone.

'Lord Mervyn Hamilton himself,' replied Richard, completely bemused.

'What did he want?'

'He would not say over the telephone, but he wants to see me Thursday.'

'Oh goodie, then you can take me and Millie with you, it will save us the train fare.'

'Why not?' said Richard, his mind racing, 'but what can he want with me?' With that he seated himself and picked up his book and as his wife readjusted the sound on the television, he knew that he would not read another word, his mind already wandering off in other directions.

# CHAPTER 11

The following morning found Richard and his wife seated at the breakfast table. 'What are your plans today' asked Richard.

'Millie is coming for lunch and then perhaps we may go to the cinema—there's that new film, some sort of follow up to Love Story and I know in advance that you will not be interested in it'

'Right there, my old darling, prefer my own love stories or are they lust stories?' joked Richard,

Smiling, Susan said 'You and your one track mind,' causing them both to burst into laughter. 'And you my love what does your day hold in store for you?'

'Murder, rape and pillage' replied Richard grinning 'and that's only for starters.'

'I see,' said Susan knowingly, 'you have nothing of particular interest today'

'No, but undoubtedly there will be some flak and fallout over the visit the other day.'

Their conversation was interrupted by the discreet toot of a car horn and Richard, seeing the Jaguar pull up outside the window, rose to his feet and, after a brief kiss and 'love you babe' to his wife he left the house, to begin yet another working day.

On arriving at his office, he found his friend and deputy Chris waiting for him. 'Nice to see you old love' he said by way of greeting, Chris reciprocated with 'You too, me old ducks,' 'What brings you to this hallowed place' asked Richard; amused by the old Northern greetings, 'come to look it over in case I get the boot.'

Chris laughed. 'The idea is appealing but I would imagine that is not for the near future' he said. 'No it's to discuss, would you believe, work.'

'Work, what's that?' replied Richard, 'don't tell me that after all these years you've started to get a conscience?'

'Get me a coffee chief and I'll bring you up to speed,' said Chris, imitating a well known actor in one of the ever increasing hourly, we can solve them all American series, which were currently flooding the television services.

'Ok doctor Spock' laughed Richard, at the same time picking up the telephone to ask his long suffering secretary for two coffees, which, miraculously as always, appeared two minutes later, complete with biscuits at no extra cost and with a lovely smile to boot. 'Thank you Barbara and try not to disturb us for the next few minutes.'

The two men tasted their coffee and then Chris said, 'I've had Bill Bowler on the phone already this morning and he's looking for a meeting as soon as possible into this Priest business. Apparently somethings come up which has excited the old sod and he's looking for some backing. I told him to be here in, let me see . . . .' his speech being cut short by a knock at the door and Bill poked his head into the room.

'Come in' said Richard, 'would you like some coffee?'

Bill entered and seated himself next to Chris, placing on the floor the package he had received the night before. 'Christmas come early this year?' asked Richard indicating the parcel.

Bill smiled. 'With a bit of luck perhaps'.

Barbara entered with yet another cup of coffee plus the coffee pot and Richard thanked her saying 'Very astute this morning, Barbara, could be that we will be in need of that before the morning is through.'

After Barbara had departed, the three men turned their attention to the problem at hand. 'So, Bill, what gives?' asked Richard, and Bill, after carefully placing his coffee cup on the saucer, related the events of the previous evening; When he had finished, Richard asked, 'Have you done anything about a search for the body?'

Bill replied, 'No, it's not a priority at the moment and I don't want these bastards warning, nor do I want the press tramping all over Teddington Lock.

There are still the explosives somewhere and I would love to get my hands on them before these so and so's can do anything nasty with them.'

'Couldn't agree more, Bill,' said Richard, 'but what do you propose and what is the secret in your package?'

'Perhaps the means to open the mouths of the Priest brothers' said Bill, picking up the package and carefully extracting a blood saturated football shirt.

'Always thought Chelsea played in blue,' joked Richard.

Bill replied with a smile, 'They do, there's still a bit of blue left if you look closely,' and placed the shirt on Richards desk.

'What are you proposing to do with that now Bill?' asked Chris.

'I'm hoping to get down to the nick this afternoon and have another go at those two close lipped bastards. I've got a bad feeling about this business, nothing I can put my finger on, but I'm beginning to wonder if we are not getting out of our depth here,' Bill replied grimly.

A long silence followed as the three men digested this information, then Richard said, 'But the Priests have never been looked upon as being a serious threat to us or anyone else. They are always a bit tightlipped, even when they are caught bang to rights, but there is nothing in their pedigree to suggest that they are in or approaching the first division.'

'Couldn't agree more', replied Bill, 'but what I'm thinking is that this time they have seriously strayed into a major league event and they are scared shitless of the future. I've known them since they were bits of kids, but this silence, coming from them is eerie. Can't be sure, but if I were to hazard a guess, I would think it possible that they have become involved in something way over their heads, with people on a completely different level to them. I must confess it is worrying me somewhat.'

'Strange', said Richard, 'the Twat, when he was here the other day, said that he wanted this thing taking over by the Met.'

'Hope you didn't agree' said Bill, 'not with our friend being part of this group. He's playing a very dangerous game and I would never forgive myself if anything should happen to him.'

'No, no rest assured', replied Richard, 'there would be no way would I hand over to the Met like that. However, I do think the time has come to bring pressure to bear on the Priests. Can our man in the field help at all?'

'The problem is,' said Bill, 'is one of identification. We know of various addresses where they have met, but they only meet once at each one. These places can best be described as accommodation addresses, used once and once only. As to the identity of the various persons, we have artists impressions and pseudonyms, but nothing concrete. The greatest danger is that something gets out of the bag alerting them, which would prove fatal for our friend and put our investigation back by weeks if not months. No, it is imperative that we get something from the Priests, something solid that we can work with.'

Again a silence fell in the room as the three men considered the various ramifications of Bills statement. Finally, Richard said, 'There's nothing else for it Bill. Get down to the prison as soon as possible and let's hope for a bit of success.'

Bill gathered up the blood covered shirt carefully, replacing it in the evidence bag in his possession. 'I will let you know the minute I have something,' said Bill, standing. With that he left the room, leaving the others deep in thought.

Finally Chris said, 'What do you think?'

Richard replied, 'I always try to stay upbeat on this type of investigation, but I must confess that in this case, especially with Bills' pessimistic outlook, I am also beginning to feel a trifle uneasy. Still, there's no point in getting downcast at this stage. Let's wait and see what Bill can come up with this afternoon.'

'In that case,' said Chris, 'I'll hang around the office today in case he needs a bit of help. I haven't very much on at the moment and you still have the aftermath of the Twats' visit to deal with.'

'Trust you to brighten up my day, I had nearly managed to get that business out of my mind.'

With that Chris left Richard, returning to his own office and the pile of paperwork which he knew awaited him there, leaving Richard to ponder his thoughts on the dilemna involving the Priests and the reasons behind their silence.

# CHAPTER 12

'Did you sleep well, my friend,' said Mansour, as he stepped from the bathroom into the bedroom. They were in a comfortable hotel bedroom in a small Bayswater hotel and Ali was still lying amongst a pile of very rumpled bed clothes. He looked up, seeing once again Mansours magnificent naked body and started feeling aroused yet again. 'No time for that now' laughed Mansour, 'now there is work to be done and much arranging to do. Come, get dressed and after breakfast I will drop you off in the City. I have a small shopping list and I would like you to do the shopping whilst I am elsewhere.'

An hour later the two men were in the West End. Handing a list to Ali, Mansour said,'Try and find everything on the list, but do not buy everything at the same place. The items are not very bulky and I will see you at the arcade in say two hours time. Here's some money, there should be enough to cover the costs,' and he handed over a hundred pounds in small denomination bank notes.

With that Mansour departed and Ali looked at the list in his hand. Electrical batteries, small ball bearings and two pounds in weight of nails, plus a quantity of electrical cable, all items readily obtainable in the area. With a spring in his step he set off on his shopping expedition; looking forward to being reunited with his new lover in a few hours time.

Mansour, meanwhile, had driven, not to the arcade, but to an address in Holborn, not far from Fleet Street. Having parked his car he was greeted at the door by a distinguished looking Pakistani, who, on seeing him, seized him in his arms and gave a friendly hug. 'My son, how good to see you. It's been so long and you know your mother worries so. Come in, your brother is also here, this calls for a celebration.'

'Father, you do exagerate, it's less than a week since I was last here,' laughed Mansour.

'That may be' replied his father, 'but it seems much longer.'

With that the two men entered the house to be greeted by a small, slender woman who said, 'Look at him, so thin and he owns a restaurant but does not eat.'

'Momma, you are beginning to sound like an Italian, always eat more, get fat. Believe me, I am fit and feeling very well, just like my brother,' said Mansour, embracing his brother who had risen to his feet at his brothers entrance.

'Give me an hour, and lunch will be ready' said his mother, bustling away in the direction of the kitchen.

Mansour looked around the room, never failing to be impressed by the spaciousness and comfort of his parent's home. His father, a retired minor diplomat, was ostensibly in the process of writing his memoirs, but never seemed to progress very far, yet no one seemed to mind and Mansour loved to come and talk to his father about the old days in Pakistan, the troubles with India and the present day problems with the terrorists. He often wondered what his father would do if he ever knew of his and his brothers involvement in terrorist activities.

'My brother, how goes your studies? Are you ready for your finals or have you still much work to do?' asked Mansour of his brother, Hassan, who was hoping to qualify in law smiled and replied,' With luck and the help of Allah I hope to qualify this year. Then I can start to work and repay my parents for their donations to me over the last few years.'

'What nonsense' said the father, 'your success is reward enough for me and your mother.'

Hassan took Mansour by the arm and pulling him gently said, 'Come to my room. I have a legal problem to deal with and I believe with your knowledge of Council procedure, you may be able to help me.

'Go, go you have the time before lunch' said Mr. Ahmad and his two sons left the room.

Once in the bedroom with the door firmly closed, the two brothers sat side by side on the bed and Hassan asked 'Did everything go well yesterday?

Mansour replied, 'Yes, very well. That problem has been dealt with and with luck our main project shall be executed within the next two weeks.'

'This project, what is it? Will I be a part of it?' said Hassan, excitedly pulling at his brothers sleeve.

'I cannot tell you anything as yet. When I have finalised my plans, I will be in a far better position to know who will be needed to do what. If I need you I will contact you in the normal way, but otherwise do and say nothing. Discipline is all so important and therefore the less who know the better it will be.' Whilst saying this he squeezed his brothers biceps as though enforcing the power of his words.

'But I am your brother. Did I not do well yesterday? I should be your right hand in all this planning,' whined Hassan pleadingly, wincing as his brothers fingers dug into his arms.

Releasing his grip, Mansour said, 'Listen. This is not a game we are playing. I have been involved a long time with the group, and the reason you know nothing more than I tell you is a deliberate ploy that guarantees complete secrecy for our projects and the prople involved in them. This is a deadly business, a war if you like, being fought by determined men, men who hope, that in the not so distant future, that Islam will prevail and become, for everyone the one and only religion, with those who do not agree being put to the sword. You must have noticed that over the last few years the movement is getting stronger, revolution brewing all over Africa and soon there will uprisings and riots all over. Finish your exams for you will be needed to help in the future planning and structuring of governments in the Islamic Way. Yes, my brother, I am a simple soldier, but you will become one of the future leaders.'

'I hear you, and, like you, I want to see Islam throughout the world. But you know, to a young man, the need for action is ever present and I know I can be of use to you,' complained Hassan, hoping his brother would relent.

'Yesterday, you were of great use, but that was yesterday. If I can use the others, who have all been trained in the camps, then I will use them as they are trained and also expendable. You are too valuable to be lost in a simple action for, as you know, we take losses as well. Now, enough of this, pass your exams and I promise you that a whole new future will be opened up for you. You will meet people, some of whom you have heard me speak, but also others, who have devoted their lives to the cause. That my brother is your future.'

'Lunch will be served shortly and I would like to take this chance to pray with my sons,' called their fathers voice, and the two brothers left the bedroom to join their father in midday prayers.

# CHAPTER 13

After leaving Richard's office, Bill had immediately returned to his own, first confirming that the Priest brothers were still in the same remand prison. Picking up his telephone he called his assistant, Superintendent Jock Boyd and asked him to call the prison and arrange an interview with the two Priest brothers.

Then he sat back in his chair and reflected on the enquiry to date.

All had started some fifteen months before, when the local uniformed police, on car patrol duty, had stopped a van on a routine check and had found a small amount of explosives, which enquiries later showed had been stolen from a colliery explosives store in Yorkshire. The two men in the van, both of Asian origins, refused to speak to the police and refused to give any sort of explanation for their possession of the explosives.

The explosives found were only a small part of the total amount stolen from the colliery and, eventually after the two men were formally identified and their respective homes searched, a further small amount of the stolen explosives were found. Also found were instructions copied from web sites on the methods used to construct simple bombs and other papers indicating that the the men could belong to an organised terrorist group. However, the men had constantly refused to speak and were now serving a prison sentence for the possession of explosives.

During the course of the investigation it became clear that over a period of time, explosives of a combined weight exceeding a ton, had been stolen from explosive stores throughout the Country. Despite a huge police investigation and an appeal for public help, no information whatsoever had ever been received, either as to the whereabouts of the explosives or the identities of the perpetrators.

Help had materialised in a very unexpected way, when Bill had received a telephone call from an old contact from his army days.

This contact was now chief of counter terrorism in the Punjab region of Pakistan and was ringing as he believed he could identify the two men who had been arrested and imprisoned in England.

He told Bill that the men were members of Al Qaida, who had been sent to England to liaise with an existing senior member, who was having difficulty finding members for his own group.

Armed with this information, Bill had visited the two men in prison. They had simply laughed in his face and refused to have any sort of conversation with him. Finally, Bill, having nothing further to go on had telephoned his contact in the Punjab, who, whilst commiserating with Bill on his lack of success, suggested that he could send one of his best operatives to England, if Bill could fix this with the powers that be.

Bill had not hesitated an instance, and after speaking to Richard and submitting a lengthy, very confidential report, he had met and spoken with Mohsin Akbar, who, as Mustapha, was installed in a small flat in East London, with an open contract to try to make contact with an active terrorist group.

Mohsin Akbar had been in place for several weeks, when he met an Afghan who used the name Umar and who was later identified as Umar Razad, a terrorist who was being sought by the Spanish police for questioning into the train explosions in 2004 in Madrid in which 191 people were killed.

Umar was working as a van driver for a local parcels delivery company and, after striking up a friendship with Mohsin, actually got him a job with the same company. Over the ensuing weeks, Mohsin worked hard on improving the friendship and finally, after many long and complicated convesations about religion and terrorist activities, he was introduced, by Umar to Mansour, who was known to Umar as Zanzibar.

After the first meeting, Mansour had immediately called for a very in depth check into Mohsin and was surprised when the information came back that he was a well known soldier in the organisation, completely trustworthy and loyal.

Mansour decided that he would test him as soon as possible, as he was only too well aware that the anti terrorist forces in Great Britain were well organised and were constantly trying to gain access to his group and his identity. To date, Mansour, who was himself a very fine technician, had managed to stay several steps ahead of the investigating forces and intended that it stay that way.

Several nights later, using one of the company delivery vehicles, the three men, Mansour, Umar and Mohsin, broke into an explosives store just outside Southampton and stole in excess of two hundred kilos of plastic explosives.

They then visited a naval base and stole a number of rifles and some ammunition from a loosely guarded arms store. After driving to an all night service station, where they were met by two more Pakistanis, the explosives and arms were unloaded with their help and placed in a small lorry which was parked in the car park. The lorry then drove away and the three men returned to London.

Although Mohsin contacted Bill as quickly as he could, subsequent enquiries proved negative, these enquiries being carried out by Bills' best officers as the protection of Mohsin was of the highest priority.

Three weeks later, Umar told Mohsin that Zanzibar had contacted him and had a little job for the two of them. That same night they had visited an address in the Nottingham area and been given twenty Soviet manfactured AK 47 assault rifles, capable of firing six hundred shots per minute and a quantity of ammunition. These they had transported to an address in Luton, helping the occupant of the house to secrete the arms in the cellar of the house. Unfortunately, owing to the fact that it was necessary to protect Mohsin, no action other than observations on the two addresses could be carried out at this time.

Thus had begun the observations and enquiries that had finally ended with the arrests of the two Priest brothers. If only they would crack, thought Bill, then he could hopefully find a lead back to the organisers and the explosives.

To date, a big, fat nothing and it was not from the lack of trying, but obviously the opposition were well organised and even Mohsin, with all his expertise could not find anything more than what he had already come up with. Until the shirt and that, with a bit of luck could be the key to this enquiry, mused Bill. 'This afternoon should reveal all' he said to himself, getting to his feet and setting off for the canteen and an early lunch, not knowing when his next meal would be.

# CHAPTER 14

Ali, having bought all the items on his list had decided to get himself a little bit of lunch. He found himself seated in a small coffee shop and after ordering a sandwich and coffee, seated himself close to the window and started to eat. What a change this last few weeks had made to his life.

From being a simple soldier in the Islamic army, he was now a tried and trusted member of a very close knit group in one of the Worlds' great centres, a centre which had always been a prize target; owing to the fact that it was Great Britain that had created the enormous British Empire, thus occupying his Country along with many others and forcing their methods onto his forebears. The fact that this occupation had helped drag his and the other countries into the twentieth century, did not seem to enter into the equation, the only thing of importance now being the supremacy of Islam and the prophet Mohammed.

He was sure, after having spent the night with Mansour, that not only was he now an important group member, he was also in love and he was certain that Mansour harboured similar feelings towards him. Congratulating himself on his apparent good fortune, he looked at his watch, realising that he had just enough time to reach the arcade for his meeting with Mansour. Gathering up his purchases, he left the coffee shop and made his way on foot to the arcade.

Mansour was already there and greeted him with a quick embrace, before enquiring if he had managed to find all the items on his list. 'Of course', replied Ali, 'your word is my command.'

Smiling broadly, Mansour took the purchases and handed them to the engineer, Wahid, saying, 'Put these with the rest and we'll check the total later. I'll be gone for a few hours and when I return I should be in a position to tell you the where and the when of our next operation.'

With that Mansour and Ali left the arcade, walking slowly through the shopping crowds to the parked Audi. 'Fancy a drive in the sunshine?' asked Mansour, and with that set off in the direction of Harrow.

After a few minutes, Ali broke the silence, asking 'Why are you so interested in the two women you have asked me to follow,' having forgotten that Mansour had ordered him never to ask questions.

Mansour did not answer immediately, then said, 'I will make an exception and answer your question, although I had expressly told you never to ask questions. However, in this case I will answer as it is a subject very close to my heart.'

Suddenly, the traffic started to slow and Mansour transferred his attention, noting that they were approaching trafic lights which were showing red. The lights changed and Mansour took up the conversation once again, saying, 'You remember the explosions here in London some five years ago.'

Ali replied, 'Yes, who could forget the bravery of those who gave their lives to our cause.'

'One of those' continued Mansour, 'was my cousin, 'and one of the investigation team was that bastard Grant, who is now a Chief Constable, very respected and an ideal target for us as he caused us great problems after the explosions with his enquiries and investigations. We would like revenge, but he is too difficult a target and therefore I have decided to attack his family to teach him and all like him not to mess with my organisation.'

'I see' said Ali 'and these women are his family or his friends?'

Mansour answered, 'One is his wife, the other is the wife of his friend and colleague. I had been planning to kidnap them by using the Priest brothers, but those stupid bastards got themselves arrested and you know what happened to the other one. The first lesson I learned is that in future I will use only those who are members of our faith and that is why you are so valuable to me.' Ali felt a warm glow embrace his body at these words of confirmation of Mansours' love and respect for him.

'When will this be and what will I have to do?' asked Ali, thinking how fortunate he was to be included in the forthcoming plans.

Mansour replied, 'Enough for the moment. I am still in the planning stage and will reveal everything when my plan is formulated and ready for execution. Until then, you know nothing and will ask no further questions. Do I make myself perfectly clear.?'

Ali did not reply, stung by this rebuke, then realised that Mansour was simply showing him that too much knowledge was a dangerous thing and he said, 'No more questions, but I can assure you of my loyalty.'

'I could ask no more and rejoice once again that you are a member, a much trusted member of my little group.' Once again Ali felt that warm glow he had felt earlier, persuaded that this must truly be love on its highest level.

# CHAPTER 15

That same afternoon, after a quick lunch, Detective Superintendent Jock Boyd, accompanied by his boss, Bill Bowler, were making their way to the prison reception rooms, where they were to interview the two Priest brothers.

On entering the room, the two men were not surprised to see that the Priests were in the company of their solicitor who immediately said, 'My clients have absolutely nothing to say about the fire arms or their arrest and have instructed me to file a complaint of Police harrassment. Am I clear?'

Bill looked at the solicitor as one would regard a pile of dog droppings on a pavement and replied, 'Shall we just wait until I have stated the reason for my visit?' and with that pulled up a vacant chair and sat down. Jock did likewise and waited for his boss to open the debate.

'Danny, I have always thought of you as the one with the most intelligence so therefore I will direct my questions to you. However Billy, if you should wish to say something then do not hesitate.'

'Fuck off' said Billy loudly.

Bill, non plussed, ignored the remark, saying, 'Now you understand why I said I would pose my questions to Danny,' with just enough sarcasm that even Billy could understand.

'You are both here awaiting trial for various offences, all relating to firearms and suspected terrorist activities. You will, in due time, appear before the Crown Court and hopefully go down for a long time. If you wish to help your case, you may decide it is better to cooperate with us.'

Danny Priest said, 'Listen. Our Billy has told you to fuck off so why don't you just fuck off.' This caused a smirk to cross the face of the solicitor, the smirk being removed by a single, withering glance from the Chief Superintendent.

'Now you have got that off your chest' said Bill, 'I would like you to tell me the whereabouts of your elder brother.'

'You hear that our Billy' laughed Danny, 'he would like us to tell him where to find Eric. These bleeders couldn't find a drink in a brewery, no wonder they can't find Eric.' He looked round the room to see if his humour was reflected in the faces of those present, and, on seeing that the police officers were unmoved by his wit, he said,

'Just fuck off, we're telling you fuck all.'

A short silence followed, broken only when Bill said, 'If I was to tell you that he was dead, what would you say?'

Danny replied angrily, 'I would say that you are a fucking liar.'

'I object to this line of questioning,' piped up the solicitor, 'you are trying to frighten my clients into confessing.'

Once again a silence fell until Bill finally said, 'I am not here for a confession as that is not necessary when I look at the amount of evidence I have against your clients. I am interested in the whereabouts of their brother and I have reason to believe that he is dead, probably killed by the people they were working with. Your clients are, I may add, in my opinion, way out of their depth in this case and that is why I was hoping that one or the other may see the light of day. I am convinced that the persons they were working for are part of a formidable terrorist group, who are planning further atrocities. They are, I believe in possession of a large amount of explosives, part of which were stolen by your clients . . . .'

Bill was interrupted by Danny Priest leaping to his feet shouting 'You have no proof, we are guilty of fuck all.'

Bill waited until calm was restored then continued, saying, 'Before I was so rudely interrupted I was explaining the seriousness of this case and the unenviable situation of your clients. Their associates are obviously very dangerous people who seem to stop at nothing which will interfere with their plans and that includes cold blooded murder. Can you try to explain to your clients the seriousness of all this and the consequences if they should wish to help us with our enquiries. Who knows it could lead to a lighter sentence. I would not bet any money on that, but it may help them to stay alive.'

'Look here, Chief Superintenent' said the solicitor, 'I cannot allow you to continue threatening and frightening my clients with your declarations of violence and death. If you have any sort of proof for these wild allegations and assumptions then show it, otherwise this interview ends here and now.' With that he started to place his notes into his attache case.

Ignoring the solicitor, Bill said, 'Danny, your brother was a Chelsea fan, wasn't he?'

Danny replied, 'What do you mean was. He still is and so am I.'

Bill reached into the carrier bag he had brought with him and pulled out a paper wrapped parcel. Placing this on the table, and with all eyes on him, he removed the paper revealing the heavily blood stained football shirt. 'Recognise this' he said.

Danny stared at the shirt before saying 'You bastard, trying to trick us like that. I would know our Erics' shirt because its signed by Frank Lampard. That could be anyones shirt,' he said defiantly, looking at his brother for confirmation.

'Look at it' said Bill, 'pick it up, examine it. Do you think I would come here with any rag bag shirt. My time is very important, far too important to waste time with people of your ilk. Look at it and tell me that it is not your brothers shirt.'

Danny reached out and picked up the shirt, turning it in his hands, stopping when he noticed something written with a marker pen. 'Look at this our Billy, that's Frank's signature, isn't it?' queried Danny, with a quaver in his voice.

Billy snatched the shirt from his brothers hands and stared at the bloodstained signature. To Bills' amazement tears started to roll down his face. He pressed the bloodstained shirt to his face and sobbed 'They killed him, those bastards killed him.'

'What bastards are those?' Bill asked gently.

Before Billy could reply, his brother shouted

'Shut your mouth Billy, we're telling them nothing.'

A long silence fell in the room, each person struggling with his emotions and then Bill said, 'Come on lads, this isn't a game;'

'I want to talk to my solcitor' said Danny, 'alone just with our Billy.'

'In that case, we will leave you' said Bill and both he and Jock rose and left the room.

'What do you reckon?' asked Jock, as he closed the door on the interview room.

Bill replied, 'I honestly don't know, but I was amazed to see young Priest crying. I thought those bastards were without emotions, now I know better. Let's go and get a cuppa whilst they are chatting with their mouthpiece.'

'This way' said a waiting prison officer, 'there's always a mash on in here. They'll be a few minutes yet as you sure shook them up somewhat. Is he really dead, the brother or are you having them on?'

'We believe so, yes' replied Bill, 'but that's between us my good friend.'

'Mum's the word' came the reply.

The two detectives had just finished their tea when the door of the interview room opened and the solicitor called to them saying, 'Could you two gentlemen join us?' Immediately Bill and Jock crossed to the interview room and closed the door, seeing the chastened expressions on the faces of the two Priests brothers.

'My clients have charged me with an enquiry, which will take me perhaps two or three days to complete. Until such time, neither wishes to make any form of a statement to you gentlemen, but, depending on the result of my enquiry, they may or may not wish to see you again. Can we leave it at that for today?' asked the solicitor.

'That will be fine by me' replied Bill 'but try not to take too long. Time is of the essence and I am afraid it is quickly running out on us.' With that the two detectives, after having repacked the shirt in the carrier bag left the room to return to their car.

Driving back to the Police Station, Jock said 'What do you think now?' We wait or we continue our enquiries?'

Bill, who was seated in the front passenger seat, turned to look at Jock and replied, 'I am convinced we have shook them up somewhat. The problem now is I only wish that I knew what the enquiry is that bloody solicitor is charged with. I'm convinced that if we knew that, we could considerably shorten our enquiry and save a lot of people a lot of pain.'

'Trouble is' replied Jock, soberly, 'we live in a democratic world and even bits of shite like the Priests and their so called solicitor have rights, mores the pity.'

The rest of the drive passed in silence and, on returning to his office, Bill immediately called Richard. 'Come down to my office, my old friend and join me in a snifter, unless you've signed the pledge,' said Richard, already reaching for the bottle and two glasses.

'Couple of minutes and I'll be there, especially if you are buying,' he laughingly replied.

Several minutes later found the two men seated in Richard's office, with heavily charged glasses of whisky and Bill recounted the result of his afternoons visit to the prison. 'So what do you make out of it? Richard questioned.

Bill replied, 'Without a doubt they were thoroughly shaken by the news and certainly by the sight of the shirt. The only problem is the enquiry that the solicitor is going to make as I am afraid it may let the cat out of the bag if he speaks to the wrong person, but we can't do anything about that. You know better than most the problems associated with this sort of enquiry and at some stage a decision must be reached and we simply hope we made the right one.'

Richard reflected on this for several moments and then said, 'Can we contact our friend?' and when Bill replied that it was at Mohsin Akbars' strict request that all contact must come from him and him alone, Richard finally said, 'I will back you to the hilt on this one. Your judgment has always been sound and the stakes are such in this case, that risks must be taken. Let's just hope that for a change it goes our way.' With that Bill finished his drink, wished Richard a good night and left the office in order to return to his own to burn a little more midnight oil.

When Bill had left the office, Richard called Chris who immediately came to see him. After serving him a severe dose of Black Bottle and recharging his own drink, Richard appraised him of the visit to the prison and the current situation relating to the Priest brothers and their solicitor.

'It is worrying' said Chris, 'as these so called terrorists are becoming more organised and certainly more dangerous. There is no other information filtering through from our other sources, and in spite of what the Twat says the Met. and the security forces have nothing either. As you know, but there again of course you know, it's you who set it up, the old grapevine is devoid of all fruit and that is very worrying and frustrating as time is pressing and we are no further forward. It's such a pity we can't tap into the solicitors' phone call as I'm sure that would fore shorten our enquiry considerably.'

'No can do' replied Richard, 'only TV cops have that option and we have not been included in their systems and we will never be as long as the Twat and his mates rule the roost. I often wonder if Joe Public knows the full extent of our powers and if he would be seriously aggrieved should he find that we cannot legally do much of what he expects us to do.'

'You're waxing lyrically now,' said Chris, reaching across the table for the bottle in order to replenish their glasses.

Richard replied, 'No, it's not that at all. We try to do a job with our hands and feet bound firmly together and a gag tied tightly in place, whilst the likes of the Priests and even worse than them, yes in some cases, much worse, have rights to silence, solicitors, appeals, family visits to jails, televisions, further education etc. etc. whilst the poor bleeders who work hard all week at menial jobs, for poor pay, who scratch around to find enough money to pay their way for them and their families, for those people and there are millions of them, we do absolutely fuck all. It's galling seeing those triple chinned, smooth, well dressed bastard politicians holding forth on whatever is the flavour of the month on the goggle box, whilst the salt of the earth struggle to keep themselves alive. Add to that all these so called fucking immigrants who cost an absolute fortune to maintain, some of which, agreed, are good citizens, but you will agree with me, that many are simply criminals who come here to rob, steal and even kill, as their outlook on life and civilisation is so far removed from our own'

'Wow' said Chris, 'is that the Black Bottle or the thoughts of Chairman Mao? I've never heard you go off like that before. On top of which I believe you make quite a lot of sense, but I would not recommend you speak like that in official circles.' Settling back in his chair, he waited for Richard to continue.

My old dad' continued Richard, 'always used to say, 'Charity starts at home' and these so called bastard politicians who rule over us ought to memorize that. I'm convinced that the whole idea behind Europe is a political one, created by the politicians for the politicians. They hope to create a political class to rule over us and that is why they keep trying to put the Royal Family out to grass. When I think of what out forebears did to create an Empire it's enough to make me want to emigrate to somewhere quiet and unknown.'

'Know what you mean' said Chris, 'Milly and myself say the same thing. The only problem is, where shall we go?

'Could always go to one of the Arab countries' said Richard, 'there are so many of the so and so's over here there must be some room over there.'

'I'll drink to that' said Chris raising his glass and draining it. Looking at his watch he exclaimed 'Is that the time. Promised the wife a night out tonight.'

'Then away with you my man' replied Richard 'or else I will be in your wifes bad books.'

'How do you mean, you've never been out of them' laughed Chris as he walked from the room.

# CHAPTER 16

The solicitor, after leaving the prison, returned directly to his office. He had a lot of unfinished work to do and was hoping to get rid of the Priest business as quickly as possible.

Once in his office he took out the piece of paper on which he had written the telephone number supplied by Danny Priest. No name, just a number, like in the films he thought. He picked up the telephone and dialled the number, waiting several seconds before a voice replied 'Hello'. 'Who am I speaking to?' demanded the solicitor, angry at the thought of being a messenger to the likes of the Priests.

'How did you obtain this number?' asked the voice of a well educated male, fluent in English, but with a slight Asiatic accent.

'I am a solicitor acting for clients who seek information relating to the whereabouts of their brother and I am led to believe that you or someone connected with this telephone number may be able to assist in this enquiry.'

'I do not think I can be of any assistance, but if you will leave me your number, I will make my own enquiries and come back to you,' replied the voice on the telephone.

The solicitor supplied his office number and ended by saying, 'The Police indicated during the interview with my client that their brother was dead? Can you confirm this?' In reply, he heard a click as the connection was terminated.

Puzzled the solicitor sat and started to read through a pile of papers marked 'urgent' which his secretary had left on his desk and was soon engrossed in this occupation. After several minutes the telephone rang.

On answering, the solicitor heard 'I am calling back regarding the telephone call you made to me a short while ago. Why do you think I can be of any form of assistance in this matter?'

The solicitor thought quickly and said, 'My clients are involved in an incident involving firearms and the Police believe this to be connected to a possible terrorist activity. When the Police indicated that it was very probable that their brother was dead, my client gave me this telephone number and asked me to ring and confirm or otherwise, the information relating to their brother.'

'I see' replied the voice on the telephone, 'and did your clients say anything to the Police about the investigation in hand?'

'No they said nothing whatsoever. However, the Police showed them a bloodstained football shirt which they alleged their brother was wearing at the time of his death.'

'You may tell your clients that their brother is alive and well and in hiding. His address, for the moment, is a secret and must remain so. If I can think of anything else which may assist you, I will contact you. The number you have contacted me by, will cease to exist after this conversation is terminated. Good day.' With that the communication was cut.

'What on earth are they mixed up in?' mused the solicitor, trying to bring some understanding into the conversation that he had had.

Mansour, on the other hand was inwardly raging. What was this all about. He had left specific instructions about the disposal of the body, now this. If the Priests decided to talk to the Police then the shit would really hit the fan.

But what to do? The solicitor was unknown to him and he had no intention of revealing his identity or involvement in this matter. Finally, he called Ali. 'My friend, this evening I have two very nice seats for the cinema, perhaps . . . .?'

Before he could finish Ali said, 'Just say where and when, I'll be there.' With that Mansour gave him the time and place and broke the communication.

# CHAPTER 17

Richard was seated in his office trying to complete his annual report for the Police Committee, a task which, as he reflected, was a necessary evil. To date he had always enjoyed the backing of the chairman of the committee and he hoped that this state of affairs could continue. He realised that at some stage some flak would come following the official inspection of the Force, but he was confident that he could handle anything which came his way.

The telephone interrupted his report writing and on answering, his secretary said, 'It's the Home Secretary for you.' Perplexed, Richard replied, 'Better put him through my dear,' and an instant later found himself saying, 'Home Secretary, what a pleasant surprise. What can I do for you?'

'I'll not beat about the bush,' came the reply, delivered in the deep resonant tones of Sir Peter Swift, the Home Secretary, 'but I would like to see you at your earliest convenience, let me see, tomorrow if that is possible.'

Richard replied, 'Tomorrow is Wednesday and I have the Police Comittee Annual Review meeting. However, Thursday I shall be in London in the afternoon.'

'I would have preferred tomorrow, but Thursday, at say 4pm. would be convenient,' came the cold reply.

'I have noted that Mr. Home Secretary. May I enquire as to the nature of the proposed meeting,' asked Richard.

'I would prefer not to discuss this over the telephone, but suffice to say that my friend and colleague Mr. Thompson will be present.'

'I see' said Richard, 'until Thursday. Good day Mr. Home Secretary.' With that he replaced the receiver and leaned back in his chair, thinking that Thursday afternoon could be a very interesting one.

He returned to his report writing and quickly finished, calling to Barbara to type it up, copy it and deliver the copies for the next day's meeting. Looking at his watch and seeing that all urgent matters had been dealt with he decided that for once he would finish early and rang for his chauffeur to prepare the car for the ride home.

An hour later, found him seated with his wife in the drawing room. Both were reading, he the local evening newspaper and Susan a novel. Suddenly Susan said, 'Is it still on for Thursday?'

Richard replied 'Is what still on?'

'You know' said Susan, 'you said you would be in London on Thursday and that Milly and I could drive down with you.'

'Oh yes,' said Richard, 'but I have another meeting in the afternoon and I do not know at what time that will finish.'

'That's no problem, darling, we can come back on the train,' said Susan.

Richard glanced at the clock and saw that it was nearly seven o'clock. 'Fancy a drink my love?' he asked his wife who replied that a glass of white wine would do very nicely. Pouring himself a whisky and a Chardonnay for his wife, Richard switched on the television to listen to the news broadcast. Nothing untoward was to be heard until suddenly Richard noticed a familiar photograph appear on the screen, a face he had not seen for several years, the face of the man who had been in charge of the Interpol Bureau in Lyon.

'That brings back memories' said Richard, indicating the television screen.

'Why it's Marcel,' exclaimed Susan.

Marcel Polidor, it was announced, had just been promoted to head the new joint police bureau in Paris, following the decision to bring the various French Police departments closer together and to also include the gendarmerie, the military side of the police in France.

'Have to give him a call tomorrow,' said Richard, 'as he can certainly obtain seats for this year's six nations.'

'You and your rugby' said Susan softly.

Richard replied, 'I've yet to hear you complain about a weekends shopping in Paris,' looking to his wife for confirmation.

Laughing happily, Susan said, 'How about a salad and an omelet this evening, something light and who knows, there's nothing on the box this evening and an early night may be beneficial.'

'Beneficial for who?' questioned Richard.

Susan, arching an eyebrow, said seductively, 'With a bit of luck for both of us. Come into the kitchen with me and we can start by breaking the eggs.'

# CHAPTER 18

After the film, Mansour took Ali to his favourite club and, after choosing their drinks, they found a comfortable seat. 'It was a very good film,' said Ali, 'thank you for inviting me.'

'Ali, you know I like you a lot and this way I can kill two birds with one stone. I would like you to answer me a question which has been bothering me all afternoon,' said Mansour, regarding Ali squarely in the eyes.

Ali did not flinch and said 'Ask, I have no secrets from you, Zanzibar, my friend. What would you like to know?'

'It is regarding the little river trip you took the other day. What happened to the clothes you took from the fish food?'

Ali laughed at the phraseology used by Mansour and said, 'Mustapha took them to burn as he has access to a large burner which he assured me would completely destroy all trace of those clothes. Why do you ask?'

'Simply because I am very thorough in my preparations and executions. I do not like loose ends,' replied Mansour.

'Do not worry,' said Ali,' I have faith in Mustapha as I am sure you do.'

'Yes, yes of course' said Mansour, smiling and lifting his drink, 'a toast to a fine ending to a very nice evening.' Both men smiled knowingly, each thinking of what the perfect ending should be like.

After replacing their glasses on the table, Mansour said, 'Oh, I nearly forgot. Have you seen Mustapha recently?'

'No, I haven't, I have not seen him since our boat ride. I was thinking of ringing him tomorrow. Is there a problem?'

'No problem at all. It is just that I like my operatives to keep in touch as much as possible, as I believe we operate better when we know and trust the person by our side. Do you not agree?

'Whole-heartedly' replied Ali with a smile 'and to date I trust Mustapha and naturally yourself. In the training camps great emphasis was placed on comradeship as I am sure you know.'

'Comradeship and the teachings of Mohamed are all we require for victory,' Mansour said fervently.

'I agree with you. Do you want me to ask if he burned the clothes?'

'No, that will not be necessary. Like you, I have my utmost confidence in him. 'Come, let's finish our drinks and go to find a little solitude.'

# CHAPTER 19

The next morning found Richard in his office in company with his secretary, Barbara. She handed him his neatly typed report for the Police Committee and said, 'All copies have been distributed and the meeting is confirmed for two o'clock at the Town Hall. Is there anything else you would like me to do?' Richard thought for a moment and then said, 'Can you try and find the telephone number of one Marcel Polidor, who has, apparently been nominated chief of all the Police for France. Start with the Quai d'Orsay, they should have some idea where he will be hiding.'

'Is this an official enquiry or personal?'

'I've known Marcel since I was a young detective and that was a long time ago. You could say it is a bit of both and it will give you the chance to air your French.'

'Merci beaucoup, I'm sure,' said Barbara, leaving Richard smiling to himself.

Five minutes later, his telephone rang, and, on answering he heard 'Bonjour mon ami' how are you keeping?'

'Marcel,' exclaimed Richard, 'that was quick. I did not expect to hear from you so quickly.'

'You know how it is in France', Marcel replied, 'if it is friends it is done straight away, business always takes a lot longer. C'est la vie, as we say here in France.

Now tell me, why did you call, because if it was for rugby tickets that's already been taken care of.'

'You never forget, do you, and I admire your courage as you know you will get another arseholing this year.' This last statement was greeted with a burst of laughter.

'Oh you English, deep down you know that this year is the year of the French.'

'We'll see after the game, now let me congratulate you on your promotion. You must be proud to be named as the first chief of the joint police services.'

'If only, but I fear that it is a political ploy. Before, the politicos had to discuss with various heads, now there's just mine.

I don't know how this will all pan out as you say, but I will try to bring our various police together and hopefully just have one police force, one day. You know I have always admired your system in England,' he concluded.

Richard laughed. 'You buggers are too undisciplined to be like us.'

This time it was Marcel who laughed.

'I am afraid you may have a point there. Now tell me, when are we going to meet up?'

'At the moment I'm a bit stretched,' said Richard, 'but we might be able to make it in three or four weeks. Susan would love to go shopping in Paris again.'

'The last time she came I said that she was a bad influence on my wife, after she had showed her how easy it is to spend a fortune with a piece of plastic,' complained Marcel.

'How do you think I feel as she is constantly practising in London for her next visit to Paris.'

Marcel let out a huge peal of laughter.

'I'm going to have to go, but you have my number so let's keep in touch. Now that we are in Europe together, I believe we should start looking at ways to improve contact between our Countries.'

'Could not agree more' Richard stated emphatically, 'so I will be back to you in the next few weeks.'

'I've left my personal numbers with your secretary, and so until the next time, ciao baby.'

'You remember that mad Italian bastard?' asked Richard, referring to one Luigi Carlino, chief of the Italian carabinieri.

Marcel replied, 'Remember, I see him more often than I see my wife. He's like us you know, how do you say it, a real bobby.'

'Yes, there's not many of us left,' concluded Richard, replacing the telephone on his desk. He picked up the report that Barbara had earlier brought him and after a moment's reflection on his telephone conversation, started to read.

# CHAPTER 20

That same morning, Mansour after having dropped Ali in London in order that he could attend his college, drove to the arcade in Oxford Street. It was early and there were very few people in the arcade. Wahid, the engineer was seated in the office, examining various machine parts on a work bench. 'How is the work progressing?' asked Mansour.

'Which work, the arcade or our work?'

'The arcade is simply a way of making money as is my restaurant. However, our special work is what interests me.'

'In that case, this may interest you' said Wahid, indicating a portable telephone which lay in pieces on the work bench.

'What is it? asked Mansour.

'I have been working on micro chip technology,' said Wahid, 'as all these machines now work on chips. I've found that this chip, which comes from that jackpot machine over there, can be altered simply, and, when installed as part of a detonator, can be activated by a simple telephone call. Also, I have discovered that in case of multiple bombs, I can use the same altered micro chips in all of them and detonate them all with one call.'

'That is fantastic,' exclaimed Mansour, 'I do not know how you do it.'

'Each to his own,' replied Wahid, 'you like to lead and organise and I like to experiment. Allah needs us both my friend.'

'Well said' replied Mansour; 'I think I may be able to use your new invention in our forthcoming event.'

'It will be ready and waiting' replied Wahid.

Mansour then left the engineer and the arcade, returning to his car. Once seated, he took out his telephone and called his uncle in Basingstoke. On hearing his uncle's voice, Mansour said, 'I think there may be a problem and I would like your advice. Can I come down to see you?'

'My favourite nephew,' replied his uncle, 'you know you are always most welcome. Your aunt will be pleased and I am sure she will prepare us a nice meal.'

'I will be there for about noon', said Mansour, then switched off his telephone and started the car for the drive to Basingstoke. 'At least it's a nice day' he said to himself, putting the car into gear and driving away.

An hour and a half later found him parking his car outside his uncles' home. His uncle was waiting for him and, after a warm embrace, led him into the house. 'Where's auntie?' asked Mansour.

'Where else but in the kitchen. Come and refresh yourself with some freshly pressed lemon juice. We will be eating in a few minutes. Do you want to discuss your problem straight away or wait until this afternoon?' enquired his uncle.

'I'll tell you now, because you may wish to reflect on the problem, before giving me a reply,' said Mansour, gravely. 'I am very worried I can tell you.'

'Then come into the garden where we will not be disturbed', his uncle said, leading the way through the French windows and onto the patio at the rear of the house, which, was for once, full in the sunshine. Indicating two comfortable reclining seats, the uncle seated himself and waited patiently for Mansour to begin.

'You will recall the night we obtained the guns and explosives,' began Mansour, 'I was accompanied by three brothers, the Priests. They were believed to be trustworthy. When we came later and collected the guns, they assured me they had a safe place to store the guns and I left them to do the storing. However, the police somehow knew and were waiting'.

'You have a traitor in your midst?' asked the uncle, looking into the worried face of Mansour.

'No it's more complicated than that.'

Taking a long drink from his glass, he continued saying, 'Two of the brothers were caught by the Police, but the third one got away. He gave me a story which I did not believe and for security reasons I had him executed.'

'That was a very serious decision you made, you could endanger the operation,' warned his uncle, 'and you know that a lot is riding on the success of that. Was there no other way you could have acted?'

'I believe not,' replied Mansour, 'but that is not the end of the problem. You see, I gave orders to two of my most trusted soldiers to dispose of the body, which they did apparently, leaving it in the Thames at the usual place. However, I have now heard that the Police are in possession of an item of clothing that was on the body and that could only have been given to them by one of my soldiers and I do not know for sure which one.'

A silence fell as his uncle tried to digest this very disagreeable news. 'It is very unfortunate and as you have said potentially dangerous, but our plans are so well advanced, there could be serious repercussions. Will the two brothers who are with the police keep their mouths shut?, asked his uncle, very concerned about these revelations.

'That is a question I keep asking myself, my uncle', said Mansour contritely, 'I just do not know. If they should think that I had their brother killed, and I think this is the idea the police have planted in their minds, then it could be disastrous as they know one hell of a lot, especially the whereabouts of the explosives. As to the two soldiers I have already formulated a plan, so that problem I can take care of. However, as to the two brothers, they are on remand in prison and I am at a loss as to what to do about them.'

'I am glad that you have come to me with this news. I will give it a lot of thought and we shall speak later, after our meal,' said his uncle, who, on hearing the approaching footsteps of his wife, said in a louder voice, 'With luck those footsteps herald the news of 'lunch is ready' so come my nephew, let us eat.'

The two men got to their feet, Mansour going to his aunt and greeting her with a warm smile and a firm, loving embrace. Smiling in return, she led the two men to the dining table.

After the remnants of the meal had been cleared away, the uncle announced that he had some urgent telephone messages to make and suggested that Mansour should accompany his aunt on a digestive stroll. Mansour, accompanied by his aunt left the house, saying they would return in an hour or so. 'Take your time' said the uncle, 'your auntie sees little of you as it is. Let her take pleasure in your presence.'

With that Mansour and his aunt left the house and the uncle went into his small study. Satisfied that he was alone, he picked up one of several portable telephones lying on the desk and consulted the list of encrypted numbers.

Selecting one, he dialled, waiting for his connection. After three rings, a recorded voice asked for his reason for calling, and, after hearing the list of options, he pressed number four and a voice answered, saying, 'Give your code and I will return your call?'

'Balthasar' replied the uncle, cutting the communication and settling back in his seat.

Five minutes later, another of his phones rang and, on answering a voice said 'Zafran, my old friend, what can I do for you?'

'There are two men, brothers, on remand in Brixton prison and they may be a very great risk to our forthcoming operation' said the uncle, Zafran Razaq, 'and I wonder if you could be of assistance.'

'We are all of the same faith and therefore I shall help if I can. How do you see me being of help to you.'

'I remember,' said Zafran, 'a little time ago you helped some of our friends escape from a prison in England and I thought that you may be able to assist.'

'That is true my friend,' said the voice, 'but that was from an open prison. Brixton is different, very different. How important are these two brothers of which you speak?' queried the voice.

'They are in possession of knowledge which if known will endanger our forthcoming operation and the identities of our group, myself included,' said Zafran.

'I will enquire and return to you as quickly as possible,' replied the voice. 'I cannot promise anything, 'the voice continued, 'but I will contact you within the next twenty four hours, hopefully with good news.' With that the communication was broken.

After replacing the telephone, Zafran leaned back in his chair and closed his eyes, replaying the conversation in his mind.

'Look at him' said Mansours aunt, indicating her husband apparently asleep in his chair; 'I tell him to take it easier but will he listen?'

'Shut up, woman' said Zafran, opening his eyes, 'Iwas only resting my eyelids.'

With a chuckle, his wife went to the kitchen, saying 'I don't suppose you thought to wash the dirty dishes did you?' and without waiting for a reply, entered the kitchen and closed the door.

'Mansour, I have contacted someone, but we shall have to wait for a definitive answer,' said Zafran, 'so try not to worry too much. Continue with your planning and I will ring you the minute I know something. Do not try to do anything on your own regarding the Priests, it will be far too dangerous.'

'Thankyou, my uncle, for your help. I shall try not to worry, but time is running short now. I will bide my time and curb my patience and just hope that with the help of Allah a solution will be found. Now, I must return to London as I have still much to do.'

Zafran came towards him, took him in his arms and said, 'You are one of us destined for great things. Do not worry—I feel it in my old bones that a solution will be found. Now, go quickly and drive carefully.'

Mansour embraced his uncle and then said his goodbyes to his auntie, once again thanking her for a lovely meal. With that he left the house and was soon safely esconced in his car on his way back to London.

Two hours later saw him once again in the amusement arcade. Wahid had been replaced by another engineer, having finished his shift for the day, and Mansour waited until the engineer had vacated the office, before taking out his telephone and ringing Ali. He replied on the second ring and Mansour said to him, 'How did the college go today?'

'Not too bad' was the reply, 'it will soon be exam time so I will study all the harder.'

Mansour thought for a moment and then said, 'Can you contact Mustapha. It is important that I see you both tomorrow. Try to make it for say eleven in the morning at the arcade and bring your telephones with you. Time is running out and we must finalise our plans.'

'I hope I can contact him', said Ali, 'but if I experience any problems I will contact you straight away. I did try him this morning but his number was occupied.'

Mansour stayed in the arcade a little longer but found that he could not concentrate. Always the spectre of failure should the Priest brothers start talking to the Police. He knew he could do nothing, but he found the waiting unbearable. He finally decided to go to his restaurant, which was nominally run by a director, some old friend of his fathers, who was in need of money. Not wishing to eat alone he called his brother and they agreed to meet at the restaurant, which was in Stepney, at eight o'clock that evening.

Glancing at his watch, Mansour saw that he had time to go to his flat for a shower and a change of clothing. He said goodbye to the engineer and left the arcade, still worrying over the Priest brothers.

Later, in the restaurant, the two brothers were seated at a nice table for two in a corner, relatively secluded, where they could speak without being overheard. 'I went to see uncle this afternoon,' said Mansour by way of conversation.

'I wish that I had known, I would have come with you. The course this afternoon was boring and it is such a long time since I last saw my aunt and uncle,' moaned the younger brother, letting his feelings show.

'You concentrate on your studies, there will be plenty of time for socialising in the future, but right now your exams are all important. You pass all your exams and you have a chance of finding a position in our government, a position that will help our cause in the future,' said Mansour, fervently.

Before his brother could reply, his telephone rang. Looking at the visual display, he recognised his uncle's number.

'Yes, my uncle,'said Mansour., 'have you any news?'

'Listen to the news broadcast tomorrow morning.'

'What does that mean?,' questioned Mansour.

His uncle retorted 'You know better than to ask questions. Simply obey.'

'Very well,' replied Mansour, chastened by his uncle's tone. The phone went dead in his hand and Mansour replaced it in his pocket.

'You look shocked' said Hassan, 'was that bad news,'

'No, on the contrary I am hoping it is very good news. Now, let's order and enjoy our meal.'

Whilst Mansour was eating with his brother, Ali was contacting Mustapha. Finally he located him, and passed on the message from Mansour. Mustapha said, 'Where are you at the moment?' and on hearing that Ali was fairly close by he said, 'Come and join me. I'm at the New Delhi restaurant; you know where that is don't you?'

'I'll be there in about fifteen minutes,' replied Ali.

It was actually twenty minutes before Ali arrived and he quickly joined Mustapha who was seated alone, close to the kitchen. 'Not the best of tables,' he said, 'but at least it's nice and warm. To what do I owe this pleasure?'

Ali seated himself before replying.

'I have instructions from Zanzibar. He wants to see us both tomorrow at eleven o'clock in London.' 'Where abouts in London?' asked Mustapha and Ali replied, 'Don't worry, I know the address. If we meet at say nine, we will go down on the train.'

'That's fine by me,' replied Mustapha, I'll be waiting at the station. Now, let us order, I'm famished.'

When they had finished their meal, Ali said, 'That was very enjoyable and this is certainly an address to remember. However, I suppose we should not use the same restaurants too often.'

'You can never be too security conscious,' replied Mustapha, 'because one simple mistake could lead to everyone's downfall.' 'That reminds me,' Ali said as he reached into his pocket for his wallet, 'Zanzibar wants us to have our telephones with us when we meet tomorrow.'

'Perhaps he is going to give us the latest in portable telephones,' joked Mustapha, 'although in all honesty I believe we will end up with something functional rather than beautiful.'

After they had paid the bill, they said their goodnights and each went his separate way. Immediately, Mustapha realised he must try to contact Bill in order that he could mount a surveillance operation in order to try to identify the other members of the group.

However, when he tried to contact Bill, all he heard was a mechanical voice saying that all numbers were disconnected until seven thirty in the morning.

'Suppose I'll try tomorrow' he said to himself, having no other means of contacting Bill. With that he returned to his bed-sit flat, where he watched television, whilst wondering what Zanzibar had in store for them the next day.

# CHAPTER 21

The following morning found Richard and his wife breakfasting at seven o'clock, as Richard had arranged his car for eight, thus giving them plenty of time to drive down to London. They were both dressed and ready when Susan said, 'Here's Milly', and Richard turned to see Milly at the wheel of her Mini Cooper. 'Is she still the most dangerous driver in the district?' asked Richard and his wife replied, 'I've not noticed any amelioration lately, but she's not killed anyone as far as I know.'

Richard went to the door and opened it just as Milly was about to ring the doorbell. 'Beat you to the bell', joked Richard and Milly replied, 'You were always a fast operator, or at least that's what Chris says.' 'Have to have a word with that man of yours regarding his use of scurriolous remarks,' replied Richard, warmly and at the same time bending to plant a kiss on each of Millie's cheeks. 'Oh you are a one', she mimicked, trying to kiss him in return. 'Now Millie, you know the rules, no lipstick,' laughed Richard, and his wife cried out, 'Have you two finished?'

'Come and have a cuppa' said Susan to Millie, 'we have plenty of time.' With that Millie joined them at their breakfast table, awaiting the arrival of the official car.

Fifteen minutes later, Richard, who was seated facing the window, saw the Jaguar saloon turning into the driveway. He finished his tea and slipped into his suit jacket, ensuring he had put his wallet in the inside pocket, alongside his warrant card.

'Here he is, so come on girls, on with your coats and lets be away,' and they left the house settling into the comfortable seats of the car for the ride down to London.

The two women were chattering away in the back of the car and Richard switched on the car radio. A modern pop tune was being played and, when the record was finished, a newscaster announced a news flash.

'Last night, in Brixton prison a disturbance broke out on the remand wing, believed to have been caused by racial tension which is ever present in this over crowded section of the prison. When peace was finally restored, the bodies of two prisoners Danny and Billy Priest, were found, both suffering from what appeared to be stab wounds.

In spite of immediate medical attention, nothing could be done for either man who were both pronounced dead at the scene. Enquiries are continuing and we will bring you further information as and when we receive it.'

Richard, completely forgetting the presence of the ladies in the car exclaimed, 'Fucking hell the shit will hit the fan now.'

'Richard' screeched his wife, 'your language.'

'I'm very sorry my dears, but that was just about the worst piece of news I could possibly receive. Bill, stop at the next auto stop, I've got a call to make.'

Ten minutes later Richard was in urgent conversation with his secretary who informed him that Bill Bowler had already received the news and had gone to the prison in an effort to obtain some more details. 'There's nothing more to be done until Bill returns. Ask him to contact me as and when he can please.' With that he returned to the car and continued the journey to London, his earlier good spirits completely dampened by the news he had received.

As they neared the centre of London the chauffeur asked, 'Where should I leave the ladies, Sir?'

'Will Bond Street do you for starters, my dears?' asked Richard, turning his head as though seeking confirmation.

Susan replied 'That'll be just fine, kind Sir.' Several minutes later found them in Bond Street and after depositing the ladies to begin their shopping spree, Richard said, 'Now, if you could take me to the Judge's Chambers please and then pick me up at say one o'clock as I have a meeting with the Home Secretary.'

'Very good, Sir,' came the reply, and fifteen minutes later, Richard found himself in a very well appointed reception area, waiting to be summoned into the presence of Lord Hamilton.

Several minutes later, a door opened and a tall, distinguished figure in an immaculately cut dark suit entered with his hand outstretched and said, 'I am very sorry for keeping you waiting.' The two men shook hands and Lord Hamilton said, 'Come on into my warren, it is nice and private.'

Richard followed his host into a superbly appointed room, furnished with deep leather armchairs, an imposing desk and an even more imposing number of books and files. 'Park yourself over there', said Lord Hamilton, indicating an armchair to one side of the desk. 'A snifter whilst we chat?'

'Most kind, a whisky please.'

Lord Hamilton poured out two man sized measures into crystal whisky glasses, handing one to Richard. The two men warmly toasted each other and settled into their respective seats.

'You have not changed much since your days in Crown Court,' said Lord Hamilton, alluding to the period in the early seventies when the Crown Court superseded the Assize Courts.

'A pity they had to change the system,' replied Richard, 'as it certainly diluted the level of Justice as we knew it.'

Richard raised his glass to his lips, appreciating the aroma of well seasoned whisky, and took a sip. Nectar! He let the amber coloured liquid trickle slowly down his throat, a feeling of well being enveloping his body.

Looking at his host, he noticed that although he must be at least seventy years of age, he looked several years younger and still maintained his imposing presence, a presence that had sent fear down many a spine in the old Assize Court days. 'If I may so,' said Richard, 'you yourself my lord, appear to be in very good shape. Indeed, apart from the white hair, there is very little change from our Court days.'

'You are too kind, but now that we have complimented each other, perhaps we should get to the point of this meeting. I have been hearing various rumours about you and I was wondering whether they were founded or not?'

'Rumours?' queried Richard, 'rumours about what?'

'About your fitness to manage a Police Force' replied Lord Hamilton. 'You see, I have always maintained an interest in people who I find interesting and you are one of these persons. I am an excellent judge of character and I always found you to be perfectly honest and frank in your expressions and your application to your duties was always first class. You are apparently popular with your men and you enjoy the confidence of your Police committee. However, I now hear that you have upset an Inspector of Constabulary and that he in turn is demanding your head.'

'It is nice to hear that your lordship has maintained a good information service,' replied Richard with a smile. 'I did have a little difference of opinion with an Inspector, which I regretted afterwards as I realised that my manner was very antagonistic. However, you know me my lord and you know that I do not suffer fools, gladly or otherwise, and unfortunately this particular inspector is a buffoon who, if given his way, will destroy the Police force as we know it.'

'I can appreciate what you are saying, for I have seen the same movements in the Judiciary. The changes are so drastic that I have decided to retire and search in other fields for the satisfaction I crave. Like you, I do not suffer fools and when I look at our political masters of today I fear that the future will be anything but bright. Once, long ago, we had a political system where men of honour and resolve pledged themselves to raise and maintain standards and to keep this Country in the forefront of World affairs. Today we have a sort of professional politician with very few thoughts other than for himself and friends and I have decided to go into politics in an effort to restore a little balance. I am, as you know, a member of the House of Lords and I will shortly be named Home Secretary as the present occupant is destined to move onto higher spheres.

'Why that's wonderful but I fail to see what that has to do with me. I have never harboured any ambitions to be a politician as I have always been on the side of the weak and the oppressed, as opposed to the present government, which, although pretending to be the representative of the working class, seem to spend more time on wasting the taxpayers money and fiddling their expenses. Once upon a time there were Statesmen, but today, like the dinosaurs, they seem to be extinct.'

'Very well put,' replied Lord Hamilton, 'and you are, of course, perfectly correct. We now have with this Europe rubbish, a new class system, the political class, all parties included. They look upon themselves as a superior race, which they are most certainly not, and dream of the age when they can rid all countries who maintain a Royal family, of the Royal image. You, like myself, are a confirmed Royalist, if my memories of our chats in days gone by are accurate, and if you look across Europe today, you will notice that those countries which still maintain a Royal family are far more stable than those that do not. How long this will last I do not know, but I hope that somewhere along the line people will start to realise that we have been invaded by numerous foreign countries and that unless something drastic is done, we shall soon be on a level with many third world countries.'

Rising to his feet, Lord Hamilton picked up the cut glass decanter of whisky and refreshed their glasses. 'Now to the reason for my asking to see you. Have you considered taking retirement as you have passed the thirty year service mark?'

'My wife would be only too pleased to see me retire, but I would look upon it as a betrayal to the people I serve as there is so much unfinished business. There are not many of us left from the old school and I am afraid that the future of the Police service will be in the balance when the new brooms of Whitehall with their lackeys start to sweep clean. Already there are so few experienced officers to train the newcomers and I am afraid we will be offering a second class service in a few years time unless something drastic is done.'

'I understand your point of view, but I must say that I believe you are wrong to adopt that attitude. Whatever you say or do you will always be a minority and, at the end of the day it's the likes of your Inspector of Constabulary who will rule the roost. I know having seen it with the demise of the Assize Court and the advent of Crown Court,' continued Lord Hamilton, 'but having analysed the whole thing, I decided to get out and change direction, which is something I think you should consider.

After a moment's reflection, Richard said,' I have been a policeman all my working life and I must confess that I have never given a moments thought to retirement or a change in direction. What do you have in mind my Lord, as I imagine that you have something to offer.'

'I certainly do have something and I hope you say yes, as you are the finest qualified person for the job. I am a member of the governing body of a very select security organization, who, over a period of time have become very well known throughout Europe. This organisation specialise in all types of security involving governments and personalities who for whatever reason, fear for their lives. The organisation is used widely in this and most other European countries owing to its very low profile and excellent results.'

'Are we speaking of the Exec organisation?' asked Richard, 'as they are the only ones I know of who can fit the description you have given me.'

'We most certainly are,' replied Lord Hamilton, 'how astute of you. How do you know of them?'

'I have had dealings from time to time with various members,' said Richard, 'normally on a need to know and you scratch mine and I'll scratch yours basis. If you were to ask me where have all the good policemen gone, I would suggest Exec. Their reputation is second to none in the very specialised work they do and I do believe that in many instances the countries for which they work prefer them to their own in house organisations.'

'You are correct in everything you say and the reason for today's meeting is that I have been charged with finding a successor for the managing director and I would like you to consider the position. What do you say?' questioned Lord Hamilton, looking Richard in the eye, 'would you be interested? I can think of no finer person than yourself to take the post and, under the present circumstances I think it could be an ideal choice for you to make.'

Richard paused, thinking hard as to the best way to reply. It was true that he had never considered retirement before now, but the post he was being offered was one that most senior police officers worth their salt would leap at.

'My Lord, it comes as a complete surprise. I am flattered that you would wish me to take this position, but I must ask for a period of time to consider, and additionally, I would like to discuss the ramifications with my wife.'

'Naturally, but I must have a reply within three months, as the present incumbent is retiring. Such things as salary and conditions of employment will be discussed as and when, but I can assure you that you will not be disappointed. We are looking for growth and you are just the person needed to assure the future.'

'I promise you that I will give your proposition every consideration and I will be back with my reply well within your time scale. I have some unfinished business, but as you have so rightly pointed out, at some stage others will take control. Added to that, I have, after leaving here, a meeting with the Home Secretary, a meeting which may help me to make up my mind.'

'Do try to control yourself as he is such a pernicious individual.' added Lord Hamilton with a knowing smile. 'Soon, I will replace him, but until then . . . .'

The two men looked at each other, each feeling the current passing between them as it had done since their first meeting. Satisfied, Lord Hamilton said, 'Well the morning has flown by and I now have a lunch appointment, so I must leave you. It has been good seeing you again and having this little chat. I am sure you will give the matter your full consideration and I look forward to seeing you in the not too distant future.' With that the two men shook hands and Richard took his leave.

On arriving in the entrance lobby Richard noticed his chauffeur was enjoying a cup of tea with the doorman. Seeing his chief, the chauffeur said, 'The cars right outside Sir,' and picking up his hat and gloves, the chauffeur led the way to the parked car.

'Take me to Scotland Yard' said Richard 'and then go find yourself something to eat. I have some time to kill, so if you can pick me up at the Home Office at say, five o'clock, that will be fine.' With that he settled back in his seat, thinking over the proposition that had been made to him that morning.

# CHAPTER 22

At eleven o'clock that same morning, Ali, Mustapha, Mansour and Wahid found themselves in the office at the amusement arcade, which was fairly quiet at this time, but the office door had been locked to deter any intrusion.

'Firstly,' Mansour began, 'can you give me your telephones please.'

Bemused, Ali and Mustapha handed over their telephones and were amazed when Wahid seized them and smashed them into smithereens with two well aimed blows of a claw hammer.

'Do not worry my friends,' Mansour said quietly and reached into the safe, extracting a small packet.

Opening the packet he took out two brand new I-phones saying, 'A little gift to replace your broken telephones. These phones are for your own personal use. This one,' he said, handing over a second, small portable telephone, relatively mundane in appearance, is to be kept with you at all times. It is an operational receiver and not a telephone. Although to all extents and purposes it appears to be a telephone it can only receive. Only I know the number so only I can call you. To answer simply press on the green button.'

Mustapha smiled broadly before saying, 'Only last night I said we would receive a functional phone and now we have the best of both worlds. Thankyou, do not worry, I will take great care of both of them,' and with much ceremony carefully placed a phone in each pocket.

The others laughed at his exaggerated actions and Mansour said, after allowing the laughter to die down, 'We may be using them quicker than you think because I am bringing forward our next operation. Today we will do a dry run and next week we shall carry out the operation.'

Turning to Ali he said, 'Which train did you take this morning?'

'The same as always, but the women were not aboard today,' he replied, noticing a flash of disappoint cross his interlocutors face.

Mustapha, on the other hand was all ears. 'Trains' 'women', what were they planning? He settled himself more comfortably in his chair, not wishing to miss anything that could indicate what their plan was.

Mansour turned and stared out of the office window as though seeking inspiration. The window was filthy and the weak morning sun was having difficulty piercing the grime to illuminate the office. Finally he said, 'It is only a trial run so it will not matter if they are there or not.'

Mustapha thinking quickly said, 'Can you not tell us what the operation entails? Will we require any special equipment or clothing? I ask this as naturally all my things are back in my flat.'

'Do not worry, all is being organised here. I still have one or two calls to make so if you want to go and eat, go now and be back for one o'clock.' With that Mansour unlocked the office door, indicating that the meeting was, for the moment, over.

Ali and Mustapha left together and decided to try a restuarant, a barbecue and grill, a short walk from the arcade. The day had brightened considerably and they were both pleased to be out of the arcade office and able to breathe the fresh, if somewhat polluted, air of London.

Reaching the restaurant they entered and selected a table near to the window, where they could watch the shoppers and sightseers passing by. It was early and there were few other customers. After refusing the offer of an aperitif, they both ordered steaks and settled back with a bottle of iced water to await the arrival of the food.

'What can it be about and who are the women you mentioned?' mused Mustapha. 'Do you have an idea of what this is all about?'

'The only thing I can tell you is that I have been following two women each Thursday for the last few weeks. They catch the same train down and the same train back. I must be careful not to say too much as Zanzibar plays things very close and would not be happy if he knew I was telling you everything, so when we get back just play dumb,' said Ali, regretting already having spoken so openly.

'My friend,' Mustapha sighed, reaching across the table to grasp the other's forearm, 'do not be worried on my account. We work together, we trust each other and we must be ready together when there is something urgent or dangerous to do. What is so special about these women?'

Ali hesitated, caught between his loyalty to Zanzibar and his friendship to Mustapha. Finally he said, 'One of the women is the wife of a police chief who Zanzibar hates but what he has planned I do not know.

Undoubtedly he will tell us more when we return. Now, look at those two beauties,' he continued, indicating two young women who were window shopping, thus deflecting the attention of Mustapha, in the hope that the conversation would change.

Happily, it was not necessary as their food arrived and they were soon both engrossed in devouring their steaks.

-o-o-o-o-o-o-o-

Whilst they were eating, Mansour was engaged in more delicate work with Wahid. On the workbench, in the workshop behind the office and out of sight of the arcade public, they had just finished putting ten pounds of plastic explosive, several bags of nails and a detonating device, in a smart leather suitcase.

'Wahid, tell me, you are sure that the detonator is not connected and that under no circumstances can this device explode,' Mansour said worriedly, with beads of perspiration running down his forehead and dripping off the end of his nose.

'I have told you there is nothing to worry about. This cannot possibly explode until the detonator is correctly installed,' replied the engineer. 'You can drop it on the floor, hit it with a hammer, even set fire to it, but it will not explode. There now,' he said, closing the case and locking it, 'you have the keys and the case is ready for transportation.'

Mansour placed the key carefully in the ticket pocket of his jacket and then placed the suitcase on the floor behind the door, out of sight of inquisitive eyes. He then glanced at his watch, noting that the afternoon engineer would soon be arriving.

'Wahid,' he said addressing the engineer, who was in the act of changing his clothes prior to terminating his day's work, 'you are sure you know exactly what you have to do this afternoon. After the last cock-up I want this operation to go just as I have planned it. That is why I must insist and check and then double check.'

'Rest in peace, my friend. The parcel is in my car and I will place it myself at the time and place agreed. Do not worry. All will go well and people will start to realise that we are a force to be reckoned with,' answered Wahid proudly.

'We have come a long way together, yet there still remains much to be done,' Mansour stated, looking keenly at Wahid as he spoke. 'You and

I started on this long road together and soon we shall be welcomed by those who went before us to open up that road which will lead to Islam being recognised as the one true religion. Those unbelievers who refuse to change will be made to change or will die.'

Wahid approached Mansour and embraced him before leaving, saying, 'Tomorrow will see the start of our road to victory. Courage, my friend, courage.'

The two men saw that the afternoon engineer was wending his way through the arcade towards them and Wahid broke the embrace and, without another word or a backward glance, left the arcade. Mansour left the office taking the suitcase with him and went to his car, locking the suitcase firmly in the boot.

On checking his watch, he saw that it was nearly one o'clock and was strolling slowly back towards the arcade, when he saw Ali and Mustapha walking towards him. He joined them and together the three entered the arcade and settled themselves in the office.

'This afternoon I have decided to do a dry run for a future operation, but it will not really start before this evening. You will not require any special equipment or arms and therefore I propose that we meet back here in an hour and a half which will give me time to find a bite to eat and for you to stretch your legs.'

The door to the office was suddenly thrust open and the engineer entered, looking suspiciously at the three men in the office. Seeing that Mansour was one of the three all suspicion left his face and he stepped aside to let the three men, who had risen to their feet, walk past him and out into the arcade.

Once outside, Mansour strolled away, leaving Ali and Mustapha standing undecided on the pavement.

'What do you fancy, Mustapha, a film or a bit of window shopping?'

'It is such a nice day that it would be nice to stroll in the sunshine and perhaps find an ice cream parlour, as I love ice cream.'

In reality, Mustapha was in a turmoil, trying to think of how he could contact Bill Bowler, whilst realising that he knew very few details of the proposed operation. Finally he placed his arm over Ali's shoulder saying, 'Come, I will find you the biggest and tastiest ice cream and we can sit and enjoy the sunshine,' hoping at the same time that Ali could tell him more of what was to happen.

# CHAPTER 23

Richard, having spent time on a lazy lunch with his ex—London colleagues, during which they had discussed the rapidly changing face of the Police Force, left Scotland Yard, finding himself with time in hand for his appointment with the Home Secretary. The day was warm and fine and he started to stroll in the general direction of Westminster.

Why not the Abbey, he thought to himself, it's been a long time, and without further ado, he took out his telephone, on impulse, and called his wife. She answered on the third ring, and finding that she and Milly were quite close by, they agreed to meet at Westminster Abbey.

Ten minutes later found the three of them standing in the sunshine as they admired the wonderful building that had withstood the might of the German Air Force, during the dark days of the second World War.

'I'll tell you what,' said Richard, 'my meeting should not take too long. We could meet here at say five o'clock and with a bit of luck we could beat the trafic. What do you say to that?

Susan looked at him quizzically. 'Just in case, we must have a contingency plan. If you are not here by five fifteen, we must be away to catch the train. Also, do not forget the children are meeting us at the station. Are you sure you will be on time?'

'I can't be certain of anything, but if I find that I cannot be here I will ring you and let you know. Now, there's a pub across the road, let us have a quick drink, then I will leave you to continue spending.'

After finishing their drinks, Richard kissed his wife and Milly goodbye and started on the walk to the Home Office and his meeting with the Home Secretary. He strolled along Great Peter Street admiring the buildings before turning into Marsham Street where sat the Home Office. Before entering, he telephoned his driver instructing him to be available at a quarter to five. That done he entered the building and was quickly ushered into a small waiting room, comfortably furnished with leather arm chairs, a deep woollen carpet and a coffee table with up to date newspapers and periodicals. 'Better than the dentists' thought Richard picking up the Times, and willingly accepting the offer of a coffee from a very well turned out young secretary.

Half an hour later, with still no sign of the Home Secretary, Richard began to realise that he was being punished by being kept waiting, a deliberate ploy, yet one which he personally found to be juvenile and insulting. However, he did realise that now he would not be able to meet his wife as planned and reaching into his pocket he took out his telephone and called her, only to hear the engaged tone. Cursing to himself, he replaced his telephone in his pocket and settled himself, determined not to let his anger show.

Nearly an hour after the original appointment time, the secretary reappeared and indicated that the Home Secretary was now available to see him. Straightening his tie and fixing a smile on his face he followed the secretary to a conference room where he was confronted by Sir Peter Swift, Home Secretary, and his old acquaintance Thompson, better known as the Twat.

'Mr. Grant, so sorry to have kept you waiting. Mr. Thompson of course you know,' said Sir Peter, making no effort to shake hands whilst indicating an upright chair, which was facing the two upholstered seats on which he and Thompson were seated. Still smiling, Richard seated himself and regarded the two men, showing no trace of his inner emotions.

Thompson was dressed in civilian clothes, a dark double breasted suit and, naturally, a Bramshill College tie. He was also wearing a very smug expression as he regarded Richard, waiting for the interview to begin. The Home Secretary, on the other hand was in his shirt sleeves, with a very determined look on his face.

Finally, the Home Secretary broke the silence. 'I have asked you here today as I am concerned about certain remarks you apparently made to my Inspector of Constabulary the other day. Is it really true that you suggested drugs should be legalised?'

Richard looked from one to the other and replaced the smile on his face with a a a more serious expression. Seeing that a reply was expected, he cleared his throat and said,

'My views on drugs are well known and for some time now I have been saying that legalisation is the only way to end this problem.'

The Home Secretary appeared bemused then finally laughed to himself before saying, 'Rubbish. With dedicated men and forceful politicians, drugs will be eliminated altogether. Only the other day our leader was expressing his joy with that seizure of five tons of cocaine here in London. To speak of legalisation is defeatism,' he finished with a theatrical striking of the table with his clenched fist.

Quite unmoved, Richard replied, 'There are millions of drug users in the United Kingdom alone. Five tons may seem a lot, but in reality it is the tip of the iceberg. I said to Mr. Thompson, that the drug problem has now existed for some fifty years and is growing yearly. No matter how many arrests are made, there are dozens of people waiting to take the places vacated. Punishments do not deter, the profits in drugs are vast and in my opinion the huge amounts of money that are spent on so called drug prevention could be far better spent elsewhere.'

'I would agree that an astronomical amount of money is set aside to fight this problem, but the public reaction to any suggestion of legalisation would be one of unprecedented fury. This is an international problem which is being fought throughout the World by responsible countries such as ourselves and I personally would never give my vote to legislation. The Prime Minister himself has stated that with a concerted effort this drug flow could be stopped. Mr. Thompson has done an in depth study and assures us this is so.'

Thompson smirked at these remarks then glared at Richard, firmly believing he had been put into place. Richard composed himself, cast a glance at Thompson, then addressed the Home Secretary. 'Firstly, I would like to say that you could not be more wrong. Drugs are entering this Country in huge quantities, proved by the fact that in spite of the drug seizures, the price of the product to the consumer is dropping, indicating that there is a price war between dealers. This is a problem that has existed for years and in my opinion the only alternatives are, to legalise, secondly, to buy each year the entire World production and destroy it, which I am sure you will agree is a non starter or thirdly to employ sufficient persons to search each and every mode of transport entering the Country. That also I would argue would be so costly that it is also a non-starter.'

'My dear Chief Constable, the public would never stand for it. Surely, even you must see that?'

'The consumers are the public from all walks of life. You say they will not accept legalisation yet I would argue that they have not even been asked.

When you consider this problem as I have from the criminal viewpoint, the huge sums of money made, the numerous crimes committed by users wanting money for their next fix, and the numerous killings and shootings involving traffickers battling for territory, then you will see that something must be done. It will take courage and daring to legalise, but at some stage someone with that courage will prevail. Roosevelt ended prohibition and I think one can say that he was a great Statesman.'

A short silence followed whilst the Home Secretary considered the statement made by Richard. 'I cannot say I am convinced, but I will certainly reflect on your comments. Now, onto this so called terrorist investigation. I personally instructed Mr. Thompson to inform you that I wanted this whole matter passed to the Met. Police as they are far more qualified to deal with it. From what Mr. Thompson says your enquiry is relatively a minor one and one which could be handled easily here in London in conjunction with other ongoing terrorist enquiries.'

Richard sat rigidly in his chair thinking furiously of how best to reply.

Thompson was watching him with a sardonic smile, hoping to see him squirm under this questioning. Revenge is sweet was the thought running through his head, as he remembered the humiliation he had suffered in Richard's office.

'Sir Peter', began Richard, 'I honestly believe that Mr. Thompson has made an error in judgment in reporting to you that our enquiry is of a minor nature. To date, the terrorist organisation has stolen firearms and over a ton of explosives. We have recovered some of the firearms, but we do not know where are the explosives. Two men were arrested in relation to these offences, but whilst on remand in prison custody, both have been apparently executed. If my information is correct, a third person, brother to the two dead men, was also executed on the orders of the head of this organisation. We have a man inside the organisation working in very close colloboration with my chief of detectives and obviously this man would be in great danger should his true identity be revealed.'

'That is all very well Mr. Grant, but as I have said the Met have the men and the experience and they can take over your informant as they are used to dealing with the criminal elements who rat on their pals.'

'This informer is a senior Pakistani officer who has spent a long time on this enquiry and has put his life on the line to help us. He had a great deal of information from Pakistan which has dove tailed with our enquiries and I am convinced that we are within an ace of identifying this terrorist group. We know that this group would like to surpass the atrocity of the eleventh September and that is why I must urge you to leave this enquiry with us.'

'Mr. Thompson must have overlooked the business of the informant, but I have already ordered that this enquiry be handed forthwith to the Met. If my instructions have been heeded and I hope they have, your chief of detectives, with whom I have personally spoken this morning, should by now have handed over everything to the Met.'

Richard was dumb struck. How Thompson could have done such a thing—then he realised that was why he was called the Twat. With no active police service to speak of, he had now endangered the whole enquiry and especially the safety of the informant. Thompson was once again smirking and Richard was hard pressed not to leap to his feet and hit him.

'Why, Mr. Grant, you look ill. Here take a glass of water. I can personally assure you that everything will be all right. I trust the Met to deal with this little matter and it should release your men to deal with other things, especially public order offences which are creating a lot of interest in many constituencies throughout the Country. What are your thoughts on the subject?'

What could he do, what could he say? Richard was in a quandry.

'Mr. Home Secretary, I am aghast that you have taken the line of action that you have just outlined to me. Only a couple of hours ago I was speaking with members of the serious crimes squad and they informed me that they are over run with work at the moment. Our enquiry has reached a critical pitch and I must confess to say that I am astounded by the arbitrary action you have taken.'

'Chief Constable, the subject is closed and now, if you please, reply to my question regarding civil disorder. It is a subject very close to my heart and I am impatient to hear your views.'

Richard looked across at Thompson, who was thoroughly enjoying himself, seeing Richard, normally so confident, being brought into line, and not before time, he thought. However, breathing deeply to calm himself, Richard settled more comfortably into his uncomfortable chair and, having composed himself, he said, 'In all my years I have never before seen such a cavalier attitude taken by anyone, and certainly not a Home Secreatry and his Inspector of Constabulary, interposing in this way in an on going enquiry. Only time will tell what the consequences will be, but I have a nasty feeling that something not very nice will come of all this.'

Sir Peter was already on his feet, pointing at Richard, saying,

'You are damn right there, the nasty feeling will be felt by you when you are relieved of your duties. I will not condone being spoken to in such a manner. I was ready to accept your excuses for having insulted my good friend here, but no longer. The quicker I find a replacement for you the better it will be for everyone involved.'

Richard sat unmoved by this outburst. 'I really am extremely hurt by the manner in which I have been received and treated here. When I arrived, I was quite prepared for a hostile reception, but I was certainly not prepared for what I have heard today.

When I was promoted Chief Constable I decided that my allegiance to my superiors would be unquestionable and that my duties were to the public and the persons serving under me.

I joined the Force some thirty years ago when Police Officers were visible, unarmed and doing a very good job in difficult circumstances. Unfortunately, politics interfered and successive Home Secretaries, obviously wishing to leave their personal hall mark, continually chopped and changed, until we have the Police Force of today, confused, in the main badly led and suffering from a lack of guidance and training. Funds are constantly being cut, whilst we are exhorted to increase arrests and maintain a steady contact with the public, whilst keeping a low profile in order to keep complaints to a minimum.'

The Home Secretary, having regained his seat, started to rearrange the papers on his desk. His eyes fell on a comment that Richard had apparently made to Thompson. He picked up the paper and indicated for Thompson to join him. Thompson immediately jumped to his feet and scurried to his mentors side. Together the two of them read the paper and then carried out a whispered conversation, which Richard was not able to hear.

'Mr. Grant,' began the Home Secretary, after indicating to his minion Thompson that he could be seated, 'I will repeat myself and say that there is only one chief here and that is me. I am Home Secretary and shall certainly not be critcised by a simple Chief Constable. I hope this is clear. Now, I would like you to explain what your plans are to increase public confidence in your Force.'

'Mr. Home Secretary, I believe that my Force has a reputation second to none, regarding good relationships with the public. I keep as many officers as possible on their feet, on the beat and in close contact with the public. Policing is based more on prevention than prosecution in my Force and I can say that reported cases of public disorder criminal damage and general devilment, is constantly declining.'

'Unfortunately you do not seem to understand what I, as Home Secretary, am trying to achieve. With the help of Mr. Thompson, I am working towards a National Police Force, with less men, but with better transport and equipment. Too many policemen are tied up in routine office jobs, which could be easily handled by civilian staff, thus releasing them for outside work.'

'I am wholeheartedly against a National Police Force,' said Richard, who had now decided to let his feelings be known. 'Local knowledge is one of the mainstays of our Service and naturally this would be lost if a National Force was formed. I will argue that people of today have not changed and, with one or two exceptions all crime and public disorder offences are committed by local people. A man on the beat sees and hears things that a man in a car would ignore and officers, being human and having a comfortable car to travel in, would be loathe to leave the warmth and comfort in order to brave the elements. As to replacing officers with civilians, I would like to point out that many office jobs can only be done by persons with Police experience and that many of those officers are people reaching the end of their service or are unfit for outside duties.'

'Are you telling me, Chief Constable, that you are keeping slackers and wastrels in office jobs. If a man is unfit he should be pensioned off. We are not running a rest home or holiday camp. Let me have a list of any persons in your Force who fall into those categories you have just outlined and I shall soon make short shrift of them.'

What an insufferable, bigoted prick this man is, thought Richard, looking at Sir Peter. I can now see where Thompson has been spending his time, but I shall not let them grind me into the dust. 'I will simply say in reply to your insinuations that any long serving officers in office jobs have given their best years and in many cases their health, in serving the public and that the experience gained is used countless times a day, in fighting crime.'

Sir Peter gazed at Richard for several seconds, then, after brushing away a piece of imaginary fluff from his tie, he said, 'You protect your men, but according to Mr. Thompson here, you are only too ready to attack this institution and the persons who work within it, people who have indeed been electecd by the democratic system in force in this Country.'

'Not knowing what Mr. Thompson has said, makes it difficult for me to reply, but if he is relating to comments made about elected officers fiddling their expenses and or otherwise lining their pockets by fraudulent means, I would submit that such information is common knowledge and makes me wonder what he had in mind when he reported this to you. It is quite true today that the man in the street is far better informed of what is happening in this Country and many of them are sick of seeing such acts of dishonesty going mainly unpunished, whilst a different means is reserved for them if they should stray from the straight and narrow. People are also up in arms about different decisions that are made, affecting their daily lives, and would love to have the chance to have a say in these decisions.'

'The people vote in order that people like myself can be elected to make decisions for them. Can you imagine what would happen if we were to let ill informed and uneducated people have a hand in decision making. Chaos, absolute chaos, that is what we would have,' stated Sir Peter, triumphantly, turning to Thompson for his appreciation of the remarks he had made and being pleased to see Thompson enthusiastically nodding his head and smiling.

'In my opinion, Mr. Home Secretary, you could not be more wrong. People of today are better educated, well informed by the medias and the internet. The majority of people, as I pointed out to Mr. Thompson, simply want a job, a house, a wife and two point five children with a bit of spending money and a car if possible, and they would be happy.

Unfortunately, successive Governments have not supplied these simple needs, preferring instead to go onto the World stage. Huge numbers of immigrants, many of them unemployed, being supplied with housing, financial aid and health care, whilst native English men are losing their jobs, their families and finally their homes . . . .'

Furious, Sir Peter leapt to his feet shouting, 'This is scandalous, you have no right to voice such opinions in this office. You are politically very incorrect and what is more your comments are bordering on racism. I shall not stand for this, do you hear me?'

'Loud and clear' replied Richard, smiling inwardly at the horrified expression on Thompson's face. He waited until the Home Secretary had regained his composure and then said, 'Unfortunately, the truth can hurt and what I will now say will probably shock you even more, but in my opinion and in the not too distant future, we are going to be embroiled in civil problems as the population is becoming extremely agitated. Unemployment, racial problems and family breakdowns are reaching critical pitch and something will happen to set the ball rolling.'

'What rubbish. I know nothing of this and I am far better informed than you are. There are some racial tensions, but all in all the situation is certainly not drastic. I am actually informed that in the main racial problems are diminishing.'

'May I suggest that perhaps your advisers are telling you what you would like to hear and not the truth, as I can assure you my information is very good.'

Sir Peter paused as though in thought then said, 'Perhaps you would like my job, Mr. Grant, but I cannot see you making a success as you lack the intellectual know how necessary in holding a seat in Government and you certainly do not have the charisma to hold such a post.'

Richard looked at Sir Peter who was preening himself, whilst waiting for Richard to reply. What to say. He looked likely to lose his job, a job he had done faithfully for over thirty years and yet he could not let this self opinionated person ride roughshod over him.

'Sir Peter', began Richard, 'I have always believed that I would finish my career and then retire to write my memoirs. Today, having been threatened with losing my job, I would have to find something else, so why not politics. Irrespective of your views on my capabilities, I do have certain ideas of what a real democracy should be like and, if given the chance, I would love to show yourself and others like you, that there is a different form of democracy that would work, in my opinion, better than the one in place today.'

Smiling encouragement, Sir Peter said, 'Go on, this should be interesting. I love debating and although I do not look upon you as a suitable debating partner, I will humour you. So carry on, let's hear your ideas, my dear Sir,' this latter being served with a liberal sprinkling of sarcasm.

Completely non plussed, Richard gathered his thoughts; then, straightening himself, he squared his shoulders and addressed himself to Sir Peter.

'I have always served the people, and if given my way, the people would have a very big say in ALL subjects governing their daily lives.

Health, employment, housing and immigration would all be put to the vote. Naturally, before a referendum, all available information on the subject at hand would be transmitted to the people, but it would be their vote that would decide the issue. Right or wrong in the Governments mind, the decision would stand and time will be the only judge.

If I had my way, the first referendum would be whether or not to restore the death penalty for all cases of murder, and I am confident that there would be a resounding 'yes' vote.'

A silence fell in the room as these words were digested.

Finally Sir Peter leaned forward and looking intently at Richard, who easily maintained eye contact, said, 'Twaddle. Utter rubbish. The death penalty is abolished and will stay that way.

There is no proof whatsover that the death penalty will reduce the number of murders and I for one would never condone its return. A barbaric practice and what if an innocent were to be convicted and executed. No, it's gone and will stay gone.'

'Each person,' said Richard, 'has one life. If you should take a life, why should you keep your own? In my mind the question is as simple as that. Whether or not less murders would be committed I do not know, but I do know that convicted murderers would not commit further crime. In addition, to the best of my knowledge, no innocent person has ever been executed as even in the case of Evans, if Christie did kill his wife he, certainly killed the child,' continued Richard, making allusion to the Rillington Place murders and the execution of Timothy Evans in 1953, who was convicted of murdering his wife, a murder later attributed to Christie, who had killed a number of women. Evans, although never charged; was believed to have killed his only child.

'No, I am convinced that given a vote, the result would be sixty to forty, if not more in favour of a return to Capital Punishment. I am not advocating treating the guilty ones to the same measures of violence or depravity that they themselves dispensed. No, any form of execution will suffice, we could even give the accused a choice, as long as the end result is death.'

'Well let us hope that you never come to power,' laughed Sir Peter, 'as I am sure I would not like to see your vote put to the test. That is why the existing system is so good as people such as myself, born to lead and decide, have been placed in high office to ensure that the right decisions are always made.'

By this time Richard was tired of playing political games with this pompous personage and his fat acolyte and he simply said, 'Only time will tell, but I am convinced that sooner, rather than later, we are going to see trouble in many cities and in many countries, as the problems are not only in this Country but throughout Europe and perhaps even, the World. There are no statesmen, only politicians, and there main aim seems to be to create a Europe for the politicians, to create a ruling political class which on present showing will lead to catastrophe. Happily, we are not in the Euro zone, but we risk to suffer harm if Europe is not controlled quickly."

You seem fairly well read, Mr. Grant, but I cannot possibly agree with you. Our strength comes now from the fact that we have twenty seven countries arm in arm, putting on a united front against the States and other great countries. Alone, we could never do that.'

'My knowledge is much the same as the majority of the adult population of this Country,' replied Richard, carefully selecting his words. 'I am one of the millions who regret the Europe of today. I am English born and bred. I admire the traditions of this Country, I love my fellow men and I believe that throughout Europe others are regretting the fact that their National identity is being lost.'

'By being European,' replied Sir Peter, sweeping Richard's views under the proverbial carpet, 'tells me that I am a small part of an enormous family. Europe will go from strength to strength and I shall take huge pride from the fact that I was instrumental in bringing this about.'

'As for myself, I am English but classed as British on my passport,' stated Richard looking at the two men facing him. 'To any suggestion that all Europeans are equal is an insult to many.'

'Two thousand odd years ago,' he continued, 'the Italians, or Romans if you prefer, were the finest fighting machine in the known World. Their armies conquered, enslaving the peoples in many cases, taking their riches, thus multiplying their own wealth by many times over. With the passage of time, they then introduced change and modernisation, whilst still maintaining their force, showing that to be rich and powerful was to be respected and feared. They were destroyed from within, something which could happen in Europe as there are far too many individuals vying for position or power, and not being particularly bothered how they achieve it.'

'Today, what do we have? Five or six rich countries who, having formed what was the Common Market, then invited all these poor countries to come and join the fun. Now instead of rich and poor we now have lots of poverty and a very few extremely rich people, who tend to be very close friends with the political classes. Sir Peter, the people are not dupes and as they see their living standards falling, they are constantly seeking the where and whyfore.'

With as much sarcasm as he could muster, Sir Peter said,

'Naturally you have the answer, I suppose?'

'Unfortunately no. Firstly I cannot understand why you need to project a united front against the United States. They are the best allies we have and they have proved their worth for the last one hundred years. Irrespective of what you may think, I believe we are no longer a major power and will remain that way until we leave the European market and return to our own ideas and ideals. The only thing that could change my mind, is that we form a European Government, and that the individual countries making up Europe become Federal States, much as in America today.

'One of the first things that needs to be done is to sort through all the strangers and immigrants in this Country, and to expel all those who do not have the good of this Country in their hearts. I, like many of my fellow men, am disgusted to see these Islamists in England, calling for uprisings and deaths whilst promulgamating their prophet Mohamed, and no one in this Government says or does anything to stop them.'

Sir Peter seemed bemused. 'My dear Sir, we have freedom of speech in this Country and they have as much right as any other to vent their feelings. That is democratic.'

'I would argue that they are inciting others to commit breaches of the peace, or even worse, and I wouild certainly not stand for it in my Force. In addition, if we are so set on free speech, why are white, English born and bred persons, convicted and quite often jailed, for making racist remarks. Once again, double standards, or, worse still, do our present day politicians not like their fellow men.'

'There you go. You just do not see the big picture. A few hotheads shouting should not affect you like that,' teased Sir Peter, who after glancing at Thompson, said, 'We, the men of the World ignore them for they are of no consequence.'

Richard felt his hackles rising, realising that Sir Peter was baiting him. Suppressing his anger he said, 'That may well be, but I like many redblooded Englishmen, feel shock and outrage that these people can act with impunity when they should be thrashed then thrown out of the Country. We are fighting on many fronts against these same Islamists and our soldiers are dying for what? The enemy is already here, on our shores and we do nothing to stop them.'

'Stop, stop,' cried Sir Peter. 'I can see that you will never understand that politics are dictated by events throughout the World and that it is seemly at the moment to ignore these minor incidents. Do not worry, our Government is well aware of the problem and is certainly not bothered by it.'

'In that case,' retorted Richard, 'I prefer to remain silent as I can assure you the majority does not agree with that point view.'

'Then we shall agree to disagree,' said Sir Peter, getting to his feet, thus indicating that the interview was now at an end. 'However, before you go I would like you to give me the tape recording that you apparently have of your interview with my friend, Mr. Thompson. No point in leaving ends untied is there?' said Sir Peter, in a tone which could be best described as jocular.

'Unfortunately, the tape recorder and the tape are my personal property,' replied Richard, straight faced, but forcefully restraining the urge to laugh, 'and therefore I must refuse. Having been threatened with dismissal today I may well need that tape to defend myself in the future. I am sure that you can appreciate my position.'

Sir Peter looked as though he would explode, but managed to hold his emotions in check.

'So be it, the weekend looms and a few days of reflection may produce a solution. Thank you for coming this afternoon, Chief Constable,' declared Sir Peter, whilst maintaining the distance of the desk between himself and Richard. 'My secretary will see you out. Good day'. With that Sir Peter turned and started to talk to Thompson in lowered tones.

Richard, realising that he had been dismissed, simply said,

'Good day gentlemen' and walked swiftly across the room, closing the door on the whispering duo. 'The sooner Lord Hamilton replaces that prat, the better it will be for everyone. What a strange day this has been' he thought to himself, starting to replay parts of the conversation in his mind whilst realising that his day was far from over, with the long drive back to his headquarters to be completed before he could regale his wife with the days events.

Thinking of his wife, he looked at his watch and saw that it was now past five thirty. Smiling at the seated secretary as he crossed to the main door, he reached into his pocket for his telephone.

His wife answered on the second ring. 'Don't bother' she said, 'I knew we would need a contingency plan. The children are with us at the station so we will take the six o'clock as usual. Don't worry about us, we are old enough to look after ourselves.

I will see you when you get home. Love you' and with that she cut the communication.

Richard went in search of his driver who he found in the gate keepers lodge drinking tea. 'Right with you Sir,' said the driver jumping to his feet. He picked up his cap and driving gloves and led Richard to the parked Jaguar.

# CHAPTER 24

The sun was still shining brightly as Ali and Mustapha made their way back to the arcade. Despite various ploys, Mustapha had not managed to prise any more information from Ali and realised that he must bide his time. Zanzibar appeared to be the main spring of the terrorist group, yet try as he might, he had not managed to find his true identity.

Before they arrived at the arcade, they were joined by Mansour, who indicated that they should accompany him. He led them to the yard where his Audi motor car was parked and, after opening the doors, indicated that the two men should get in. Ali made a beeline for the front passenger seat and Mustapha installed himself on the back seat, taking in the luxury of the car. 'Nice wheels' he said to Mansour, who acknowledged the compliment with a smile and a nod of the head.

Mustapha glanced at his watch and saw that it was now past three o'clock. Zanzibar started the car and carefully reversed from the yard into Oxford Street, turning left in the direction of Bayswater. Trafic was fairly heavy and they travelled relatively slowly, the windows open to let in a bit of fresh air.

'We have plenty of time,' said Mansour, 'and I just feel like taking a pleasant drive. In addition, it is nice to have good company as too often I find I am alone. What about you Mustapha? Do you enjoy good company?'

'I suppose I am very much like you, Zanzibar. I am all too often alone. I have no family except you and the other group members and my friends I could count on one finger.'

'Have you been alone a long time?' asked Ali.

Mohsin did not reply immediately, instead he reflected on his cover story. Thinking he may not have heard, Ali repeated his question and Mohsin, who had by now collected his thoughts, said, 'I am sorry my brother, I was lost in thought. It is a long time since my family was exterminated by those bastards in the Punjab.'

'Which bastards are you referring to?' asked Mansour, not wishing to be excluded from the conversation.

'The Government lackeys, the soldiers who kill to order and enjoy it more each day. I was once proud to be Pakistani, but no longer. It was only by luck that I escaped execution, and since then I have promised that I shall not rest until my enemies are defeated and Allah is recognised throughout the World.'

'Then you are in good company,' replied Mansour, 'as we are all sworn to eradicate the non-believers. Plans have been laid and very soon we will all be put to the test as there is still much to be done. If everything goes according to plan, within six months our names will be linked with that of The Prophet; that much I can promise you.'

'What are your plans?' asked Mansour, hopefully, only to be rebiffed by the ferocity in Mansour's voice as he snarled, 'All in good time. When I am ready I will explain and not before.'

A silence fell in the car and Mansour, in a lighter tone said, 'Let's enjoy the drive,' and with that he turned right into Gloucester Place and started to accelerate. They crossed the Marylebone Road, continuing along Park Road until they turned right at the round-a-bout and into Prince Albert Road.

Seeing the sign for the Lords cricket ground, Ali said, 'One thing I miss is playing cricket. The joy of standing in the sunshine, ever alert for the ball and after with the bat in my hands facing fast or spin bowling. My childhood was spent on playing and watching cricket and I am sure that if this Holy War had not started I would today be a great cricketer.'

'Patience, my friend,' said Mansour, 'the War will soon be over and then we can all play together,' this last said in a suggestive tone which made Ali's skin tingle.

'Interesting' thought Mohsin, 'so our leader is a queer. Strange how so many violent, vicious types, who have the charm and panache to lead, are roaring puffs.' With that he settled back in the seat and pretended to sleep, closing his eyes and regulating his breathing, whilst at the same time honing his nerves and hearing to maximum pitch.

'Our friend appears to have dropped off,' remarked Mansour, and Ali turned in his seat to see that Mustapha did indeed appear to be asleep. 'A pity that there is not enough time to renew our friendship this afternoon, but there will be other after noons, I am sure.'

Ali moved in his seat until he was close enough to touch Mansour, happy to be in such close proximity to his hero and lover. Through half closed eyes, Mohsin saw Ali start to stroke Mansour's thigh. Anything but that, thought Mohsin, and with a realistic snort, he appeared to wake and look around as if in a daze. Ali had quickly moved back into his seat as Mohsin said, 'I must have dozed off.'

Mansour, completely unmoved said, 'You missed the cricket ground, but as you can see, we are close to Regents Park. A walk in the sun should do us good and I may be tempted to buy us all an ice cream.'

Finding a parking space, he secured the car, and the three men strolled into the park. There were not many people around and Mohsin decided to try to gain further information about Mansour and, if possible, his future plans.

Looking around and seeing that there were no people close to them he said, 'Zanzibar, tell me have you been involved in this work a long time?'

Mansour, who was still in a quandry about a traitor in their midst thought carefully before answering. Perhaps he may learn something more about Mustapha, a man who had been sent to him with glowing references, but someone he knew very little about. He had proved himself during the various operations they had carried out together, showing a cool head when under pressure and certainly not squeamish when it came to violent death.

'I have been involved in this work nearly all my adult life,' he began, 'and I have carried out operations all over Europe. The biggest operation I have been involved in was the Madrid train bombings in March in two thousand and four. What a day and what brave comrades fell for the cause. I have always sworn, although I am not a vengeful man, to bring down one of the investigators from Interpol, who traced us to our safe house. I escaped, but unhappily the others were killed in an explosion'

'Have you managed to bring this person down? asked Mohsin, interestedly, 'or is he still waiting to be dealt with. I have people I would like to see dead as well. Perhaps we could work together. What do you think?'

'Patience, that is what I think. I rush into nothing. Planning is all important as I never try to under estimate the law enforcement agencies.

Richard Grant proved that much when he traced us to our safe house in Madrid.'

Richard Grant, thought Mohsin, is Bill's Chief Constable. What is going on here? Taking the bull by the horns he said to Mansour, 'I bet you already have plans to take him down, don't you.'

'Take him down, yes, but kill him, no. What I have in mind is far better than that. He is going to suffer for the rest of his life and he will know that his suffering will be traced back to Madrid. Yes, revenge for my friends will be very, very sweet. Come now, there's an ice cream stall and I have promised to pay.'

There were several people standing around the stall and it was not possible to bring the conversation back to Richard Grant. What had he in mind for Bill's boss? If I can't find out, I'll get hold of Bill as soon as possible and see if he can shed some light.

He was brought back to reality as Mansour handed him a large cornet of vanilla ice cream. 'Daydreaming again, Mustapha, we cannot have that. There is work to be done shortly and we must all have our wits about us.'

The three men retraced their steps to the parked car and Mansour immediately drove away, turning right into Albany Street and then left onto the Euston Road, coming to a halt several minutes later close to St. Pancras railway station.

'I'll be gone for a short time with Ali,' said Mansour, 'so could you keep an eye on the car for me please. The police and wardens round here are evil.

I'll leave the keys in case you have to move the car. If you do have to, drive around the block and come back to here. I should not be more than twenty minutes.'

With that, he left the car, but not before taking the suitcase from the car boot. Together with Ali, he walked away towards the main entrance to the railway station and Mansour watched them both disappear from sight.

Mansour got out of the car to stretch his legs. He admired the station building, an absolutely marvelous construction dating from the mid to late eighteen hundreds, and mainly constructed of red bricks. The magnificent portal entrance leading to the vast interior was a work of art in itself, with the whole building being covered by a gigantic glass roof. 'To think they wanted to demolish this' thought Mohsin, 'that would have been a crime in itself. Thank goodness commonsense and the Channel Tunnel happened' making allusion to the fact that St. Pancras now houses the Eurostar trains.

Turning back to the car, he slipped into the front passenger seat and, ensuring that Mansour was nowhere in sight, he jotted down the registration number of the car in his little pocket notebook. With one eye on the railway station, he swiftly opened the glove compartment, only to be disappointed, as the only objects in there were the car handbook and a pair of sunglasses. Looking at his watch, he saw that the others had been gone for about ten minutes.

Reaching into his pocket, he took out the brand new telephone, which Mansour had given him. Ensuring that he was not being observed he quickly dialled Bill's private number, only to be rewarded with the unobtainable signal. Slipping the phone back into his pocket, he made a mental note to try again at the first opportunity.

Several minutes later, Mansour returned alone to the car, without Ali and without the suitcase.

Pretending concern, Mohsin said, 'Where's Ali?' There has not been a problem has there?'

'Don't worry, all is under control,' replied Mansour, smiling a reassuring smile. 'Did you have to drive the car?'

'No, worse luck,' replied Mohsin ruefully, 'I have often dreamed of driving such a vehicle, but it is way out of my price range.'

'Then today is your lucky day my friend as we have a journey to make and I am feeling a little tired. I also think better when someone else does the driving, so move over and let me in.'

So doing, Mohsin slid across into the drivers seat and Mansour took over the passenger seat. He waited until Mohsin had adjusted the driver's seat and the interior and exterior mirrors, pleased to see that he was meticulous in everything he did. Mohsin switched on the engine and Mansour said simply, 'Follow the blue signs to the M 1 North,' and then settled himself in his seat and closed his eyes.'

Mohsin noticed straight away the sign for the motorway and after slipping the car into gear, he expertly moved the car into the heavy trafic.

# CHAPTER 25

Soon he was driving through Harrow, thoroughly enjoying himself, reveling in the power of the Audi. Mansour appeared to be dozing and Mohsin started to let his mind wander onto how he could contact Bill as quickly as possible.

He was suddenly brought back to reality when Mansour said, 'Watch the speed, we don't want to bring attention to ourselves this late in the game.'

Mohsin realised that he had better keep his wits about him, as it was apparent that Mansour had not been sleeping at all. He saw the entrance to the M1 North and steered the sleek car onto the outside lane, accelerating smoothly. 'What a pleasure this is' he commented, as he skilfully steered the car past a line of speeding lorries.

Mansour smiled. 'I do so enjoy seeing people enjoy themselves. You are a very skilful driver. Where did you learn?'

Be very careful, Mohsin thought to himself. I don't think he would appreciate the knowledge that the army and the police taught you to drive. Instead he said, 'Before I was recruited into the organisation I was a well known, but never convicted car thief. I have driven dozens of different vehicles but this Audi is a very nice car. You are a very lucky man,' he concluded, thinking that a bit of flattery could not do any harm.

'Thank you my friend. Now I know that you are a good driver, perhaps we should consider making you my official driver.'

'I would enjoy that,' replied Mohsin, whilst thinking at the same time he would be able to ingratiate himself, thus being in a position to gain sufficient information to allow Mansour to be locked away for a long time.

'I suppose you would like to know where we are going?' Mansour suddenly said, 'so I will tell you. We are going to a town called Bedford.'

Hoping that Mansour would think him more dumb than inquisitive, Mohsin after a moments hesitation, said, 'Why?'

'I am putting the final touches to a plan I have been working on for a long time. Today is the final dress rehearsal and next week everyone will be talking about us.'

'Can I ask what it is or is it simply on a need to know basis?' asked Mohsin, whilst keeping his eyes on the road.

'I have always been very careful about my plans, but I feel that I can trust you implicitly. You proved yourself with the operations involving the guns and explosives and I was particularly pleased to see your reactions after the demise of Priest.'

'You can trust me, honestly you can,' replied Mohsin, introducing a wheedling tone into his voice. 'With Ali, I have a very good team mate, someone trustworthy and brave.'

'I know, I know and that is why the pair of you are involved in this operation. Oh look, it's the turnoff to Bedford,' exclaimed Mansour, indicating the junction with the A421.

Mohsin flipped the indicator switch and reduced speed as he entered the slip road leading to a round about, where on seeing the road was clear, he took the A421 in the direction of Bedford.

Bedford is the County town of Bedfordshire, and lies about a hundred miles north east of London. With a population of some 80,000 people, it is a quiet market town lying on the Great Ouse River. The railway station is more or less in the centre of town.

Mansour said nothing further and finally Mohsin said, 'You were going to tell me why we were going to Bedford.'

'Excuse me, my friend, I was deep in thought. Yes, Bedford. You see I am not a vindictive man, but even I make exceptions. I told you earlier about that bastard Grant. Well his wife, with a bit of luck, will be on a train which will pass through Bedford next week and her life will end there and Grant's suffering will commence. It will be a great day for me, and revenge for the lives of our comrades who died in Madrid.'

'And today, what are we going to do?'

'Simply observe. I want to know the exact time the train passes through Bedford, so that my scheme can produce the greatest number of casualities.

Ali will be on the train today to estimate how many passengers there are, as this train is a regular one and there should not be too much variation from one week to the next. It is my intention to place a bomb on the train, but perhaps you may think of a different, more interesting place to place a bomb. Where ever we place it, there must be maximum effect.'

A silence fell and Mohsin saw that he was already in Bedford and passing the Woburn Road Industrial estate. Mansour indicated that he should turn left and he noticed that the road was named Ampthill Road and that he was soon driving past a college.

'The next on the left is Woburn Road and the railway station is down there,' said Mansour and Mohsin turned left and saw before him the railway station which, he immediately noticed, was nothing like that at St. Pancras. He swung onto the car park and Mansour indicated that he should park in the middle amongst the commuter cars, of which there were very many. Finding a parking space, he parked the car, switched off the engine and said, 'Now what do you want me to do?'

Mansour made a great play of studying his watch. 'It is now 7pm. If the train left, as planned at 18.46pm. It should arrive here in about forty minutes. All I require is that you note the arrival time, the number of people leaving the train and if possible have a quick wander into the station to see how many people there are in the station. The important thing is not to draw attention to yourself.'

Mohsin digested this information and then said, 'Will you be with me or are you going elsewhere?'

'I my friend have other things to do, but Ali, who is on the train, will leave at this station and join you, so make sure you are somewhere he can see you.'

'How do we get back to London? Is there another train? Where shall we meet you in order to hand over the information we are going to obtain?'

Mansour laughed and as he opened the car door he said, 'You have proved yourself a good driver so I will leave you the car. You and Ali can drive back to London and we shall meet again at the arcade tomorrow afternoon. I trust you to look after the car. You do remember the yard where I park?' he said as a parting shot, slipping out of his seat and closing the car door dehind him. Mohsin watched him walk quickly away until he disappeared from sight behind the station buildings.

He waited a full two minutes and seeing that Mansour had apparently left the vicinity, he glanced at his watch. Just over half an hour and the train would be here. He took out his telephone and immediately called Bill. Fortunately he answered nearly immeditaly and, on hearing that it was Mohsin he said,'Listen I can't explain everything, but I am no longer in charge of this operation.'

'What are you talking about,' cried Mohsin, 'something is going down very shortly and we have a chance of rolling this up. I still do not know the identity of the leader, but shortly another member of the team will be joining me here.'

A short silence followed before Bill replied. 'This has been taken from my control on the express orders of the Home Secretary himself who called me today, ordering me to forward all documentation relating to this operation to the Serious Crime Squad, at the Met. I'm sorry, but I had no choice.'

'There is no way I am going to work with anyone else but you. These bastards are very, very dangerous. I have put my life on the line for you and you leave me up in the air like this.'

'Mohsin, I don't blame you one bit. Pull out now. Put your thoughts and information on paper and I'll send that to the Met. Then I shall stake you to the finest meal you can possibly eat. I don't like this any more than you, but I have no choice, for if I disobey this order I won't even have a job. Even my chief does not know as he is down in London and I hate to think what will happen when he finds out.

'Bill, listen and listen good. The person who has just left me here in a place called Bedford was one of the planners of the Madrid train bombings . . . .'

Cutting in, Bill said, 'Yes my chief was involved in that investigation when he was with Interpol. He's always said that some got away.'

'Please do not interrupt me. I have just been told that this will be a very bloody operation and the main target is the wife of your chief. Apparently they are afraid of attacking your chief directly so they are going for his family.'

'The bastards,' exclaimed Bill, angrily. 'Forget everything I said before. Even if it costs me my job, I can't let anything happen to my chief, who is also a very dear friend. Where are you exactly and how will I find you.'

'I am sitting in a very nice Audi motor car on the main car park outside Bedford railway station. I should be joined by a fellow terrorist, but I can get rid of him whilst I speak with you. How long will you be?'

'Provided that traffic is favourable,' said Bill as he started to put on his coat, 'I should be there in about an hour. Give me the number of your car so that I can find you easily.' He wrote down the number, picked up his car keys and said, 'I'll be with you in a hour at the latest. And thanks, thanks for everything.' With that he cut the communication and ran to his car.

# CHAPTER 26

Ali had accompanied Mansour into the railway station at St. Pancras, wondering what was in the suitcase. However, he said nothing as he was only too aware of Mansour's temper if questioned. Mansour looked at his watch and said, 'The train you normally take is the 18.46, isn't it. What I want you to do is take the train today and take this suitcase with you.'

He handed a piece of paper to Ali, saying,' When you arrive at Bedford station, I want you to leave the train and take the suitcase to the address written on the piece of paper. Mustapha will be waiting for you on the car park in my car and he can take you to the address. Afterwards he will drive you back to London and we shall meet up at the arcade.

The suitcase is locked and the contents are very valuable, so look after it. Here are the keys,' he said, handing over the suitcase keys. 'There is no message. Simply hand the case over and leave.'

Ali felt a pang of disappointment, thinking that he was being treated as a delivery man, whilst Mustapha would be driving with his lover. 'Are you sure I cannot drive with you and Mustapha can deliver the case', he said somewhat peevishly.

'No and for one very good reason. I am still very interested in the women you have been observing and if, by chance, they should show up today, I need to know. You know these women, Mustapha does not. Do not worry, what I am asking of you is of the utmost importance to my future plans.'

Still feeling a little put out, but having accepted the explanation given, Ali took the suitcase. Mansour grasped his forearms, smiled, and said, 'Until tomorrow. Have a good journey and do not forget that we are all fighting for the same ideals.'

Mansour turned and strode swiftly away and Ali, seeing that he had at least an hour to kill before the train was due to leave, wandered into a snack bar and ordered a sandwich and a coke. Finding a seat and ensuring that the suitcase was close at hand, he started to eat.

The suitcase was heavy he thought, what could be in it?

He was by nature curious, but even though he had the keys, he was afraid to open the case, firmly believing that Mansour was capable of rigging the case in such a way that he would know if it was opened by someone other than the person destined to receive it.

As he ate he ruminated. His lot was not too bad. Having been accepted as a trustworthy member of Mansour's group and as his lover, he reflected that things could be a lot worse. He finished his sandwich and coke, realising that the snack bar was rapidly filling with commuters and, glancing at his watch, he saw that the train would be leaving in about twenty minutes. He was about to leave his seat, when, completely by accident, he looked towards the door in time to see the two women he had been following, entering the snack bar. He kept his face averted and the women walked past him, taking no notice of him whatsoever, and joined a younger man and woman who were seated at a corner table.

The young couple got to their feet and embraced the two women and Ali, suddenly noticing a resemblance, realised that they were the children of the woman known to him as the wife of the police chief. 'Something to tell Zanzibar' he thought to himself, and making sure that he was not noticed, he picked up the suitcase and left the snack bar.

Glancing at the screen on which was displayed the trains and their departure times, he saw that the train he required was already taking passengers. He hurried to the ticket office and bought a one way ticket to Bedford and then made his way to the train, selecting the carriage the furthest away from the first class carriage.

He quickly found his seat, and, after placing the suitcase on the luggage rack in full view from his seat, he looked around at his fellow passengers. He found he was sharing with a young woman with two small girls and after politely saying 'Good day', he looked across to the snack bar that he had recently vacated. He was rewarded in seeing the two women, accompanied by the young couple, stroll across to the first class carriage and climb aboard.

After seeing the women board, he was amazed to see the arcade engineer, Wahid, leave the first class carriage and hurry away from the train. How strange, thought Ali, what could he have been doing?

The imminent departure of the train was announced and Ali settled back in his seat as the train slowly started to leave the station. The other passengers, after arranging their affairs, started to read whilst several took out portable computers which they began to study. Ali, feeling in his pocket, took out the brand new I-phone that Mansour had given to him and started to look at all the different features which the phone displayed.

He was so engrossed in this occupation that he was surprised to hear the announcement that the train was approaching Bedford station and that there would be a two minute wait. He got to his feet, as did other passengers, and he started to make his way towards the luggage rack in order to reclaim the suitcase.

He was standing in the middle of the carriage, when suddenly the other telephone, the one Mansour called the receiver, started to ring. Instinctively, Ali took the phone from his pocket and pressed the answer switch as he lifted the phone to his ear.

His right hand and part of his arm disappeared in a cloud of bright red blood as the telephone exploded, joined by bits of brain and flesh as his head blew apart, his body being flung across the carriage. One other person received fatal injuries and several others were injured.

Although that was dramatic in itself, it was nothing compared to the enormous explosion which ripped the first class carriage apart, causing the other carriages to be derailed, whilst strangely enough, the locomotive remained on the tracks. The explosion occurred as the train was slowing to enter the station and the derailed carriages, two of which had fallen onto their sides, helped the train to come to a halt after about two hundred yards of horrendous screeching of metal on metal.

The train came to rest with the last carriage having been thrust into the air colliding with the footbridge which connected the various platforms. A fleeting moment of absolute silence followed the stopping of the train, before the sounds of screams could be heard coming from the wreckage of the train and the railway station.

All the windows had been blown out by the explosion and bodies littered the platforms and the ticket hall. There were bodies caught in the mangled mess of the footbridge and in every direction was a scene of death and desolation. Bits of bodies were littering the platforms. Survivors started to emerge from the tangled mess of the train, shock marking their faces, as they stared disorientatedly at the chaos surrounding them.

Screams and pleas for help seemed to be coming from every part of the train and station, but it would be long minutes before rescue workers could be on hand to start the mammoth task of helping the survivors and recovering the dead. Many more would die from lack of medical attention, sorely needed for the horrific injuries that many had received.

Thankfully, as often seems to be the case, one man, a retired police officer who had been taking a leak whilst waiting for his wife who was on the train, was uninjured, and although shocked, he managed to alert the emergency services. Strangely, and when asked afterwards he could not say why, he looked at his watch and noted the time, 19.39pm exactly. Amidst all this damage and death he thought, the train was bang on time.

Within minutes of his phone call, the first fire engines and ambulances started to arrive. The first on the scene, seeing the enormity of the catastrophe, immediately recognised a very major incident and calls were sent all around the County and even surrounding counties and towns, with requests for help and blood.

Twenty minutes later, police and fire chiefs were huddled in conversation on the platform and it was quickly decided what the priorities were.

A call went straight to the Minister of the Interior, informing him of the gravity of the incident and with a formal request to mobilise the nearest army personnel to help with the rescue work.

Out of chaos came organised chaos and soon ambulances were ferrying injured persons to hospitals throughout the region. Medical personnel were called upon and they all responded brilliantly. Residents close to the railway station, who had left their homes to assist, were soon helping in any way they could, whilst others engaged in that typical English pastime of mashing huge quantities of tea and supplying that with biscuits and snacks to all and sundry, involved in the unwelcome task of trying to help the dead and dying.

The ticket hall, although having no windows, was the only suitable place to store the dead and very soon that room was filling, as bodies were brought in, after one of the many doctors present had certified death. A huge supply of blankets and sheets was found, but there were no body bags and the bodies were placed in long rows and simply covered with a sheet until such time as the difficult task of identification could be put under way.

Outside the rescue workers quickly saw that, owing to the huge amount of damage to the first class carriage, that there was no chance of finding survivors in there. However, with that knowledge, several of them volunteered to go into what was left of the carriage and among the smell of death, the pools of blood and the numerous body parts, they stoically carried out the task of removing the dead.

From time to time a cheer would go up as a survivor was found, but it was soon to be realised that the death count would be very high. Investigators from the Police and Fire Services, started to examine the carnage of the train and, although it was swiftly suspected that a bomb was responsible, it would be many hours before the truth was known.

During the examination of the other carriages, rescue workers were intrigued to find a very badly mutilated body, in a carriage which had suffered a little less than the others. However, there was no time to ponder this question as there was much to be done and so the body of Ali and the other passenger killed by the exploding telephone were placed with the other dead in the ticket hall.

# CHAPTER 27

Bill was driving as fast as he considered safe, and seeing that he was approaching Bedford, he telephoned Mohsin. Thankfully, he possessed a 'hands free' telephone system in the car and could speak whilst concentrating on his driving.

Mohsin answered immediately, and in response to Bill's first question, explained exactly where he was parked. Bill asked him if there had been any further developments and Mohsin simply told him that Mansour had left him with the car and apparently returned to London. He did hint, however, that it might be an idea for Bill to start thinking of organising a surveillance team for the morrow, as he would be able to lead them straight to the arcade and ultimately to Mansour.

'Don't worry about that,' replied Bill, feeling the adrenaline starting to run, 'I'll okay all that with the chief later this evening. Firstly, I want to see you and obtain all the information you have gathered, and then discuss with you the best way to proceed.'

'No problem my friend, I am here to serve your every need,' and Bill laughed at the comical tone that Mohsin had introduced into his voice. 'On top of which I believe I can hear a train arriving. Will you be long?'

'About ten minutes, I don't want to be nailed for speeding . . . .' but before he could finish speaking, Mohsin interrupted, saying, 'Hang on, my other phones ringing.'

Bill laughed saying, 'That's why you have two hands because you have two . . . .' then suddenly stopped speaking as he heard an enormous explosion.

'Mohsin, Mohsin, what the fuck was that,' shouted Bill, only to be rewarded by silence. Without further ado, he placed his portable blue flasher on the car roof and pushed the accelerator to the floor. In less than ten minutes he found himself amidst a huge number of emergency vehicles, all flashing lights, sounding sirens and all heading apparently, in the direction of the railway station.

He switched on his police radio and immediately heard an emergency message, exhorting all available persons to go to the railway station to assist with a serious accident.

Arriving in front of the station, he saw the entrance to the car park and swung in, already searching for the Audi. It was still quite light, but owing to the large number of parked cars it was several minutes before he found the car.

It was parked in the centre of the car park between two other cars. All the windows were smashed, as were the windows of the surrounding cars. The roof of the car appeared to be buckled and, after stopping his car, he rushed to the Audi.

The scene waiting for him was one of the worst he had seen in all his police and army service. Mohsin's body was slumped against the drivers door and Bill noticed that his upper body was badly damaged and his head had disappeared. A huge pool of blood had formed in the footwell of the car. He also noted a strong smell of cordite, suggesting an explosion.

He did not touch the car and was debating on what to do next, when he was joined by two uniformed police officers. 'What's happened here?' asked the younger of the two, then promptly vomited all over his shoes as he saw the destruction in the car.

'I am Chief Superintendent Bowler,' said Bill, producing his warrant card, 'and I would like this scene to be preserved as from now. Are you able to do this,'

'It will be difficult as there is far more important work to be done,' replied the elder of the two officers. Bill realised, that in his haste to find Mohsin, he had completely forgotten the serious incident and said lamely, 'Excuse me, what exactly has happened here tonight?'

'The evening train from London,' began the elder officer, 'has been derailed and there appear to be a large number of causalities. We were sent to start setting up a security cordon around the station.'

'Can your young friend there,' said Bill, indicating the younger officer who was in the act of wiping the vomit from his shoes, 'find a senior officer, as the person in this car has been murdered and the scene must be preserved until the car can be examined by forensics.'

The younger officer did not require a written invitation, but shot away as though in training for a forthcoming athletic event, returning several minutes later with a uniformed police superintendent. 'Hello Bill, what are you doing on my patch?'

'Tommy, nice to see you, but the circumstances could have been a lot different. The body in this car is that of someone I know well, and he has been murdered, possibly by an explosive device. It is imperative that the scene be secured until I can find transport to remove this car. Can you help?'

'Naturally, but not immediately. We have a very major incident in the station. The London train has crashed and there is tremendous damage and undoubtedly a great number of dead and injured to be rescued and treated. I've never seen anything like this, never,' said the superintendent, his voice breaking with emotion. Reasserting himself he instructed the two uniformed officers to stay near the Audi car and to stop any persons from approaching the vehicle.

'I'm here for the night,' now said Bill, and after parking and locking his car he accompanied the superintendent to the station. He telephoned his headquarters and informed them that he was in Bedford at a crime scene, and that he could be contacted there if required. Then with a heavy heart he entered the station, only to stop, shocked by the carnage confronting him.

Stepping over body parts and avoiding pools of blood, he made his way towards the ruined train. He noted that the locomotive appeared to be undamaged, whereas the carriages, especially the first class carriage, were excessively damaged. Going to the first class carriage, he immediately noticed what appeared to be a huge hole burned through the inner and outer metal skins of the carriage.

'A pound to a pinch of shit that that was caused by an explosive device', he mused, but refrained from going too close as he did not wish to contaminate the scene more than was necessary. Whilst he was looking at the damage he was joined by the superintendent, who said, 'Excuse me Sir, could you come and look at this,'

Together the two men walked to the ticket office, where already numerous bodies were lining the floor. Stopping at the side of a heavily bloodstained sheet, the superintendent said, 'It's not a pretty sight,' and lifted away the sheet, revealing the mutilated body of Ali.

Bill immediately noticed the similarities in the injuries to this body and to that of Mohsin. 'Where did you find this one?' asked Bill.

'That is the strange thing. This body and another body were found together in the first carriage, the one with the least damage and the least injuries. It seems so strange that this one is so seriously mutilated.'

'Look Jimmy, I cannot comment until such time as the bodies and the vehicle outside have been thoroughly examined. However, and this is for your ears only at this stage, I believe that this man and the one outside were killed by explosive devices, probably portable telephones which had been rigged. I want you to ensure that this body is left here, untouched until I can personally organise its removal.'

'Are you saying that the train . . . .' began the superintendent, and Bill, interrupting said, 'I'm afraid so. I just looked at the first class carriage and it appears that an explosive device destroyed the carriage. Forensics will undoubtedly substantiate that this is the case.'

'I must hurry and inform our chief and I will also ask for someone from the CID to get down to give us a hand. It looks like being a long night.'

They walked together from the hall of death and Bill, who had been thinking of Mohsin and how he was going to have to explain his death, said in a choked voice, 'Just to have two minutes with the bastards who did this. That's all I ask, two minutes.'

If Bill had only known, the person responsible was sitting in a car parked some three hundred yards from the station with the Afghan, Umar Razad, who was staring at Mansour as though he was some sort of God.

'You did all that with a telephone call,' he said, amazed. 'Allah moves in mysterious ways and may he continue until victory is ours.'

Mansour, who was feeling very pleased with himself, replied, 'Come on, you drive. I feel like celebrating tonight.'

Umar started the car, and as he drove away from the scene of death and desolation, Mansour wondered who was the traitor, Ali or Mustapha. Finally, he reflected, it did not matter, as they were both now dead, although in a way it was a pity as Ali had been pretty good in bed. He glanced sideways at Umar, who was concentrating on his driving, and thought to himself that perhaps he could replace Ali in more ways than one.

# CHAPTER 28

Richard, seated in the back of the luxurious Jaguar saloon, looked at his watch and saw that nearly two hours had elapsed since he had left the Home Office.

Traffic had been horrendous coming out of London and he could feel his eyes beginning to close.

He thought back over the afternoon and, although thinking he had acquitted himself rather well, he was under no illusions as to the power the Home Secretary could wield over him. Why couldn't the freemasons have selected better coppers to be part of their organisation, he thought for the thousandth time; then realised that the answer was simple; they wanted 'yes' men, just like Thompson. He hoped that he would have enough time to finish the reorganisation of his Force, before the axe fell, but felt deep down that moves were afoot to oust him. At least it would please his wife, he thought ruefully, and then, thinking of his wife, he remembered that he had not rung to say he was on his way.

Reaching into his jacket pocket, he took out his telephone and called his home, but there was no answer. Must have gone to Millie's he thought and started to scroll through the listings on his portable, in order to telephone Millie.

Before he could find the number, he was interrupted by his driver, who had turned the volume up on the official Police radio, at the same time as he said, 'Excuse me Sir, but this sounds important.'

'All officers able to respond to extremely grave situation at Bedford Railway Station, call in please with your availability and E.T.A.' The message was repeated and Richard, who had always been a very active police officer, felt the surge of excitement that had been missing from his life, since he had been promoted to Chief Constable.

Glancing at an approaching road indication sign, he saw that they were at the Bedford turn off and without further ado he said to his driver,

'Turn off here and go down to Bedford. It sounds important and perhaps our four hands may be put to good use. Bit of overtime for you as well which can't do any harm.'

Without question, the driver signalled his intention of leaving the motorway and slid swiftly along the exit road to the round-a-bout, where he took the Bedford turnoff. Without being told, he activated the siren and built in flashing blue lights and was soon travelling at over a hundred miles an hour, eating up the distance to Bedford. For Richard, it brought back happy memories of previous highspeed dramas and he thought how his wife would laugh when he regaled her with this story.

It was then that he realised that he did not know what the incident was all about, but soothed himself by thinking that it may be the last piece of excitement in his police career.

As they neared the railway station, Richard noticed the large numbers of emergency vehicles. His driver pulled into a car park at the side of the station and, after switching off the siren and flashing blue lights, the driver jumped out of the car and opened the door for Richard.

All around was noise and flashing lights. The electric power seemed to be out as a generator was running, in order to service numerous arc lamps which were the only source of extra light available. Richard could smell the harsh metallic odour of acetylene torches and as he neared the station entrance he saw the red blue flames of the torches in action.

'Good God, what are you doing here?' said a well cultured voice and, on turning, Richard saw Victor Mayhew, his counter part in the Bedfordshire Constabulary.

'Hello Victor, what on earth is happening? I was on my way up from London, when an emergency call for all hands was made and, you know me, can't keep away from the action.'

'When you have seen this little lot, you'll wish you had kept driving. Carnage, utter fucking carnage. Bodies all over the place, dozens with wicked injuries and we are running out of vehicles and hospital places.'

Seeing the distraught face of his colleague and hearing the despairing tone in his voice, Richard said, 'But what exactly has happened?'

'Early days yet, but at first glance it appears that some bright individual placed a bomb of some description on the London train. And some bomb. It is unlike myself to swear but this fucking bastard wants to be strung up and then ripped limb from limb. There are so many dead, so many women and kids . . . .' his voice broke as he choked back a sob, 'the bastards, the bastards.'

Richard immediately put his arm around his colleague's shoulders to comfort him and said, 'Come on old love, brave face for the men,' and together they entered the railway station.

Never would he have imagined such a scene in rural England. In a small, provincial railway station to see such devastation. All the railway buildings were damaged, the railway carriages of the London train lying on their sides, the windows gone and their sides split open like so many tins of beans. Strangely enough, the locomotive was still upright, but, in contrast, the first class carriage had been tossed into the air and was leaning as if drunk, against the pedstrian footbridge which led from platform to platform.

Although most of the bodies had now been removed, there were still huge pools of blood and blood dripping from the coach work of the upturned carriages. A scene from hell, desolation and death.

'Oh, I nearly forgot, Richard, your chief of detectives is around here somewhere. I'll try and find him for you,' said Victor Mayhew, who had recovered his composure.'

'My chief of detectives, here?' questioned Richard. What the bloody hell is he doing here. I've had a beast of a day and now I learn that my men are trespassing. What on earth is going on?'

'No, no, don't jump the gun. If my understanding is correct, he came here to meet someone only to find a dead body. Let me get him as he can explain far easier than I can.'

Victor hurried away leaving Richard extremely puzzled. Bill Bowler was amongst the best and he would not have come all this way on a wild goose chase. Impatiently, he looked around and saw Bill coming towards him, deep in conversation with Victor. Seeing Richard, Bill hurried forward and said, 'Can we find a quiet corner. I'm afraid the shit's going to hit the fan over this.'

'What could be worse than this?' asked Richard, incredulously, indicating the carnage all around them. 'Victor was saying he believes a bomb had been placed on the train.'

'I agree with him and the problem is I believe that the team who were mixed in with the Priests are responsible.'

'Come now,' said Richard, somewhat astounded, 'How can you make such a presumption. Surely our friend would have contacted you to avoid this.'

'That is the point. He did, or more to the fact he was in the process of doing so when the bomb went off.'

'You what,' shouted Richard, 'he knew and waited until it was too late to do anything about this. I'll have him shot. This is a disgraceful disaster which could have been avoided and what's more we are in part to blame.'

'Excuse me Sir, but before you say any more I think you should see something which may change your thoughts entirely.'

Leading the way, Bill took Richard to the ticket hall where the grisly business of tagging the bodies already identified, was under way. 'Good gracious, Bill, how many are there?' asked Richard.

'I honestly don't know,' replied Bill, stoically, 'but what I do know is what I am about to show you. I know you are very experienced, but be careful, because it's not very nice to look at, especially if you have just eaten.'

Having said this, Bill lead Richard to a corner of the ticket hall, where two heavily bloodstained sheets were concealing what appeared to be two bodies, which had been deliberately placed away from the other bodies. A uniformed police constable was in attendance and on seeing Richard he saluted.

Bill looked at the young officer, nodded his head and the officer lifted the sheet. 'This some kind of joke?' queried Richard, angrily, seeing the headless body.

'Unfortunately no,' replied Bill sadly. 'You are looking at the remains of my friend Mohsin.'

Richard was struck dumb by this revelation. Finding his voice he asked, 'You'd better tell me everything as I am sure that there is not going to be a very happy ending.'

Before replying, Bill stooped and lifted the sheet from the second body. Richard looked, stony faced, noting the similarities in the injuries to the two bodies.

'This body was recovered from the first carriage, the one with the least damage. Completely inconsistent with the other persons injured in that carriage. I was in the process of speaking to Mohsin on the telephone when he stated that he had another call on another phone. I remembered, because I made an off the cuff remark about him having two telephones, when I heard an enormous explosion and his phone went dead. I drove straight here and found his body in an Audi saloon which is parked on the car park at the side of the station.

'He had intimated that something was going on, that he was due to be joined by another terrorist and he was really upbeat, saying he could see an end to this business. From what he said and the subsequent revelations, I suppose that this poor sod is the other terrorist.'

'But the injuries,' said Richard, 'how on earth did they come by those?'

Bill collected his thoughts before replying. 'I'm assuming that our terrorist friends are more technologically advanced than we thought. I will not know for sure until a full autopsy has been carried out, but I believe they were both in possession of a telephone containing explosives. It would appear that when the bomb in the train exploded, their telephones exploded as well, and, going on the injuries sustained, it would appear that they were in the process of answering the telephones when they exploded. One detonator for three bombs is a first for me.'

'I've never known you to be far wrong, Bill, so I will go with your version. What I cannot understand is that you were not closer to Mohsin. You knew with the Priest business that things were hotting up.'

'You've been down in London today and I was trying to contact you all afternoon. This morning, Sir Peter Swift, in person, telephoned me and instructed me to send the whole terrorist file, immediately to the Met. by special messenger. I told him I would contact you and he made it plain that my job was on the line if the file was not on its way immediately. What could I do?' cried Bill, overcome with emotion, 'that's my fucking friend lying there and now I am responsible for his death.'

Shocked, Richard put his arms around Bill and cuddled him as one would a baby. Slowly, Bill regained his composure and wiped his sleeve across his eyes, saying, 'Sorry about that Sir, I don't know what came over me.'

'Old friend, no one should have to suffer like you are suffering. If its the last thing I do, I'll get to the bottom of who has been ordering what in this enquiry. Come on, let's go and get a drink.'

Before leaving, the two men stood in silence, each in his own way saying farewell to a brave colleague and friend. Finally, Bill stooped down and gently replaced the bloodied sheet over the badly mutilated body of Mohsin.

Turning, they started to leave the ticket office and its grisly contents. One of the several people engaged in the tagging of bodies shone an electric torch to indicate a clear path along which to pass, as evening had started to close in. A brilliant flash of green caught Richard's eye, and, on turning his head, he saw it was an emerald ring on the finger of a sheet covered corpse, which had caught the light from the torch, He bent to cover the hand, but as his eyes fell on the ring, his blood seemed to turn to ice and, without a sound, he collapsed on the floor amongst the shroud covered bodies.

Bill, who was walking behind Richard, stared down in horror then, without further ado, shouted for assistance. Several people came running across and, with their help, Bill assisted them to carry the unconscious Richard outside, where they laid him on the platform. An ambulance man ran across and after a few seconds of treatment, Richard regained consciousness.

'Thank God for that,' muttered Bill, much relieved when Richard showed signs of recovery, but the next second it was he who was in shock, as Richard sat up and let out a blood curdling scream, followed by an anguished 'No, no, no.' Before he could recover, Bill was further shocked as Richard reached up, grabbed hold of his jacket lapels and pulled himself to his feet.

He pushed Bill to one side and stumbled off in the direction of the ticket hall doorway and a rescue worker tried to block his passage. Richard savagely pushed him away as Bill caught up with him, saying in what he hoped was a soothing voice, 'Calm down Sir, it must have been the heat.'

Richard turned and once again grabbed Bill's lapels.

He pulled Bill close so that their faces were nearly touching and Bill saw that Richard looked deranged. In a strangled voice he said, 'The heat!. No, no that's my wife in there.'

With that he pushed Bill away and entered the ticket hall, making for the shrouded corpse of the body with the emerald ring. Before others could intervene, Richard had pulled the sheet away from the body and was staring in wide eyed shock, at the bloody mass that had once been his beautiful Susan.

Bill, who by this time had been joined by Victor Mayhew and several other officers stood behind Richard, powerless to help him in his grief. They could only stand looking at their friend and colleague, who was now on his knees before the mangled remains of his wife, with streams of tears coursing along his cheeks.

Finally, Bill reached down and gently tugged at Richard's shoulders, urging him to stand up. Turning his stricken face to Bill and the others he said in a hoarse whisper, 'It's my wife, I would know her engagement ring anywhere.' Then his voice rose into a scream and he shouted, 'Where are my children? They were all together.'

Bill and Victor Mayhew with the help of Richard's driver, half pulled and half tugged Richard out into the fresh air. He offered no resistance whatsoever and allowed himself to be led to his official car, which the driver had driven closer to the station.

They placed Richard in the back of the car and Victor Mayhew produced a hip flask which he placed between Richard's lips, allowing a few drops of brandy to trickle down his throat. Richard coughed, then straightened up and seemed to be recovering his equilibrium. 'Bill, Bill,' he said in a whisper, 'try and find my kids. And Millie, yes Millie, you know Chris's wife, she was with them on the train.'

With that Richard fell back into the seat and his driver said, 'I'll stay with him Sir. He'll be in good hands,' and as if to prove a point he took a travelling rug from the car boot and gently placed it on Richards motionless body.

For Richard, time stood still. For once in his whole life he felt completely drained and impotent, not knowing what to do and so he did nothing.

He had no idea how much time had elapsed nor did he care, but Bill finally returned to the car and said to the driver, 'I'll drive back with you and the chief. My car can stay here until the morning.

There's going to be no sleep tonight and perhaps not for some time to come.'

Richard, in the meantime had struggled into a sitting position and staring fixedly at Bill he said, 'The kids and Millie are they . . . .' and seeing the look on Bill's face he started to quietly sob.

'Come on', said Bill to the driver, 'let's be on our way. There is nothing else we can do here.' With that he climbed into the front passenger seat of the Jaguar and as the car drove away he turned and stared at his grief stricken chief and friend.

If it takes a lifetime, he swore to himself, I will make the bastards who did this pay. He then laid his hand on Richard's arm in an effort to comfort him, but Richard was beyond comfort.

# CHAPTER 29

Mansour and Umar were in high spirits on the way back to London. They had been listening to the regular news broadcasts about the train 'derailment', which meant that the police must be maintaining a strict control on information released to the media, but they were over joyed when it was announced that the death toll had passed the hundred mark.

'One hundred less to kill when the time comes,' exclaimed Mansour gleefully. 'When you think of all the injured who will now live in fear after this night, fear of us and of Allah, our leader and protector, it makes me wish we could celebrate for a week in my favourite London nightspots.'

Umar, who was just as excited as Mansour, said, 'Well, why not? We deserve a big celebration after this nights work.'

A faithful soldier but certainly no intellectual, Umar looked at Mansour awaiting confirmation that they would be shortly celebrating the nights activities.

He was disappointed when Mansour simply said, 'There is much work to do done tonight. Never take the Police to be fools. Soon, there will be a huge search for those responsible and we must be away from this Country as quickly as possible. However, before we leave we must clean away all signs of our involvement. That way we can fight yet another day.'

Umar continued driving towards London, whilst reflecting on Mansour's words. 'Leave the Country, but where shall I go?' he asked in a plaintive voice. 'I have no family and I have very little money.'

'Do not worry my faithful friend,' replied Mansour. 'As your leader I have sworn an allegiance to help and protect you and others like you. I have made all the arrangements, but first we have other things to do.'

'All I have in the world is in my bedsit. Can we call there so that I can pick up my things. It will only take a few minutes."

'Of course, of course, and then we shall drive to the arcade. I have much to do and you can help me. Now that I no longer have a car, I will require you to drive me.'

Umar thought for a few seconds before saying, 'This is a hire car and I must take it back tonight or else they will charge me extra. You only gave me enough money to rent the car for twenty four hours.'

'I have already told you. Do not worry. Now drive to your bedsit and pick up your gear as there is much to be done.'

With that Mansour closed his eyes and laid back in his seat, well satisfied with his nights work.

Two hours later, after having visited Umar's bedsit and removing all signs of his occupancy, the two men drove to the arcade. It was nearing midnight, and the arcade was heaving. That's good, thought Mansour, the engineer and cashiers will be busy.

Sure enough, the office was in darkness and after entering, Mansour carefully locked the door behind him. He quickly crossed to the safe, opened it and took out a bulky envelope, which he handed to Umar.

'In there' he said, indicating the envelope, 'Is your new identity and an air ticket to Algeria. There is also an address of a faithful member of my group who will supply you with everything you may need. Here' he said taking out his wallet, 'is five hundred pounds in cash to tide you over until you are installed in Algeria. I will be kept aware of your whereabouts and will contact you in the near future as I have plans for you in our next, and hopefully final operation. Now go, and may Allah bless you for your work this night.'

With that, Mansour embraced him, kissing him on both cheeks. Releasing him from the embrace he said, 'Leave me the car keys. You can take a taxi to the airport and try not to draw attention to yourself.'

Umar picked up his travel bag and with a last, fond look at his leader, he left the office, which Mansour immediately relocked behind him.

Crossing to the desk he picked up the arcade telephone and dialled his uncle, who answered immediately, saying, 'I have been impatient for your call. The news broadcasts are very good and our leaders back home are greatly pleased.'

Mansour felt himself flushing with pride at his uncle's words, and simply said, 'With luck I shall be with you in about two hours.'

His uncle simply said, 'I will be waiting' and then cut the communication.

Mansour went to a locked cupboard from which he took an attache case containing thousands of pounds; money he had skimmed from the arcade and restaurant operations. Then, going to the safe, he took out several books and disks, containing information on his English based operation, plus information on the larger, European group. He knew that in a short time he would be needing their help in the finalization and execution of his next and perhaps greatest project, something to over shadow the infamous 11th of September. If I am successful, he thought, a place will surely be reserved for me amongst the leaders of our great Islamic movement.

After a final check to ensure that nothing remained to implicate him in the running of the arcade, he picked up his attache case, the car keys, and left the office, switching off the light, but leaving the door unlocked. There were still large numbers of people in the arcade and no one paid the slightest attention to this latest mass murderer, as he left the arcade to drive to Basingstoke.

Mansour had already informed his parents that he would be leaving the Country for a short time in order to have a well earned holiday. His father had wholeheartedly agreed, saying that running a busy restaurant plus his acitivities involving the local council, must take a terrible toll on his health. Naturally, his father knew nothing of his sons activities with the arcade or with Al Qaida.

Driving the hire car, he firstly went to his rented flat, a place he had rented under a false name, and picked up his pre-packed suitcases, which he placed in the car. Making reasonable time, he arrived at his uncle's home at around two o'clock in the morning. Basingstoke was normally pretty quiet and at this hour there were no people to be seen, nor lighted windows in the suburban homes.

His uncle was waiting for him and helped him to unload the hire car. He led the way into his home, explaining that his wife, Mansour's aunt, was away for the night visiting her sister, and so they could talk openly.

Having said this, the uncle urged Mansour to tell him of the previous evenings operation, and was overjoyed by the success, especially the number of dead, which had now reached one hundred and five, with more than twice that number injured, many seriously. 'Revenge for our families and forebears, slaughtered by these European terrorists is the finest medecin possible,' jubilated the uncle.

Mansour, after waiting for his uncle to finish his praises then asked if there was a car available for him to drive to Heathrow airport. His uncle replied in the affirmative, saying that he would personally collect the car from the airport and arrange for the hire car to be returned to the hirers.

With those details sorted, Mansour said, 'Now, as regards the explosives, is everything under control for the transfer to our friends in Europe?'

'They have already been loaded onto two different lorries and, provided there are no problems, will be delivered as planned at the end of the week.'

'In that case, my uncle, I will take my leave. My plane awaits and I promise you I am looking forward to a long rest in the bosom of our family in Pakistan.

You will be kept informed of our future plans and I trust you to contact if there is any change in the planned reunion, due to take place later this year.'

'Do not worry, my nephew, all is under control. Now go and enjoy your holiday which you have so richly deserved.'

The two men embraced and Mansour took his leave, impatient to be at Heathrow Airport for his flight to Pakistan.

# CHAPTER 30

They travelled in silence until they reached Police Headquarters in the centre of town. Bill, who was dreading the next hour or two, instructed the driver to stay with Richard, who appeared to be sleeping, whilst he went to his office to find his official address book. He knew Chris Wooler slightly better than he did Richard, having been invited on several occasions to social engagements and was on particularly good terms with Chris's son, Martin. With a heavy heart he lifted the telephone and dialled the number listed for Martin Wooler.

In spite of the late hour, the phone was answered almost immediately by Martin, and, on hearing Bill announce himself, Martin said, 'I suppose you want my dad. He's playing pool with my wife, but I'll go get him.'

Bill said straight away, 'No, no, don't do that. Can I speak to you or, what's better, can I come out to your place?'

'Course you can come. You know the way. Will you be long as the drinks are dimishing very quickly,' replied Martin buoyantly.

'I'll be there as quickly as possible, but I must warn you that I am not coming with glad tidings.'

'That sounds ominous,' replied Martin, still with laughter in his voice, 'so I will save a bit of the good scotch for when you get here.'

Bill paused before replying, then said, 'I'll have the chief, Mr. Grant with me.'

'In that case I'll get out the Black Bottle as it will certainly be a long night,' replied Martin. 'So see you when you get here as I'm sure you can remember the way.' With that he replaced the receiver, leaving Bill staring straight ahead and wondering what would happen in the forthcoming minutes.

Having given the address to the driver, Bill got into the car, desperately wondering how best to deal with the forthcoming confrontation.

He was still deep in thought, when the car drew to a halt outside Martin's neat, detached home.

Instructing the driver to wait with Richard, who was still apparently asleep, Bill got out of the car and with a heavy heart, walked towards the house.

Before he could ring the bell, the door was flung open wide, revealing Chris and his son, both of whom seemed slightly the worse for drink. 'Come in bearer of grim tidings,' laughed Martin, moving aside to let Bill enter the house.

'So what's up, old chum?' asked Chris. 'The station bar closed early or what?'

If only, thought Bill, seeing the two laughing faces before him. They won't be laughing in a minute, of that I am assured.

'Can we sit down,' said Bill, 'it's been a long day for me.'

'Let's go into the lounge, the wife's making a cuppa and I'm sure you'd like one Bill,' replied Martin, leading the way into a modern, but well furnished room. 'Take a pew' he said, indicating a comfortable leather chair, whilst he and his father sat down together on a three seater canape.

'By the way, Bill, where's Richard?' asked Chris, 'my son said he was with you.'

Realising that there was no other way, Bill said as gently as he could, 'Yesterday evening, in Bedford, the London train was destroyed by an explosive device, causing huge casualities;' As he spoke he was watching Chris very carefully.

'Amongst the dead are the wife of Richard and his two children . . . .'

Fortunately he was ready as he saw all the colour drain from Chris's face as he toppled forward onto the floor, causing Martin's wife to come into the room from the kitchen, saying, 'What on earths going on in here?'

Bill looked at her, completely at a loss and said simply

'Millie died last night in the explosion on the train in Bedford.'

Mary, Martin's wife, began to sob and Martin, with an anguished expression on his face, immediately folded her in his arms and gently rocked her, as their tears streamed down their faces.

At that moment, Richard flung open the lounge door and staggered into the room only to see his friend Chris lying unmoving on the floor. Flinging himself down beside him, he took him in his arms, whispering,

'They're dead, all dead, all fucking dead. Everything we've loved and worked for dead,' and then he burst into tears as well.

Poor Bill, the harbinger of bad news, was left staring from one to the other, wondering what to do next, when he saw Richard's driver trying to draw his attention. The driver, an old police constable of some thirty years experience, waited until Bill was close to him before he said, 'It's always been my experience, Sir, that once the message has been delivered, it's better to just go and leave them to it'

With that he turned and left the house, followed by Bill who softly closed the door behind him.

Once back in the car, Bill asked the driver to drop him off at headquarters and then to get off home, remembering to thank him for all his assistance and good advice.

After returning to headquarters, and in spite of the late hour, Bill personally telephoned the Chairman of the Police Committee and the Assistant Chief Constables, informing them of that nights events. He also telephoned the Police Surgeon, who, without hesitation said he would go straight away and offer whatever condolence or medecine he could, to Richard and Chris.

Being a divorced man, and having nothing else he could do, Bill lay down on an antique Chesterfield which he had purloined for his office, and promptly fell asleep.

# CHAPTER 31

The following morning, Richard's brother, Gerald and his wife Ellen, arrived at Chris's home and took charge of Richard. Gerald was three years older than Richard, slightly smaller, but stockily built and with the same light coloured hair, which he wore slightly longer than Richard. He was a very successful solicitor and the two brothers were very close. Normally a happy go lucky person with a ready smile and a caustic wit, he saw immediately, that neither would be needed or welcome at this time.

After offering their condolences to Chris and his family, Gerald took his brother into the kitchen, where he tried to speak with him, but Richard just stared blankly at him, saying nothing. He was unwashed, unshaven and his clothes were rumpled and badly creased, him having slept in them. They were also somewhat bloodstained.

'Come on, old son,' said Gerald, 'let's get you home and into a nice hot bath. I'll stay with you and help in every way I possibly can. If we go now, Chris's kids can help to get their dad sorted out.'

He made no reply, and assisted by his brother and sister in law was installed in Gerald's new BMW saloon. Gerald collected his wife and together they drove Richard the ten or so miles to his home.

Richard allowed himself to be led into the house, offering no resistance and making no effort to speak, yet when Gerald took him into the bedroom he started to softly sob. Gerald held him until the sobbing subsided and then helped him to strip off his clothes and half pushed him under the shower, where he left him to let the water soak out some of the pain.

Fifteen minutes later, Richard, dressed in a green coloured track suit, joined his brother and sister-in-law in the lounge. His face was drawn and his complexion grey. Gerald, despite the relatively early hour, poured him a half tumbler of 'Black Bottle', which he swallowed down in one. This made him cough, but it also brought some colour back into his face.

'That's better,' said Gerald, refilling his glass and, despite the disapproving look on his wife's face, decided to help himself as well. The two men drank deeply, and after helping Richard to sit in an armchair, Gerald pulled a high chair forward so that he could sit close to his brother.

After a short silence, Richard said, 'For years I've had to comfort people who had suffered loss, but now that it has happened to me I just do not know what to do. All my family, all my hopes and ambitions, all I possessed of value gone, just like that. Bang, and it's over.' He buried his head in his hands and started to weep.

At that moment, Gerald saw Richard's official Jaguar coming to a stop outside the house. 'Dick', said Gerald, 'you have visitors. Come on, try and pull yourself together. I know it must be hellishly difficult, but I'm sure that Susan would expect you to put on a brave face.'

Richard mumbled something, but did stand up and ran his fingers through his hair. Looking through the window, he saw Bill Bowler and the Police Surgeon walking towards the front door. Giving a very wan smile to his brother he walked unsteadily across the room, entered the hallway and opened the door.

'Good to see you up and about' exclaimed the surgeon, perhaps a little too boisterously, but it seemed to have the desired effect as Richard managed another smile as he shook hands with the two men. He held the door open as they entered and courteously asked them if they would care for any refreshment. Seeing that Richard and Gerald were drinking whisky they both decided to do likewise.

Richard, feeling the soothing and warming effect of the drink, started to push his personal suffering to one side, as he remembered that he was still a Chief Constable and that others would be counting on him. Addressing himself to Bill he said, 'What about official identification? I suppose I shall have to go back down to Bedford, won't I?'

'I'm afraid so. Fortunately, I have to go as well and if I may suggest it, I could take you and Mr. Wooler with me.'

The telephone started to ring and Gerald answered it, saying 'No, not at the moment. A press statement will be issued later,' and he replaced the receiver, only to take it off the hook and leave it. 'Should guarantee a bit of peace, but for how long?' The question was left hanging in the air as the men finished their drinks.

Richard left the room and fifteen minutes later reentered, wearing a well pressed dark suit, white shirt and a black tie. Gerald said, 'I would also like to come with you to say goodbye to a part of my family,' whilst his wife elected to stay with Chris's son.

After leaving the surgeon at his office in town, Bill who was driving the car, called headquarters to inform them of their intentions. They then drove in near silence to the Bedford mortuary, where the bodies had been arranged for official identification.

On entering the viewing room, Richard was surprised but pleased to see Victor, his counter part, present. 'Heard you were coming down and thought I would like to assist. We have removed all forms of jewellery, watches and what not and I am sure there should be sufficient there for a positive identification.'

A number of items were placed before him and Richard identified his sons watch, his daughters gold chain and pendant and finally the emerald engagement ring, which, after staring at it for several long seconds, he placed in his jacket pocket.

'I would like to see the bodies please,' said Richard and Victor ordered the curtains on the viewing window to be opened.

Displayed behind the window were three very mutilated bodies and as Richard stared he realised that it was virtually impossible to recognize these bloodied corpses as the three people he had loved more than anything else in the World.

'Only wish I could have saved you that experience', said Victor softly, indicating for the curtain to be closed.

He was somewhat surprised when Richard said, 'I had to do it. I owed it to them and I owed it to myself.' Anger crept into his voice as he added, 'One day I will meet the perpetrators of this crime and I will have this image burned into my brain.'

Together with Gerald, Richard left the room whilst Chris, with Bill in attendance, identified the remains of his beloved Millie.

After all the formalities had been carried out, Richard said farewell to Victor after thanking him for his help and kindness. They were taken to a comfortable waiting room, where tea and refreshments were served, whilst they waited for Bill, who was examining the bodies and possessions of Mohsin and Ali. He also had a long discussion with the members of the crime team who were sifting through all the baggage and the ruins of the train, attempting to find evidence that could be used in any future prosecution.

Finally, having taken possession of certain items, Bill joined the others and drove them back to Richard's home. Waiting for them there was the Chairman of the Police committee together with the senior Assistant Chief Constable.

After offering their condolences to Richard and Chris, it was agreed that both men would be granted unlimited compassionate leave, in order for them to put their affairs in order and arrange the funerals of their loved ones.

Gerald and his wife left, promising to return the next day, and finally Richard and Chris were alone. They sat for a long time in silence, each lost in his own thoughts.

Suddenly Chris said, 'So what do we do now? Life must go on, but I don't really feel like continuing. We had so much planned, Millie and I, but now there's just no point.' He dropped his eyes, staring blankly at his clasped hands.

Realising that he had not spoken to Chris about his visit to London, he started to explain about his meeting with the Home Secretary. Chris listened, not interrupting, until Richard mentioned that he had been virtually threatened with dismissal. At that Chris said, 'You have enough time in. Why don't you spike his guns and resign? He would find it difficult to sack you then, especially with everything that's happened.'

'You have a point there, but what do I do if I resign? Stick a gun to my head? I have decided that until after the funeral I shall do nothing but mourn my loved ones. Then after I shall decide what to do.'

A car drew up outside the house and Chris said, 'That's Martin come to take me home. Do you want to come? Better than staying here alone.'

'No, I'll be alright, you get off. I have a lot to sort out and then there'll be the funeral to arrange.' said Richard escorting his friend to the door.

He watched their car disappear down the drive and with a heavy heart he entered his silent home, mounted the staircase and entered their bedroom. Picking up a photo of his dead wife he flung himself onto the bed and burst into tears.

# CHAPTER 32

The following morning Gerald and his wife arrived, this time carrying a couple of suitcases. 'I have a few days owing to me and we have decided to keep you company and help with all the arrangements,' said Gerald, by way of explanation.

'Come into the kitchen, I was just about to make a cup of tea,' replied Richard, leading the way. Ellen, seeing that he seemed disorientated and was still dressed in the same clothes as the day before, surmised that he had not washed, changed or perhaps not even slept.

Pushing in front of her husband, she took Richard firmly by the arm, saying, 'You are not doing yourself any good by neglecting the basics. Get yourself upstairs and into the shower whilst I see about a proper breakfast. We are all suffering, but I know that Susan would give you a bloody good bollocking if she was here to see you in that state.'

Gerald was about to remonstrate with his wife, but Richard, with a tremble in his voice said, 'You are right Ellen. I needed that,' and he disappeared upstairs.

Twenty minutes later, showered and dressed in slacks and a black polo shirt, he reappeared, saying, 'That smells good. I could eat a horse.'

Ellen smiled at the compliment and soon all three were enjoying a real English breakfast, washed down with strong tea. Although Ellen and Gerald tried to engage Richard in small talk, they soon realised that he was not interested in useless chit chat.

Finally, with breakfast finished and the dishes packed into the dishwasher, Gerald said, 'I know it is very difficult, but it is necessary to contact the funeral people and a church. Have you anyone in mind?'

Richard, after some contemplation, suggested that Gerald contact the same funeral directors that had provided such good service when their father had died and this was done without delay. The funeral home said they would see to all the paper work regarding the recovery of the bodies and the work necessary in preparing them for burial and also asked if there may be a problem regarding a probable inquest. Gerald said he would contact the coroner, who he knew personally, and would inform the funeral home in due course.

Fortunately, the coroner was in his office, and he stated that all the bodies had been autopsied and the certificates giving cause of death processed.

It was decided that the funeral would be held the following week and Richard asked his brother to contact Chris and ask him if he would like the service for Millie to be held at the same time.

Chris, when contacted said he thought that would be the best way, the two women having been such good friends, and he suggested that perhaps the church of St. Thomas, where his son had been married, may agree to conduct the funerals.

That same afternoon, Chris telephoned to say he would be coming across and two hours later, he arrived at Richard's home, with the Reverend Jennings, Reverend of St. Thomas's church, which was to be found some three miles from Richard's home.

Reverend Jennings, a portly gentlemen with ruddy features and a receding hairline, was wearing a dark grey suit and his dog collar. A quietly spoken man, he explained that he would be only too happy to help, in what was to say the least, a very distressing occasion and asked if the bodies were to be cremated or buried. Chris immediately said that his wife had always said she wanted to be cremated, whilst Richard hesitated.

Finally, he asked the Reverend if there was a possibility of his family being buried in the small cemetery adjacent to the Church of St. Thomas.

Reverend Jennings said that there were still plots available and the whole party left in two cars to visit the cemetery.

On arrival, Richard was struck by the silent beauty of the church and graveyard. Although the church was relatively small, it had a tall spire topped with a weathercock and the graveyard was neat and well tended. In silence, the party meandered along the paths leading from the church to the graveyard, Richard noting the well kept graves, many with headstones. In a corner of the graveyard was a weeping willow tree and Richard suddenly said, 'There, under the willow, would it be possible?'

Reverend Jennings, after a few moments thought, looked at Richard, seeing before him a broken man. 'I will personally ensure it', he said. 'Now as to a date. Have you decided when you would like the funeral to take place?'

Gerald broke in, saying that he had spoken with the coroner and that all was in order, and asked if it was possible to arrange the funeral service for the following Wednesday. The date was agreed and, after once again expressing his sadness, Reverend Jennings took his leave. The others, after a last look at what would be the final resting place for the wife and children of Richard, returned to the cars.

During the next three days, family, friends and colleagues were contacted, with Richard simply stating that he wanted a simple funeral, with just family and close friends present.

On Wednesday morning, Richard entered the kitchen, already dressed in a dark suit, white shirt and a black tie. He declined breakfast, much to the chagrin of Ellen, but did accept a cup of tea. The others ate their breakfast in silence, each lost in their own thoughts.

At nine thirty a limousine, supplied by the funeral home arrived and Richard, accompanied by Gerald and Ellen, were driven sedately to the church.

To Richard's horror, he saw what appeared to be hundreds of people gathered outside the church and a television crew busily setting up their equipment. He stepped out of the car and the crowd fell silent, parting to let him and his party pass into the church.

The church was packed with people and Richard, somewhat unsteadily, started the long walk to the pew that had been reserved for them. At the sight of the four flower bedecked coffins, he stumbled and would have fallen had Gerald not been prepared. Catching him by the shoulders, he steadied him until Richard whispered, 'It's OK', and they continued to wards their pew.

Richard had recognised many of the people in the congregation, but there were many more he did not know. He was also surprised by the huge Police presence. Once seated, he whispered to his brother, 'I only wanted close family and friends to be present. I did not want all these crowds.'

He then looked up and saw once again the coffins and, realised that this was the final act in his families' life. Full of self pity, he started to sob and Gerald handed him a handkerchief, saying, 'Susan would be ashamed to see you blubbering like that. Think of good times and wipe your eyes.'

The organist started to play and the Reverend Jennings entered the main church from a recessed door beside the altar. Everyone stood and the service started, the Reverend Jennings being true to his word by delivering a glittering sermon to the memories of the deceased. Finally, the service ended and the pall bearers took up the coffins, leading the mourners outside into the sunshine.

What a nice day for such a grim occasion, thought Richard, ironically. Once again, his thoughts turned to his family and the weight redescended on his shoulders as yet again the truth hit him, 'Yes, you are all alone.'

He did not have chance to dwell on this, as Gerald helped him to follow the coffins to the willow tree, where the wet piles of earth indicated the final resting place for his family. Reverend Jennings recited a short prayer and the three coffins were lowered into the grave. Richard picked up a beautiful red rose, part of a wreath and walked slowly to the open grave and looked down.

The three coffins were lined neatly in the grave and Richard, as he looked, realised that it was the final contact he would have with the three people he had loved more than life itself. He was sorely tempted to throw himself onto the coffins, but restrained himself. Instead, with tears trickling down his cheeks and with several hundred mourners gathered around him, he said a last goodbye and tossed the rose into the grave.

Accompanied by his brother, he walked to the cemetery gate, where he waited, head bowed, to thank the gathered mourners for their assisting in this, his saddest moment.

He shook hands and listened to whispered condolences but was later unable to remember anyone he knew, until suddenly his hand was grasped firmly. Looking up he saw the composed features of Sir Peter Swift, with his Special Branch bodyguard hovering behind him, and a television camera and commentator in close attendance.

Sir Peter muttered something, which Richard took to be his condolences and then made to pass on. Richard however, held on firmly to his hand and pulled him closer. A look of surprise crossed Sir Peter's face, but owing to the presence of the television camera he hastily readjusted his features. With their faces only inches apart and with Richard keeping a firm grip on Sir Peter's hand, Richard finally spoke. Afterwards, Gerald who was standing next to Richard said that he had not heard what was said, but did notice the colour drain from the face of the Home Secretary.

Pulling Sir Peter even closer, Richard said in a very clear whisper, 'Thompson has an excuse, because he is a twat. You are just a self opinionated prick who should have been drowned at birth. I have never hated anyone before in my life, but I say that I hate and detest you. I am convinced that my family and all those others would be alive today had you not interfered. If there is Justice, I hope that somehow you will suffer as I and many others are suffering because of you. Now get out of my sight and my life.' With that he let drop Sir Peter's hand and turned to acknowledge the following mourner.

Sir Peter, rubbing his hand vigorously, walked swiftly from the graveyard, his face an absolute mask. The television commentator was roughly handled as he tried to speak to Sir Peter and the bodyguard hurried his charge to the waiting chauffeur driven car, which immediately departed. Richard, however, took no notice, until he had thanked all the mourners. Then, accompanied by Gerald, he returned to the church to thank the Reverend for his understanding and compassion.

The limousine was waiting for them, but instead of driving him to his home, the driver took them to Richard's favourite restaurant, where Chris and Gerald had arranged a meal for them and their friends. The room was packed and Richard quickly had a whisky thrust into his hand and, without thinking, he downed it straight away and held out his glass for a refill.

'Hey, steady on old boy,' said Victor Mayhew, surprising Richard because he did not even realise he was present.

'Sorry,' said Richard contritely, 'but it's been a very stressful time. On top of which I was amazed to see so many people there this morning.'

'Perhaps it may not be of great comfort to you at the moment, but that indicated the love and respect that the people hold for you and your family.

You are held in great esteem and I only hope that as time goes by, you realise just how much people will be ready to help and support you in the future. I can say,' continued Victor, 'that all the Police Officers present this morning were there of their own volition, none of them were ordered to attend. It may seem strange at the moment, but in many ways you are a very lucky chap and I for one, having known you for a number of years, will confidently say that, after your period of mourning, you will retake the bit between your teeth.'

With that, Victor shook Richard's hand and took his leave, leaving Richard very sad, but also, perplexed.

# CHAPTER 33

Finally, Richard found himself alone, Gerald having been obliged to take his leave, owing to pressing business matters. However, before leaving, he had extracted a promise from Richard to stay in touch and get himself back together and back to work.

Ellen, before leaving, had arranged the kitchen and vacumed the downstairs rooms and Richard, after looking around him, picked up a bottle of whisky and wandered upstairs into the bedroom. The moment he opened the wardrobe door and he caught sight of his wife's clothes, his spirit dissolved and he slumped down onto the bed, whereupon he opened the bottle and began to drink.

The telephone rang and he threw the telephone across the room and carried on drinking. Later he heard the door bell ringing and then someone tapping on the windows, but he ignored this as well.

Feeling more and more depressed, he continued to drink until finally, he fell back in a drunken stupor.

He had no idea of the time or even the date, but he noticed that it was dark outside. He got unsteadily to his feet and waited until the room had stopped spinning, then wearily, he made his way to the bathroom.

Later, he had no idea how much later, he managed to walk down the stairs and methodically he went from room to room, drawing all the curtains. He then opened his drinks cabinet and selected another bottle.

Much later, another day or even two, he had no idea, but was aroused by someone banging on the doors and windows of the house. Blearily, opening his eyes he shouted 'Go away, go away.' He half recognised Bill's voice, but just shouted for him to leave.

He must have fallen asleep for he then saw his wife, who was berating him for neglecting himself. Opening his eyes, he realised he must have been dreaming.

The image of his dear wife stayed with him and, in his half drunken stupor, he decided to visit the grave of his family. Without looking in a mirror nor even noticing that he was badly dressed and in dire need of a shave, he picked up another bottle of whisky and left the house.

He had no idea of the time although it was light, and with a rolling, stumbling gait, he made his way to the cemetery. Several people saw him, but no-one spoke nor tried to intervene. Finally, he reached the church and made his way to the newly turned grave beneath the willow tree.

Clutching his bottle of whisky, he sank to his knees, full of self pity, and as he stared at the grave, the tears started to course through the stubble on his cheeks.

How long he was there he did not know. The sun was up and warm and Richard, who was still on his knees, became aware of someone walking along the path behind him. He ignored the footsteps, preferring to stay on his knees and to wallow in self pity.

After several seconds, he became aware that the footsteps had halted behind him. He felt a hand gently touch his shoulder and a very cultured voice, softly said, 'Come along old friend, the time for mourning is over. We have to get you back into the land of the living and back to work.'

His body wracked with tears as he recognised the voice of Lord Hamilton, but he made the effort to stand upright and turn to face him. Wiping his arm across his eyes, his said, 'It's no good. I'm finished. The quicker I join my family the better.'

Lord Hamilton, who was of a similar height and build to Richard, took him by the shoulders saying, 'What a defeatist attitude to adopt. I would never have believed it possible for you to utter such words. I am a very good judge of character and I know you far better than you could imagine. So, let's be having you home and we'll get you sorted out quicksticks.'

'It's easy for you to say, but when you have suffered as I have, you would understand and just leave me alone,' replied Richard, still wallowing in self pity.

'If I believed for one minute that you sincerely mean what you say, I would simply leave you to suffer alone. You are not the first and you certainly won't be the last to suffer loss. Come, you need sorting out and I think we'll start with a shower, a shave and a change of clothes for you.'

Taking him gently by the arm, Lord Hamilton led Richard, who followed meekly to his car, which was parked in front of the church. After installing Richard in the front passenger seat, he took the wheel and a few minutes later they were entering Richard's home.

Lord Hamilton surveyed the disarray, the unwashed dishes, the scattered clothes and sniffed distastefully at the sour air in the curtained room. Opening the curtains and flinging open wide the windows, he said, 'Get yourself upstairs and washed and changed. We have a lot of work to do and before starting I think a meal and a chat are in order.

So, be a good chap and bobby off, no pun intended, and come back as quickly as you can.'

Richard was both shocked and amazed by the treatment he was receiving at the hands of the Judge, but did as he was told. Fifteen minutes later, freshly showered and shaved he entered the kitchen to see Lord Hamilton wearing one of his wife's aprons as he cooked a richly smelling omelette. Realising he had not eaten for some time, having preferred the bottles of alcohol, Richard quickly set the table as his friend spooned the omelette onto two plates.

After finishing their meal Richard made a coffee and the two men went into the lounge and settled into two armchairs. Lord Hamilton, after sipping his coffee and remarking on the quality, said, 'Earlier, you made allusion to the fact that I could not understand your suffering. How did you arrive at that conclusion?'

'Quite simply by the fact that I know your lovely wife and I am sure she is still with you in body and in health.'

'You are quite correct. What do you think of my children?' asked Lord Hamilton, directing his piercing gaze onto Richards emaciated face.

Richard wondered where he was going with this conversation as he knew that Lord Hamilton had no children. He made no reply, simply waiting for the Judge to continue.

'I see you are perplexed, so I will explain. I am now seventy two years of age, and I qualified for the bar when I was twenty eight. Two years later, I married my wife, and eight years on I had two sons, aged four and six. A blooming career, a lovely wife, two sons and a very promising future you may say and you would be correct.

'However, one evening the boys went to stay with one of their school friends and it was decided that they would sleep over. It was the first time they had been away from home and they were very excited, but my wife was apprehensive as mothers of young children tend to be.'

Lord Hamilton paused to take a drink of his coffee and Richard wondered where he was going with his story. Wiping his lips carefully with a napkin, Lord Hamilton placed his cup on the coffee table.

'Where was I. Oh yes, the wife worried but I, like you supremely confident in all I do, simply laughed it off, telling her she was worrying over nothing.

The following morning, the children were on their way to school with their school friend and his mother, when their car was struck by a speeding car which had been stolen earlier by a fifteen year old boy. Both cars were badly damaged, but whereas the fifteen year old was uninjured and even ran away, my two boys were killed outright as was the driver of their car. Fortunately, their friend who was seriously injured, later made a full recovery.'

'Needless to say, the young boy resposible for the accident was a product of a broken home and had indeed absconded from a Young Offenders Institution.

He pleaded not guilty to everything and was cleared of blame for the accident, stating a defect in the cars braking system was the cause of the accident. He was found guilty of stealing the car and was simply returned to the institution from which he had absconded. When you are involved in the law as I am, you wonder how justice can arrive at such decisions. That, more than anything else pushed me to join with the judiciary.'

Richard noted that as the Judge spoke, his voice started cracking and he was certain he could see tears glistening in his eyes.

'That was nearly forty years ago and as you can see, I still suffer. There is not a day goes by that I do not think of my sons and wonder what they would be like today. No sons, no grandchildren, just like you, but as you will find out, life goes on and you must go on with it. You are still relatively young and there is so much to be done and you have far too much talent to spend the rest of your days belittling your lot.

'I do not say this cruelly, but you may even find that now you can invest in things, simply because you are alone, with no family responsibilities to hold you back. Now tell me, if you wish to, that I cannot understand your grief.'

Silence fell. Richard dropped his head, staring at his slippered feet, then, on looking up, he said, 'I feel as though you have just kicked me in the balls, and, yes, you are right, I needed and deserved it. I also thank you for explaining your personal loss as it will help me put my life into perspective.'

Rising to his feet, Lord Hamilton stretched then said, 'On your feet my man. I can still remember my army training and as the sergeant major used to say 'Let's get this shit tip tidied up.' With that Lord Hamilton vanished into the kitchen and started to clean the table and arrange the dirty dishes.

When he had finished, he went in search of Richard, and found him standing in front of a wardrobe full of his wife's clothes. 'What can I do with these,' he asked, despairingly and Lord Hamilton simply said, 'Leave it to me.'

He left the room and Richard heard him talking on the telephone. Returning to the room he said to Richard, 'We'll clean the bedrooms and the bathroom and we'll leave the clothing disposal to the experts. So come along, I haven't got all day as my wife would say.'

For an hour the two men worked as hard as any chambermaids, and soon the house was looking and certainly smelling more like a home. They were interrupted in their work by a ringing at the doorbell, the door being opened by Lord Hamilton, who ushered in two well dressed, elderly ladies.

He introduced them to Richard as two stalwarts of the local charity shop and then led them upstairs to show them where all the clothes, both those of Susan and the children were kept. Leaving the women to work, he returned downstairs to Richard and, after consulting his watch, he said, 'I think we've deserved a drink, but mind you, only one.' Mesmerised, Richard went to the drinks cabinet and was pleased to see that he had not drunk all the whisky.

They drank in a comfortable silence, until Lord Hamilton said, 'Have you given any thought to my offer of employment?' and Richard had to admit that he had not.

'The reason I ask, is that from next week I shall be Home Secretary and may find myself less available than at present.' Richard was astounded but stuck out his hand, saying 'Let me congratulate you, but it was a bit sudden, wasn't it?'

'My dear chap, if only you had been following daily National events instead of feeling sorry for yourself, you would know why. However, as I am in a benevolent mood, I will explain.

'The day of the funeral, you had words with Sir Peter, my predecessor, in the church yard. Unfortunately for him, as he was the person responsible for the presence of the television cameras, the whole thing was captured on television and beamed on the National news. Unbeknown to Sir Peter, the news crews are in the habit of taking lip readers with them when on outside interviews and your whole speech to Sir Peter was recorded for the Nation to hear. A huge public outcry followed and Sir Peter did the only thing he could do, and that was to resign.'

For the first time in a long time, a smile creased Richard's face. 'So there is Justice still, even though it cannot bring back the dead. I am so glad that you came today and dragged me back into reality. I still have some things to tidy up, but I feel that my time with the Police Service should come to an end. With you as the new Home Secretary, would it be too much for me to ask you to consider Chris, my deputy, as my replacement? He is a fine chap and will be a credit to the Service.'

'Consider it done and should I also understand that you will accept the proposition I have put to you.' Seeing that Richard was now beaming from ear to ear, the Judge also smiled, saying 'You see, we make a good team.'

They were interrupted by the two ladies asking them if they could help carry the cartons they had prepared, to their waiting vehicle. With willing smiles, the two men went happily upstairs to assist the ladies, who, in turn were left wondering just what they had been drinking.

Finally, the ladies departed and Lord Hamilton said,

'You will soon see that today is your first day on the road to recovery. Now, I must leave you, but we will be in touch very shortly.'

With that the two men shook hands and Lord Hamilton drove away in the direction of London, to rejoin his loved, but childless wife.

Richard on the other hand, still in a buoyant mood, picked up the telephone and called his office. On hearing Barbara's voice, he said, 'Hello Barbara, Grant here. Tell my driver to have the car here for seven in the morning. I have much to do.'

He then called Chris, who was still staying with his son. 'I have decided to return to the land of the living and would love to take you and yours out for dinner. Will eight be fine?' As he replaced the receiver he thought he could hear Chris's smile and his own dear wife congratulating him.

# CHAPTER 34

How nice it felt, thought Richard, as he settled back into the rear seat of the Jaguar and allowed himself to be transported to his office. It was a beautiful day, and he looked at familiar sights through new eyes.

Only too quickly, he arrived at headquarters and his driver, on opening the door, said emotionally, 'It's great to have you back, Sir.' Thanking him, Richard entered the building, expecting to have the time to acclimatise, only to find, on entering his office, that Chris and Bill were already there.

'Good gracious,' exclaimed Richard, on seeing his two friends and colleagues, 'what got you up and about so early.'

Smiling, Chris said to Bill, 'There's thanks for you. We've been keeping the ship afloat and that's all the thanks we get. Do you believe you are indispensable?' this last being aimed at Richard.

Richard, who was still standing holding his raincoat and attache case, laughed and replied, 'Indispensable! That's a big word for you so early in the morning and I bet you don't even know what it means.'

'Then it's your day for surprises as not only do I know what it is, I know how to measure ones indispensability in any given situation,' Chris stated proudly.

'Go on, I'll buy it,' sighed Richard, resignedly.'

'Quite simple really. You take a large bucket of water, roll up your shirt sleeve and plunge your hand to the bottom of the bucket. Wait several seconds, then withdraw your hand, and the hole remaining in the water is your indispensability.'

'Wow, that's a mind boggler so early in the morning, but on reflection, so true,' said Richard as he crossed the office, placing his brief case on the desk and draping his raincoat over the back of a chair.

'Would you care to talk about the tragedy now,' asked Bill apprehensively, 'as we have been and still are making numerous enquiries into this matter.'

'Thought that had been taken out of our hands,' said Richard, remembering that the last he had heard was that the Met Police were going to be handling the enquiry from now on.

'That's the strange thing,' replied Bill, 'but shortly after the funeral, the Home Secretary resigned for health reasons. Then, the strangest thing of all was the Inspector of Constabulary visited and asked for me personally. He handed me the file that I had sent to the Met and told me that there had been a mistake and that I should never have sent the file in the first place. He then gave me a bollocking saying that precious time had been lost and for me to pull out my finger or suffer the consequences.'

'Well, well well,' said Richard, amazed by this revelation, 'so the Twat is not as thick as I thought. As we are on the subject, can you fill me in on the enquiries?'

Before starting, Richard, on realising it may be a long morning, asked Barbara, who was also, miraculously, at work so early, if she could provide coffee and biscuits for three. Several minutes later, she entered and, after placing the tray containing the coffee on the desk, she surprised everyone by embracing Richard and, after planting a huge kiss on his cheek said, 'It's just so nice to see back in harness.' She then left the office.

Richard was somewhat embarassed by this show of sympathy, but it was Chris who said, 'You will see in the coming days just how much you mean to everyone and how sorely you have been missed.'

Turning to the window in order that the other two men could not see the tears that had sprung into his eyes, Richard composed himself before turning to face them again. 'You be mother, Bill,' he said pointing to the coffee tray and Bill, with a huge smile did the honours.

Once seated and having tasted their coffee, Richard said, 'Well come on then Bill, let's be having the news or I may be tempted to telephone your friend Mr. Thompson, to tell him that you have not been following his explicit commands.'

Composing himself, Bill said, 'To date we have the following. After the dead and injured had been moved a forensic team went in with a fine tooth comb and did a really thorough search of the scene, which in itself took up several days. Their findings are in this file,' he said, placing a three inch thick folder file on the desk, 'but the main points are as follows.'

He paused and took a sip of his coffee before continuing. 'A close examination of the first class carriage, showed massive evidence of a very large explosion and from the tests made, it seems to be the same type of explosives which were stolen from Southampton. Further tests of the carriage and the bodies which were taken from there, also showed that nails and ball bearings had been packed in with the bomb, which, in turn we believe was contained in a suitcase which had been placed on the luggage rack inside the first class compartment. Everyone in that compartment,' here he paused out of respect for Richard, 'were killed outright.'

Richard felt his bile rising, but contained himself, saying simply, 'Go on and do not spare me any details, especially details relating to deceased persons. Chris and I were only two of many people who lost loved ones that evening and yet we are the ones that can, if we do our jobs correctly, find the perpetrators of this horrific, cowardly attack.'

'Now we come a to very interesting bit. The person decapitated in the first carriage is unknown, but believed to be a Pakistani. In the carriage, we found a suitcase and in the pocket of the deceased the keys to this suitcase.' Here Bill paused as if for effect, and Richard, ever impatient urged him to carry on.

'The suitcase contained a very sophisticated bomb, which had been deliberately constructed so that it could not explode.' Before he could continue, Richard interrupted.

'Are you saying that another bombing was planned or do you think it was someone trying to send a message?' he queried.

'After much reflection,' continued Bill, 'I believe the latter. The fingerprints of the deceased were all over the suitcase, the ball bearings packed around the explosives also bore his prints and we had found the keys to the case in his pocket.'

'And the message. To whom was it addressed and in which form?'

Bill consulted his pocket book, then said, 'If I were to say that the explosives in the suitcase were Goma-20 ECO, would that ring any bells?'

Richard felt his blood start to ice over as his mind went back to the train bombings in Madrid. 'Madrid, of course, some got away.'

Then he froze and his mind worked feverishly as he suddenly remembered the meal in the Asian restaurant and his wife's expression when she saw the young Asian come into the restaurant.

Chris who had been listening carefully to the exchange between his two friends said, 'You alright Richard? You look as though you have just seen the reaper go by.'

'No, no it all makes sense now. The explosives were the same as the explosives in Madrid. The worst part now is that I think I saw your headless body some weeks ago, here in the town.' He then went on to relate what had happened in the restaurant, the day he had eaten with his wife.

Bill was busily scribbling in his note book saying,

'As soon as we are finished here I'll be onto this. Like yourself, I have promised to have these bastards and have them I will.'

'Is there anything else at this stage?' enquired Richard, 'or are we all finished'.

Once again Bill consulted his notebook. 'Yes, that's it. In the pocket of Mohsin's jacket we found a notebook, absolutely soaked in blood. Its contents are quite illegible and the forensic chaps have it now. They are confident that within a few days they will be able to decipher the contents.'

'Why that's great news,' said Richard, feeling his excitement rise, 'and what about the car? Do we know the owner.'

'The car,' replied Bill, 'poses other questions. It is a hire car taken on a long lease by a London based company. The Company exists, but they say that the person who used this car, a certain Walid Benghazi, was running an amusement arcade in Oxford Street. Naturally the arcade was visited, but this Benghazi, his description is here,' he said handing a piece of paper to Richard, 'appears to be a sort of ghost figure, flitting in and out of the arcade. There is no address for him and apart from a description, nothing else.'

'More's the pity,' said Richard, 'I thought it was too good to be true.'

'There's one final thing. The car has been thoroughly examined and here is the interesting bit. Among the fingerprints we have identified Mohsin, the headless corpse with no name and we have numerous prints which we believe to be that of the famous Benghazi. For the final we have this,' said Bill, who always liked to introduce a bit of drama into his enquiries, 'we have the prints of a man which match perfectly with the prints of a suspect in one of your own reports, a report dating from Madrid. You called the person in your report 'The Expert' whereas I call him Wahid Umar, known Al Qaida member, explosives expert, and the subject of an International arrest warrant.'

'Good work, Bill,' exclaimed Richard excitedly, and then his ardour was dampened when Bill said, 'All in all, with the evidence to date, we believe that the subject Benghazi is the brain behind this, possibly the brain behind Madrid and God knows what else and we have no idea where or who he is. The only other thing we have are a number of fingerprints from the car which match to a certain Umar Razad, who was declared killed some eight years ago and yet seems to be very much alive. The only problem is that we have no idea where he is or what part he plays in all this.'

Bill stopped and looked across at Chris, saying,'Do you want to tell him or shall I?'

Richard looked from one to the other and Chris finally said, 'Our conclusion is that all this was to get back at you for being too efficient in Madrid.'

Burying his head in his hands, Richard let his mind flash back to the restaurant, the Asian entering, his wife recognising him and he, the great Richard had pooh poohed the whole thing. Now over a hundred dead and double that number injured.

Composing himself, he looked up and said, 'I've cried enough for ten lifetimes these last few days. Now, we shall attack. No stone will be left unturned until these bastards are in jail for life or, even better, dead.'

# CHAPTER 35

'Death to British Imperialists.' 'Islam will rule the World.' These and many other scandalous slogans were being carried by young Arabs of different Countries who, like many young people were often carried away by the occasion. This demonstration was in aid of a group attached loosely to Al Qaida, members of which had been arrested for conspiracy to cause explosions. Passersby started to taunt the demonstrators who in turn turned violent and soon the police intervened with tear gas. As the demonstration was being held right outside the main entrance to Scotland Yard, the officers did not have far to go with their prisoners.

After a half dozen or so had been arrested and taken away, the other demonstrators seemed to lose heart and the demonstration broke up. One of those arrested was the younger brother of Mansour, Hassan. He along with the others, was arraigned and detained in custody until the next day when they would appear before the court.

Lord Hamilton, who had been advised of these arrests, telephoned Richard to ask after his health and to also inform him of the arrests that had been made.

He invited Richard down to London the next day, saying that it could be constructive if he and his men could question these would be terrorists in order to glean information on the recent train explosion. When he followed up with an invitation to dine Richard did not hesitate and informed the Judge that he and Bill would meet with him at midday on the morrow. The Judge also intimated that it would be the last case in his long and honourable career.

The following morning, Richard and Bill, arrived at the holding cells and held a long conference with their counterparts from the Met. Police. It was decided that owing to the refusal by their solicitors to allow the detained men to be further interviewed they would wait until after they had appeared before Lord Hamilton who was to hear their pleas.

The two men went to a nearby coffee shop and Bill asked Richard what he thought of the detained men. Richard replied that the problem of today was one of fanatacism regarding the Islamic faith and that it was very difficult to identify the hardliner from a simple' hangeron.' 'Let's just wait and see' said Richard. 'If you can work out some plan of action with the Met. lads, I want to pop up and have a quick word with Lord Hamilton, before the Court session starts. I am intrigued as to the reason why Lord Hamilton should have called me, as this has really nothing to do with us.'

Leaving Bill to go and see the officer in charge of the case involving the unlawful demonstrators, Richard made his way to the Judges Chambers, where he found the Judge in the act of reading some case papers before going into Court. After shaking hands, the Judge looked at Richard appraisingly saying, 'You are a different man. I am looking forward to us working together in the future, aren't you?'

'A few days ago I would not have known how to have answered that question,' said Richard softly, 'but now that my decision has been made to leave and to take the post you have offered me, it is as though a huge weight has been lifted and I am thrilled to bits at the thought of us working together.'

'Good, well at least that's settled. Now, as to my ringing you yesterday. This is obviously between us and to go no further, but one of the accused, a certain Hassan Ahmad, is the son of an old friend of mine, a retired diplomat, who has been living in London since he retired some ten years ago.

'He asked if I could help his son, who is studying at University here, to escape a possible prison sentence as this would obviously affect his studies and indeed his position at the university. Personally, I do not know the son and I thought that you, as someone I would trust with my life, could possibly have a word and assess the son for me, obviously unofficially and off the record. What do you think?'

'Before Court, that will not be possible as the solicitors involved in the case have already instructed their clients to say nothing and refuse to be questioned. Perhaps if you could order them to be detained until this afternoon saying for instance that you require a Social Services report or something along those lines, I should be able to get in and have a little chat.'

'Knew I could count on you. Now, if you will excuse me, I must robe up for Court. We'll be eating at my club so if you could be outside the Judge's entrance at half twelve that will give us time to enjoy a decent lunch.'

With that Richard took his leave and went to find Bill in order to put him into the picture. Before going into the main body of the building, he decided he needed to relieve himself and went into the public toilet. Whilst he was standing at the urinal, a group of four young Arabs, hard looking young men, similarly dressed in trainers, jeans and sweat shirts entered the toilets and went to the far end of the room where they huddled together in conversation. Richard, who was well dressed was probably taken to be a solicitor by the four, as they paid him little attention.

After zipping his trousers, he went across to the washbasin and started to rinse his hands, keeping an eye on the four men through the mirror set over the wash basin. He saw one of the men show what he thought was a knife to the others and then the four 'high fived' with clenched fists and left the toilets. Following them, Richard saw them walk into the Court where Lord Hamilton would soon be officiating.

'There you are.' Turning he saw Bill with another man coming towards him. 'This is Dave' said Bill, 'who is in charge of this little investigation. He tells me that none of the arrested are known to the Police and he thinks it more youthful exuberance than hard line Islamic demonstrators.'

Shaking hands, Richard said to Dave, 'I may be wrong, but there are four young Arabs who have just walked into the Court, and, whilst I was in the toilet I saw them huddled in deep conversation. In addition, although I am not one hundred per cent certain, I am sure at least one of them is armed with a knife.'

'Thank you, Chief Constable,' replied Dave, 'just leave it to me. I'll make whatever arrangements are necessary to contain them.' With that he hurried away and Richard, accompanied by Bill, walked into the Court room.

There were already a number of members of the public present plus solicitors, barristers and various Court room staff. The four young Arabs were seated together, quite close to the dock area, where soon would appear the accused. The two men took seats in the public area, close to the four Arabs who were sitting quietly, waiting for the Court to come into session.

A few minutes later, Lord Hamilton made his appearance and Richard took the opportunity to look around him, satisfied to see a heavy Police presence in the Court room.

Once the Court had been called to order, the accused demonstrators were led into the dock. Richard noticed that they seemed like young men from good family backgrounds, judging from their dress and general demeanour. He identified Hassan immediately from the description the Judge had given to him, a good looking, well groomed young man, but as Richard knew from experience, first appearances could be misleading.

The charges were read to the Court and each accused pleaded 'Not Guilty' and in turn the defence solicitors made applications for bail to be granted.

When all the pleas had been heard, Lord Hamilton announced that before considering the bail applications, he would like Social Service reports on all the accused, and that all would be retained in custody until the afternoon, whilst these reports were prepared.

Immediately, there was confusion in the Court room as the accused leaped to their feet in anger and the four young Arabs seated in the well of the Court also jumped to their feet, shouting abuse at the Judge. Richard and Bill stood, in time to see Hassan and another of the accused, push their guards out of the way and vault over the dock and into the well of the Court.

Screaming defiance, the young men started to move menacingly towards the judges bench and Richard and Bill moved swiftly to put themselves between the advancing Arabs and the Judge. Hassan launched himself at Richard and before he could defend himself he received a hard blow in the face, causing one eye to immediately close.

Instinctively, Richard struck out, catching Hassan with a hard blow to the shoulder; Hassan lost his balance and half fell to his left and Richard, quick as ever, as he afterwards thought, thrust his right hand between Hassan's legs and, taking a firm grip on his testicles, squeezed.

Hassan screamed in agony, but Richard, keeping a firm grip on this very tender part of Hassan's body, steered him towards the advancing Police officers who had been instructed to assist in the Court room. Once Hassan had been handcuffed, Richard released him after a final squeeze, which left Hassan blubbering like a baby. The other accused and the four other Arabs had all been restrained and were led away.

Richard, who could see nothing through his closed eye, was helped by a uniformed officer to seek medical attention. The officer, a long serving stalwart, looked admiringly at Richard saying, 'I bet you did not learn that restraining hold in Police College, Sir. A pity some of our young sprogs were not around, as I am sure they would have enjoyed that.'

In spite of the damage to his eye Richard smiled, wincing with pain at the same time. 'You are dead right, but seeing we are of similar age I am sure that you must also have a trick or two up your sleeve. Am I not right in that assumption?'

'You certainly are, Sir, but those days are gone. Today we are expected to turn the other cheek and drop our trousers at the same time. I'll be glad that within two months it will be over and I can start to enjoy retirement.'

'Good for you,' replied Richard as he accepted a seat, 'but if you decide to take another job, look me up at the Exec Organisation.' Smiling his thanks, the officer said he would do just that.

By this time order had been restored. Bill joined Richard, remarking on his now firmly closed and discoloured eye, saying, 'You know, I think we are getting too old for this type of life,' whereupon Richard, turning his head to see through his one good eye said, 'I agree, but it was good fun. Did you notice how easy it is to persuade someone when you have his bollocks in your hand?'

After receiving medical treatment from the Court nurse, the two men went in search of a drink in a local public house, and at half past twelve precisely met up with Lord Hamilton who expressed concern at Richard's injury, only to be reassured as Bill regaled him with the tale of the 'Old Bailey' massacre.

On reaching the gentleman's club, of which Lord Hamilton was a founder member, the three were soon in a very comfortable lounge bar, sunk deeply into luxurious leather armchairs. After hearing of everything that had occurred, the Judge having been moved to safety immediately the trouble had erupted, indicated that there was only one form of action he could take, regarding the accused. 'Won't put me off my lunch though,' he said, accepting the proffered menu card. He ordered for the three of them and, after finishing their drinks, the three men were lead by the head steward to a well laid out table, where they enjoyed an exceptionally good meal.

Whilst drinking their coffee accompanied by a very well seasoned brandy, the Judge thanked the two men for their assistance and asked if they had enjoyed their meal. 'I can assure you, my Lord,' replied Bill, 'that your canteen is several notches higher than our own.' Laughing, the three men rose and left to return to the Court.

True to his word, after the accused, this time including the four others who had also been detained, were newly arraigned on charges including affray and a whole list of offences relating to assaults and disorderly behaviour in a Court of Law, Lord Hamilton promptly ordered them all to be kept in custody. This time they were all handcuffed and there was no further trouble as they were taken away.

'Let's get going Bill, to try to beat the traffic, or it will be midnight, before we get home.'

'Right you are, Sir,' replied Bill, as he went in search of their driver. Richard, on the other hand had stopped, thinking' why rush,' as there would be no one waiting to greet him or hear his tales of derring do, at the Court House.

# CHAPTER 36

The next three weeks flashed by for Richard. So much to do, so many people to contact and during which the enquiries into the train explosion, seemed to be grinding to a halt. Bill had interviewed, or at least visited the accused Arabs remanded in, custody but to no avail, the only reply to his questions being, 'Allah Akbar' meaning God is the greatest. When Bill asked to what God they were referring, they laughed saying 'There is only one God, Mohamed.' Try as he might, and he was a formidable interviewer, he got no further.

The only positive piece of evidence came from the surveillance cameras at St. Pancras. They found images showing an Arabic type leaving the first class carriage of the fated train, minutes before it left. Other images showed him on the platform with a suitcase, whereas when he left the train, he was empty handed. Photographs were enlarged and distributed throughout the Police agencies, but no identification was forthcoming.

On Richard's last day of work, Bill came to see him, saying he would continue with the enquiry and that Richard would be kept up to date with any new developments. He then reached into his jacket pocket and took out a sheet of typewritten paper.

'This has just come through from forensics. You may remember that I had mentioned finding a blood soaked pocketbook in the jacket belonging to our poor friend, Mohsin. The lab. people have managed to decipher some of the things written and have come up with the following.

'He makes mention of of someone named Ali, which is believed to be a pseudonym, who appeared to be friendly towards him. The other headless corpse we believe, may be this Ali. His fingerprints were identified by the Police in Pakistan as one, Mohamed Ramzan, a known local criminal. We are still waiting for confirmation, photos; etc., and when these are received we will see where we go from there.

The only other thing of any note is of a certain, Zanzibar, described as their leader with a footnote saying 'stinking breath.' To date we have nothing further on this person, and what he means by stinking breath defeats me. Probably never cleans his teeth.'

Richard sat in silence, thinking, then asked if any visits had been paid to the homes of the accused Arabs in custody.

'Now I know why you are the chief, never miss a thing. I completely forgot, but on the other hand nothing was found of interest at any of their homes. On visiting the home of your Judge's friend, I found the parents devestated at the arrest of their son. They said they could not understand him and only his elder brother can control him correctly.'

'So what is big brother going to do about it? asked Richard, 'Beat the living daylights out of him I hope, but that would be hoping for too much.'

'As a matter of fact the problem seems to be that the elder brother is away on holiday at the moment and the parents are at their wits' end as what to do with him. On top of which they seem a very pleasant couple, and their house is very nice.'

'Bill, my boy, just keep trying your best. Something will come out of it in the end, just you wait and see. Keep focused, you can't do more than your best.'

Someone knocked on the door of Richard's office and, before he could answer, Chris stepped into the room. 'Come to see that I've not nicked the ashtrays,' laughed Richard and Chris replied that that was the sole reason for his visit.

'However,' said Chris, 'I am glad to see Bill is here. I received a phone call a short while ago from the chairman of the Police Committee who wishes for you and us two, to present ourselves at the City Hall at seven thirty this evening, I suppose for a farewell drink. I can arrange to have you picked up and brought home afterwards, as driving may be a little difficult.'

'Shouldn't think so,' laughed Richard, 'for if it's the chairman who is paying, it will surely be a round of orange squash.'

At that moment the phone rang and on answering, Richard was pleased to hear the soft tones of Lord Hamilton. He enquired after Richard's health, and then asked if he knew the whereabouts of Bill. 'Right in front of me, my Lord,' replied Richard, handing the telephone to Bill.

Chris and Richard watched as Bill's face broke into a huge smile and then they heard him say, 'Is that not a bit much' and a few seconds later he said,' I see. That makes sense and thank you.' With that he replaced the receiver.

Seeing the bemused smile on Bill's face, Richard said,

'Come on, spit it out. What did he say?'

'That laddie Hassan, the one you demonstrated the ball crushing on, the 'Old Man',(referring to the Judge) gave him five years in the slammer. Five years. That'll keep him quiet for a while.'

'Rubbish. He'll appeal and be let out in next to no time' replied Richard. 'The only reason he did that was to send out a message to others not to follow the example of our young friend, but you know that in this day and age, if the agitators in the Al Qaida organisation don't immediately start a campaign, there are always 'do-gooders' ready to jump to their defence to the detriment of their own Country.'

'Blimey, I knew you were good, but not that good. You are either psychic or telepathic as that is exactly what the Judge said,' exclaimed Bill.

Looking at his watch, Richard said, with a lump in his throat, 'Well you two, I must throw you out now as I have some last minute things to do before I finally leave this hallowed building. You,' he said, addressing Chris, 'can wait until tomorrow before you move in and change this office around.'

The two men left Richard's office and after several minutes of silent contemplation, Richard checked to make sure that he had cleared out all his personal effects. After a final look at the culmination of thirty years of heartache and devotion, he picked up his briefcase and, for the last time switched off the office light.

Barbara, his secretary, rose to her feet as he entered her office and the two met in the middle of the room, where they fondly embraced. 'It will be so hard without you,' she said, 'but I must continue, as I have my aged mother to look after,' whispered Barbara, still holding onto Richards shoulders.

'I thought your mother lived in London,' replied Richard.

'She does, but her pension is not enough to live on and she prefers London, owing to the fact that the few friends she has, all live there.'

Richard thought for a few seconds, then, releasing his hold on her shoulders, he said, 'Tell you what and you don't have to make a decision straight away. I have been offered and have accepted a new position in London and I am sure to need a good secretary, one I can trust implicitly. Obviously with London weighting the pay will be a lot higher than here, probably twice as much or thereabouts. As I said, no need to make a decision straight away, but the offers on the table.'

With tears in her eyes Barbara stared at him and then said,

'You know, you are such a good man and with all the awful things that have happened to you, you still find time for others. I will certainly consider your offer and give you my answer as soon as possible'.

Finally, after saying goodnight, Richard descended into the front lobby where his driver was waiting for him. Without a word, the driver preceded him to the Jaguar staff car and for the final time as Chief Constable, Richard allowed himself to be driven home. On arrival, the driver, after opening the door and allowing Richard to step out of the car, held out his hand to Richard saying, 'I will be retiring shortly, Sir, and I would like to say what an honour it has been to have served you for these last few years and I wish you all the very best for the future.'

Overcome, Richard thanked him warmly and then took his leave, watching the tail lights of his ex official car disappear down the driveway.

At seven o'clock, Richard was showered and changed and, as he descended the stair case, he saw headlights coming up the driveway. Checking that he had his wallet and credit cards as he knew he would be expected to pay a round at least during the evening, he opened the door to see his ex-driver holding the door open for him. 'Couldn't turn down the overtime,' said the driver stoically and with a smile, Richard climbed into the car to join the new Chief Constable Chris, and Bill.

'I can't understand why they should choose the City Hall', remarked Richard, 'as it must be the ugliest building in this town. The Germans would have done us a favour if they had bombed it.'

'Probably because it's big and big is beautiful to some people,' replied Chris. 'Anyway, at least we can park in the official underground parking lot.'

Twenty minutes later the car entered the underground lot and the three men took the lift to the first floor, where they walked towards the big double doors leading to the largest of the three reception rooms. Richard noticed the silence and wondered if he was coming to a farewell party or a wake.

Bill stepped forward and rapped on the door and then stepped aside to allow Richard to pass in front. At the same time the doors were flung open wide and Richard was blinded by a spotlight aimed at the double doors and coming from the centre of the room.

He was obviously startled, but before he could react, an enormous cheer went up from the room and a thunderous round of applause broke out. Blinded by the light, he stood dumbfounded, as the people inside the room broke into singing, 'For he's a jolly good fellow' followed by a deafening rendition of 'Why was he born so beautiful'.

Turning, with tears of joy streaming down his face, he saw Chris and Bill smiling broadly. 'You bastards set me up and I fell for it. Shows I've taken the right decision, to leave,' and as the spotlight was extinguished and his eyes adjusted to the lights of the room, he saw a crowd of hundreds. Pushed from behind by Chris, he made his way through the room to a dais which had been set up at the end of the room, where waited the Chairman of the Police Committee and the Lord Mayor, who warmly welcomed him.

He then turned to face the sea of hundreds of faces which all started to chant, 'Speech, speech' and Richard went to the microphone and as silence fell he said,

'I just do not know what to say?' and before he could gather his thoughts, an anonymous voice from the crowd said, 'Say nothing and get the drinks in', which brought a laugh from the others present.

When quiet returned, Richard addressed them saying, 'My anonymous admirer has hit the button on the head. I promise you all that I shall personally thank each and everyone of you for coming here tonight and I now declare the bar open.' To yet another thunderous round of applause, the crowd headed for the bar, where a phalanx of waiters waited apprehensively to serve them.

The Lord Mayor approached him saying, 'You got your speech just right. Perhaps I could interest you to enter politics. We are always on the lookout for good candidates and with the following you apparently have, you would be voted in on a land slide.'

'Perhaps, one day, but at the moment I have other things on my plate, but I will certainly keep your offer in mind,' replied Richard and, on turning to face the other invited dignitaries said, 'The drinks are on me.' A hand signal summoned a passing waiter who swiftly supplied filled glasses to them all. A band struck up and, as promised, Richard started to make the rounds in the room, shaking hands until he thought his own would drop off. 'Wonder how the Queen manages?' he thought after about the four hundredth handshake.

Some three hours later, people started to drift away and Richard positioned himself by the door to thank them for giving him such a great send off.

Barbara, was one of the last to leave and as she gave him a kiss on the cheek, she said, 'I have spoken to my mother and she is delighted, so the answer to your question earlier is, yes I will.'

Finally, there was just Richard, Bill and Chris left, with a small army of workers who were in the process of clearing up. Richard noticed a pile of gift wrapped parcels at the side of the dais and said, 'Someone's birthday?'

Laughing, Chris said, 'No they are all for you, all bought and paid for by your friends and colleagues. I do not know if you are aware or not, but nearly every officer in the Force, except those on duty or off sick, was here tonight. Some even changed shifts in order to be here as they wished to show their appreciation to you. I would say it borders on love. What about you, Bill, do you not agree?'

'I certainly do. Everyone chipped in. The Mayor gave us the City Hall free of charge and the rest was paid for by your ex-officers. You know, Richard, you are the last of the dinosaurs and the men and women of this Force know that and needed to show their appreciation in the only way they could, and that was by turning up here tonight.'

Overcome, Richard allowed himself to be taken to the car and to be driven home for the last time in the beloved Jaguar. After saying goodnight to his friends he climbed the stairs and, after stripping, climbed into his empty bed. However, he could not sleep as his emotions were running so high and so he started to talk to Susan explaining his hopes and fears for the future, much as he would have done if she was alive.

Finally, he fell asleep and was rewarded by Susan coming to visit him in his dreams.

# CHAPTER 37

M ansour was relaxing on a sunbed beside the luxurious pool of a suburban palace in Pakistan. He was surrounded by beautiful young people of both sexes, as well as the older, ruling order of Al Qaida. He was well rested, bronzed and fit, six weeks after the train bombing. He had been greeted as a hero and had been included in very important private meetings, where future operations were discussed and vital decisions taken.

After leaving his uncle, he had driven to Heathrow Airport and there had boarded an Air Pakistan flight to Lahore, the capital of the Punjab region of Pakistan.

Lahore has been the capital for over a thousand years and has a reputation as the cultural, academic and intellectual centre of Pakistan. In the early fifteen hundreds, it was the centre of the Mughal Empire and during the decades that followed many beautiful palaces, gardens and mosques were created. Later, during the British reign, Victorian structures were added which blended well with the existing buildings.

Mansour looked at the new Rolex that adorned his wrist and noticed several of his age group, especially the men, were casting their eyes over him. He knew he was handsome with a well sculpted body and his sun tan, coupled with the very brief swimming trunks he was wearing, showed off his body to perfection. He stretched out languidly on the well sprung sun bed feeling the morning rays of the sun warming his body.

His mind went back to his university days in Cambridge.

Having a father who had been a successful diplomat, meant that he had received a very private and very expensive education and it was a well educated, handsome undergraduate who arrived in the hallowed halls of Cambridge.

From the start he was very popular, excelling at cricket and rowing. He was later to win blues in both sports. However, one of his weaknesses was women, as he did not like them at all. From his earliest days at boarding school he had felt sexually attracted to other boys and had not waited to start experimenting.

It had been at the end of his second year at Cambridge, when, with his then lover, an Egyptian politicians son, he had decided to enrol in an Al Qaida training camp in the Afghanistan mountain region. He had drunk up the indoctrination lessons and had also discovered he had leadership qualities, which did not go un-noticed by the training staff at the camp.

During the last week in the camp, he was wakened by the sound of helicopter engines and found himself face to face with American Marines who instantly opened fire. A short but very savage battle was fought, leaving dead and wounded on both sides.

Mansour showed great bravery, but even he was not able to save his lover who was blown apart by an American grenade. From that time on, he had sworn revenge against the enemies of Al Qaida and undying loyalty to their cause.

He was disturbed by a servant who, after politely asking him to follow, led him to a shaded area, where he indicated a telephone that was lying on a bureau.

Taking the telephone, he was pleased to hear his father's voice until his father explained the reason for him calling, explaining that his brother was in prison.

'I am worried about your mother, she cannot sleep and you know she has problems with her heart. What could have got into your brother? I always thought we had taught by example. Britain is our adopted Country and I would give my life for it. Look at you, a son to be proud of, a businessman and councillor, and your brother. What could have got into him? What can we do? I even spoke with the Judge after he was arrested. The Judge told me not to worry, but then after he assaulted the Police Chief, in the Court room, the Judge would not have had any choice. But five years in prison, how will he survive?'

Mansour was shocked by these revelations. His brother, his baby brother, what had got into him? He had always been headstrong, but never stupid.

'Father, I have friends in high places and I will put the wheels in motion straight away. But tell me, who did he assault to warrant five years in prison?'

'It was that poor Police Chief who lost his wife and family in that cowardly train bombing some weeks ago. The Judge was Lord Hamilton, who is an old friend of mine, but he had no choice.'

Overcome by anger, Mansour shouted 'There is always a choice,' but on hearing the exclamation made by his father, he apologised, saying 'I'm sorry, my father for my outburst. Of course the Judge was right, but Hassan had never been in trouble before and I was shocked by the sentence. I will ring you later, but leave me time to telephone my contacts.' With that he broke the communication and instead of returning to the pool, he went up to his room, where he lay on the bed, gazing at the ceiling.

'That bastard, Grant. First Madrid, now my brother. Not even killing his family can keep him quiet. By Allah, I promise that the next time I will make him pay, along with the Judge. These unbelievers have to be taught that there is only one God and that is Mohamed."

He took his address book from the bedside table and started to make a list of persons to contact, in order to try to gain early release from prison for his brother.

–o–o–o–o–o–o–o–

Back in England, Richard, after a short break with his brother and his wife in a comfortable South coast hotel, had started installing himself. The headquarters of the Exec Organisation were in Trafalgar Square in a listed building, known to the people who worked there as Fort Knox, owing to sophisticated security systems in place inside the building. On the exterior was simply a small brass plate marked 'Exec Org.'

His office was on the fifth floor looking out on the famous column bearing the statue of Lord Nelson, who in turn supplied a splendid resting place for the dozens of pigeons that inhabited the square. The office was sparsely, but comfortably furnished, as Richard did not believe in opulence in a working environment. Barbara would be joining him shortly, and he had overseen the planning of her office, knowing her likes and dislikes. Piles of papers were waiting for him on his huge modern desk, but before he could start on them, his phone rang.

'Settling in, old chap,' said the pleasant voice of Lord Hamilton, and on hearing that Richard was pleased with his accomodation, he said, 'I am in the process of installing myself in my new abode in Marsham Street and was wondering if you could pop across some time to give me some advice. Tomorrow perhaps?' asked Lord Hamilton, wistfully.

'Not a problem', replied Richard immediately. 'Shall we say ten thirty?'

The next morning, the two men met in the new Home Secretary's office. Spacious with large, comfortable looking armchairs, a huge desk, obviously a very valuable antique, and a wonderful wall to wall, floor to ceiling bookcase to the right of the desk.

On the other side of the desk were huge picture windows looking out onto the morning London skies. The room was about 45 sqare metres in space and Richard remarked that if the Lord's wife should throw him out, he could quite easily move into his office.

'By the way,' Richard continued, 'when I was here to see Sir Peter, we were seated in another room, certainly not this one.'

'Ah, yes, that would be the ante chamber. Come, I will show you one of the little secrets of this room.' Leading the way, Lord Hamilton left his office, turned right and walked about 20 meters to another door, which he opened.

'This is the office where I met with Sir Peter,' said Richard, recognising the rather rudimentary furnishings after the flamboyant luxury of the Home Secretary's domain.

'Thought so,' replied Lord Hamilton. Moving to the wall behind the desk, he stopped beside the fireplace, and invited Richard to join him. When Richard was by his side, he placed his hand under the marble mantlepiece and pressed a concealed button.

Soundlessly, the wall to which the fireplace was attached swung inwards on well oiled hinges, and Richard saw that it allowed access to the Home Secretary's office, actually opening into the book case to the right of the desk. Richard whistled appreciatively and Lord Hamilton, smiling, said, 'Rather neat I think. Good to have a back door in case the opposition come looking for blood one day.' The two men passed through the opening and Lord Hamilton showed Richard the button secreted in the bookcase and closed the opening.

'Marvellous. Not even a join to be seen,' remarked Richard running an experienced eye over the bookcase. 'Now let me see what recommendations I can make to increase your security.'

After a thorough scrutiny of the room, Richard suggested that possibly a more secure telephone system could be installed and noted to have the windows checked for their strength in deflecting bullets. 'There is bullet proofing and there is bullet proofing,' he said. 'Now, why is the room soundproofed? To stop noise entering or leaving?'

Lord Hamilton laughed, saying that as the sound proofing was already installed, it may as well stay there. Richard remarked that it could be useful for questioning recaltrican prisoners, which brought a wry, but knowing smile to the Home Secretary's face.

'I have also brought this little gadget with me. As you know I will invest in men, but am loathe to invest in technology, but this little beauty is something else. Here try it,' he said and in so doing, handed a small, black plastic object, smaller than the smallest portable telephone. There was a grey coloured press switch in the centre and a connection to which one could fix a battery charger.

From his pocket, he took a similar sized object, only this one had a screen. Richard walked to the far side of the room, leaving the Home Secretary beside the fireplace. 'Now,' said Richard, 'press the grey button.'

A high pitched screeching noise emitted from the object that Richard held in his hand, and Lord Hamilton, holding his ears, shouted, 'Switch that dreadful noise off.' Richard silenced the object, glanced at the screen and then joined his friend beside the fireplace.

Richard held out the object he had in his hand and Lord Hamilton saw a large number five, printed in the centre of the screen. 'Well, what is it,' he asked somewhat exasperated.

'If at any time you are in danger, you press the button and you will alert everyone of my men within ten miles of your position. The number five indicates your personal alarm. In my secretaries office is the master receiver and with that we can pin point your exact position. Please keep it with you at all times.'

'I will show this to the Prime Minister,' said Lord Hamilton, enthused by this little piece of technology.

'Please don't,' said Richard. 'Can you imagine, the Prime Minister would want everyone to have one, people would give it to their kids to keep them quiet, and before you know it, my men would be racing about all over the place on wild goose chases. No, let's just keep it between us.'

'All right by me. I can promise you that I will always carry it alongside my inhaler. Now, it must be getting on for lunch time, so . . . .'

The two men, comfortable in each others company, left the room together, to go in search of sustenance.

After a quick drink in a local public house, they decided to try a local restaurant set in a large detached house in Pimlico. Once comfortably seated, Lord Hamilton asked Richard how he was settling in. Richard replied that it was different to being a Chief Constable and brought the conversation round to necessities.

'What bothers me at the moment is that I have no fluent Arabic speakers and certainly not in the Pakistani dialects. I have feelers out, but I fear it could cost a lot of money.'

Lord Hamilton laughed softly, then said, 'The first thing you have to remember is that you are no longer a Chief Constable with a budget to balance. Exec is an organisation paid for by very rich companies who want the best, Governments included. You need something, you buy it. There is no budget as far as you are concerned. You spend whatever is necessary. Now, what is the real problem as regards the lack of your Asian dialect speakers?'

'Information is trickling in from my different contacts throughout Europe, of an uneasiness being felt by those involved in surveying possible Islamist trouble makers. It would appear that in certain locations during meetings, veiled messages are passed regarding a World shattering event which is in the process of being formulated.'

Lord Hamilton, after a moment's reflection, said, 'Seems a bit vague to me. Are you sure it is not some doom and gloom merchants trying to further the distrust between the Europeans and the Arabs, as there are plenty of those about.'

'No, simply because all the information is coming from the Arabs themselves, not our normal informants, but Arabs who sense unease because of the tone used in these certain locations. Unfortunately, although some are prepared to tell us little bits, we have found no one who will work for us in an effort to infiltrate some of these meetings.

You will remember our friend Mohsin who lost his life at the same time as my family. Well, to try finding someone of that calibre is not easy and that is why I needed to know how far I could go financial wise.'

'You, personally, Richard, what do you think. Do you believe that something major could be being planned? I have had no information whatsoever from my official sources and Lord knows they are numerous and well equipped. Why do you think that is?' queried Lord Hamilton, becoming intrigued by this information.

'I would imagine,' replied Richard, 'that the official bodies, MI5 and the like, do not want to be seen as alarmists. They would demand confirmation and that is very difficult to come by, hence my wish to recruit specialists who can mingle freely in Islamic circles, without drawing attention to themselves and to, hopefully, ingratiate themselves to such an extent that they could possibly be taken into confidence. It is a long hope, but one I am willing to try, as I have this horrible, inner feeling, that someone out there has plans for an Islamic World domination. It could possibly be the same person who planned the train explosion, as I now know that he was also involved in the Madrid bombings.'

Lord Hamilton lowered his head as he considered the various implications, political and otherwise, that could be forthcoming should Richard be proven to be wrong. Heaven alone knew the pressure that could be inflicted the moment someone started to criticise or attack the Islamic movement.

Finally he said, 'Look, Richard, I have the utmost confidence in you and I will support and follow your suppositions with great interest. However, I cannot in the existing political climate come out and repeat what you have just told me. I must have proof or confirmation.'

'I know, and that is why I must have these extra bodies. It is of the utmost importance that they are credible and able to mingle and, most importantly, that they want to do this work. They must be one hundred per cent trustworthy and I will require at least forty to cover the ten biggest countries in the European Community. It would be safe to say that if the feedback is positive as I unhappily believe it will be, it will be fair to say that if the answer is the same for the ten, then the seventeen others will follow suit.'

Showing that he was au fait with his generation, Lord Hamilton said, 'In that case, as the well known sports shoemaker would say, 'Then just do it.'

# CHAPTER 38

'Hello, my favourite, nephew, and how are you?' Mansour jumped to his feet and on turning saw his uncle coming towards him. It was a beautiful morning and the swimming pool was already occupied by a number of visitors, wanting to experience the luxury of a swimming pool in the heart of the Punjab, where luxury was not available to everyone, only the chosen few.

'My uncle, what a surprise and a pleasure to see you here. Have you come with some good news of my brother? I would cut off my right arm if I could free him from the Imperialist prison,' cried Mansour, looking at his uncle with beseeching eyes.

'Your brother is paying the price for his stupidity and with the help of Allah, he will be soon freed a much wiser man. Now, to more important matters. Do you know why you are here?' asked his uncle. 'Has anyone explained anything to you?'

'Explained in what way? You gave me the air ticket and the address and I have been here ever since. I am now waiting for instructions as I will revenge my brother if it is the last thing I do.'

'Revenge is for idiots. You are here for one reason and one reason alone. You have been chosen, having proved yourself for the last ten years, as capable of taking a leading role in our quest for World domination. We were fifty one, but with the demise of Bin Laden, we are just fifty, which does not leave us with a choice in case of difficult decisions.

You have been selected, to replace Bin Laden himself, and, I for one am pleased at this choice, for I am convinced that you have the stamina and moral turpitude to help us achieve our aims.'

'What aims, I know nothing. How can I help if I am not informed?'

'Today is the last day of your holiday. From tomorrow you will be under constant surveillance and you, like myself, will be accountable for all your actions relating to our forthcoming decisions. You have been chosen by Allah himself.'

Mansour was astounded. All his dreams and aspirations were to be realised and he looked at his uncle with a huge smile lighting up his face. He had already forgotten about his brother, with the excitement that his uncle's news had brought him.

'But uncle,' began Mansour, 'how do you know all this when you live so quietly in Basingstoke? It cannot be possible that you could have been involved with the ruling council, when you were thousands of miles away.'

'You have much to learn. With modern telephones, you ring me and you think I am in Basingstoke, but I could be here or anywhere else in the World. Modern transport is such that in a few days you can travel the World, and no one has even noticed that you are not at home. Now, I have much to do, but you will be called before morning prayers tomorrow for the meeting of the Council.'

With that the uncle took his leave and Mansour, exploding with joy, leaped into the swimming pool and started swimming lengths in a fast crawl. At last, a full member of the ruling council. He could not wait for the morrow to find who the other members were and could not get it out of his head that his uncle was a member, whilst he, Mansour, had thought his uncle an old, retired pensioner.

It was three o'clock the following morning, when Mansour was wakened by an armed guard, who stood silently in the room, whilst Mansour hurriedly dressed.

The two then left the room, the guard leading, him taking Mansour to a large, basement room, where the guard indicated he should wait. Impatiently, Mansour waited, noting the lack of decoration and furnishings and, when he thought he could stand the tension no longer, the guard returned and ushered Mansour into an adjacent room.

The room was well lit and he saw that everyone present was seated on cushions on the floor. Tea was being served and Mansour looked around, recognising amongst the seated persons, several members of various European governments, two or three that he had worked with at different times and even a well known film star. His uncle was seated to the right of the council president, jolting Mansour who had never even dreamed that his uncle could be holding such an exalted position within the Al Qaida organisation, and to be seated next to Oussama Bin Laden's successor.

The president, an elderly man wearing traditional robes and sporting a very long beard, clapped his hands to draw attention to the presence of Mansour and to silence the other council members, who in turn regarded Mansour. He suddenly felt very self conscious being the only person standing in the room. Several members nodded, indicating that they knew him and the president indicated that Mansour should take the one vacant place amongst the members, a place directly in front of himself.

Once seated, Mansour waited expectantly as the president addressed the Council, briefly identifying Mansour and explaining his previous involvement within their movement. He then signalled to a waiting secretary, who stepped forward and handed each member a folder marked 'Secret'. Each member took his folder and waited for the President to issue his instructions.

'My friends, things are moving at a goodly pace,' he stated, in a quiet, well modulated voice. 'Many years have passed since the World Trade Centre, and I, like many of you here, believe the time is now ripe for us to remind our enemies that we are still present and prepared for action. Our training camps, for the past ten years, have trained thousands of volunteers, who are now, in the main, waiting in their selected towns and cities throughout Europe, for the call to take up arms.

'Thanks to our wealthy neighbours and friends, arms and explosives are in plentiful supply and are just waiting to be put to good use. Today, we will decide what the next target will be and once that decision taken, plans will be drawn up for its execution. Now, you all have a a dossier and inside you will find a number of suggestions for the next target. Today you will each, individually, select one target, indicate that you are personally willing or not to participate actively in its execution and, once you have marked the target selected, I wish you to place the sheet of paper bearing the details of your selection in the urn provided.

'You will then join me for prayers. May Allah guide each of you in your decision making. We three,' he added, indicating himself, Mansour's uncle and the man to his left, 'have already selected our targets and will wait patiently for each of you to make your decision.'

With that, the three men rose and left the room. No one spoke and, as one, the remaining Council members, opened their dossiers and started to study its contents.

Mansour counted nine sheets of paper. The first suggested an attempt at disruption of the forthcoming Olympic Games, another an attempt on the Royal Family, during their summer holiday in Scotland. Others covered major sporting events in various European centres and one even suggested an attempt on a nuclear power station.

However, there was one suggestion that over shadowed all the others, and that was a planned meeting of all the twenty seven member states making up the European Union, together with a suggested twenty eighth member, Turkey.

On the 14th of April, 1987, Turkey had made its first official demand to join the European Economic Community. They had signed a customs union agreement in 1995 and were recognised as a candidate on the 12th. December, 1999. Finally, negotiations began on the 3rd. October, 2005, amidst much controversy, and these negotiations were still ongoing.

The main problem appeared to be that whilst some countries were wholeheartedly behind their application, others had certain reserves, involving their attitude to civil liberties and also towards women. In Germany, for instance, the Turkish population had grown from seven thousand in 1960 to over two million forty years later, thus making up over two per cent of the total population of that Country.

An ex-French President, Jacques Chirac, was reported to have said at the time, that it was his 'dearest wish' to see Turkey in the European Union. Finally, the 'ayes' prevailed and it was decided that Turkey would become the 28th. Member State.

It seemed that a suggestion had been made by the European president that he would like to host a huge meeting of all the Governments of the member States, plus a certain number of opposition members and, naturally all the European Commissioners and Deputies, to celebrate the entry of Turkey into the European Community. Mansour roughly calculated that would mean somewhere between two and a half and three thousand people.

Apparently, the French President had been approached and asked if he would be willing to supply a location for this historic meeting, and he naturally had agreed, especially as the European President had intimated that all costs, including travel, accomodation, wages etc. etc. would be paid from central European funds, meaning the French tax payers would not have to pay, at least, not directly.

When Mansour saw the suggested location, he knew that this target would be his selection and that he would volunteer to be involved and even to be in charge of the operation. The reason, the target, the Château at Versailles, close to Paris in France. A mythic location and Mansour nearly wet himself in excitement as he thought of the accolades that would be awarded to he who successfully launched the attack on such a target.

Seeing that several members had already left the room, he took his pen and endorsed sheet number seven, indicating that he wanted to be involved with the planning and execution of the proposed meeting of European Governments at the Château of Versailles.

Carefully folding the signed sheet of paper, he did as the others had done before him, placing his paper in the urn and leaving the rest of the dossier on the floor. He left the room to join the others in prayer, already praying that his selection would be the one chosen.

After morning prayers, Mansour was seated at breakfast with other members of the Council. No one spoke of that mornings meeting and Mansour did likewise. He was interrupted by a messenger, who handed him a piece of paper. On opening it he read, 'Telephone Wahid ASAP'.

After finishing his breakfast, Mansour went in search of a telephone. There were the usual delays in getting a connection, but finally he was in contact with Wahid.

'Greetings my friend,' began Mansour, 'what can I do for you?'

The line was crackling, but he heard Wahid reply, 'You know your brother is in prison, don't you,' and on hearing the reply in the affirmative, he continued, 'The person who put him there has now left the Police and is working with a private company. He has also left his home and is living at the moment in a hotel room in London. It would be an easy matter for me to leave him a small present, but before I do anything, I would need your support.'

Mansour realised that with all the excitement of the last few hours, he had forgotten his poor brother who was locked away for five years. Quickly, he thought that he would like to be instrumental in the death of Grant, but realised he would be jeopardising future plans for a simple question of vengeance.

'If you think you can do it, then do it with my blessing,' he said, and the communication was cut.

He made his way back to his room, reflecting on his morning. A full Council meeting, a World changing decision and the icing on the cake, the proposed death of that bastard Grant. He opened the door to his room and immediately saw a sealed envelope lying on the pillow. Opening the envelope, he extracted a piece of paper and read, 'Unanimous decision. Target number seven.' He felt his bladder about to burst, but managed to reach the bathroom before embarassing himself.

# CHAPTER 39

S everal days later, Richard found himself, once again, seated in the Home Secretary's office, waiting for the Home Secretary who was on the telephone.

When he had finished he turned to Richard and asked if he had made any progress in the recruiting of his Asian speakers.

'I am very fortunate,' began Richard, 'to have people of the calibre of Bill Bowler who I can count on implicitly. He went straight back to his contact in Pakistan who immediately supplied a list of candidates. Apparently, Mohsin, the poor chap who was killed, has been named a National hero and was given a hero's funeral. He was also a very popular man and there were no shortages of volunteers. So, they will be shortly in place and, with luck, we will be soon receiving information.'

'Why, that's wonderful news,' exclaimed Lord Hamilton, 'and how is it being received in the other countries?'

'As you are aware, we are doing this on a strict need-to know basis and only my contacts, who are also personal friends, and yourself are privy to this operation. However, it was whilst we were planning this operation, that something else came up and I have been asked to put the idea to you.'

'Intrigue, eh! Wait whilst I serve the drinks, then you can explain.'

Lord Hamilton served very generous measures of Talisker single malt, fifteen years aged and indicated to Richard that they would be more comfortable in two leather armchairs in front of the fireplace. Having toasted each other and sampled the excellent brew, Lord Hamilton settled back and waited for Richard to begin.

'This idea originally came from Werner, my old friend and Police Chief in Berlin. Apparently when the Wall was still standing, they had an unofficial ad hoc arrangement with other police chiefs throughout West

Germany and also with certain contacts at the highest level in the military, to warn each other in case of attack from the Soviets.

Naturally, under normal circumstances, any form of mobilisation of police and armed forces to face a threat to National Security, would be decided by the political leaders.

'However, it was noted that owing to the very close proximity of the enemy, a situation may arise where for whatever reason, political intervention may prove difficult or even impossible and so they decided on their own early warning system. Thankfully, it was never used, although on several occasions during the occupation of East Berlin, the system was tested and found to be successful.

Today, Europe is a collection of twenty seven different countries, each with its own police and military, some, naturally far superior in quality and quantity, to others. The scenario was suggested that if a major problem involving national or international security was to occur, precious time could be lost whilst ministers were located and informed. In some way this was to be seen in New York during the World Tower tragedy where there were difficulties due to the fact that no one had ever anticipated such an attack and therefore precious minutes were lost, which unfortunately proved fatal for many of those who died. However, that is only conjecture, but there is no doubt that if those who are charged with security are the ones who are able to make immediate decisions without referral to political intervention, perhaps situations could be contained.'

Both men reached for their glasses and drank deeply, Lord Hamilton, letting the whisky wash around his teeth as he reflected on what Richard had said.

Finally, he looked across at Richard and said, 'I suppose you are speaking of problems which could come from our Islamic friends as I must confess to being somewhat confused by my fellow ministers and their lack of will power in dealing more strongly with some of the more blatant acts of these terrorist types.

'I have,' he continued, 'been constantly amazed how they can demonstrate, burn flags and threaten death and mayhem and no arrests are made and no judicial punishment handed out. However, white demonstrators, especially the ones from the National Front party, are quite harshly dealt with, under similar circumstances and I for one can commiserate to some extent at this apparent unfairness in the application of the judicial procedures. It almost appears that many of my colleagues are afraid of these creatures.'

'Demonstrators are one thing, but the bastards who blow up trains or plant huge bombs in parked cars are a different proposition altogether. You know as well as I do, that there are many Islamists in this Country who are proud to be British and we in turn are proud of them. The problem is the others, for we do not know who they are or how many they are.' Here Richard paused, whilst he consulted some handscibbled notes.

'I have sorted out some rough figures. In the UK the total number of Police and army personnel is about four hundred and twenty thousand. According to the Pew Report of two thousand and nine, there were one million, six hundred thousand Islamists living in the Country and representing two point seven of the total population. What percentage is dangerous? That is the unknown factor. Seeing the number of shootings that take place involving these people, indicates that they have easy access to weapons, many of which are weapons of war.

'This trend is repeated throughout Europe with France and Germany between them having some seven and a half million Islamists and one and a half million police and military. When seen in this context, it becomes worrying, because there are too many unknowns.'

Getting to his feet, Lord Hamilton stretched and walked over to the window and stared down into the street. Richard, seeing that he was deep in thought, wandered over to the bookcase and started to look at the various titles on display. He was interrupted when he heard Lord Hamilton cough and, on turning, saw that he had regained his seat.

'You are right of course and the problem is that for years, successive Governments have ignored the problem, until now it has reached such proportions that a solution is virtually impossible. In addition, judging by the rate that they reproduce, in twenty years they will outnumber us. I doubt that I will see it in my lifetime, but the risk is there, that one day a Government will be formed by an Islamist party, and that will be game, set and match.' Lord Hamilton, having delivered this forecast for the future, allowed himself to slump into his seat whilst regarding Richard opposite him.

'It's not all doom and gloom,' Richard replied, 'but I am worried about the unknown quantity of Al Qaida supporters. They will be certainly organised and possibly armed and could cause much damage and loss of human life before any form of serious resistance can be put together. If there could be any other way of dealing with this I would naturally consider it, but to date I have not found one.'

'You are right. I will help in any way I can and will simply ask that I be kept informed of your plans and arrangements. Now, is there anything further on the train explosion as I know that you will have more up to date information than the official investigators.'

'Unfortunately, not very much. Everything possible has been investigated, but, the problem is that the opposition have become far more professional.

They appear to have perfected the cell system where everything is self contained on a need to know basis. The only thing of any note is that the pocketbook in Mohsin's possession, although very heavily bloodstained, has to some extent been deciphered.

'All the information regarding vehicles used and the various addresses has come to nothing, the only interesting piece of information being that of the believed leader of the group named as Zanzibar. His description could fit about half the Arabs in the Country, there being one salient point however and that is that he has smelly breath, possibly halitosis. He is also suspected of being a homosexual.'

Finally Lord Hamilton smiled, albeit somewhat wanly, saying, 'Well, I suppose you could go around the Country kissing all the arabs you crossed, but I would not recommend it.' Even Richard managed to smile at his friends attempt at humour.

The two men shook hands and Richard took his leave. The day was fine and he decided to walk back to his office. He did not notice that he was being followed and a half hour later he arrived at his office in Trafalgar Square. Barbara had made fresh coffee and the pair of them sat in her office drinking and discussing the result of the meeting which Richard had held that day.

Barbara agreed to contact the security chiefs, be it Police or military and to arrange a meeting as soon as possible at a secure location. Seeing that there was nothing of note left to be done that day, Richard decided to go to his hotel suite and sort out some of his personal problems.

The advantage with the hotel suite was that, being situated in Knightsbridge, he could walk everywhere and have no need of a car. The disadvantage was that he was easy to follow.

On arriving in his room he stripped and showered and dressed neatly but casually. He realised that he had not eaten since breakfast and decided to go to Harrods, where he knew the produce and service were first class.

After eating, he wandered around like one of the many tourists, calling into a pub which caught his eye. He realised that he was lonely, but no one could replace Susan, and so, feeling sorry for himself, he had one last drink and made his way back to the hotel.

Before he reached the reception, he heard someone call his name and noticed the night manager of the hotel signal to him from the bar.

He walked across to him and the manager said, 'It's probably nothing, but the chambermaid who was engaged in turning down the beds, reported seeing a man loitering in the corridor near to your room. It's probably nothing, but our night security officer is up there checking. So, if you will allow me to buy you a nightcap . . . .'

'That's very kind of you, I'll have a small whisky,' replied Richard, and smiled yet again when the manager indicated to the barman to make it a double.

Meanwhile, outside the hotel, Wahid and his companion, an extremely efficient and very dangerous terrorist, were watching the hotel window on the second floor. Suddenly, the light in Richard's room lit up and a male figure came to the window and began to draw the curtains.

Wahid looked at his companion and smiled as he took his telephone from his pocket. He started to dial as his companion walked away to fetch his car from a nearby parking lot.

Richard had just started to taste his whisky, when an enormous explosion shook the hotel. Everyone in the bar ran to the exits and Richard, stunned by the explosion went to the staircase. He raced up to the second floor, noting the huge amount of damage, but thankfully no human debris. However, when he saw that the explosion had completely destroyed his room, he suddenly felt very sad for the night security guard.

Wahid, who had joined his companion in the car simply said, 'Adieu, Mr. Grant' and burst into laughter.

# CHAPTER 40

The emergency services were soon on the scene, followed by the press and television. It did not take long for a loosemouthed fireman to breathe 'explosive device' and once the press got wind of this they arrived in force. A very well known BBC interviewer was soon esconced in a neighbouring hotel, where all the guests from the bomb damaged hotel and staff, had been offered temporary shelter. Once it had been established that the explosion was due to a bomb that had been placed in Richard's room and, that the hotel security officer had died in the explosion, Richard found himself, accompanied by the senior police officer present, seated before the television cameras.

Richard had become a nationally recognisable figure, following the deaths of his wife and children, and he was treated like a star by the interviewer. He patiently answered questions, always waiting for the police officer to indicate that he could do so, as he did not wish to interfere in their enquiry, or to innocently supply ammunition for a defence lawyer in the event that a suspect would be arrested.

'On a personal note,' asked the interviewer, of Richard, 'have you anything that you would like to say about this terrible tragedy?'

Richard composed his features, feeling the beads of sweat breaking out on his forehead, owing to the reflected heat of the television lighting, and was pleased when a makeup girl deftly wiped his forehead for him.

Smiling his thanks, Richard looked straight into the camera and said, 'I firmly believe that we in this Country and in Europe in general, are facing a threat from the growing forces of Islam. There are millions of Islamics living in Europe, the vast majority being well behaved, integrated into the European system and a credit to themselves and their neighbours.

'Unfortunately, there are others, and we do not know how many they are, if they are trained terrorists or simply fanatical in their quest for World domination. I would urge each of you, in your daily comings and goings, to keep your eyes and ears open and to report to the Police, anything of a suspicious nature. This threat involves everyone, as a bomb does not differentiate between the sexes, the ages or the colour of people's skin, when it explodes.

The people responsible for these atrocities, will almost certainly kill or maim their own members, even their friends or families, but their determination is such, that such peccadilloes are swept aside.

Finally, I would like to address myself to the cowardly individuals responsible for the atrocity this evening.' Here, Richard paused for effect, then continued, saying, 'I have retired from the Police Service and am therefore no longer involved in the hunt for those responsible. However, I am still alive and kicking and will do all that I can to assist the law enforcement people, to rid our society of these sick, perverted individuals.'

With that, he got to his feet and walked outside into the fresh night air, which still smelled of spent explosives, wiping the makeup from his face with a hand towel, supplied by the BBC. He had only walked a few paces when he was stopped by a plain clothes police officer, who indicated that he should accompany him.

Together, they walked some fifty yards, Richard noticing the familiar bulge under the officers jacket, indicating that he was armed, to a waiting BMW saloon car. The officer opened the rear door and Richard saw Lord Hamilton smiling at him from the back seat. Richard seated himself and the officer took the front passenger seat, the car drawing silently away from the kerb.

'My wife and I,' began Lord Hamilton, 'have decided that until things are sorted out, we shall be responsible for your well being.' Seeing Richard preparing a reply, he held up his hand saying, 'It's no use. You may win an argument with me, but where my wife is concerned, you would not stand a chance. So, for the foreseeable future we have organised a self contained flat in our country mansion, which, owing to my position as Home Secretary, is well protected. So, welcome to my world.'

Richard smiled at his friend saying, 'I see that you still remember 'The King', 'he said, referring to Elvis and the title of one of his many hits.

Smiling in return, he replied, 'Like you, I believe that popular music died when he died, but the youth of today would not understand that.'

Reaching into a concealed drinks cabinet, he extracted a bottle, two glasses, and poured two generous measures, before settling back in his seat, to enjoy the long drive to his home. The two friends continued to discuss the change in musical tastes, agreeing that the modern youth was very badly served by the 'zing-zang' of modern day electronics, or worse, the Rap.

-o-o-o-o-o-o-o-

At five in the morning, several thousand miles from England, Mansour awakened, refreshed and in high spirits, having dreamt of forthcoming glory.

He dressed and as he stepped from his room, he was stopped by a guard who indicated that he should follow him. Intrigued, Mansour followed the guard to the second floor, where he was led into a well appointed sitting room, and was even more intrigued when he saw his uncle seated with the President of the Council.

Without any preamble, his uncle tossed him a pile of newspapers and Mansour blanched as he saw the headline, 'Ex-Police Chief Escapes Terror Bomb.' His uncle rose to his feet, making an obvious attempt to keep his temper, saying, 'I told you not to engage in revenge attacks, and now this,' indicating the newspapers. Mansour did not know what to say and simply hung his head in shame.

The well modulated voice of the President caused him to lift his head, as he heard the leader say, 'Come, old friend, we were young and foolish. What Mansour must do is learn from his mistake and ensure that nothing, and I repeat nothing, interferes with our plans.'

Mansour could have embraced and kissed the old man on hearing these words and was then overjoyed when he heard him say, 'Mansour, you have proved yourself in combat and your time for greatness is near. The forthcoming operation in France will be your responsibility and I know in advance that you will not let us down.'

He felt a shiver run down his spine, in spite of the heat, as he sensed the veiled threat in that last spoken statement. 'I am honoured to have been chosen and I promise you both, before Allah, that I will succeed, even if it costs me my life.'

His uncle was now smiling and the President, with an impatient wave of his hand, indicated that the meeting was over. Mansour accompanied his uncle for the ritual of morning prayers.

After they had eaten breakfast, his uncle said, 'There is much planning to be done and I have been chosen to accompany you. This should impress on you the importance of the mission. Now, you must pack, because we leave for Europe tonight.'

# CHAPTER 41

Several days later, saw Richard seated in his flat, adjacent to the home of Lord Hamilton. He was surrounded by travel brochures and was only too pleased to hear the intercom buzzer interrupt his thoughts. On answering, he heard the voice of his friend asking if he wanted a breath of fresh air.

'Wish I could, but I'm busy with some paperwork problems which I must solve as quickly as possible. The doors open if you want to see someone swamped with work.'

A minute later, he was joined by Lord Hamilton, who on seeing Richard surrounded by piles of travel brochures, could not repress a smile. 'Those your paperwork problems? Wish mine were so easy. The States, Mexico or somewhere closer to home. What decisions to make,' he ended with a laugh.

'If it was for my holidays, it would have been finalised days ago. No, what I am trying to find is somewhere I can meet in private with my International Police colleagues in complete secrecy. I am starting to receive information from my Arab infiltrators, which is causing sleepless nights and it is imperative that we get together quickly, and in secret, as unfortunately recent incidents have pushed me into the limelight, causing me to be tracked by the media 'greyhounds'.'

Lord Hamilton joined Richard at the table and with a smile said, 'I have already told you. Stop thinking like a Chief Constable on a meagre budget and try putting yourself in the shoes of a business mogul or even a business moguls' mogul. You are sitting on billions, which each day make millions and in turn more billions. I know, your working class background and the wish to economise at every bend and turn takes a bit of overcoming.

'Are you prepared to let me help you find your secret location? You are, good, for it will mean making a telephone call and then having to go into town and force down a wonderful meal at my club. Now, forget your travel brochures for it is a nice day and I want to pick your brains, as I have been given a task by the Prime Minister which I know you can help with. I also think better on my feet and it is so nice outside, a walk would do us both some good.'

Richard knew there was no point in arguing and went to fetch a cardigan as it was somewhat chilly, in spite of the sunshine. Once dressed, the two men stepped outside and started to walk through the private park surrounding the house, followed at a discreet distance by an armed police bodyguard and his dog.

After a short silence, Lord Hamilton said, 'The problem I have been handed is complex, involves the whole Country and for years has defied successive politicians. The problem is the youth of today, the lack of employment and the massive increase in crime, vandalism and general public disorder. Whilst you are thinking about it, I'll make my telephone call.' With that he took his telephone from his pocket and dialled a number.

Two minutes later, he cut the communication and replaced the telephone in his pocket. 'Have you assimilated the problem?' asked Lord Hamilton.

'It did not take me very long as I have been considering those issues most of my working life, and I can tell you that the answer is simple and extremely difficult at the same time. In short, there is no easy answer, but there are things that could be done straight away in order to attack the problem.'

'Sounds very mysterious to me,' replied Lord Hamilton, 'perhaps you could enlighten me?'

Richard, folded his hands behind his back, bent his head as though in thought and said, 'For years we have heard the same voices saying the same things. It is the fault of the Police, or the education authorities, or poverty, or individual families, or the lack of employment or problems in the National Health Service. The reality is that it is a piece of all of those problems and no one has ever thought about getting everyone around a table to try to hammer out a solution. Not on a local, regional or even National basis and, I would argue that this has to be instigated at a very high, National level, for it to have any hope of success.

Over the years various things have been tried, lowering standards, trying to animate inner City areas, creating jobs with no interest for anyone.

One I know of, was employing youngsters to MOT pushchairs and another counting street lamps that were not working. The time has come for the various organisations to stop blaming each other and to work together, but, as I said, it has to come from the top, has to be serious and to include people who will stick at it until a solution is found.'

'You are quite right. I was looking through some files of my predecessor and I saw that he favoured attacking the education system and the lack of firmness by the Police.'

This brought a short, barking laugh from Richard, who said, 'The French have a saying for people like Sir Peter, which is 'Il pète plus haut que son cul.'

'I must confess that languages were not my forte. What does it mean?'

'The nearest translation is 'He farts higher than his arsehole,' this bringing a cry of laughter from Lord Hamilton.

'You will have to write that down for me as I can think of several more people who could be classed the same.'

Richard then said, 'I hope I do not cause offence, but there is one point I would like to make, that is very salient in certain parts of the Country and which undoubtedly helps to contribute to deliquancy, and that is the different sorts of Justice which is meted out, at different levels. A poor person steals to eat and finishes in prison, a rich person steals to become richer and receives a slap on the wrist. A poltician steals or cheats or both and he is very rarely punished, whereas they are where they are to serve the people who put them there.

For people, and let me tell you there are lots of them, who are poor and living, quite often in atrocious conditions, this type of behaviour creates a psychose where they simply give up. They feel, and possibly quite rightly, that they have helped to put these people into power on the promises made, only to be shatt on from a great height (excuse my French), once those people attain the dizzy heights in politics.'

'Of course I will forgive your French and at the same time thank you for increasing my vocabulary. There are things that could and should be done, but many of these would cost so much money that it would not be feasible.'

By this time the two men had reached the lake in the park and stopped to watch trout rising to the settling flies. Richard laughed and Lord Hamilton asked him why?

'Seeing the trout rise to the fly reminds me of the Twat,' replied Richard, and then had to spend two minutes explaining a Twat and why Thompson bore the nickname. This left his friend spluttering with laughter.

Glancing at his watch, Lord Hamilton said they must make tracks for the house if they were to make their luncheon date and they turned, retracing their steps.

After several moments thought, he asked of Richard, 'Can you suggest anything that could be done almost immediately, so that I can put it to the Prime Minister and get him off my back?

'There is one thing that I personally would try if I had the power to do so.' Seeing Lord Hamilton indicate that he should continue, he said, 'One of the greatest problems is civil disorder, lack of respect to persons and property and petty crime in general. Young people today, especially those with no jobs, find themselves at a loose end with no money, few prospects and in the main with a vigour and health which surpasses that which we enjoyed when we were younger. Burning cars, destroying beautiful objects, insulting or even attacking authority, is often the result of frustration caused by circumstances outside their control and quite often by a lack of 'savoir vivre'.'

'That one I know, knowing how to live correctly. Tell me, you have obviously given this matter some thought. Is there a solution?'

'I have one, but it would take someone in the highest position to put it into effect.'

'Come on man, you have my interest, spit it out. We are nearly home.'

'When National Service existed, the youth of the day spent two years in one of the armed services. I always thought this too long, but the truth was, that after completing their service, the majority were quite happy to quickly find a job and settle down.

Today, I would not like to see the return of National Service as I think it criminal to send our soldiers to places like Afghanistan in order to satisfy some politicians personal ego and to see so many of them coming back in boxes or wheelchairs.'

'Look, we are already at the house and I still do not have a solution,' cried Lord Hamilton. 'It is so frustrating.'

'I promise you my Lord,' replied Richard, making a mock bow, 'that I will have given you not one, but two ideas by the time we reach your club.'

With that the two men entered their respective residences in order to change for their lunch appointment.

Half an hour later, they were seated in the rear of the Home Secretary's official car and Richard, after making himself comfortable, said, 'Now to business,' and the Home Secretary turned to face him.

'In place of National Service, I would introduce a twelve month period of Civil Service. In the case of youngsters who finish school at 18 years of age, they could do their service straight away and in the case of University graduates, after they have finished their studies.'

'Quite, but what form would this service take?' asked Lord Hamilton, somewhat irritated by the slowness of the replies. Seeing his obvious discomfiture, Richard smiled to himself before replying.

'The youth of today insult the Police and throw stones and insult the firemen, often after they themselves have started the fires. My idea is simple. The Civil Service they would undertake would be with the Police or the Fire Service or with other services which have a direct contact with the public. I think that from throwing stones to ducking to avoid them, could have a very salutary effect on our young people.'

Silence fell whilst Lord Hamilton digested this idea. After several minutes contemplation, he said, 'So simple and yet it could be so effective. Of course we would pay them. It could also help in recruiting for those services, as well.'

Seeing that Lord Hamilton had apparently bought that idea, Richard said, 'I promised you two ideas. The second one is one which I would love to see come to fruition. May I put this one to you?'

Indicating that he should continue, Richard said, 'My second idea is to revolutionise the prison system, which I find archaic, extremely expensive to run and judging by the numbers who commit further crime, inefficient. In addition, I often feel that the victims get a very poor deal out of the system as often, having been granted damages or compensation, they are not paid owing to the apparent insolvability of the perpetrators of the crimes.'

'Very difficult, old chap, to make them pay when they have nothing. Blood from stones and all that.'

'I said the system would have to change. There are certain criminals, murderers, violent or dangerous persons, who cannot be dealt with otherwise than by a custodial sentence. For such persons, prison as we know it is the only choice.'

'Could not agree more, perhaps even make their prison life even harder. Go on, you interest me.'

The prison population is full to overflowing and them some. To build a prison as we know them would cost a huge amount of money. My idea is this.' Here he paused for effect.

'In place of a sentence of imprisonment, I would sentence them to a fine, for example in the place of six months inside I would fine them two thousand pounds. If there were damages or compensation, that would be added.

If the convicted person is fortunate enough to have sufficient money to pay his fine, then he would pay and be free to leave. In the case of those who do not have the means to pay straight away, they would enter into my new prison system.'

'Go on, go on, you are so infuriating with your slow replies. I will make you pay for lunch if you do not hurry.'

'Patience is a virtue,' began Richard, but on seeing the scowl on his friend's face, he continued.

'In the place of recognised prisons, I would take over and transform existing, abandoned, Army and Air Force bases, turning them into secure camps, much on the line of prisoner of war camps. There would be fully equipped workshops, where the prisoners would manufacture whatever was demanded, possibly articles to help the aged or infirm, road signs, etc. etc.

They would be paid full rates, as much overtime as they like and naturally would pay tax. A further sum would be deducted for board and lodgings. Someone who would wish to get out as quickly as possible would work to do so. Others, would stay until their debt is paid. I would submit, in conclusion, that such a system would be far cheaper to run, would create employment, would probably have a positive effect on the wrong doer and would most certainly satisfy my primary condition, that is, the victim would be reimbursed.'

'What a bloody good idea,' said Lord Hamilton. 'May I say it was my idea, if I should be asked?'

'If it means that I do not have to pay for lunch,' replied Richard, noticing that the car was drawing up outside the Club.'

'Not to worry. Now come and meet someone who will solve your problem even quicker than you have solved mine.'

The two men entered the club and were led to a secluded table, where was seated a well known City figure, who immediately stood to welcome them. After he had shaken hands with the Home Secretary he turned to Richard saying, 'I have read so much about you, that I think I know you already and if I can help in my modest way, I certainly will do.'

After sitting, Lord Hamilton set the tone of conversation, by addressing Richard, saying, 'You are in the presence of one of the World's biggest bullshit merchants who would have your last cent if he needed it. His only redeeming factor is his love of good food and wine and an endless expense account.'

Laughing good naturedly, their guest replied, 'One of these days there will be the big ears of the tax man in the vicinity. I will most certainly be sorted out and you yourself may find yourself in the shite.'

The lunch continued in this light hearted vein, until coffee was served, whereupon Lord Hamilton outlined the predicament facing Richard, saying, 'Do you still have your boat?'

'Which one?' asked their guest, 'for we have bought another one for our corporate guests. The latest, 'The Philanderer' is at present in Monaco. How many people would be using it and for how long?'

Lord Hamilton looked at Richard who said, 'Possibly as many as twenty and for two or three days.'

'The Philly' can sleep seventy five guests in comfort so that should be big enough and you can have it for up to a week if you like as it is not in use and we pay the crews wages, whatever.'

Richard could not believe his ears. 'But how much would it cost?' he asked, staggered by the suggestion.'

'My dear chap, money is the means to an end. Now, if I understand it mum's the word, so how will you get to Monaco and aboard the boat?'

Seeing the bemused expression on Richard's face, he continued,

'Let me have a list of your guests and a place which supports a helicopter landing pad. I will see to the rest. The easiest way would be for the boat to put to sea and you and your guests be ferried there by helicopter. Would that suit you?'

Richard was completely stunned. Fortunately, Lord Hamilton said,

'Forgive him, he is still in a transitional phase. Those arrangements will do us just fine. Yes Richard, I've decided to come along as well.'

Turning to Richard, the third guest said, in all sincerity and with great seriousness, 'Nail the bastards who blew up the train and I'll probably give you the boat.'

# CHAPTER 42

Mansour and his uncle arrived at Heathrow and went immediately to Basingstoke, where a welcome had been planned. Various neighbours and friends came, including Mansour's father, who was soon engaged in conversation with his eldest son. He had visited his younger son who was suffering badly, due to his incarceration, and Mansour promised him that he would leave no stone unturned in liberating his brother as quickly as possible.

The following morning, Mansour returned with his father to London and was soon immersed in local politics, which he had neglected somewhat. He was popular with the local electorate as well as with his fellow councillors. His aide informed him of a forthcoming engagement where the Lord Mayor of London himself would be present and Mansour informed him that he too would be there.

In mid-week he received a call from his uncle who told him that a provisional date had been supplied for the meeting in Versailles and that they should leave for France the following Tuesday, to meet with their in-house contact and, if possible to visit the château. Mansour told his uncle of the forthcoming evening involving the visit of the Lord Mayor of London and his uncle told him to act normally at all times and to bring no suspicion upon himself, as the operation in France would catapult their organisation into the same category as the 'Super-powers'.

On the evening of the Lord Mayor's visit, Mansour, dressed in evening suit and highly polished shoes and wearing a dazzling white shirt which set off his suntan to perfection, caused many heads to turn during the evening. Espying the Lord Mayor, deep in conversation with someone, he made his way across the room, to offer his greetings.

The Lord Mayor, on seeing Mansour approaching said to his unidentified guest, 'This is one of our shining lights for the future' and as the guest turned, Mansour and Richard Grant met for the first time.

The two shook hands as the Lord Mayor made the introductions and Richard, on regarding the other, had the impression of an inner strength, well masked by his handsome good looks and perfect smile.

'Ah, yes,'said Mansour, 'I heard about your terrible loss. Please accept my condolences and, if at any time you may require assistance, do not hesitate to contact me, as I have many introductions into the Asian communities.'

Richard thanked him for his kind offer and Mansour drifted away to greet others who were arriving for the festivities. The Lord Mayor also excused himself and Richard, finding himself alone, started to take stock of the evening. Having already attended several such engagements, he was becoming used to the small talk and as he crossed the room spoke to several people he had met on other occasions.

After speaking very briefly to a heavy set, elderly lady who was wearing a very strong smelling perfume, Richard was suddenly struck with a thought associated to smells. Who had mentioned to him someone with very bad breath, as the man Mansour, he recalled, had such a problem which he tried to hide behind mint sweets or breath spray. He looked around the room, but could see no sign of him and he saw that the Lord Mayor was in the process of leaving and decided that he too would leave.

His path crossed that of the Lord Mayor as they both neared the door, and, as they said goodnight, Richard asked after Mansour, causing the Lord Mayor to break into laughter. Puzzled, Richard asked the Mayor what was so funny about his enquiry and the Mayor replied that he was the brother of the man who had assaulted Richard in the Court House some weeks previously, and he had thought that Mansour had shown great restraint during his short conversation with Richard.

The penny dropped. The blood stained pocket book and, what was the name, yes, 'Zanzibar' with smelly breath. Feeling the excitement starting to course through his body, Richard intensified his search, but Mansour had obviously left.

He left the building, his senses heightened, but there were no suspicious persons in the area and soon Richard was seated in a taxi. He quickly took out his notebook and noted down all he could remember of the meeting with Mansour, fully intending to contact Bill Bowler in order that he could start the long and difficult process of investigating Mansour. Such investigations could take time, certainly owing to the fact that he Mansour, was a public figure and could be difficult to approach.

It was past midnight when he arrived at his new home, and after saying goodnight to the on duty security guard, he retired for the night.

The following morning he spoke with Bill and the two agreed to meet at the Scratchwood Service area on the M1 motorway, a place where they could reasonably expect not to be seen or overheard.

It was a beautiful day for a drive and, although the service area was only an hours drive, Richard set off early, in order to enjoy the drive in the sun shine. He was in his Mercedes, with the roof down and soon started thinking of his dead wife and how she had so enjoyed riding with him in this car.

Feeling a depression coming on, he selected a disc and was soon listening and singing along with Elvis, until the song, 'Wonder of You' started to play and he felt his eyes start to moisten. Thankfully, he saw the entrance to the service area approaching and signalled that he was turning, at the same time, switching off the music in his car. Seeing Bill, he parked alongside him and the two of them entered the cafeteria for coffee.

Richard took out his notebook and recited the passages relating to the previous evening and his meeting with Mansour. Bill took copious notes and when Richard was finished, Bill, consulted his own notes.

'Firstly,' he said, 'I visited the restaurant and spoke to Mr. Khan the owner. He is very pro-British and proud to be a member of this great Nation, certainly seemed to be more proud than myself. He told me that his son had returned to Pakistan for a holiday and has promised to let me know the moment he comes back.

The man you and your wife saw in the restaurant, would appear to be a certain Mohamed Ramzan, who is known to the authorities in Pakistan as a fringe member of Al Qaida, but has no convictions. He was enrolled in college here in London, where he was known as a quiet, studious sort, not brilliant by any means, but a good student. We are waiting for confirmation from fingerprints, but I am quite certain he is the second headless body that we found in the train. Apart from knowing the restaurant owners son, he appears to have no friends or family in this Country.'

'Just keep digging away, something will come up, it nearly always does. The man, Walid Benghazi, have you anything on him?'

'The description of this man Mansour Ahmad could fit him and once I can get hold of a photograph, I'll do the rounds to see if we can get a positive identification. I'm feeling very confident about this enquiry as the public, for once, are really behind us.'

'Well', said Richard, 'things seem to be taking a turn for the better. All I can say is that Mansour has stinking breath and as regards his sexuality, I would say he is as queer as a clockwork turnip. It would be nice if we could get a positive identification and be in a position to question him about terrorist activities, especially regarding those damned explosives that are missing.'

Glancing at his watch, Bill stood, offering his hand to Richard. 'I must go as I have another appointment in an hours time and I've nearly a hundred miles to go.'

'I think I'll grab a bite to eat,' replied Richard, 'so drive carefully and, Bill, thanks for all you are doing in this case. Keep in touch and if I get anything further, you will be the first to know.'

Whilst Richard was eating a snack in the service area cafeteria, Mansour and his uncle, Zafran Razaq, were beginning the approach to Charles de Gaulle airpport in Paris.

They left the aircraft and, after completing the passport formalities, entered the main concourse area, where they were approached by an elegantly dressed Algerian gentleman, who Mansour recognised as a well known French politician.

'Zafran, you old goat, you certainly do not look any older. How are you? And this, I suppose is your nephew of whom so many good things are being said.'

Mansour shook hands and the politician took them to a waiting limousine and, once they were comfortably seated, they started the forty kilometre drive to Versailles.

Trafic was fairly light and an hour later they entered the sleepy, wealthy town of Versailles. The stunning architecture was set off by the blue skies and the sunshine, and Mansour could not withhold an expression of delight on seeing the magnificent château for the first time.

'It is very beautiful, isn't it,' stated the politician, 'and so much history. Built by King Louis the fourteenth, also known as 'The Sun King', in the latter half of the sixteenth century, there is so much history attached. When I come here I can almost forget my upbringing, but fortunately I manage to remain faithful to our Leader and guide, Mohamed. Now, I have been instructed to help in any way I can, so do not hesitate to ask me.'

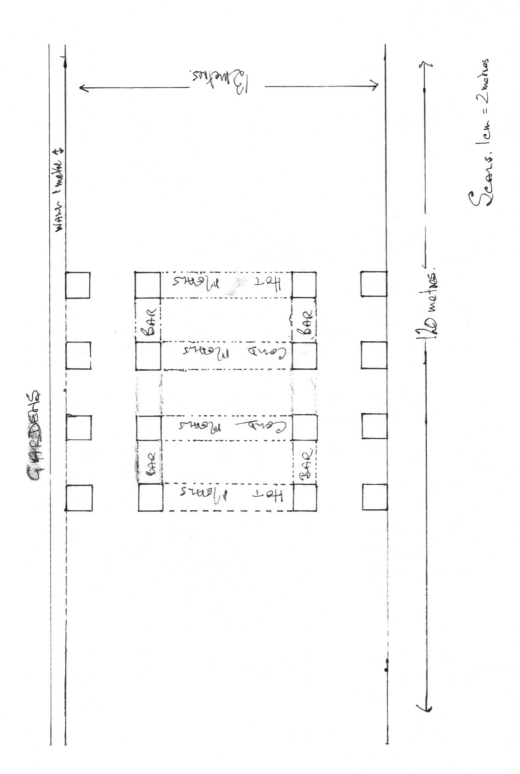

13 metres

Wall 1 metre

Hot Menus

BAR

BAR

Cold Menus

Cold Menus

BAR

BAR

Hot Menus

GARDENS

120 metres.

Scale. 1cm = 2 metres

213

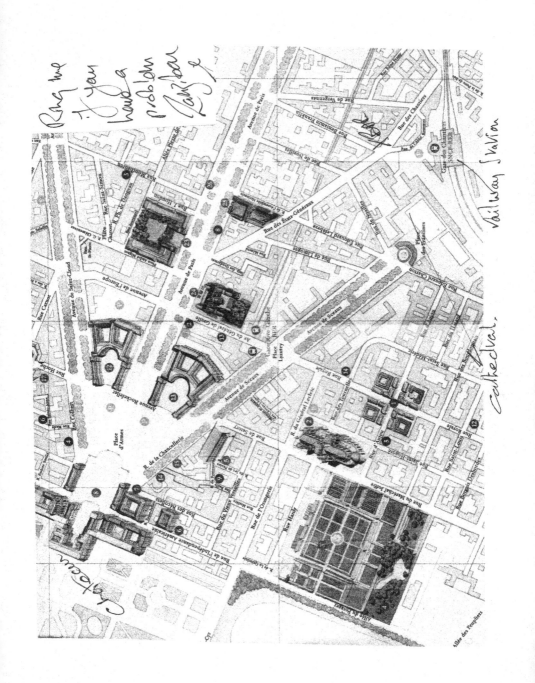

Ring me
if you
need a
problem
solution

railway station

Cathedral.

Château

214

'It is my nephew who is running the operation and I am sure he will let you know the moment he requires anything.'

Mansour who had listened carefully to this exchange asked, 'What exactly have you been told?'

'Simply that an operation is being planned which will shake the World and propulse our Organisation into the spotlights. For the rest I have been asked to make myself available and to help in any way I can. As you know I am an advisor to the French President and I have many contacts throughout France and even Europe.'

Mansour could not decide if he liked this man very much, but having seen that his uncle obviously knew him very well and trusted him, he decided he would do likewise. 'Firstly,' he said, 'I would like to visit the château and see its layout, especially the Hall of Mirrors.'

The politician produced three very official lapel badges and together the three of them entered the château, marvelling at the size and luxury of the rooms and their contents. On arriving in the Hall of Mirrors, which is on the first floor, overlooking the gardens, Mansour was fascinated by the reflections caused by the presence of of the seventeen, huge floor to ceiling mirrors, lit by the sunshine coming through seventeen huge windows. Looking at the visitors brochure he had been issued with, he saw that the room was seventy three meteres long with an overall surface of seven hundred and thirty meters.

They continued their visit and, on the first floor, but on the opposite side to the Hall of Mirrors, they entered the Battles Gallery. This room was far bigger than the Hall of Mirrors, being one hundred and twenty metres long by thirteen metres wide. In the centre of the room were eight marble pillars, all equally spaced and Mansour just knew this was the room he wanted.

There were few windows, but there were two large, glass skylights and the walls were covered with huge paintings depicting famous scenes of battles won by the French.

'A meeting is to be held in the château and there will be between two and three thousand people attending. I had thought of suggesting the Hall of Mirrors as a good meeting place, but this room is far better suited,' said Mansour.

That is very astute,' replied the politician, 'as this is the room the President always chooses when he is hosting official functions.'

Mansour's attention was drawn again to the eight marble columns and, with the aid of a laser measuring tape he took the measurements between the pillars.

'If food and drink were to be served at a reception, who would organise the catering services?' he asked.

'For the last thirty odd years, the catering company is always that of Daniel Allary, who is now a personal friend of the President. What do you want him to do?'

'A very important target will be here and it is necessay that he does not leave the recption alive. We would like his death to be as natural as possible and the easy way would be for him to be served a toxic product in his food and or drink. I would like to offer to this caterer therefore, a superb mobile bar, with both hot and cold meals and drinks on offer, as we do not know if the target would drink or eat hot or cold food and beverages.'

'I foresee no problem there, as the caterer, I am sure, would be only too pleased if someone were to offer him such a magnificent gift,' replied the politician. 'Tell me, when will this reception take place?'

'We think within the next six weeks and that is why we must act quickly, in order that all can be in place. Would you also be a guest?' he asked innocently.

'Without a doubt, as I am normally part of the official party, whenever functions are held on behalf of the State.' As he spoke he preened himself and Mansour found him liking the man less and less. Still, if he was to be present during the meeting, he should soon be joining The Prophet in Heaven, so let him have his day. With that Mansour gave him a winning smile and even took his arm as they continued their tour of the château and gardens.

'Absolutely fantastic,' said Mansour as they regained their car. 'It goes to show what can be done when you have unlimited man power and an unlimited money supply. Such a beautiful building in a sumptuous park and all that history.

In actual fact, the château of Versailles was an ancient hunting lodge, built by King Louis 13th, and was subsequently transformed by his son, Louis 14th. It was the official Court and seat of Government of France from 1688 until the Revolution in 1789, covering a total floor space of some 6300 square metres. In all, there were 2300 rooms. After the Revolution, the seat of Government moved and, in 1830, the château became the

Museum of French History, having been donated to the Nation by King Louis Philippe.

In the beginning, the original château was surrounded by woods, prairies and swamp land. In 1661, André le Notre, was commissioned to create the gardens that exist even today. Hundreds of tons of top soil were laid, a canal was constructed, leaving a view from the Hall of Mirrors of fantastic gardens which disappeared into the far distance. In addition, the fountains set in the Versaille Gardens are a wonder to behold, especially when one thinks they were constructed some three hundred years ago.

'Are you going back to England today?' asked the politician, desirous of making himself indispensable, and at the same time breaking the reverie of Mansour and his uncle, who were both astounded by the outrageous beauty of the château.

Mansour's uncle, Zafran, looked at Mansour as though for confirmation, then said, 'All work and no play . . . .' and the politician said 'I will arrange everything, starting with a hotel.'

Taking a telephone from his pocket he dialled a number and several seconds later said, 'The George Cinq? Good, for this evening I will require a suite for my friends. No problem, we'll be there in about an hour.'

Turning to his two companions, he said, 'I will try to make it a weekend for you to remember.'

# CHAPTER 43

'Nearly, Easter my friend,' said Lord Hamilton, as Richard was working on his proposed meeting. 'How far have you got with your planning?'

'Just about finished. The five Police chiefs were no problem and all I am waiting for now is confirmation regarding the Chief of Staff of the German Army and some General friend of Marcel's who is having wife problems. However, I should have it finalised by tonight, which could mean in forty eight hours. You are still coming along so I will make you coordinator with your poor business friend, to ensure that everyone arrives in one piece.'

'Excuse me for smiling, but when you said 'my poor business friend,' it reminded me of an occasion several years ago when I happened to call him a poor bastard. He looked at me with those gimlet like eyes and said, 'Hamilton, you can call me whatever you like, but never poor.'

Richard finally put down his pen, looked at his watch and said, 'Time for a quickie before lunch.' Seeing the look of anticipation on his friends face he took out two glasses and went in search of a suitable bottle.

-o-o-o-o-o-o-o-

Mansour and his uncle, having spent a very entertaining weekend in some very classy Parisien night spots, were getting ready to leave the hotel, when the telephone rang. On answering, a voice which was used to commanding respect, said, 'Come to Pakistan straight away,' and the communication was cut.

Zafran, who was packing his case, enquired as to who had called. On being told he immediately contacted the politcian, requesting two seats on the first available flight to Lahore. So it was that within twenty four hours of the telephone call, the two of them were seated with the Council Preseident.

'How was your Paris trip,' he asked. 'Have you formulated a plan that would have pleased my dear departed friend, bin Laden?'

Reaching into his travel bag, Mansour removed a writing block which he opened and began to read. 'The Château at Versailles is a wonderful example of European decadence. I believe I have found a way of introducing an explosive charge into the room where the meeting and subsequent festivities will be held. With one ton of high explosive, I believe that everyone in that room will be killed.'

'That will be how many people?' asked the President.

'I estimate about two thousand five hundred of whom the majority will be European politicians and, of course those Turkish dogs who would betray the Islamists in order to share in the decadence of Europe.'

'What have you planned once the bomb has exploded?'

'In every European country we have devoted and dedicated soldiers, all trained in our own camps. Before continuing, can you tell me if a date has been arranged for the meeting?'

'Yes, the date is the second Saturday in May and so you have only about six weeks to arrange everything and have it all in place. Will that be enough?'

'If I remember correctly, we part own a factory in the Italian town of Milan, who specialise in the manufacture of all types of refrigerated and kitchen units. If I give you the specifications, can you order the construction and for it to be completed in three weeks.'

'You are referring to Guillemins. It is all ours now, but obviously it is wiser to keep the Italian name. How do you wish your elements to be finished? I would suggest marble, but that is heavy.'

'Exactly what I will require. The measurements are all in my report and I would suggest marble from Brescia as it is far superior in quality.'

'So it will be. You have done well. Now, after the explosion, what do you forsee happening?'

Mansour paused and looked at his writing block. Closing it, he looked with admiration at this elderly, bearded, stern faced man, who he knew he loved more that life itself.

'I was saying earlier, that we have many followers, most of them trained and many of them armed. Their leaders should now be in constant contact with the people who are loyal to our cause, and to all those who help us with information and money.

These people are the ones who will pass the final message for action, but I want that to be kept a secret until the final seconds.'

'You are speaking in riddles. Be plain and to the point.'

Mansour, seeing that his leader was getting impatient said, 'The European meeting is going to be televised. When our followers see the explosion, that will be the signal for them to pick up their arms and cause as much mayhem and death as possible. I would also urge that you tell their squad leaders to select high profile targets, police stations, army barracks and all places where many people may be found.

I would estimate that within twenty four hours, Europe will be on its knees in a bloodbath and that it should be a relatively easy thing to take control with all their main politicians lying dead.'

'We have already planned with our loyal supporters who are involved in local or regional politics, to make themselves available to aid and assist the fighters once their victory is complete,' said the President. 'Then, myself and other leaders of our great movement will travel to Europe to help reconstruct it in our image.'

'May I be named overall Commander of our Islamic army?' asked Mansour, as he saw himself being elevated to great position and power if this operation was a success.

'That and much more. If your planning bears the fruit we desire, I will name you as my successor. Now go, there is much still to be done.'

Realising that they had been dismissed, the two of them kissed the President's ringed hand and took their leave, returning to their hotel.

On reaching their room, Mansour was surprised to see Wahid waiting outside in the corridor. 'What brings you here, a holiday?' he asked, and was interested when Wahid told him that the police were asking questions amongst the Asian Community in an effort to find the perpetrators of the Bedford train bombing.

'I planned too carefully, nothing will lead to us. We are so near the fulfillment of our objectives, that nothing must stand in our way. Wahid, I will go with you to Italy where I can help you to build the bomb that will change the World. Are you ready to travel?'

'I have no baggage,' he replied, 'and as I am very fond of pasta, a trip to Italy will be an excellent idea.'

'And you, my uncle. What will you do. Go back to England and dig your garden?'

'Do not worry on my account. I have much to do as I am the main liaison officer between our leaders and our soldiers. Now, let us pack and leave quickly. I will require some time with my wife, before I can start supporting you lot,' replied Zafran.

He reached for his suitcase and started to pack for his return to England. Once his suitcase was ready, he took an envelope from his pocket.

'Mansour, this is a perfectly good passport, showing your new identity. All you have to do is stick on a photograph.' He handed him the passport and the two embraced. 'I will settle the room bill,' said Zafran. 'You two get off to Italy and make sure that you are successful, as our leader is a very dangerous person if things do not go according to plan.'

The two men embraced and Mansour said, 'My uncle, I felt so proud when I realised that you were so close to our leader. Do not worry about the operation as I have planned for all contingencies and Wahid is here to help.'

Mansour and Wahid left the hotel and were soon seated in a speeding taxi on their way to the airport. At such short notice, it was not easy to find a convenient flight, but finally, after much cajoling of airport staff and a hefty tip, they found a flight which would get them to Milan in the middle of the next afternoon.

The two men slept much of the way and although feeling jet lagged, made their way to a clean but non descript hotel near to the centre of Milan, where they took two adjoining rooms.

Once showered and changed, the men felt invigorated and settled down in Mansour's room, to formulate their plans for the construction and delivery of the state of the art bomb that was going to change the face of the World and the direction of millions of people.

'Wahid, where are the explosives at the moment and what is their condition?' questioned Mansour, 'as it is of the utmost importance that the materials we use are in pristine condition and undetectable, once they become a composant part of the mobile bar, which is, at this very moment, being built to my specifications, here in Milan.'

'You chose me, Zanzibar, because I am a perfectionist. The explosives, just over one ton, are at this moment stored in a high security warehouse in Ambrogio di Valpolicella, in the Verone province. That is the area where the best marble in Italy can be found and it is there that I wish the completed bar assembly be transported in order that the final dressing, the marble, can be installed.'

'I do not understand why it is necessary for you to go to all that trouble, when we can simply have the marble brought to Milan and installed here.'

'Zanzibar, you are a great planner and leader of men, whilst I am a technological perfectionist. It is necessary that the marble is cut and polished to perfection, before it is installed, and the experts in this form of art are in the region where the marble is quarried.

I want to see the whole unit finished and assembled, before I put my finishing touches to it. It would be a good idea if you could arrange for the finished unit to be officially presented to the French caterer here in Italy, with the press and television, if possible, in attendance. With a large reception, and perhaps using the unit to supply the food and drink, this unique bar installation will be seen to be efficient, thus satisfying the mind of the caterer and aesthetically beautiful when it is suggested that it be installed for the European reunion in Versailles.'

'You cunning beggar, what a brilliant idea. No one will suspect anything, but how are you going to get the explosives into the units and then into the château?' queried Mansour, who's own technical ability left much to be desired.

'Scagliola,' said Wahid with a smile.

'What on earth is that,' cried Zanzibar. 'Keep it simple as you know my shortcomings on anything technical.'

'It is derived from the word 'scaglia' meaning chips, in this case, marble chips. Using selenite, glue and natural pigments, we can make an imitation marble, which you cannot differentiate from the real thing, without physically testing it. However, the imitation marble is much lighter than the real thing.

Before we can transport the units to France, the Italian customs will come to examine the finished article and may well weigh it as part of their examination. Once the officials have completed their examination, the units will be loaded onto a lorry, which will be sealed by the customs officers.'

'We cannot allow that to happen,' said Zanzibar, 'as once sealed the explosives cannot be inserted into the units.'

Wahid could not contain himself and let out a huge guffaw of laughter. 'When you say you are not technical, I honestly do believe you,' he said, wiping the tears from his eyes. 'It is necessary that the customs officially signal the fact that the cargo has been correctly inspected, documented and sealed for delivery.

Once that has been done, my driver, a man of my own family and one of us since the outset, will drive the lorry to the warehouse containing the explosives. In the meantime, I will have made the imitation marble slabs, which, because of their composition, are much lighter than the original marble. The difference in weight will be made up by the explosives, which will be concealed under the imitation marble slabs. Once in place, they will be undetectable unless someone decides to dismantle a unit and I do not think that would be done, seeing as how the units have already been exposed to the public gaze.'

'But the official seals, how will you get past those,' queried Mansour. 'If the security people in Versailles examine the seals, surely they will be seen to have been tampered with?'

'Once again, you forget that I am a perfectionist. With a drill using dental drill bits, I can drill out the seal and with a little molten lead, replace it, with no-one being any the wiser.'

Mansour looked at Wahid with admiration shining in his eyes. 'Allah was smiling on me the day I met you. Together, we will help to conquer the World and show that Islam is the only path to follow. Now, we have just under six weeks to execute this plan, so the quicker we get started the better.'

# CHAPTER 44

'Finally, my Lord, we are ready to go. Everyone who is invited is simply waiting for the off. If you could contact your friend so that the final preparations can be put into motion, we can get started. You are still coming on the trip, are you not?' Richard sat back in his chair, surveying the mountain of paperwork on his coffee table.

'Just try and keep me away. I've even packed my swimming trunks as the Mediterranean sea is heaven at this time of the year.'

'But we are still in April,' protested Richard.

'Do not compare the sea off Monaco with the North Sea at Blackpool. Chalk and cheese. You will see when we get there, clear blue, warm water; azure blue skies, brilliant sunshine. Once you have tasted it you will not want to come back to this lot,' indicated Lord Hamilton, pointing to the low, grey clouds emitting a wet drizzle that would seep right through to the skin.

'It is what makes us British,' retorted Richard. 'To accept the weather and eat the food, sets us apart from the other races.'

Lord Hamilton seized the proffered papers, setting out the proposed times and pick up areas and placed them in his pocket. 'I will drop by about six to let you know how I have gone on' he said, leaving the room.

Richard leaned back in his chair and closed his eyes. His job was going well, Exec Association being the finest of it's kind, with a worldwide reputation, second to none. The only problem on his horizon was this Islamic business and it was worrying him. Despite having numerous men in place throughout Europe with instructions to report back on unusual activities within the Islamic communities and meeting places, all he was getting were garbled reports relating to a World shattering situation and the coming of the terror.

Feeling lonely, he picked up the telephone and called Chris, who was delighted to hear from him. 'How about meeting up for lunch?' suggested Richard. 'It's been a long time since our last chat.'

The fact that they spoke on the telephone nearly every day, obviously did not count, thought Chris. 'Sure, why not. Try the Travellers, it's about halfway between us? Got to be careful with my expenses now I haven't got you to okay them for me,' he said with a laugh in his voice. 'I'll bring Bill. It'll do him good to get out and see what is happening in the Country today.'

Two hours later, in the Travellers, a well known, former coaching house, now transformed into a very chic restaurant, the three men sampled their drinks, whilst choosing what they should eat. Finally Richard relented, saying he would pay, which miraculously caused the others to try items on the menu that normally they could only dream about.

Over coffee and brandy, Richard asked if there was any advancement in the train explosion enquiry. It was Bill, who, after tasting his brandy and smacking his lips, said, 'I think we've just about run this into the ground.'

'But the Ahmad fellow. You get nowhere with him?' asked Richard.

'A pillar of society, well liked by friend and foe. He is still apparently in Pakistan. I obtained a photograph of him, but noone has come forward to identify him as being in any way involved in the explosion. We have confirmed the identity of the headless corpse, identified the explosives and are reasonably satisfied that the bomb was detonated by using a portable telephone. The experts tell me that whoever put the bomb together and prepared the suitcase with the unexploded bomb, is himself an expert or even a genius.'

'The guy who did the Madrid bombs was good. Wonder if it could have been the same person?' said Richard, toying with his brandy glass. 'I would really like to spend a few minutes in his company, before dispatching him to his Paradise and his vestal virgins.'

'If you are entertaining those sort of ideas,' said Chris, 'then don't forget to count me in. I'm short on target practice too and I am sure a live target such as he would help me get my eye back into focus.'

Richard picked up his glass and swirled the contents around, apparently deep in thought. He looked around him and saw that they could not be overheard. Leaning forward, he said, 'I am going to confide in you as I trust you both implicitly. What I am going to tell you is in utmost confidence and at least I know that you can accept what I say without searching for confirmation.

'In the near future, somewhere in Europe, an incident is going to take place which will have earth shattering repercussions. We do not know where, nor what, nor when. We do know that it is intended to overshadow the eleventh of September, that it is planned by the successors of bin Laden and that the object will be World domination.

There are so many possible targets, that we can do nothing in the way of prevention, as that would only cause suspicion and panic and would also show our hand to the Islamists. No, the only thing we can do is be watchful, alert and be prepared for any and all eventualities.'

Chris and Bill looked at each other, both shocked by these revelations. Chris said, 'I can see what you mean. In our County alone there must be at least a dozen or so events due to take place in the coming weeks, which could be possible targets. I suppose the only thing we can do is keep the old ear to the ground and pray.'

'I'm afraid you are right, old pal,' said Richard. 'It's causing me a lot of sleepless nights. The only thing I can suggest is, whenever possible, try keeping mobile teams, armed if possible, on the ready, but as I said earlier we cannot afford idle talk to cause panic.'

Bill sat deep in thought. Suddenly he said, 'This Ahmad fellow, if he is still in Pakistan, could feasibly be involved, certainly in the planning. I will ask the Border guys to keep an eye out for his return from Pakistan and I'll try to have a little chat with him. Outside that, I cannot think what else we can do.'

'And there,' said Richard, taking a quote from Shakespeare, 'is the rub. The only other thing I can say is that our informants talk of the coming terror. I have decided that our warning will simply be 'terror' and the moment I hear anything the word will be passed to you and then you must act as you see fit.'

'You know, Richard,' said Bill, 'I was feeling quite happy with a glass of brandy in my hand, but you have sobered me up.'

'Don't worry. When this little lot is over I will buy you a bottle of the stuff.'

Rising together, the three men left the restaurant, and, after saying their goodbyes on the car park, Richard climbed into his pride and joy and drove back to his country residence. Lord Hamilton was waiting for him in the garden along with his dogs, and, on seeing his car, walked across to the garage.

'Had a good lunch, I hope,' said the Home Secretary, and Richard replied, seeing the flushed face of his friend, 'Not as good as yours I think.'

'That's hardly fair, old boy, especially as I was working for you. Anyway, it's all fixed for this Friday and everyone should be on the boat in time for dinner at eight thirty. I've arranged for us to be picked up here. Aviation didn't like it, but I thought there's little point in having rank if one cannot exercise it from time to time.'

-o-o-o-o-o-o-o-

Thirty six hours later saw the two friends seated in an extremely comfortable helicopter, flying over the blue seas, under a setting sun, aiming for a beautiful looking ship which appeared to be stationary.

Lord Hamilton drew out a sheet of paper and started to read. 'The Philanderer' a copy of the latest yacht ordered by a well known football club owner'. Over five hundred feet in length, two helipads, swimming pool, at least twenty cabins for guests, cost over three hundred million pounds and even costs around eighty thousand pounds, just to fill it up.'

'So, we'll be slumming it. Beggars can't be choosers as they say,' replied Richard, as he waited for the helicopter to touch down on this floating palace below them. What would the others think? Then he came back to reality as he remembered the reason they were there. Still, he thought, beats sitting around in an office waiting for something to happen.

The pilot placed the helicopter exactly in the centre of the helipad, and the two men stepped out into the warmth of the setting sun. 'Seems strange, does it not, to have left the cold and the rain four hours ago and now to be stepping into the setting sun,' said Richard, who had very little experience of foreign travel and certainly not in this luxury market.

Cabin staff were waiting for them and they were each escorted to a private cabin, where they were informed that the captain would be waiting to greet them at cocktails in half an hour's time. Both men showered and changed and a half hour later, Richard was introducing Lord Hamilton to his old Police friends, who in turn introduced them both to the visiting armed forces officers.

Marcel Polidor set the tone when he said, 'We don't know why we are here, but if we have to be somewhere, here's as good as anywhere.' Drinks were served and after a short welcoming speech from the captain, an ex Royal Navy man, the group descended to the dining room, where they experienced a culinary treat, rarely seen in even the best restaurants. At eleven o'clock, they retired for the night, satiated and ready for bed, each of them with their memories of an evening far exceeding anything they could have dreamed of.

Luigi Carlino, nick named 'The Latin Lover,' by the others, summed it up succinctly when he said, 'There are millions of us throughout the World and a very, very few live like this all the time. What do I have to do to join them?'

Uproarious laughter burst forth, as several suggestions, some unprintable and others physically impossible were put forward, but each was sobered when Richard said, 'Let us hope we are still laughing tomorrow after I have told you the reason we are here.'

The following morning, the weather was fine and clear and, after breakfast and a walk around the decks, they seated themselves around an enormous oak table in the main conference room and waited for Richard to open the debate.

After studying yet again the pile of papers in front of him, he cleared his throat, looked around him at the expectant faces and said, 'Let's get down to business.'

'Before coming to the reason for this meeting, are there any amongst us who may feel uncomfortable in the knowledge that what I am about to tell you, must not be divulged to anyone, including your employers. Something very sinister is being planned by Al Qaida and if we are to have any success at all, we must say and do nothing until we know exactly what is planned, where and why.

'I have informants in place in all the main European countries, including yours, and the information which is being fed back is scant, but applies to each Country. I know for a fact and Lord Hamilton here would confirm this, (at this juncture Lord Hamilton nodded his head in confirmation), that if I were to go to the Prime Minister with the information he would either laugh in my face or tell it to the press. I believe that each of you here know the various foibles of your Country's leaders and obviously I would have to accept that if all or each of you feel that you must, through loyalty or whatsoever, go to them with this information, then obviously

I can do nothing to stop you. However, I will say, please, please think very carefully before you do, for any form of visible action will be spotted by the opposition, as they apparently, are everywhere.' Richard paused, seeing he had their attention.

'I have known most of you for years and we have always worked well together. To my knowledge, I have never lied to you and believe you me, I am certainly not going to lie now.'

A deathly silence followed as each digested what Richard had said. Werner Gierschick, the all powerful Berliner finally broke the silence, saying, 'I have an excellent relationship with my Chancellor and have never been let down. I will say this. I will listen very carefully to what you have to say and afterwards I will decide if in all true conscience, I can keep this information to myself or not.'

'We all know and trust you Richard,' said Marcel Polidor, 'but Werner does have a very good point. Each of us here are employed by our respective Governments and we must show allegiance, even though in many cases it is mostly lip service. You on the other hand, work now in private industry and there is a great difference,' here there was a burst of laughter as with an expansive gesture he indicated the surroundings in which they were meeting, 'but like Werner I would like to hear what you have to say before I can make a decision. You are right in so far as that our leaders today, do seem to lack the class and statesmanship of their forebears, for as you know in my Country there are at least a dozen or so postulants for the post of President, when the next elections come around.'

The Swiss, Pierre Jiguel, a very attractive man in his mid fifties, always debonair in manner and dress stated, 'Marcel, that goes to show that the position is a comfortable one. I have always wondered, in circumstances such as exist in your Country, why all those candidates do not get together. If they each have something which they believe would make them the perfect candidate, then they should throw their ideas into a melting pot, until they were all satisfied that the best ideas could be put forward for the benefit of your Country and its people. As to the president, they could decide amongst themselves or take it in turns.'

'That's easy for you to say, my Swiss friend. You only have to look after all the World's money. Our politicians have to make sure that they are well served first,' retorted Marcel.

A general discussion then started about the merits or otherwise of their respective Government representatives, until Richard tapped on the table to regain their attention.

'I will obviously agree to your demands, simply because I have no choice. But first let me tell you what I know.'

His companions fell silent, waiting for him to finally divulge the reason for them being in this lap of luxury.

'Two years ago, a report was drawn up showing that over the last thirty years, the Muslim population, in Europe, had doubled. It is estimated that in another five years it will have doubled again. Owing to the very sensitive nature of this report, very few details have been allowed to be given to the general public.

For instance, there are over one and a half million in the United Kingdom, which represents two point seven per cent of the population.' Here he halted as he noticed that his colleagues were all writing down this information.

'In comparison, there are only about four hundred and fifty thousand police and army personnel. In France the figures are three and a half million, representing six per cent of the population whilst in Germany there are four million representing four per cent. In your two countries the police and army have about seven hundred thousand personnel. Just from an interest point of view there are sixteen and a half million in Russia and a staggering twenty two million in China of all places.

Those are official figures, but what we would like to know is what percentage is allied to Al Qaida or other terrorist organisations and what numbers can be classed as active. We all have our different calculating systems, but this total is vital to us and we have no idea what that total is.'

Once again he paused until they had each finished scribbling their notes. After pouring himself a glass of water and drinking deeply, he continued.

'We do know that over the last few years, those organisations have been recruiting and training, but we have no idea on what scale. We know, from the increase in armed robberies and murders perpetrated mainly through gang battles associated with the illicit drug trade, that they do have weapons, including military weapons. However, and here is another unknown; we do not know their commitment, their local leadership or their professionalism in the art of combat, nor their level of information and communication. Is there anyone here who could enlighten us if, anywhere within your own organisations, there is a means of calculating the threat potential that I have outlined.'

Sitting back in his chair, Richard studied the others.

The majority of the armed service members were mainly unknown to him, whereas the Police members were all personal friends, who he hoped he could trust implicitly. The various discussions finally died down and it was Manuel Costello, the Chief of the Guardia Civil in Spain who answered.

'You are all aware of the train bombings in Madrid,' he started, glancing across at Richard as he did so, noticing his face harden and his eyes start to glisten with tears, 'and you know that some of the terrorists were killed, some arrested, whilst others seem to have got away. Following these atrocities, special teams were set up throughout the Country in an attempt to monitor the Islamic communities and to obtain information or even better, proof, of terrorists and their activities. As you are probably aware the results were in the main, negative.

'We liaised with the American authorities who do not like to give information, some say because they do not have any, only a large supply of bullshit, and though they supplied us with certain details, this information was, in the main, inconclusive.'

Richard then once again took over the narrative. 'Now I come to the only seemingly solid fact that I have. Apparently it is planned that somewhere in the World and, I believe personally that it will be somewhere in Europe, an event is planned to take place that will far over shadow the tragedy of the World Trade Centre.

This event is supposed to be the signal that will lead eventually to World domination by the Islamists. The problem is, I have no idea at all what is planned. I have a large team of loyal Asian informers working in the various communities, especially within the religious sections, but to date their information gives us no idea of what is planned. However, I do know that the terrorist organisations are being kept up to date through various channels. My men have been trying to ingratiate themselves into these organisations, but with very little success as they are treated with suspicion, even though they have excellent cover stories and speak the various languages fluently.'

Luigi interrupted saying, 'I know that in my Country there are far less Islamics than in your respective Countries. We could always pick up some of them and try to extract the information.'

'The Americans have been trying for years, eventually kidnapping them and taking them to Guantanamo, but they have come up with zilch,' replied Richard. 'Similarly, if you were to do what you have just suggested you would be very politically incorrect, probably breach the Geneva Convention and at the end of the day simply tell the opposition that we know something is afoot, thus pushing them further underground.' This last brought a burst of somewhat strained laughter.

'Before opening the discussion, I would just like to add this. We do believe that the event planned is for soon, that it will be grandiose and that the subsequent happenings will instill terror throughout Europe. This information, although pretty general, is coming to me from all over Europe. When I think in the coming weeks, the number of possible targets, the problem you will see is vast. How many sporting events, concerts or even commercial centres where many hundreds or thousands of people could be gathered? What will happen? An explosion, a gas attack, bacterial weapons, large scale poisoning or a combination of all those? The problem is infinitesimal. Unless anyone here can come up with some ideas, all we can do is wait.'

This time the silence was deafening as each considered what Richard had said. Each of them held responsible positions, positions which could, and certainly would in this case, put their fellowmen at grave risk. In normal times, they would simply pass on the information to their political leaders, but they all realised that Richard was correct when he said that in this case it would create more problems than it would cure.

General Schwarz, a military man through and through, renowned for his Teutonic stubborness and bravery in battle said, 'It is clear we must do something, but what. I can think now that if we start to plan ahead, one of the first things to do is draw up lists of possible targets and see how we can best protect them. This will not be easy as others would have to be brought in to help with the planning, so cover stories would have to be made. It is possible to start with strategic and public buildings as we already have certain contingency plans, but as to covering everything . . . .'

Richard looked around at the glum faces staring back at him, then glanced at his watch. 'How about a break. We can keep the boat for a week if we like', this bringing knowing smiles, 'and I could certainly use a drink. How about meeting back after lunch at say, three o'clock'

With that he stood, as did the others and they all made for the cocktail lounge.

'You have certainly given them food for thought,' said Lord Hamilton, as he reached Richard's side.

'That may be, my Lord,' replied Richard with a smile, 'but I do not think they will refuse the alternative food which is being prepared for lunch.'

After a couple of stiff whiskies, Richard went for a stroll around the decks, beathing in the fresh sea air whilst feeling the sun warming his back.

'I suppose, with a bit of an effort I could acclimatise myself to this life,' he said to himself, before going to his cabin to freshen up before lunch.

# CHAPTER 45

Richard left his cabin and walked slowly, deep in thought towards the dining room. He could already here the muted voices of his colleagues and, yet again, wondered where all this would lead to. On entering the room, he saw a beautifully laid out table, with the personnel waiting to serve lunch.

Each person took their seat and then the door opened and the Captain walked in. 'May I join you?' he asked, 'as it is customary for the Captain to officially welcome aboard all visitors. I know that you are here for a very special reason, but my experience has shown that all work and no play . . . .' Here he stopped, looking around him expectantly.

'You are more than welcome,' replied Lord Hamilton, rising and shaking the Captain's hand. 'Let me make the introductions.' One by one, he introduced the visitors to the captain, each in turn shaking the Captains hand.

'How does he do it?' thought Richard. 'He's only met them once and he remembers all their names.'

The meal was lavish and after coffee and liquers had been served, the Captain turned to Richard and said, 'It would be a pity that whilst you are here with us, you did not partake of the pleasures. Before returning to your business, I would suggest that a few hours of play and relaxation may do wonders for you and your colleagues.'

'What do you have in mind?' asked Richard and the Captain, started to tick off on his fingers examples of the joys aboard his vessel.

'Firstly, there is the swimming pool with the sun beds and we do have a qualified masseuse on board for those who may fancy a massage. After, we have the jet skis; waterskiing, power boat rides or simply swimming in this beautiful sea. It's a bit early for the dolphins, but one never knows.'

'Thank you, captain, that is an excellent idea.' Turning to the assembled group, Richard announced the suggestion made by the Captain and was rewarded with smiles of anticipation. 'Let us say six thirty this evening to continue our discussion.'

With that the group broke up, each going to change. The afternoon passed in a whirl of fun and laughter, making Richard realise how necessary relaxation was.

Finally, at the appointed time, the group once again found themselves seated in the conference room and, when they were settled the French Field Marshall opened the debate, saying, 'We have spoken together and separately as, it is possible, each of us has different views on what is important and what is secondary. Apparently, at this juncture, secrecy is imperative, and therefore any sort of contingency plans, must have a convincing cover story.'

'I'll start to make a list,' said Richard, 'reaching for paper and pen. 'Good, please continue.' He sat back waiting for the Field Marshall to continue.

'Firstly, we must try to protect our lines of defence and communication. This would include many public buildings, plus broadcasting stations, fuel stores, arms and explosive stores etc. You will appreciate that the list can be extensive without being exhaustive, but, it must be accepted that the main activity must take place in the different capital cities as to attempt to cover the whole Country would be virtually impossible. Naturally, such installations as nuclear reactor centres would also have to be included, which will complicate the problem, but that cannot be helped.'

Various ideas on subterfuge have been muted and I personally think that if we can keep our activities in line with the present World situation, our activities would go relatively unnoticed.' Here he paused, noting that he had the full attention of those present.

'For instance, increasing security within certain strategic buildings, can be put down to Government departments wanting their individual responsibilities upgraded, something which is often done on a whim and costing a fortune. In this case it is necessary and the installation of additional security items can be carried out by our normal contractors, without drawing any special attention to ourselves.'

'Can my company put in tenders?' asked Richard flippantly, bringing a retort of 'Cheeky bugger' from Lord Hamilton. The ensuing laughter helped the men to relax and the Field Marshall waited for order to be restored, before continuing.

'Turning now to the opposition. We have no knowledge of numbers or weapons, but we must assume that the weapons, in the main, will be hand held guns, grenades and even knives. Irrespective of what people may think, weapons of mass destruction are not something that your urban terrorist would possess, simply because the delivery and activation of such weapons are beyond their comprehension.'

'I would agree with you one hundred per cent,' said Richard, 'but I will add this sobering thought. If at the time of the World Trade Centre destruction, several hundred or even thousands of conventionally armed terrorists running amok in New York, shooting and killing indiscriminately, would have been a very difficult problem for the Americans to contain.

Whilst still reeling from the shock of such an unexpected attack, to be then faced with this secondary problem, would more than have stretched their ressources to the limit. Bringing sufficient reinforcements from the Army or Police would have taken time and think of the damage which would have been done before a positive reaction could be formulated.

When you look at the scale of destruction in London recently, by a band of youngsters, unorganised and in the main, unarmed, what would have been the outcome if they had been organised, armed and with a specific object in mind. Simply thinking of it frightens me.'

Luige Carlino broke in, saying 'I think such a scenario would frighten all of us. I remember the terror caused by the 'Brigade Rouge' in Italy as I am sure Werner will remember the Baader Meinhof group. There were not many of them, but they were armed, organised and determined in their actions and, before they were stopped they had created an atmosphere of terror and suspicion throughout the Country.'

Once again, the Field Marshall took up the narrative. 'I believe one advantage we do have, is that our men are better trained and armed. Although the opposition do have the advantage of surprise, provided we can respond quickly, we would possibly blunt their attacks. If we cannot react fast enough, the danger will be, as we have all seen throughout the years, that the fringe types will join in, thus complicating our problems.'

The Spanish Chief of Staff broke in. 'This leads to another problem and that is the number of Moslems in our different armed services. Would they be loyal or would they be persuaded to change sides. There is also the added risk, that if we talk about contingency plans, the information could be leaked with disastrous results.'

'Marcel had a good idea,' replied the Field Marshall. 'He has suggested that we tell our staffs that the Government is considering sending our men into Africa to help with the different revolutions which are happening there. We could then increase training in urban guerilla tactics and even create groups, several of which are available at any time, so that we can react the second we know what is going to happen.'

Werner then spoke up. 'What about us activating our own sources of information? We have many Turkish Moslems and they know that it is not in their interest to upset the apple cart.'

'The only problem I can forsee,' replied Richard, 'is that if word does get out, all our planning is for nothing. I can only say that if you feel you have to and you think that you can trust your informants, then do as you think fit, but I would urge each of you to consider very carefully such a course of action.'

'But we must do something,' broke in Manuel.

'And so we will,' replied Richard,' and here is what I suggest. Think of what the Field Marshall has said and consider how best you can implicate his suggestions into your own Countries systems. For my part, I will suggest the following.'

Seeing that he now had their full attention, Richard continued his discourse. 'Firstly, we must install a foolproof early warning system. Even a few minutes warning may be enough to give us time to react efficiently.'

'What I suggest is this. We will have coded into our own portable telephones a number which can be dialled by any of us and which will simultaneously cause all the other telephones to ring. On answering you will hear only a recorded key word, I would suggest for example 'Terror', which will immediately tell you that whatever is planned has happened and that you must react as quickly as possible. There is no need for you to know what the incident is at this time, simply that it has happened. Naturally, one person will know exactly what has happened as that person will have dialled the number.'

'How will we get this high tech equipment?' queried Marcel, 'for I know that any additional expenditure, certainly at this time, will cause questions to be asked."

Looking to Lord Hamilton for confirmation and getting it, Richard said, 'Our company will foot the bill. I will have installed in my offices the necessary telephone and transmitting devices in order that simultaneous warnings can be given to you all.

I would also like a list of names of people you can trust, in those countries which are not present here today. If such persons exist, then each of you must explain the reasons and I will see that they are properly equipped. It must be realised that perhaps the incident planned may take place in one of these countries and it will be better that they be warned, but only if they can be trusted implicitly.

With there being no frontiers now between member States, we can also perhaps push a point and send our forces to assist in case a member State is having problems due to lack of suitable response teams. You can always inform your Government masters after the event.'

This last comment brought general laughter and knowing looks and Richard said, 'I think that is enough for today. You will undoubtedly talk with each other or even with me this evening and tomorrow at ten we will meet again to finalise our plans.'

'I am not known for my public speaking,' said General Schwarzkopf, 'but I am very impressed by what has been said and decided today. We are all professionals and I think we can work well together.

'With one of my most trusted aides, I have been working on urban terrorist problems for some time and we have devised various means of approaching the different problems. Civilians, in the main are not armed and must be defended vigorously. In Germany we work at speed and efficiency and have devised various scenarios using light tanks, armoured personnel carriers and helicopters.

'I would suggest, as I think it of the utmost importance, that each of us take one of our assistants into our complete confidence. This is necessary in order that there is always one person who can react immediately the alert is given. All of us here know that our duties are such that we may be away from our base for any number of reasons and it is imperative, as you so rightly point out, Richard, that we act immediately.'

'On reflection I will agree with you whole heartedly. If you could, at a later date, inform me of the details of your assistants, I will include them in my operational file.' Richard then made note of this last suggestion.

'Now, I think we have covered nearly everything and I am sure that after the day we have just spent, sleep will come easily tonight, especially if we eat yet another of those gourmet meals. I don't know about you lot, but I could soon become accustomed to this style of living.'

A chorus of 'Hear, Hears,' went up as the group got to their feet and started to leave the room, preparing to spend their last night aboard, and fully intending to enjoy it.

# CHAPTER 46

Mansour and Wahid left their hotel and walked a few hundred yards to their favourite restaurant, in order to eat yet another plate of pasta. Wahid was happy, because now the units were completed, Mansour had contacted their French/Algerian politician, who had promised to arrange a suitable, well publicised reception of the new units.

Local television, radio and journalists had been contacted and all had promised to come, especially as a couple of football players from Milan A.C. and a female film star would also be present.

The politician would naturally bring the caterer, Daniel Allary to the reception, along with several well known French 'hangers-on', to bolster the numbers.

'Money is no object' the President had said when briefing Mansour. Never one to look a gift horse in the mouth, Mansour had spent a small fortune on the reception, but he was now basically assured that the units would be accepted without question by the personnel at the château of Versailles.

When they had finished eating, Mansour asked Wahid how much time he would need to install and prime the explosives in the units.

'I would think two days. There are four units measuring six metres by one metre and four units measuring two metres by one metre, and I shall distribute the explosives evenly between all the units. They will detonate simultaneously.' There is no need to insert extras such as nails, as the force of the explosion will shatter the contents of the units, which are nearly all made of glass or porcelain. Added to that the cutlery in and around the units and I would estimate that what the explosives don't kill the flying shrapnel will.'

'In that case, we have five or six days to complete the work and then count a couple of days to transport the units to Versailles. That will give them about ten days to install the units, before the planned meeting takes place.

'It would be better if you were not seen hanging around here during the presentation and I shall not be present either. Our French Presidential representative, who just loves publicity and himself in equal doses, is only too happy to do the presentation himself and has even persuaded the French President to lend him a plane for the journey.

'I would like to meet up with my Afghan friend, who you know as Umar Razad, who will accompany me to Versailles the day before the meeting. We have much to discuss and to decide on what weapons to take with us. Can you let me know how many of our soldiers will be mobilised after the blast?'

'On the day of the meeting, there will be at least 200 in and around Versailles to attack those not killed in the blast, because with so many countries involved, there will undoubtedly be huge numbers of soldiers, police and other security personnel in attendance. There will also be huge crowds of spectators as well who will swiftly fall victim to our brother's bullets.'

'In the other countries,' asked Wahid, 'what will happen?'

'The explosion is the signal for all our soldiers, over two hundred and fifty thousand in all, armed and devoted to the cause, to take to the streets. They are mainly in the capital cities, but there are others in smaller cities and towns. Many have been trained in guerilla warfare and have specified targets to go for. The others are simply instructed to cause as much death and destruction as possible.'

'The security forces will react quickly,' said Wahid, thoughtfully.

'Without a doubt, but I estimate that they will require a half a day at least, to mobilise. During that time, I am confident that many other Moslems, on seeing what to them is a revolution, will join in on our side, multiplying the problems for the security forces.'

'What of our leaders in Pakistan and Afghanistan? Have they plans to intervene?'

Mansour paused before answering. 'I must report back to them before the day of the meeting for a final briefing. I understand that they will try to force through a ceasefire agreement in order to prevent further loss of life amongst the civilian populations, and that then they will try to form an Islamic state. We have the element of surprise and this time we have the backing of thousands of warriors.'

'At last our hard work and devotion is going to bear fruit,' said Wahid, 'and I will have played my part. I can only hope that we can come through this unscathed and help to form the new Islamic World.'

'Will three days be enough for you to do your work in Rome?' asked Mansour. "I have work to do here and will see you back in the hotel in three days. Then we can see to the transportation of the units and the inserting of the explosives."

The following morning, after breakfast, Wahid left to meet Umar Razad in Rome, whilst Mansour spent the day helping the manufacturer of the bar and kitchen units to assemble them in the main showroom, situated in the heart of this state of the art factory. What a glorious piece of work these units were, burnished steel with gold cloured handles and trim, finished off by the dull sparkle of the marble tops and sides.

Mansour returned to his hotel room and continued working on his master plan, which would start with a big bang and finish in a crescendo of accolades for himself. The body count did not bother him as he himself had little respect for human life, except his own.

He worked late into the afternoon, marvelling at the simplicity of his plan and dwelling on the moment when he would be declared a hero of the Islamic Revolution. Had not the revolutions in North Africa worked in much the same way?

The dissatisfied citizens, wanting a share of their country's wealth, were more than willing to collaborate with the Al Qaida activists who stirred them to such a pitch that they truly believed they were oppressed. The beauty of that plan was that the stupid European politicians and their inept leaders had then assisted them in getting rid of the ruling parties, the only Arabs feared by Al Qaida, who knew that they would be ruthlessly put down should they attempt a head to head struggle with them. Now that the work had been done for them by their European enemies, who firmly believed that democracy would be embraced by the Arab people, little realising that the Arab World did not know the meaning of the word, and it was certainly not Al Qaida who would teach them.

Finally, his work done, he telephoned the politician in Paris, once again feeling his revulsion for the man, even over the telephone. Saying that all was ready for the handing over ceremony, he contacted the factory owner who promised that he would see to suitable transport for the politician and his guests from the airport to the reception, whilst presenting his regrets that Mansour could not be present for the handing over ceremony.

That done, Mansour telephoned a very private, select club for discerning persons desirous of fulfilling their various fantasies, and booked in for the next three days.

# CHAPTER 47

After their final breakfast aboard the 'Philanderer' the men said their farewells, each wanting to hasten back to their respective countries in order to start putting into effect the necessary precautions in order to better protect their peoples. For the next two hours a series of helicopters ferried the guests back to their various destinations, until only Richard and Lord Hamilton remained. They in turn, said goodbye to the captain, thanking him for his wonderful welcome and for the agreeable time they had spent in his company.

Safely and comfortably seated in the helicopter, they rose into the air to begin the flight back to England. They spoke of their last two days and of the arrangements made for the future, each hoping that in the end, nothing would happen, but feeling deep down that the die had been cast and that it was now simply a matter of time.

'My Lord', began Richard, 'I have a question that I have been longing to ask you ever since you became Home Secretary, and that is 'Why'? You could have taken retirement and spent the rest of your days with your wife and perhaps even written your memoirs. Why choose this post at this time?'

'You must be aware that I am one of the chosen few as regards lands and possessions. I am also gifted with a good brain. Although politics as such do not interest me greatly, I do feel that I can still make a substantial contribution in helping my fellow man.'

'There is also the hundred grand plus a year that goes with it as well,' said Richard, only to be rebuked by the Judge, who insisted that money was not an important issue regarding his decision to serve his Country.

'In your case, I suppose I can understand your willingness to serve as your years in the judiciary must have given you certain insights into the devious workings of the human mind. I am sure you will do an excellent job, but I still cannot think why you should wish to when you could simply retire and enjoy a few years of the good life. We have just spent a very agreeable two days as I am sure you will agree.'

'I could not agree more, but I already enjoy such a life style; it's just that you have never noticed. But honestly, can you imagine me wanting to spend the rest of my days in the sole company of my wife. I love her dearly, but she would drive me to distraction.' Suddenly, realising what he had just said, he turned to Richard, saying, 'Forgive me my friend for those thoughtless words. How idiotic of me.'

'Do not worry, my Lord,' replied Richard, 'as I too have learned to live with my loss. By immersing myself into work I find that the pain, although always present, becomes more bearable with the passage of time.' Here he paused in reflection.

'What I am really getting at, is why do people enter politics? Is it a driving force, a willingness to serve or simply a reasonable way of making a living without having to dirty ones hands.'

'I would imagine there is a bit of each. Most politicians have some sort of ideologic inspiration, which quite often dissipates with the passage of time and the acceptance of an easy way to make a living. Others appear devoted to their ideas or their political parties and spend the rest of their lives trying to fulfill their ambitions.'

'What I cannot understand is what I refer to as the square peg/ round hole syndrome. How on earth can a person become a Minister when he has no experience of the subject he is supposed to be advising on.'

'That is simple to answer. To start with, Ministers are normally personal friends of the Prime Minister. They are normally well educated, presentable persons, although there are exceptions and their main function is to protect the Prime Minister.

When you see a Minister making a speech, you have to realise that the speech was written by a professional writer who is advised by various aides as to what to put into the speech. The Minister will then spend a considerable amount of time in front of a mirror, practising his speech and working on his facial expressions. It is a little bit like being an actor. Tell me, why this sudden interest in politics?'

'I have always been interested, but never in a position to question someone in such an exalted position as yourself. When I see the numbers of politicians who live well and the service they provide, I cannot help but wonder if there is not a different way to govern. As you say, there are people who truly believe, but there are many others who simply pay lip service whilst collecting their pay and allowances.

Simply by watching television, one can see that on the programmed television discussions, the House is full of well dressed, important looking people.

On other occasions, when it is simply by accident that the television is present, there is hardly anyone present and half of them are asleep.'

The Home Secretary regarded Richard with a quizical expression; Finally he said, 'If you were not too important in the job you hold, I would propose you to our political leader as you would be a fine recruit. You wear your honesty and devotion like a suit of armour and one can almost feel the goodness emanating from you. I believe that you would make an excellent politician, but you would make many enemies as there are those who do not share your passion and devotion. However, I can say this in all sincerity and that is that I am proud to be your friend as I have a feeling that if I was your enemy I would be faced by an implacable force.'

'So you would say that politicians can come from any walk of life and be successful. It takes some believing that does.'

Lord Hamilton smiled at Richard as one would to an ignorant child. 'Example', he said. 'Take Madoff the American financier. He would have made an excellent President of the United States had he been willing to try for it and others were there to help him in the race.'

'Now I know you are pulling my leg. The man's away for the next hundred years or so,' laughed Richard. 'Come, be serious. It is a subject that interests me.'

'I have never been more serious. How many men have you known, well educated, beautifully attired, who could shake your hand and look you squarely in the eye whilst stealing billions. I personally do not know any, but there are lots of succesful political figures who come near to that description.'

Richard mulled over these words and was so lost in thought, he did not realise that his friend had fallen asleep beside him. 'Might as well join him' he thought, and closed his eyes.

They woke almost simultaneously as the helicopter descended onto its pad at the airport, and very soon were seated in Lord Hamilton's official car on the drive back to their joint homes. 'The next few weeks may prove interesting', said Lord Hamilton, 'and there is something that has been troubling me. We have discussed over the last few days proposed plans for other countries, but what about our own?'

'I can see to the Police side,' said Richard, 'and could you help on the military?'

'Consider it done. The Chief of General Staff was at school with me and I can soon put him into the picture over lunch somewhere.' With that, Lord Hamilton closed his eyes and went back to sleep.

# CHAPTER 48

The day of the unveiling of the state of the arts units, was destined to be one of the finest days in that Italian spring. The day was warm, all the celebrities came as planned and the television and other media present had an absolute field day of interviews and photographs.

Daniel Allary tested the functions of the units which he found to be first class, and all declared the day a roaring success.

Wahid, as promised, rejoined Mansour three days later and they organised the lorry to transfer the units to his secure warehouse and workshop, where he would remove the marble panels and replace them with the false ones and the explosives. The device to be used to detonate the bomb would be similar to the one used in the train explosion, and could be activated from distance by way of telephone.

'How long do you estimate to do your work?' asked Mansour, 'as I must arrange for my flight to Pakistan.'

'Say three days, four at the most. Delivery should take a maximum of four days, which leaves us nearly two weeks before the day of the meeting. That should be ample time for the units to be unloaded, cleaned up and installed for the meeting. You make your arrangements and I will contact you in Pakistan, when the units are installed and operational.'

The two men embraced and Mansour left for Rome Airport after ensuring that Wahid had the means to contact him quickly if necessary.

Once in Rome, using the new passport supplied by his uncle, Mansour booked a flight to Lahore, arriving the following day. He went straight to the home of the President, only to be told that he was absent and would be for several days. Mansour was instructed to rest and replenish his strength, for the forthcoming operation.

Wahid, in the meantime, had transported the bar units to his secure warehouse, where, for three whole days he worked on the transformation of the units into the most powerful bomb he had ever constructed. He inserted his favourite form of detonation and added a secondary detonator which could be activated by a 'suicide' bomber, should the first detonator malfunction.

He spent the final morning on inspecting and comparing the false marble decor with the real one and, when finally satisfied that the two were identical in every way, he installed them, completely hiding all evidence of any change in the units.

Once his work was completed to his entire satisfaction, he contacted the driver who, on arrival, helped him to load and secure the units for the journey to Versailles. He had checked and rechecked the weight and specifications as recorded by the Italian customs, ensuring that they were correct in every detail, and then he resealed the customs seal, thus showing that the load had not been tampered with. Normally, if stopped, provided the seal was in place, no one would open the lorry until it's arrival at Versailles.

The lorry driver, a member of Wahid's own family, was a very experienced driver, used to Continental roads and systems. Firstly, they drove to the factory where the units had been manufactured and there took on board their lorry, two skilled installation fitters, who would be responsible for the placing, securing and connecting of the units in the prearranged site inside the Château of Versailles.

Two days had been reserved for the transfer of the units, and the manufacturer had contacted the caterer, Monsieur Allary, to inform him of the proposed date of delivery. Wahid, in the meantime had contacted his friend, Umar Razad, instructing him to go to Versailles and book two hotel bedrooms and to await his arrival in two days time.

The journey was uneventful and two days later, exactly nine days before the proposed meeting of the European Governments, the units arrived at the Château of Versailles. French customs, security officers from the Château and Government security personnel, together with the site director, were all present to receive the lorry and to supervise it's unloading.

Once the units had been transferred to the Battles Room, the technicians began the delicate work of unpacking and installing them. The caterer, Monsieur Allary arrived and exclaimed in glowing terms at the sight of the units in place.

During the afternoon, a further disturbance was caused, this time by the arrival of the President of France, accompanied by several ministers and the Algerian political adviser. Each proclaimed their pleasure at the beauty of the units, which actually added to the beauty of the room, owing to the skills of the manufacturing team to harmonise with the somewhat spartan decor of the Battles Room.

Monsieur Allary was called upon to explain the functions of the units and he wasted no time in his explanations, praising the state of the art workmanship and the multi-functions of the units. The President expressed reserves about the ability of the units to cope with two and a half thousand guests, but was reassured when Mr. Allary explained that the total operation had been meticulously planned and would work to perfection on the day.

Congratulations were then given and accepted by the various parties present and arrangements made for Monsieur Allary and his staff to have ready access to the units, in order to start the preparations for one of the most important and prestigious meetings ever to be held in the Château of Versailles.

Wahid had left earlier and joined up with his friend Umar, who had secured two rooms in a small, non descript hotel in Versailles. He had booked for two weeks to ensure that they would have the rooms as, with the planned meeting at the Château, rooms were extremely scarce. 'Eight days to victory', said Wahid as the two friends embraced and began their meticulous planning for the day of the meeting.

The following day, Wahid telephoned Mansour to inform him that all was in place and ready for the meeting. Mansour expressed his delight and told Wahid to enjoy a few days rest with sightseeing as, if their plan went to perfection, the shape of the Château would be changed forever.

# CHAPTER 49

Exactly one week before the meeting at Versailles, another meeting was being held in the President's home in Pakistan. The full Council of Al Qaida was present, as, on the day of the planned explosion, each would have specific duties to perform, to ensure that the operation was successful and that the ensuing transitional period and putting into effect of an Islamic ruling force, would go smoothly.

When all had been discussed, the President turned to Mansour saying, 'You are to be congratulated. Your planning has been perfect and I can see no reason whatsoever why success should not follow. On the day of the operation, where do you intend to be, may I ask?'

Mansour had been waiting for this question, as he had very specific plans for that day. 'In London,' he replied, calmly, 'for as a legal representative of local Government in England, I believe I can be of more use playing a background role, than in involving myself in the fighting which will follow the explosion. In addition, I am in the process of finalising plans for joint televised tranmissions throughout Europe, instructing the people to stay calm and not to involve themselves in the fighting.

In this respect, we are fortunate to have television personalities who are supporters of our cause and who will facilitate easy access to the transmitting stations.' His personal plans would not interfere with the successful concluding of the operation and therefore he decided not to speak of them to the others.

'If no one has anything to add,' said the President, 'then may Allah go with each one of you and give you the strength and courage to see this operation to its final conclusion. For centuries we have dreamed of World Domination and, if successful in Europe, I am sure that the rest will follow in due course.'

The meeting broke up and the members started to leave in small groups. Mansour went to his uncle and together they left the room.

'What will you do now, my uncle,' asked Mansour. Will you return to England or have you some other plan in mind?'

'At my age we do not make long term plans. Your aunt needs me like I need her. No, I will live my days out in England, especially now that we will have an Islamic State. I may even be selected to sit on the Council, who knows?'

'I will be leaving today,' said Mansour, 'as I want to go by way of Paris to check with Wahid, that all goes well. I will then most likely travel by car from France, as controls are far less severe on Channel crossings.'

'Then we may see you in Basingstoke before the blast, shall we?' asked his uncle. 'You know you do my wife's heart good when you come to visit.'

'Depending on time I shall certainly try to and, failing that, I will visit after our victory.'

Mansour left his uncle and mounted the stairs to his room, packed his suitcase and left immediately for the airport as now there was very little time left to complete his plans before the big day, next Saturday.

Wahid was waiting for him at Charles de Gaulle airport, and together they drove to Versailles. During the drive, Wahid explained his plans for the coming Saturday and also stated that the Afghanistan controller had promised more than a thousand trained 'suicide' bombers, who would be spread around Europe to await further instructions.

He then went on to say that all member countries were sending their governments, plus various guests and members of the opposition, plus the Turkish Government and European deputies. He estimated the final count at around two thousand six hundred. Added to that would be numerous security personnel, police and military, the majority of which would be outside the building.

Mansour then told him he had planned for a minimum of two hundred and fifty faithful, armed to the teeth, but disguised as tourists, to be in the vicinity of the Château and to attack the moment the explosion was heard. 'When you think,' Mansour added, 'all the security people will rush to the Château thus leaving their backs exposed. It will be like a duck shoot.'

Chortling to themselves, they completed the drive to Versailles, Wahid taking Mansour into a bar situated across the road from the railway station and some four hundred yards from the target. Wahid pointed to the three television screens mounted in the bar, perfect for them to judge the most opportune moment to explode the bomb.

The following morning, Mansour telephoned Lord Hamilton. 'Mr. Home Secretary,' he said after introducing himself, 'I would like to meet with you in order to discuss various plans and ideas I have for helping the deprived children of East London.'

'It will be my pleasure to receive you,' replied Lord Hamilton. 'When would it be convenient to you?'

'I am, at the moment, out of the Country,' replied Mansour, 'but I will be in London by Friday morning.'

'Friday's out, I'm afraid,' said Lord Hamilton, 'but I will be available Saturday, as I have declined the offer to attend the acceptation of Turkey into Europe. You have, of course, heard of this plan, have you not?'

'I like you, do not agree with Turkey joining the European Community,' replied Mansour, 'and, if it is possible I could meet with you at say eleven o'clock.'

'That will be fine. My secretary will be absent, but the security guard will direct you to my office.'

Thanking him, Mansour replaced his telephone in his pocket, smiling to himself. No secretary, no witness, one down and one to go. How would he get within range of Grant?

-o-o-o-o-o-o-o-

Whilst Mansour was congratulating himself, Richard was chairing, what would prove to be, the last security meeting between the various security services in Europe. Nothing concrete had been forthcoming, although increased activity had been noticed in and around various locations. Also, an increase in telephone calls and internet activity had been recorded, especially in calls to Algeria and Pakistan, although once again, nothing of substance was forthcoming.

However, Richard was pleased when all those present regaled him with the preceautions they had taken. Increased security on public and vulnerable buildings, armed teams in civilian clothes and vehicles always on duty, tanks and light armour ready to roll at the drop of a hat and a twenty four hour watch on all television services.

'Personally,' said Richard, impressed by the seriousness and professional approach that all had taken, 'I cannot think of anything to add except perehaps, good luck. So good luck it is and let us hope this is all for nothing, although I am convinced that those fanatics will continue until they have their Holy War for Islamic domination.'

The meeting then adjourned to a nearby bar, where for the next two hours, all thoughts of World Domination were forgotten, as old rugby games were replayed and even Werner Gierschick tried to upset Richard by saying that the World Cup Final at Wembley had been fixed. 'Bollocks' was the last word on that subject.

# CHAPTER 50

The second Saturday in May was a beautiful day. The sun was shining from a clear blue sky as Lord Hamilton came out of his house to see Richard in the process of starting his car.

'I say Richard, could you drop me at the office. My chauffeur is not working today and I cannot be bothered with asking for a 'pool' car. We could go for a drink after down at the Club.'

'No problem. I'm going into the office to do a bit of dictation with Barbara and to try to catch up on my paperwork. I'll just drop down the soft top and we'll be away.'

The drive, as usual was extremely pleasant and uneventful, and at half past ten Richard left his friend outside his office building. As he was about to drive away, Lord Hamilton said, 'Why don't you stick the car in my place. It's a lot easier to walk to your office from here as you know that Saturday trafic is always bad.'

Lord Hamilton gave Richard his underground car park pass and Richard drove into the car park and left his car in the Home Secretary's spot. On returning to the street he saw that his friend had already entered the building and, slipping the card into his pocket, he strode off towards his office.

He was soon esconced in his office with Barbara and started dictating the minutes from the last security meeting.

The Home Secretary was reading a proof for a proposed law on litter dropping, when his phone rang. On answering, he heard the security guard say that his eleven o'clock visitor was waiting in the lobby and he instructed the guard to bring him to his office. Three minutes later, after shaking hands, the two men were seated across from each other, each studying the other. Mansour saw an elderly, refined looking gentlemen whilst Lord Hamilton was impressed by his visitor, a very attractive Asian wearing a dark grey Armani suit.

'In what way may I be of assistance to you?' asked Lord Hamilton pleasantly, smiling at his visitor as he did so. He noticed that his visitor did not return his smile.

A few seconds ensued and then Mansour said,'I require an explanation as to why you sentenced my brother to five years in prison for attacking that piece of vermin, Richard Grant.'

Lord Hamilton was stunned. Then it dawned on him that the person seated across from him was the first born son of his friend, Ilyas Ahmad, the retired diplomat. Recovering his aplomb, he said, 'I invited you here today to speak of other matters. I am not in the mood for a discussion on decisions I made whilst a member of the judiciary.'

Mansour regarded him with disdain. 'You, like Grant are a worthless piece of shit which needs to be exterminated. My brother is worth ten of you and I am going to make you pay for every second that he has spent rotting in your prison.'

Recovering quickly from this verbal attack, Lord Hamilton reached across his desk to ring for the security guard. Before he could reach the bell push, he found himself staring into the barrel of a Smith and Wesson revolver and froze, unable to believe that this was happening in his own office.

'Just in case you feel like attempting that little trick again,' said Mansour, 'I will give you something to contemplate on.' Jumping to his feet and, before the Home Secretary could react, he struck him a violent blow across the side of his head, drawing blood and causing the elderly man to topple from his chair to the floor.

Ignoring him, Mansour opened his brief case and took out a small cine camera which he placed on the desk facing the window. He then took a small slate from his case and started to write on the slate.

Lord Hamilton, although dazed, half opened one eye and saw Mansour engaged in writing something at his desk. Very slowly, he slipped his hand into his jacket pocket and felt the small plastic box Richard had given him. He pressed the button on the box and withdrew his hand, closing his eye as he noticed that Mansour appeared to have finished writing.

Mansour went round the desk and saw that his victim appeared to be unconscious. Without ceremony, he lifted him into his chair and wheeled the chair in front of the window, so that his face was in shadow. He then took a roll of tape and attached Lord Hamilton's arms to the chair. At the same time he wrapped the tape several times around his body in order to hold him upright in the chair.

Seeing that he was still apparently unconscious, he crossed the room and switched on the television set which was on the opposite wall to the bookcase.

Selecting the channel Al Jazeera, he perched on the desk, watching the news items whilst waiting for Lord Hamilton to regain consciousness.

Richard, who had finished his dictation, realised that he had left his brief case in his car. Cursing to himself, he explained to Barbara that he would have to return to his car for the brief case and that, if she had finished typing his report she could leave.

With that, he went out into the warm sunshine and started the short walk back to his car.

He was still several hundred yards from the car park when the alarm in his pocket started to screech. Taking the alarm from his pocket, he looked at the screen and saw the number five staring at him. He broke into a run, something he had not done in a long time and, as he reached the Home Office building he took out the parking card his friend had given him earlier and, on entering the garage, made his way to the lift.

The lift took him swiftly to the second floor and as he ran into the corridor he saw that the 'do not disturb' light was illuminated, outside the Home Secretary's office. He could hear no sound and then remembered the sound proofing inside the office. Without further ado he went further along the corridor to the interviewing room, breathing a sigh of relief when he found the door unlocked.

He entered the room and crossed to the fireplace, quickly locating the button which opened the hidden door, concealed in the bookcase. The door opened silently revealing a man perched on the desk with his back to Richard, apparently watching television. Then he saw his friend, his face covered in blood and apparently immobilised in his chair in front of the window. Suddenly, Lord Hamilton moved his head.

'Back in the living I see. You will soon regret that you have not answered my question, but before I have finished with you, you will be pleading with me to end your worthless life.' With that, Mansour lifted his arm and Richard saw that he was holding a gun.

He brought the gun barrel down hard on the side of his friends face, drawing fresh blood and causing his friend to cry out in agony. He lifted his arm to strike again and Richard, who had drawn his own pistol, a

Glock automatic, took aim and fired, the bullet striking Mansour on his right elbow, smashing the bones and causing him to drop his gun on the floor.

Screaming in pain, Mansour whirled round to see Richard facing him with a gun in his hand. 'Yooouuu' he screeched and tried to leap at Richard, who calmly shot him in the left knee. Mansour flopped to the ground howling in agony as Richard went swiftly to his friends aid, after first picking up and pocketing Mansour's revolver.

Richard quickly cut through the tape binding his friend to the chair and then examined his injured face. He was pleased to see that he appeared to be conscious, but was obviously suffering badly from his injuries.

Mansour spoke. 'You are too late as usual. I may be injured, but what I have put into motion cannot now be stopped. World domination will be with you shortly, Grant, and there is nothing you can do to stop it.'

Richard immediately took his phone from his pocket and speed dialled Barbara who answered immediately. 'Barbara, activate 'Terror' straight away,' he shouted into the phone, before turning back to Mansour. 'What is to happen?' he asked with a measure of menace in his voice, which was unmistakable to Mansour.

Mansour laughed, a harsh, grating laugh, which made Richard's hair stand on end 'He's mad' thought Richard, but Mansour continued his laughing.

'I asked you a question', said Richard and Mansour replied 'Watch the television with me. We will see together the catalyst which will unite the Arab World, leading to Islamic domination as promised by the Prophet.'

Hearing his friend groaning, Richard turned and saw that he had regained full consciousness, but was in great pain. Then the telephone on the desk began to ring.

Richard answered, to hear the security guard announcing the arrival of one of Richard's mobile teams, answering the alarm call. Stating that everything was under control, Richard asked the guard to give the telephone to his security officer.

'Go straight to headquarters and take control until I can arrive there. Barbara is there and should by now have activated the 'Terror' programme. Help her as much as you can and I will be back to you as soon as I know what is planned.'

Mansour again burst into laughter, despite his gunshot wounds. 'You, Grant, you are so good you could not even stop me from killing your family. What a celebration that was. Beats a good kick in the balls any day.'

A stony silence fell in the room, broken by Mansour who said, 'Yes, my brother is in prison because of you, but your family is dead because of me.' His next burst of laughter finished in a scream of pain as Richard shot him in the groin.

Ignoring the screaming, writhing figure on the floor, Richard returned his attention to his friend and started to clean his injuries as best he could.

Whilst he worked, he realised that the programme on the television had changed and turned his head to look at the screen. What he saw made his blood run cold.

The television commentator was standing in brilliant sunshine in front of the Château of Versailles, and Richard suddenly realised what the proposed target was to be. As he watched, he saw the television cameras inside the château, showing the huge number of politicians gathering together in the Battles Room.

Reaching into his pocket, he took out his telephone and quickly found the number of the Twat, Thompson. He was relieved when the call was answered on the second ring. 'Thompson,' Richard said, 'I believe you are one of the guests at the meeting in Versailles today. Is that correct?'

'I do not know how you obtain your information, Grant,' replied the oily voice of Thompson, 'but as a matter of fact I am. What can I do for you? Collect an autograph or two?' This last was followed by sardonic laughter.

'Listen, and listen well. I believe that something terrible and earth shattering is going to happen there today. I beg you, for once, use your position and authority and evacuate the building as quickly as possible as you are all in grave danger.'

'You are even more stupid than I thought,' replied Thompson. 'There are so many security people here, no one not invited could get within a mile of the place. I have always said you were an alarmist, but you are worse. You are a used up has been, Grant, so piss off, and leave those that are capable, to do the jobs at hand.' With that, Thompson cut the communication.

Richard could only stand and stare at the silent telephone in his hand. 'The stupid, stupid twat,' he whispered to himself, then turned and faced Mansour on the ground.

'What is to happen' Richard asked Mansour, who replied by saying 'Go fuck yourself.' Richard again fired, the bullet smashing Mansour's other knee.

More screams of pain and agony filled the room, but Richard was completely unmoved. You will tell me' he said, 'or your suffering will get worse.'

'Did you love your wife? Do you miss her?' taunted Mansour, and was rewarded when his left elbow dissolved into mushy bone and flesh.

Finally, Mansour seemed to lapse into unconsciousness and Richard called his office, telling his security officer to contact Marcel Polidor and tell him that the proposed target was to be at Versailles.

# CHAPTER 51

Wahid and his friend Umar were seated in the bar across from the railway station, eating a leisurely snack and watching the preparations for the meeting on the television. The television commentator was inside the Battles Room, interviewing any politician who would talk to him. Soon, the meeting would start and already the room was nearly full.

The commentator announced that the Heads of State of each of the member Countries, were in the process of taking their places on the raised dais at one end of the room. Silence started to fall, as the European President rose to his feet and approached the battery of microphones in order to deliver his historic speech, welcoming Turkey into the European Community.

Wahid, seeing the President about to begin his speech, reached into his pocket and took out a portable telephone. He nodded his head to Umar, who got to his feet and went to the toilet, carrying a small back pack in his hand. Returning a minute later, without the backpack, he sat opposite Wahid and started to open the large rucksack which was on the floor between them.

The President started to speak, and the people in the bar fell silent to listen to him, whilst Wahid dialled a number on his telephone. Several seconds later, an enormous explosion was heard, the televisions went blank and outside could be heard sirens and people shouting. Umar, meanwhile, had taken from the rucksack two Uzi sub machine guns and, after handing one to Wahid, started to spray the interior of the bar with bullets.

Screams of pain were heard as pandemonium broke out in the bar, people diving to the floor to try to escape from the blazing guns. Umar stopped firing, grabbed the rucksack and shouting 'Allah Akhbar' raced from the bar accompanied by Wahid. Some twenty yards from the bar, the bomb that Umar had left in the toilets exploded, destroying the bar and all those inside it.

The two men ran swiftly towards their secondary target, the Cathedral St. Louis, some four hundred yards away. As they ran they saw smoke billowing out from the Château, and they could hear the sound of sustained gunfire coming from the same direction.

Grinning to each other, Wahid and Umar raced into the square in front of the Cathedral, noticing that the huge doors were open and that dozens of people were standing on the Cathedral steps, absolutely bewildered. Shouting, the two men recharged their weapons and once again opened fire, cutting down the people massed in front of them. They raced into the Cathedral still shooting and Wahid took out another prepared bomb from his rucksack and hurled it onto the altar. The two men then retraced their steps, racing through the Cathedral and down the steps, leaping over inert bodies and slipping in pools of blood.

The bomb thrown by Wahid exploded, shattering the altar and the beautiful stained glass windows.

Outside to the right of the Cathedral, was the statue to 'L'Abbé de L'Epée', 'the Abbot of the Sword', and Wahid could not refrain from placing a piece of plastic explosive with a twenty second detonator and blowing the statue to pieces.

The two men continued running until they came to their car, which had been parked some distance from the action on a large, municipal car park.

Throwing their guns and unused explosives into the car, they drove away in the direction of the motorway, leaving behind them death and destruction on a scale not seen since the Second World War. As they drove away, heavy fighting was still going on around the Château, but they had other plans and were intent on putting as much distance between themselves and Versailles as they could.

# CHAPTER 52

Lord Hamilton appeared to be in shock and had lost some blood, but not as much as Mansour. He was pitiful to behold, but Richard felt complete indifference.

To think that this blubbering, bleeding mess on the floor had deprived him of the woman he loved, the children he cherished, all for some mad scheme about World domination.

But was it a mad scheme or was there some hope of success? Mansour, had been very confident earlier that what was to take place would have Global consequences. What was the final plan?

The television was still broadcasting in the Arab language and Richard noticed that the image had changed and that the cameras were now inside the Château.

He could see various members of Governments, some of whom he knew, milling around inside a large, sparse room, with huge paintings adorning the walls. A movement caught his eye and he saw Mansour, though obviously in great pain, straining to see the television screen.

'I've won,' cried Mansour,' for you did not kill me and even though I may not live, I shall live to see the beginning of the end.' He broke down in a fit of coughing and then said, 'You see Grant, I've won, your wife and fam . . . .'

The last word was never finished as Richard put a bullet right between his eyes, thus silencing him forever.

A silence fell on the room as the television commentator stopped speaking, and Richard saw the President of the European Community approaching a battery of microphones, clutching his speech in his right hand. He was wearing a huge smile, obviously pleased by something, but as he started to speak there was a loud explosion and the television screen went blank.

Richard turned and saw that Lord Hamilton was also looking at the screen. Suddenly, the screen came back to life, only this time there was a newscaster, surrounded by armed Arabs, all of whom were smiling and obviously happy about something.

He picked up the remote control for the television and started to zap through the channels, stopping when he saw a well known, coloured broadcaster, surrounded by heavily armed, mainly young Arabs, all of whom seemed to be excited.

Turning up the sound, he heard, 'you will come to no harm if you do not interfere. This is a popular uprising by oppressed young people who want a say in the way their lives are run. So stay indoors. Keep your televisions switched to this channel. You will be kept informed of the progress of this popular movement.'

Richard was stunned. This was happening in London only minutes after the incident in Versailles. He looked at Lord Hamilton who was staring slack jawed at the television screen.

Reaching into his pocket he took out his telephone and speed-dialled his office. 'What the hell is happening,' he cried, when the phone was answered.

He listened intently and then said, 'Can you get an armed team over to the Home Office. The Home Secretary has been injured and requires urgent medical attention.'

He listened for several more seconds, then replaced the telephone in his pocket. Going to the window, he saw very little movement, but on opening a window, he could hear small arms fire and explosions, similar to those of hand grenades. As he looked he heard the sound of racing engines and suddenly an armoured troop carrier and ambulance turned into Marsham Street, screeching to a halt outside the Home Office. Heavily armed soldiers raced into the building, whilst others protected the medical team which was leaving the ambulance.

'My Lord, I do believe the cavalry has arrived,' and he was rewarded by a wan smile. He went to the door and opened it, shouting 'In here.' Several seconds later he was joined by an army officer and two soldiers who were with the medical team.

'Looks like you have been fighting your own private war in here,' stated the army officer, quickly appraising the situation. One of the medical team looked at the body of Mansour and said, 'Nothing to be done for him,' and appeared shocked when Richard, in a low menacing tone said, 'If only you could rescucitate him I would have the pleasure of shooting him again. That', indicating the body on the floor, 'is responsible for all that is happening at the moment. I want you to leave the body exactly where it is. He won't be going anywhere now.'

The medical team looked strangely at Richard and the doctor in the team asked if he needed anything. 'Only for Lord Hamilton to receive the finest treatment possible. He is a true hero, a very courageous man, who stood up to that,' once again indicating the body on the floor. 'As for me, I have felt better, but there is much to be done. Can you transport me to my office in Trafalgar Square, as I fear that what is happening here, is happening all over Europe.'

Seeing that his friend was now in good hands, Richard, accompanied by the army officer, raced for the staircase and was soon safely protected inside an armoured personnel carrier.

The vehicle raced through the streets, occasionally firing and receiving fire, from hidden gunmen. 'We'll sort those boyos out,' said the officer, 'as soon as the support arrives. There has been a lot of indiscriminate killing in the centre of London, the main shopping areas having been particularly hard hit.'

Arriving at his office, Richard was made to wait whilst the area was secured and only then was he escorted into the building. He could hear shouts coming from what he called his operations room, and on entering found several members of his staff either on the telephone or on the private radio to his armed teams somewhere in the City.

'Thank goodness, you are here at last. There's mayhem all over the Country, but especially here in London. It is as though an Arab army has invaded us,' cried one of the staff. Richard replied, 'Basically, that is what has happened.'

Taking his master plan from a drawer in his desk, Richard called to one of his female operatives. 'You will be responsible for liaising with the various persons named in the different European countries, as what is happening here is almost certainly happening there as well. Select a few people to help you as this, until controlled, can be best described as a European war.

One of my assistants will be joining you shortly in order to try to co-ordinate actions throughout Europe, especially with a view to helping those countries who may not have the forces that we have here. Having said that, it is far from a forgone conclusion that we will win, as we have no idea of the strength of the opposition.'

More people started to arrive and Richard left his deputy in charge, to organise the office staff in such a way that as much information could be received and transmitted as quickly as possible to those in need of that information.

Seeing that everything was slowly being controlled in the office, Richard went into his own office and changed from his suit into camouflage army clothing, not forgetting to equip himself with the finest body armour available.

Returning to the main office, he quickly sought out the army officer who had earlier transported him to the building.

'How long will it take to get to the television station transmitting that rubbish?' he asked, 'as it is vital we stop those transmissions and replace them with our own.'

'If we leave now, say ten minutes,' replied the army officer, leading the way from the office, followed by Richard.

Parked outside was a Warrior Infantry Fighting Vehicle, a very fast, flexible means of transport. Armed with a turret mounted 30mm. Rarden cannon and equipped with eight 94mm HEAT rockets, it's armour plating would make it a very fearsome weapon against lightly armed terrorists. Once installed, Richard could only marvel at the speed, as they rushed away to the television studios.

Chaos was everywhere, vehicles having been abandoned, bodies littering the streets and footpaths, and fires burning in vehicles and buildings.

Small groups of young, armed Islams were to be seen, but they soon dived for cover as the gunner in the Warrior's turret opened fire on them.

Several minutes later they arrived in front of the television studios, only to find blazing vehicles parked in front of the main doors and were met by automatic fire coming from the interior of the building. Without slowing, the Warrior mounted the pavement, literally shrugged aside the blazing vehicles and smashed straight through the main doors of the television building. The turret gunner was raking the entrance lobby with machine gun fire and Richard saw several of the opposition falling to the ground, obviously having been hit by the hail of bullets.

The vehicle continued, smashing its way into the television studios, where the Islamic forces were in the process of transmitting their emissions urging the civilian population to surrender to them. A well aimed burst of fire soon put a stop to their broadcasting.

Leaping from the vehicle with the officer and four men, Richard started a search of the television studios. There were endless bodies strewn around the building, but in a second floor store room, they found a group of television personnel who had barricaded themselves so successfully, that the terrorists had been unable to get to them.

A quick search of the building, revealed that the terrorists had either fled or been killed.

Richard's radio crackled into life and he heard his deputy transmitting information, hundreds, if not thousands dead or badly wounded and firefights going on all over the City centre.

'Is there anyone here who can prepare a broadcast?' asked Richard.

'We are all technicians,' replied one of the rescued men, 'and provided they haven't sabotaged everything, we should be able to get things up and running in about a half hour. Before we start though, are you sure the building is clear of that lot,' he asked pointing to the lifeless terrorist bodies on the floor.

The Army officer instructed his men, and after ensuring that the entrance was securely protected, the others began a search of the building.

Richard went into an adjoining office in order to contact his office to obtain an up to date state of affairs.

# CHAPTER 53

Wahid, who was driving, was bubbling over with excitement, reliving the explosion and the subsequent killings. Umar, who was seated in the back of the car was just as boisterous as he recharged their automatic weapons and readied the grenades, for when a suitable target appeared. All passing cars were targets for the duo and they had possibly killed or wounded many more with their indiscriminate shooting.

'Look', shouted Umar,' the autoroute for Paris is coming up shortly. Let's head into Paris and join our Brothers in the fight for Islam.'

Wahid drove into a left hand bend and, as he came out of the bend, he saw a roundabout some three hundred yards ahead. Standing at the side of the road, close to the roundabout, was a group of armed gendarmes. 'What a target,' shouted Umar, lowering the window of the car and levelling his sub machine gun.

The round-about was of a type that the French love to build, with flower beds and huge rocks, topped with a small copse of trees. Increasing speed, Wahid broke into maniacal laughter shouting to Umar, 'They are all yours.'

Umar started to fire and the gendarmes dived for cover. In his exhuberance, Wahid failed to notice that there was an addition to the round-about in the form of an AML Panhard four wheel drive personnel carrier sitting amongst the trees on the top of the round-about. This vehicle, known as an M3, contained three men and two turret mounted twenty millimetre cannons. Before Wahid and Umar realised, the two cannons opened fire at point blank range, thus despatching the two terrorists to whatever hell awaited them.

-o-o-o-o-o-o-o-

'Richard,' said the voice of Marcel Polidor, as Richard lifted the telephone to his ear, 'what a fucking mess.'

'Marcel, take your time and tell me all you can about what's happened in Versailles. Here all hell has broken loose with thousands of young so called armed terrorists, creating mayhem. Fortunately, we were ready for something and the armed services are heavily engaged with the Police, but it will be touch and go. We have even called upon armed helicopters, but their use is very limited in urban warfare. To date, we have not called upon the Air Force, but they have received calls for help from Kosovo and Albania. These requests are being assessed at this moment by my office team and the London military commanders. So what gives over the water?'

'I have seen the inside of hell, and I can tell you that it is not a pretty sight. Who would have thought they would have attacked the Château of Versailles with all that security around it. Fuck it! Twenty eight countries invited as guests to my Country, to participate in what should have been an historical occasion. Instead of celebrating they are all dead.'

Silence followed as Richard tried to understand fully what Marcel was saying. Finally, he broke the silence.

'Are you saying that all those Government members, all what, say two and a half thousand men and women, are all dead? How, what on earth has happened?'

Richard could practically hear Marcel's brain whirring as he prepared his reply. All around him in the television studio, preparations were under way for a broadcast, and Richard could still hear automatic gunfire and the occasional explosion.

'Someone, somehow, managed to introduce an enormous bomb into the very centre of the Battles Room inside the Château and, when the European President rose to make what should have been an historic address, the bomb exploded.

Going by the damage we are estimating a device of at least a ton of very powerful explosive.'

'There must have been hundreds of Police, Army and other forms of security present. How could anyone have planted a bomb that size?' asked Richard, astounded by this announcement.'

'At this moment in time,' continued Marcel, 'we do not know. What we do know is that the force of the explosion was such, that the whole central area of the Battles Room was destroyed, creating an enormous hole in the floor and causing the remains of the roof to fall inside the room. The outer walls which are nearly four feet thick have been breached in several places, as have the interior walls. There may be the odd survivor, but I doubt it.

I can honestly say that I do not wish ever again to witness a scene such as that in Versailles. Imagine, between two and three thousand people were in or around the Battles Room when the explosion occurred. The whole side of the building is destroyed, with body parts littering the gardens. Streams of blood are running down the broken walls and the mess inside is horrendous. Imagine, if you possibly can, all those bodies, shattered or simply ripped apart, the blood, the stench . . . .' Here his voice cracked and a heavy silence fell.

Finally, Richard asked, 'And you say there are no survivors? Twenty eight Goverments destroyed, just like that?'

'To date, we cannot say, as following the explosion, most of the security forces rushed towards the Château. As you can imagine at an event such as this, there were huge crowds of sightseers standing on the car parks in front of the Château and, when the explosion happened, absolute panic broke out. It was then that the secondary problem started.'

'Secondary problem, what are you talking about?'

'Obviously, the explosion was the signal for a huge, vicious, completely unexpected attack by at least three hundred heavily armed terrorists. They were disguised as ordinary tourists, many with bag packs, which, as we saw afterwards; were used to carry their arms, including grenades. Do you know the amount of damage that can be done by three hundred, well armed and determined young men, to a huge, civilian, unarmed crowd. There are hundreds if not thousands dead or dying.

The security forces were taken by complete surprise and many of them were killed, before they could organise any form of resistance. Naturally, the 'Terror' programme had been activated and at the moment the biggest problems are here in Paris, with Marseille also being heavily engaged in guerilla warfare. Lyon, Bordeaux and other large towns have also got problems. At the moment we are trying a policy of containment as we have no idea how many of the enemy there are. They are well armed, but we do not know if they have substantial reserves of ammunition.

I have spoken to Werner in Germany and the same thing is happening over there. They are holding their own at the moment, but he says there is a lot of opposition, very determined, who have already created panic and havoc within the civilian population, by their indiscriminate killing of civilians. They have attacked obviously prearranged targets, City centres, supermarkets and sporting events. The body count will be very, very heavy.

Werner tells me, and I think it may not be a bad idea, that they are placing a huge amount of faith that the terrorists supply lines may be slim to non existent. They are engaging all armed groups as soon as they come across them, forcing them into firefights in the hope that they will run out of ammunition.'

'Are your television services working?' asked Richard, and, on hearing that his friend did not know, he suggested that he find out and try to put out a broadcast advising the public on what they could and should do.

'Ready when you are, Mr. Grant,' said the television technician, and Richard realised that he had forgotten all about the television as he tried to digest the news that Marcel had supplied him.

'How far will this broadcast go?' asked Richard, 'will it cover all Europe or is it just local?'

'This will give National coverage, but we can, if we receive the necessary authorisation and help, extend the transmissions to cover the whole of Europe.'

'Let us get this first transmission going. Can you record it and let it play ad infinitum? Those poor bastards out there haven't got a chance in hell if we cannot reach them and help them.'

'If you would stand over there,' said the technician, indicating a chalk mark on the floor, 'we can get started. Have you prepared a speech or something?'

'No prepared speech,' replied Richard, 'but I will be very brief and to the point.'

'Then after ten,' said the technician, as he started the countdown with his fingers.

Ten seconds later, Richard Grant's grimy, blood streaked face was being beamed throughout Great Britain. His face was heavily lined and the signs of strain were there for all to see.

'Fellow citizens,' he began, 'we are faced with a unique and very, very dangerous situation. Earlier today in Versailles in France, a bomb exploded killing all the members of all twenty eight European Governments plus the European Ministers and deputies. This explosion was apparently the signal for a well organised terrorist attack throughout Europe and as I speak heavy fighting is taking place in many European towns and Cities. In short, we are at war.

Those of you in your homes, stay there. Protect your families. Barricade your doors and windows and arm yourselves with whatever you can. Do not try to go outside, even if others are in danger, as you will simply endanger yourselves. If you have an arm, load it and, if necessary, shoot to kill. You will not have to fear any form of prosecution if you should kill any of this vermin that is currently attacking us.

We, the security forces, will soon be with you, but until then keep your heads down. I have always believed in honesty and I will be honest with you.

When this is over, there will be hundreds of thousands dead and injured. Do not add to this number. For all those persons who are not at home, form groups and try to barricade yourselves wherever you can, in cellars, secure buildings or public buildings where security forces are present.

Good luck to you all. With God's help we will prevail.'

'For an off the cuff speech, that was brilliant,' said the technician. 'I will now set it to automatic replay and it will play non-stop until further notice.'

Thanking him for his assistance and kind words, Richard called to the Army officer, asking if he could secure the broadcasting station and return him, Richard to his office.

Five minutes later, the armoured personnel carrier was making the return trip to Trafalgar Square. Joining the officer in the turret, Richard saw a scene of death and desolation, and ducked as the occasional shot was fired at them. A small group of armed Arabs suddenly appeared, running from a block of flats towards a group of shops a little further down the road. The gunner in the turret at the side of Richard switched to automatic fire and stitched a line of bullets into the armed group. Some fell, others tried to avoid the flying bullets, but the gunner, who had served long years fighting urban guerillas calmly continued firing until they were all on the ground, unmoving. Nothing was said, no congratulations uttered. This was war.

On arriving at his office, Richard was quickly appraised of the present situation. He called to the Army officer, who, when he had asked earlier, had simply said, 'Call me Ted', and Ted came over to where Richard was sitting.

'From what I can gather, Ted,' said Richard, after indicating a nearby chair, 'is that this is obviously a very well planned attack and appears to be basically a declaration of war, much as the same as Japan at Pearl Harbour. There are armed groups of terrorists attacking military and civilian installations throughout Europe, and they are causing panic in public places, shopping centres etc. by their determined if somewhat senseless, indiscriminate killing.

Whilst I am contacting my men, can you get onto your Army boys and see what the situation is like there?'

Without a word, Ted jumped to his feet and hurried away, returning some twenty minutes later, with a sheaf of papers in his hand. Calling to Richard, the two men returned to Richard's office, and regained their seats.

'There is a lot of confusion, but as you have stated, there are many hundreds, if not thousands of young terrorists armed mainly with light arms and grenades, although there are some with grenade launchers, hand held missile launchers and even a flamethrower. They appear to be organised into squads and most of them are in cars or vans, although some, those mainly in the centre of London, appear to be on foot.

Those buildings which we managed to protect, Buckingham Palace and the main central Government buildings, are safe and sound, for though they have all been attacked, the attackers withdrew when they saw that the defences were strong. This indicates that they have some sort of communication system and possibly a control centre somewhere.'

Richard intervened. 'Can we find this centre, if it does indeed exist?'

'Orders have gone out and patrols are being posted at many important junctions, in the rôle of observers. We hope that these patrols may spot a pattern in the movements of these terrorists, which could help lead us to their control centre. For the moment, there is very little else we can do, but we are getting more and more men out into the streets. Unfortunately, they have been well trained to fight in Afghanistan, but who would have thought we would one day be fighting in Central London.'

'My men are also trying to find who is controlling this debacle. The only positive note of hope at the moment, is that many of these groups, although heavily armed, are poorly led. We must continue to liaise together and, perhaps we may have a chance of thwarting them, but that is far from certain at this moment in time.'

Ted shuffled the papers in his hand and, looking at Richard said, 'There is one very grave problem and that is Heathrow Airport. Apparently the terrorists attacked in great force, by entering the underground parking system and then erupting into the terminals. They have seized control of the control tower and all the planes waiting to land at Heathrow must do so, because they literally do not have any alternative as all Europe is under attack.'

A silence fell as the two men tried to picture what could happen in the event of a major plane incident on top of everything else.

'The main problem,' said Ted, 'is that the terrorists are allowing the planes to land and then ordering them to park their planes on the airport perimeter. Once parked, they are attaching explosives to the planes and instructing the flight crews that any attempt to escape or cause any form of trouble, will result in the destruction of their planes.'

'What a set of bastards.' The words exploded from Richard's mouth. 'The other passengers at the airport, what's happened to them?'

'Quite a number were killed or wounded in the initial attack and apparently the others with airport personnel and those who work there in the shops etc. have all been herded onto the upper floor of Terminal five. There are one or two terrorists with them, but the main group is on the ground floor of the terminal buildings or in the control tower or administration buildings.'

'You appear to be very well informed,' said Richard. 'How do you do it?'

'Thanks to your early warning, a team of commandos were installed somewhere, and even I do not know where, in the airport. Their brief is to watch and report and that is what they are doing. Undoubtedly, if we ever get the chance to attack, they will be in a position to help and guide us.'

'Hey, Richard, come and look at this,' shouted the voice of one of his assistants. Richard and Ted rose as one and went into the main control room, where they saw the staff gathered round a television set. Pushing his way through the crowd, Richard saw on the screen, the face of one of the World's most wanted persons, an aged Arab with a long beard, known as 'The President.'

He was speaking. 'Peoples of Europe, stop your useless opposition and surrender your armed services to our soldiers. In that way, further killing can be avoided. Should you wish to continue, then your deaths will be on your hands as you have been forewarned.

This moment in time has taken many centuries to reach, but the time is now nigh. Islam will rule over Europe and soon, over all the World. We are unstoppable. So lay down your arms and surrender in order to avoid further bloodshed.'

The screen went dead and silence descended on the room, as each thought of the consequences which could follow.

# CHAPTER 54

A few miles away in the Broadway Shopping Centre on Hammersmith Broadway, five young terrorists, the eldest just nineteen years of age, and their leader, an Algerian freedom fighter aged twenty six, were staring transfixed at two banks of television screens inside one of the centres shops.

On one bank, was the head of their leader making his speech and, on the other bank, Richard making his. All six of them were gorging themselves on food they had taken from Tescos inside the centre.

All six were well pleased with their work so far.

Having received orders to attack the shopping centre, they had arrived at about two thirty in the afternoon, by way of the underground car park. On reaching the ground floor, they had started throwing hand grenades into the crowded shops, causing immediate panic and many deaths. They followed this up with indiscriminate bursts of automatic fire, spraying the whole ground floor area killing dozens more.

Luckily, their leader was not the brightest of individuals, and he insisted that the six of them remain together. This decision, allowed many who were on the other floors to escape. Now, as they ate they studied the carnage inside the shopping centre and commented on the amount of damage they had done in such a short time.

With the exception of the squad leader, the five terrorists were all examples of the present day youth.

A secondary education, leisure hours filled with video games, where they killed enormous quantities of whatever the enemy was, or time spent in the mean London streets where they could indulge themselves in senseless violence, often four or five against one, they were no different from other youths throughout Europe. The only thing that set them aside, was that they were all born in England.

After they had listened and commented on the speech of their leader, they turned their attention to Richard. At the end of his short speech, the squad leader undid his fly and started to urinate on the screened face of Richard. Laughing uproariously, the others followed suit. They then left the shop and as they were heading to the underground car park, the leader sensed a movement. Turning, he fired a quick burst and the movement seized.

This movement had been caused by an injured child trying to find its' mother, which seemed extremely funny to the terrorists.

They regained their stolen estate car and drove up onto Hammersmith Broadway. As they emerged onto The Broadway, they were spotted by an army team in an unmarked Ford van. Keeping a distance, they followed the car, calling for assistance, as there was very little trafic about. Soon there were four vehicles relaying each other as they followed the estate car to Canary wharf. There, the estate car drove into a huge warehouse complex.

Each of the following vehicles found a place where they could remain undetected, whilst one vehicle parked in such a way as to observe the entrance to the complex.

During the next two hours, they counted more than a hundred vehicles entering, and then leaving. Certain that they had located a command centre, this knowledge was relayed to Army Command.

-o-o-o-o-o-o-o-

In the meanwhile, Richard, with his team of assistants and advisers, were drawing up plans of containment, as information started to come in from the various teams who were patrolling whilst trying to evade contact with the enemy.

'There is little point in being drawn into a firefight,' he proclaimed, much to himself as to anyone else, 'as we have no idea of their strengths or weaknesses, or indeed what their final intentions are. We have all heard the broadcast and from what I can understand, we are already receiving calls from the defeatists, the racial societies and general do gooders, who would rather hand Europe over to a bunch of Arabs, than fight for their liberty and freedom.

'We are going to fight, but before we must glean as much information as possible. The moment we have something to go on, we shall act and act very fast.' He looked at the people around him, different races, different colours but with a sole aim, defeating Al Qaida. 'I love 'em all,' he thought to himself and was brought back to reality when a telephone was thrust into his hand.

'Waring here,' shouted the voice of the Army General Staff, 'may just have a little titbit to nibble on.'

'Anythings better than nothing, Oliver,' said Richard, somewhat warily. 'Do you want to share it with us?'

'We're all in this together old boy,' replied Oliver, 'and I owe this lot something if for no other reason than my old mucker Hamilton. He's going to be all right, but it will take time; the bastards worked him over pretty well.'

'Only one bastard did that and he is now out of action on a permanant basis,' replied Richard. 'So tell me, what have you got?'

Oliver Waring cleared his throat before replying. 'One of our spotter teams may have found one of their control centres down on Canary Wharf. They are sorting themselves out at the moment, but these are infiltration specialists and they will undoubtedly gain access at some time and give us the feedback. I have readied an assault team, backed up by missile carrying helicopters and wondered if you would like to come along for the ride.'

'That's very kind of you, but surely you are . . .

'I am what. For years my Government masters have ordered me to remain behind in command, whereas in reality it was to take the blame when the shit hit the fan. Now my masters are no longer here and this dog is off the leash. You coming or not?'

Laughing delightedly, Richard replied, 'Just try to keep me away. How long will you be?'

'With you in twenty minutes. If you have any of your special brew available, stick a few bottles in a bag. We don't have the same expenses as you civvies,' he chortled.

Smiling to himself, Richard asked, 'How do you know about the special brew?' I have only a few cases of Black Bottle left.'

'There are no secrets in London and as we share the same friend, need I say more?'

Richard quickly formed a squad, including Arab speakers, and they started to prepare for combat. He also issued orders for an update on what was happening elsewhere.

Twenty minutes later a small column of armoured vehicles arrived, and Richard could not resist a smile as he noticed Oliver Waring was taking a particular interest in the two cartons of whisky he was placing in their transport.

The column drove at speed and once again Richard noticed the piles of bodies littering the roads and footpaths and the numerous abandoned vehicles making driving difficult. There was the occasional shot, but nothing to cause them any worry.

Ten minutes later, the column pulled into an empty parking lot, some three hundred yartds from the supposed control centre. He joined Oliver who was talking into a chest held microphone. After a few seconds, he terminated his conversation and turned to Richard. 'My boys are spot on. The warehouse is full of arms and ammunition and security appears to be very lax. They will approach on foot and when they are in an attacking position, they will whistle up the cavalry, that being us. We shall drive at full speed into the complex and hope to take them all out by surprise.'

A few minutes later the call came and with a theatrical wave of his hand, Oliver signalled the attack. The column shot forward and were soon bursting full speed into the warehouse compound. Several motor cars and vans were parked, and these received very short shrift as did the bemused terrorists inside the complex.

The fight lasted a few minutes and terminated with the attacking force unscathed and the terrorist force lying dead. They quickly checked the stock of arms and ammunition, noting that in the main they appeared to have come from Eastern Europe. 'Destroy the lot', instructed Oliver, and the engineers soon had the whole complex wired. The attacking forces withdrew and the complex was completely destroyed.

'That's why we pay insurance,' said Richard and Oliver replied with a laugh that the no claims bonus would be most likely forfeited.

On returning to his office, Richard learned that reports were coming in from all over Europe. Turkey had requested assistance and Germany had readily sent forces to help. France, who have a very big Arab population were experiencing some difficulties, but Marcel assured Richard that with the help of the armed services, he believed that they would prevail. However, as with Richard, certain parts of the Country were in favour of surrendering to the terrorists.

'Not much change from the attitudes in the last war,' said Marcel. 'Anything for a quiet life, but I am convinced that the people do not understand what the Arabs mean, when they speak of World Domination. I cannot see my fellow countrymen accepting the Sharia and I certainly cannot see the women agreeing to be veiled for the rest of their lives.'

'What of the ongoing situation regarding the terrorists?' asked Richard. 'Are you gaining ground or what?'

'Very difficult to say,' replied Marcel, 'as we have no idea how many they are. We are engaging groups in firefights, but it is a very tiresome business and we are taking casualties. Night is coming on and we shall have to see what the morning brings. We are keeping our fingers crossed, but I can say there are huge casualty figures.'

'Do you need any extra help?', queried Richard, and was pleased when Marcel said he thought they could cope.

He then contacted the hospital to enquire after Lord Hamilton, and was pleased when they said he was now sleeping soundly and out of danger.

# CHAPTER 55

Night had fallen, and the sounds of fighting died away. Realising that the enemy had obviously been instructed to lie low during the night, Richard issued similar orders so that his men could be fed and rest time arranged. He was just about to go to eat when the telphone rang.

'Oliver here,' shouted the voice of the Army,'want to come across. We are working on a plan to liberate the Heathrow Airport and wondered if you would like to accompany us?'

'Just going to get a bite to eat,' replied Richard, whereupon Oliver said, 'Get your arse across here. There's loads of grub for everyone'.

Ensuring that everything was under control in the office, Richard called his active forces team together in order to go and enjoy some Army hospitality.

-o-o-o-o-o-o-o-

Zafran Razaq was ensconced in his control centre at the bottom of the garden. In a large brick built building, housing his gardening tools and mini tractor, he was busily engaged in operating his state of the art communications equipement. His excitement knew no bounds as report after report came in detailing successes throughout Europe.

Mansour had proclaimed that the element of surprise was the one major card in their pack and that appeared to be so true.

Nearly every pre-planned target had been taken, and the death toll was horrendous. Zafran had no sympathy whatsoever for the victims, as he remembered only the losses he had borne when living in Pakistan. In common with most of the Islamic extremists, his one thought was of power and domination.

Suddenly, his very private telephone shrilled.

On answering, he heard the voice of The President asking for an update of the state of affairs in the various European countries. Proudly, he exclaimed that nearly all targets had been seized and the main airports were all under their control.

'In that case,' said The President, 'I shall make arrangements to fly across tomorrow with the Council. There is much to be done and if we do it quickly and efficiently, the other major powers will leave us alone. Tell your nephew he has done well and he shall be rewarded for his work.'

Zafran was pleased for his nephew, but felt constrained to say that he had no idea of his whereabouts. 'That is typical of the youngsters today,' replied The President, 'Do not worry for he has much to do before we can sleep safely.' 'Now, tell me, can you arrange everything for tomorrow, my friend.'

'You know you can count on me,' replied Zafran. 'I will arrange a reception fit for a World Leader.'

-o-o-o-o-o-o-o-

When they had finished eating, Oliver drew Richard aside and said, 'Come up into Control, there is something we must work on.' Together, the two men entered the Control and Richard was amazed to see a huge gathering of generals and other General Office Staff.

An RAF officer had the floor and he was talking of a planned airborne invasion on Heathrow Airport. Apparently, the spotter group in place at the airport had managed to gain access. to Terminal five and had identified the terrorist group, the majority of whom were now sleeping on the ground floor, whilst a minimal group patrolled the alleys on the ground floor of the terminal. They appeared to be heavily armed, but very young and their leaders, although older, did not appear to be much of a match for the British Army soldiers.

It had been decided that the planned attack would commence at three o'clock in the morning, when resistance was at its lowest. Two hundred and fifty paratroopers would land on the airport and take up position around the Terminal Five. The terrorists had erected floodlighting all along the perimeter fence, the effect of which was to leave the runway and plane parking areas in near total blackness.

Several sentries had been posted, but their positions were identified and they would be taken out when the attack began. Heavily camouflaged foot soldiers would be rushed into the airport through the main entrances as the first of the paratroopers landed on the airport. It was hoped that the element of surprise would this time work in their favour.

At midnight, Richard and Oliver were waiting to greet the soldiers who would make up the main attacking force. 'Say a few words to them,' urged Oliver and Richard said, 'Why me?'

'Since you made that impassioned speech on the television, you have become the latest, rising star. Like it or not, the public are looking to you to save them and therefore you should get all the practice you can in public speaking. Your audience,' said Oliver, indicating the massing soldiers, 'are waiting.'

Richard was dumbstruck as he had never sought the limelight, but now it seemed he was to be thrust into it, whether he liked it or not. Banging on a table in an attempt to bring a little order, he was surprised just how quickly the noise ceased.

'Gentlemen' he started, before realising that their were female soldiers present. Coughing to hide his embarrassement, he started again.

'Ladies and gentlemen, your attention please for a few moments. You are all aware of what has happened today and of the horrendous number of casualties. I am sure that there is not a family in Great Britain who has not been touched by what has happened. Wars happen, but when the enemy is of the same nationality, it adds an extra dimension.

However, this is not a revolution, but a war based on religion. Unfortunately, many wars in the past have been fought on religious grounds, but this one is one fought by religious fanatics who dream of World Domination. Many of the enemy are young, for as usual the schemers and planners are not amongst the soldiers. They leave the dirty work to others, whilst they wait in the wings to come on stage.

Your job this night is to render these soldiers harmless and the best way to do that is to kill them. What they have done, they have done and they have done it willingly. Throughout Europe today, it is estimated that perhaps as many as one million lives have been lost. The perpetrators are to be punished and their punishment is death. Are there any amongst you not happy with that?'

Richard was pleased when there were no detractors and Oliver ended the meeting by simply saying, 'Go do your duty.'

A meal had been prepared for the combatants and everyone hurried to take a place at the huge tables which had been set up for them.

Soon the room was buzzing with conversation and the occasional burst of laughter, as these young soldiers prepared for war.

# CHAPTER 56

At one o'clock the following morning, the troops took their places in the various transports which had been arranged. Strange to think that this was London and not, Irak, Kosovo or Afghanistan, thought Oliver, as he saw to the loading of the troops. He was once again in his element, in the field and in charge. The years were falling away, and the adrenaline had started to run, just like in the Falkland Islands all those years ago.

Richard allowed himself to be seated, very pleased to have a back seat in this operation, as all things military were very vague to him. Used to giving orders, he did not like to receive them and therefore made himself as small as possible in the larger scheme of things.

During the late evening, more and more observer vehicles had been released onto the streets, and the whole of the route from Central London to Heathrow was under strict observation. In addition, further supply points used by the terrorists had been identified and plans were afoot to hit them all simultaneously as dawn was breaking.

Once night had fallen, the terrorists had apparently all gone to ground. There were occasional skirmishes, but in the main it was relatively calm, with both sides taking stock of their situations and making plans for the morrow.

Finally, the convoy got under way, driving to within a mile of Heathrow, before stopping on one of the surrounding freight warehouse parking lots. They were receiving information from within Terminal Five, most of which seemed to be good. There had been a number of incidents, mainly rape and inane violence, as the various terrorist factions tried to prove they were fighting men.

Information was coming in from the air force who were transporting the paratroopers. Their flights were on time and it was decided that the army ground force would attack as the paratroopers started their descent. In this way, it was hoped that the attacking soldiers would take the brunt of the defensive fire, protected as they were by their armoured transport, allowing the paratroopers to arrive unseen and hopefully, unscathed.

In the end it was easier than they had imagined.

The terrorists inside the Terminal, being in the main untrained and undisciplined, had spent a part of their evening sampling the goods in the duty free shops. As the armoured carriers roared into the Terminal, smashing straight through the plate glass windows and doors, the terrorists did not know what had hit them.

They scrambled for their weapons, but were already being decimated by a withering hail of fire from the attacking soldiers. Some tried to run, but were confronted by paratroopers, all clad in black and all looking for a fight.

Part of the attacking force went straight for the upper levels, in order to better protect the terrified civilians, who had been herded there like so many cattle. One or two explosions were heard and one terrorist managed to get off a missile shot, which immobilised one of the armoured transport carriers, but in the main it was a complete rout.

After twenty minutes all firing had ceased and those lights which were still working were turned on. Additional emergency lighting was brought into play and calls went out for medical teams to treat the injured, of which there were many.

There were also huge numbers of dead bodies and as Oliver and Richard took stock, they were filled with revulsion for those who had perpetrated these acts and those who had planned them.

'What should we do with the prisoners?' asked Oliver, indicating nearly a hundred young men, some of them wounded, who were now standing, all bravado having deserted them, waiting to see what would happen next.

'My first reaction is to simply take them outside and shoot them;' replied Richard, grimly. Pointing at one of the young men he said, 'Where are you from?' and the youth replied 'Camden Town.'

Richard could feel his bile starting to rise, and walked towards the prisoners, pointing at them, saying, 'And you, and you,' hearing the same refrain; they were all English born and bred. He restrained himself, as his greatest urge at that moment in time, was to wade into them, and slap them all to the ground.

'Who is your leader?' he asked, and one of them pointed to a body lying on the ground. 'See if he has any identity on him', Richard instructed and one of his men, after a quick body search, produced an old leather wallet. Inside was a passport issued in Pakistan, showing the holder to be a thirty two year old Pakistani National.

'Others will be along shortly to start the identification processes for all their victims, but I want you,' indicating one of his assistants, 'to be responsible for the identification of this lot, the living and the dead.'

Finally, one of the younger terrorists, with tears streaming down his face, said, 'And us, what will happen to us?'

'What were you feeling when you were killing all these men, women and children?' snarled Richard. 'I bet you thought you were Rambo or some other super hero. Now, you are going to find out what happens to war criminals.'

'We are not war criminals,' replied another of the prisoners, 'it was just for a bit of fun.'

'I hope you have the chance to say that to the relatives of the people you have killed and injured here,' replied Richard. 'As far as I am concerned, the simplest way to deal with you is to take you all outside and shoot you like the mad dogs you are. However, etiquette forbids that and undoubtedly there will be a trial . . . .'

Oliver interrupted Richard, finishing his speech by adding 'and then we will shoot you.' The humour of this remark was lost on the prisoners, who were now contemplating a very short future.

'Telephone for you, Sir,' and one of Richard's aides ran across, saying, 'It's Mr. Polidor.'

'Michel, how are things going over there in France? Do you require any help?'

'For the moment, we are holding our own. No, the reason I rang is because we have discovered what happened in Versailles.'

'That was quick work,' said Richard, 'congratulations.'

'More chance than anything else. Two of these so called terrorists, both of whom were wanted for terrorist activities, attacked a group of gendarmes between Versailles and Paris, and they in turn were killed by the army who were assisting the gendarmes. In their car we found arms and explosives and also reams of paper, all of which refer to bomb manufacture.

'One of the men we believe is the one you named as the Expert after the Madrid bombings. Amongst these papers, there is a very detailed plan of the Battles Room, showing the installation of a magnificent bar, made up of eight sections.

It would appear that the bomb was cleverly installed inside these units.'

'A Trojan Horse, job,' said Richard. 'No wonder no one found the bomb. What is the current state of the various Government ministers who were present?'

'All dead.'

Richard saw one of his aides, frantically trying to draw his attention. 'Got to go Marcel, but I'll be back to you as soon as possible.'

The aide immediately rushed to Richard's side, saying, 'Quickly, Sir, this is important.'

With Oliver following on behind, Richard followed the aide to a secluded part of the ground floor terminal, where he saw an enormous communications lay out. A number of his men, guarded by soldiers, were examining the material and piles of paperwork, which were strewn all over a table.

One of the Urdu speaking aides was involved in a telephone conversation when he said, 'We will be waiting. Allah akhbar.'

Richard's head jerked up at this last expletive, but he noticed that the aide was looking very pleased with himself.

'What was all that about,' asked Richard, and the aide replied, 'That was Pakistan on the telephone. We've found all their codes and their different instructions and, whilst going through them, a telephone call was received from this man.'

The aide handed a piece of paper to Richard, who saw written thereon, 'Balthasar', Basingstoke.

'It would appear,' said the aide, 'that this person is very highly placed on the Council of Al Qaida. 'He rang here a few moments ago to say that the full Council with The President will be flying into Heathrow to take charge of negotiations.'

'There is no way he would come here, knowing that we have retaken the airport,' said Richard.

'That is just the point, he does not know. I have assured him that the terrorist organisation is in full charge and that we are preparing the airport as for visiting Royalty. They should be arriving about three this afternoon.'

'Well done,' cried Richard. 'We'd better get started right away. I would hate to disappoint the Council's first and last visit to England.'

Ensuring that there was no further danger at the airport and that all the people held prisoner in the numerous airliners parked around the airport were safe and sound, Richard returned to his office with his escort. Arrangements had been made for all those terrorists taken prisoner, to be taken to Catterick Army Base in the North of England, where they would be held, not as prisoners of war, but as common criminals and mass murderers.

# CHAPTER 57

Throughout Europe, the fighting continued. France had taken a beating owing to the huge numbers of Islamists present in that Country, who thought that it was the moment to really bite the hand that had been feeding them for years.

Fortunately, Germany and Italy, one because they had so few Islamists and the other because of the huge numbers of Turkish immigrants who had rushed to aid the security forces, having subdued the attacking forces in their Countries, had immediately sent help to France and some of the smaller member States who did not have the structure in place to defend themselves from an inside attack.

Feeling that the end was in sight, Richard contacted his friends to put them into the picture regarding the situation in England and, more importantly, the proposed visit of the full Council of the Al Qaida organisation.

Satisfied that things seemed to be more or less under control, Richard turned his attention to the proposed visit of the Council.

-o-o-o-o-o-o-o-

'So, my good and loyal friend,' said the President to Zafran Razaq, known as 'Balthasar', 'our planning and daring attacks have borne the fruit we had hoped for.'

The telephone connection to Pakistan was very good; and Zafran could feel the old man's pleasure emanating from the telephone in his hand. 'All the suffering and sacrifices made are proving to have been worthwhile and, shortly, the rest of the World will be sitting up and taking notice as they see the flag of Islam flying over Europe.'

Zafran was literally beaming. All the news he had been receiving from throughout Europe and, especially from England, had lifted years from his aging body, and his mind was racing as he thought of the important post he would soon be holding in the new Islamic Europe.

'My President and friend, how soon can you arrive to take control? Your stability will be needed to inject force into our soldiers to complete the many tasks in hand and I am sure that simply by your presence, moral will know no bounds.'

'Patience, Zafran, arrangements are under way for us to fly across in one of our supporters private airliner. From what I understand, with the time differences, we should be at Heathrow at about three o'clock in the afternoon.'

'Then I will see that a suitable reception is on hand to receive you,' replied Zafran, 'and then I can show you my adopted Country.'

'I am handing the telephone to my aide who will give you all the necessary details. In just a few hours, my friend, I will be embracing you. Tell me, how is that nephew of yours? This is his doing and I would like nothing better than for him to be with you to witness our final triumph.'

'For the moment, I do not know of his whereabouts, but owing to the very fluid state of the situation here, he is undoubtedly involved with his troops. Do not worry, he will be there, I promise you.'

A few minutes later, Zafran called his control centre at Heathrow airport. Hearing a voice he did not recognise he said, 'Put Ilyas on please.'

'Ilyas is not here at the moment,' replied the unknown voice, 'he is organising the transferral of command into Central London. Who is on the line and can I help you?' This was all spoken in Urdu as spoken in the Peshawar region of Pakistan.

Excitedly, Zafran said, 'This is Balthasar in Basingstoke. Our leader and the full Council will be arriving at about three o'oclock this afternoon. Tell Ilyas to make suitable arrangements to greet our leaders at the airport and to have transport on hand to take them into London in order that they can examine their new seat of Government.'

'Consider it done,' replied the voice.

Zafran cut the communication and Richard's Urdu speaking aide handed the message to Richard.

-0-0-0-0-0-0-0-

'We have about seven hours to organise a reception committee. Can it be done in time?' Oliver who had accompanied Richard on the ride back intervened. 'For years, we in the Army have been organising this type of reception as visiting dignitaries and our own Ministers just loved the pomp and ceremony. If you like, you can leave this to me. I will arrange a reception to top any reception ever held at Heathrow.'

Smiling, Richard replied, 'You're on. You shall be stage manager and producer and director. Let me know what your plans will be. Everything must be in place, at the latest by two o'clock, so best jump to it.'

Taking his leave, Oliver turned to Richard and took his hand. 'We have only just met, but I feel I have known you for years. I won't let you down.'

After Oliver had departed, Richard, after ensuring that things seemed to be sorting themselves out throughout Europe, called his friend, Chris.

'That has been a very exciting and instructive forty eight hours,' said Chris, who had finally been located at a temporary command post inside a local army barracks. 'It was touch and go for quite a while and if the opposition had been better led I hate to think what could have happened.'

'But you are all right,' said Richard. 'How's Bill?'

'He's about somewhere,' replied Chris. 'Now tell me, what on earth happened to cause all this? There must be hundreds of dead and injured still lying around outside.'

'The same thing happened simultaneously throughout Europe,' said Richard softly, 'and no figures are known at this time, but there could be as many as a million casualities.' He then went on to explain exactly what had happened.

After he had finished his explanation he said, 'Can you get away at the moment and come straight down to my office. There is something going down this afternoon and I would love you to be present. If you cannot come, I will understand, and if you do come, travel in an armoured vehicle as the present state of affairs is still in flux.'

'Try and keep me away,' shouted Chris, 'I should be with you in a couple of hours.'

Richard then contacted Oliver. 'Can you meet me at the Home Secretary's office in thirty minutes? There is something I want to show you'

Half an hour later, the two men were standing in the Home Secretary's office, contemplating the body of Mansour, which was still lying where Richard had left it all those hours ago.

'Smells a bit ripe,' said Oliver, bending over the body. 'Good gracious, look at those injuries. Whoever did this must have had something against him. What's the story?'

Very briefly, Richard related what had taken place in this office all those, how many hours ago.

After listening to Richard's explanation, Oliver said, 'One thing intrigues me. Which shot was the head shot?'

Without blinking, Richard looked Oliver squarely in the eyes and said, 'All of them. I'm very short on practice.'

Richard then explained what he wanted doing with the body and Oliver said, 'Consider it done.'

# CHAPTER 58

'Private flight, PF 1 requests permission to land at Heathrow', said the cultured tones of the pilot carrying the Council to London. 'Estimated arrival time sixteen minutes.'

'Permission granted. After landing please taxi to main airport buildings where the official reception committee will be waiting.'

The President, accompanied by his aide, entered the pilot's cabin. Looking down, he saw acres of greenery, cultivated fields, and extensive woodlands.

'A wonderful change from the sand and rocks of our Country,' he said to no one in particular.

The pilot said, 'We are approaching the airport. There, can you see the flags?'

Going to the other side of the cockpit, the President looked down on a colourful scene of fluttering flags and marquees. There appeared to be some form of military band and a small crowd of people awaiting their arrival. 'You have done well, my friend,' thought the President, thinking back to his earlier conversation with Zafran.

A few minutes later, the plane touched down and taxied to the main buildings, stopping at the side of an enormous red carpet. The door was opened and the President stood in the doorway as the band broke into a well known Victory march.

Smiling, the President descended the stairs and on touching the ground, he knelt and kissed the red carpet. As he rose to his feet, a black Mercedes saloon car with tinted windows, drew up to the carpet at the side of him.

Stepping forward from what he took to be the reception committee, was a well dressed, fifty year old Asian. 'Welcome, President,' said the man, taking the President's hand and kissing it.

'Where is Zafran,' he asked, and was reassured when the man replied, 'He is waiting in the main building with the rest of the reception committee.'

Another man stepped forward and opened the door of the saloon and the President said, 'And my committee, is there no transport for them?'

'There is a vehicle for all of you,' replied the man, indicating a long line of identical Mercedes saloons.

Climbing into the car he settled himself on the huge rear seat, already composing in his mind his greeting for his old friend, Zafran.

The car drove slowly away, passing in front of the band, who were still playing the same tune, and turned behind the main building, and entered an underground parking. The car drew to a halt and the door was opened. The President started to leave the car then stopped, as he saw before him an armed phalanx of very determined looking British soldiers. 'Welcome to England, shithead,' said Oliver stepping forward, indicating to two soldiers to take the President's arms.

'Do you know who I am?' ranted the President, and Oliver replied in very icy tones, 'You are the bastard responsible for all these deaths in the name of your twisted views of your own religion. Do not worry, you will have time to explain before we execute you.'

The two soldiers dragged the President away as the second saloon car entered the parking. Soon, there were forty nine prisoners being held in the car park, some of them internationally known faces. 'Who would have thought,' mused Oliver.

Richard then stepped forward. 'I am Richard Grant and I am very pleased to see you in my Country under these conditions. Come, there is someone waiting to greet you who can explain much more fully your future in this green and pleasant land.'

The President and his council, all now manacled hand and foot, were forced to shuffle forward into an adjoining room, which was in complete darkness. When all were in the room, a single, harsh white spotlight was switched on, revealing the naked, bloody body of Mansour Ahmad.

'There,' said Richard, 'is your future.'

'It has cost us dearly,' said Chris, 'but if this ends the Islamic Domination plans, then perhaps the cost will have been worth it.'

'Oliver, get this shite out of here and ensure that the rules of the Geneva Convention are obeyed to the letter, no more and no less.' With that Richard and Chris left the room to return to London.

-o-o-o-o-o-o-o-

At two o'clock that same day, Zafran drove his car to London, turning off the M3 to reach Heathrow Airport. He was suddenly forced to stop, owing to the presence of a road block manned by armed Police and soldiers.

A police inspector stepped forward, saying, 'Where are you going old man?' and Zafran replied, 'To London. I wanted to know if my family are all right.'

'You cannot go into London at the moment,' said the inspector, 'until we have got this mess sorted out. I'm sorry, but you will have to go back to where you have come from.'

A police constable stepped forward to help Zafran turn and take the road leading back to the M3.

With a heavy heart, Zafran realised that all the years of hope and planning had somehow been thwarted and that now his hopes and dreams would never be fulfilled.

He drove back to his home, arriving an hour and a half later. His wife, surprised to see him, said, 'What are you doing here. You said you were going to London. Is there more trouble?'

Forcing a smile, Zafran said, 'No my little flower. I changed my mind, that's all.'

'You look tired,' said his wife, 'go and sit in your favourite chair and I will make a nice cup of tea.' Turning she started to walk towards the kitchen, and, with tears in his eyes, Zafran looked at the retreating figure of the woman he had loved for over fifty years.

Reaching behind him, he drew the automatic pistol from the waistband of his trousers and, aiming very carefully, he shot his wife in the back of the head. He then walked into the sitting room, leaving his wife in a pool of blood on the floor. Seating himself in his favourite chair, he looked round the room, memories flooding back to him.

He looked down into his lap and saw that he was still holding the pistol. Almost absentmindedly, he lifted his hand and placed the barrel of the pistol in his mouth and pulled the trigger.

Two hours later, the heavily armed 'snatch' squad which had been despatched to arrest a very wanted terrorist, found only two very dead old people.

# CHAPTER 59

'I have been lain here whilst you have been gallivanting around town having fun,' moaned Lord Hamilton, as he addressed Richard from his hospital bed. His injuries were bandaged, but judging from his general condition, he was on the mend.

'You save your strength, my Lord,' replied Richard as he handed his friend a large box of chocolates, which were immediately confiscated by a nurse hovering close by, like a mother hen looking after its chick. 'There is still a lot of work to be done.'

'How can I build up my strength, when sustenance is ripped from my very grasp.' This comment was greeted by the same nurse cheekily sticking out her tongue.

Richard laughed at this exchange of frivolities, only too glad to see his old friend well on the way to recovery. 'When you two have finished, we have things to discuss, which cannot wait.'

The nurse left the room, taking the box of chocolates with her. Lord Hamilton arranged himself more comfortably in his bed and without further ado, asked Richard what had been happening since he was attacked by Mansour. Richard quickly brought him up to date, seeing his friends eyes darken and his face take on a grim expression as Richard gave him the latest casualty figures. 'More than a million dead throughout Europe, and for what? A depraved mans' dream. Throughout history there have always been such persons and I do not expect he will be the last. Thank goodness they did not get their hands on our nuclear stocks. I would hate to think of what could have occurred if that should have happened.'

'There is still a lot of clearing up to do,' said Richard, 'as there are pockets of resistance in several countries still. They are slowly but surely being winkled out.'

'From what you tell me, it could well be a fight to the death in most cases,' said the Home Secretary, looking intently into Richard's face, noticing the dark bags under his eyes and the new stress lines around his mouth. 'You should be in bed, you know.'

'There will be time for bed when this little lot is over. Before coming here, I made yet another television broadcast, aimed directly at those misguided killers. I told them that they can fight to the death or that they can surrender and die a little later.'

'You can't say things like that, Richard,' admonished the judge, 'where is your sense of Justice? You would be immediately over-ruled by any Appeal Court.'

'When that bomb exploded in Versailles, that was taken as a declaration of war. Whilst they were killing and maiming, raping and robbing, these so called terrorists were in their element. Now they have been shown what their future is, they are far less vociferous. They will get a fair trial, but before a military court, with no press or public present.'

'You feel that this is the best way to deal with them? Surely, if we search, we can find alternatives,' said Lord Hamilton, a little shocked by Richard's no nonsense approach as to the fate of possibly several thousand young people.

'My Lord, the reason this happened in the first place is because the Council, were under the illusion that Europe had become a soft touch and was there for the taking. It was not an illusion, it was a reality. They had studied decisions made in Europe which they took to be signs of weakness and decided to play on that weakness. When one looks at some of these decisions, made by persons who have lived so long on hedonistic plateaus that they are completely devoid of all sense of reality, one can begin to understand how the Islamists came to their decisions.

Numerically, they were at an advantage and their surprise attack would have succeeded had we not been forewarned and able to organise to some extent. Even then, it was touch and go for quite a while out there.'

A long silence followed. Finally, Lord Hamilton said, 'I can see your point, but I cannot see others agreeing with you. People are conditioned today and certainly would not condone what could be construed as legal mass murder.'

'My Lord, throughout Europe there is hardly a single family who has not been touched by the fighting. The media are baying for blood and I for one will give it to them. For years, politicians have kow towed to extremist groups in the hope that by doing so they could remain in power. The vote at eighteen, sex whenever you like, punish parents who physically punish their children, court sentences so lenient as to be laughable and so on and so on. Nearly everyone of those terrorists in custody is British born and bred. Imagine!

They have received an education, they have been molly coddled from birth by a welfare state that had lost all direction, and during all this time, in the name of religion, they have been actively plotting. The old adage, 'live by the sword and die by the sword' could have been written with this scenario in mind.'

Richard then produced a copy of one of the National newspapers bearing the title, 'Rid us of these animals.' The story continued by saying that the public wanted retribution and would have it by one means or another. 'My only comment on this article, is the insult to animals, as I know of no animal that could or would behave in such a way.'

'You have changed, Richard,' said Lord Hamilton, 'in a way that I would never have thought possible. You are harder yet seem more sophisticated then before. Your demeanour is now such that you command respect when you speak, and what you say makes a lot of sense. Of course you are right. Perhaps they are fairly young, but they and they alone, made the transition from youth to terrorists. As you say, if they had won, what would have happened? I for one am too old to learn another religion.'

'Unfortunately, in their case, religion was not a cause but an excuse. It will be hard on their families, but there again many of those families are not free from blame. However, your old friend, the retired diplomat, has come to terms with the loss of his son and has actually thanked me for the fact the other son was in prison and therefore was saved from participating in what has taken place.'

'What are your present plans, Richard? Life goes on and we are like a rudderless ship without a crew.'

'The doctors tell me that you will be out of here inside forty eight hours. I am planning on calling together all the chaps that were on the boat with us, plus those from the smaller countries who took command so brilliantly at such short notice. I will require your presence as well, for you have the age and experience to help in what must be a rebuilding of Europe.'

Chuckling, Lord Hamilton said, 'You have even started to speak like a politician, one third stick, one third carrot and one third bullshit. Of course I will be with you, it may keep Altzheimers away a bit longer. Where are you holding this meeting of yours?'

'Her Majesty has kindly loaned us Windsor Castle, and I naturally accepted.'

'You have seen Her Majesty. What did she have to say about this little lot.'

'It was very strange to receive a summons to Buckingham Palace. What an extraordinary lady she is. Wanted to know to the last detail what had caused this emergency, what we had done about it and what we intended to do in the future.

She has offered any assistance we may require and she even asked after you and your health.'

'You surprise me more each time you open your mouth. What did you tell her?'

Suppressing a smile, Richard replied, 'The truth, the whole truth and nothing but the truth. Seriously, she wanted to know the whole thing with nothing left out. It made me realise just how much we take for granted in our day to day lives, whilst Her Majesty, in her own way, keeps her finger on the Nations pulse.

As I spoke with her, I was thinking of how she had lived through the Second World War, the loss of the Empire, the Falklands and all the other skirmishes big and small, yet she has retained her dignity in spite of the many and varied attacks on her and her family over the years. She has assured me of her continuing support and will offer whatever help is needed in the rebuilding of the Country and indeed of Europe.'

'When will you organise this little get together,' asked Lord Hamilton, and Richard replied that arrangements had been made for four days hence.

'Better start getting myself together, in that case. Are we all staying in the Castle?'

'Certainly are. We even have the President and his Council under lock and key there. I could not believe the accommodation. There again, I suppose Her Majesty may have loaned us The Tower if I had asked.'

With that, Richard took his leave, his mind already racing ahead to the following week and the forthcoming meeting at Windsor Castle.

Barbara was waiting for him at the Castle, accompanied by a younger woman. 'Richard, this is my niece, Hazel, from America. She came across to study English, but in effect is a very competent secretary in her home Country. Would it be inconvenient if she was to sit with me to assist when the meetings start. I could use the help.'

Shaking hands, Richard looked at Hazel, saying, 'You Americans have been trying to speak English for nearly three hundred years, but you still have not quite managed it. However, it is nice to see that at least one of the 300 million American citizens are making the effort and of course she may assist you. Do not forget to put her name on the wages list.'

# CHAPTER 60

During the ensuing days, Richard met many times with his friends and colleagues, where all aspects of what and could be done was discussed. Many retired politicians came forward offering their help, but each was thanked and told that for the moment their services would not be needed.

It was announced that a television broadcast, covering the discussions and the various decisions made, would take place at eight o'clock in the evening, the following Wednesday.

On the Monday before the proposed television broadcast, Richard was working with Michel Polidor on proposed plans to draw up a European Police Force.

They were interrupted by an aide, who stated that a Judge of the European Courts Human Rights, would like a few words. Indicating that he should enter, Richard and Michel moved from their paper strewn table to a more comfortable area, in front of a roaring log fire.

After shaking hands, Richard proposed a drink, where upon the Judge refused, saying, 'I only drink with people I like and respect, so therefore I cannot possibly drink with you.'

Taken aback, Michel and Richard stared at each other.

'I do not know,' continued the Judge, 'what you were thinking, when you blandly announced the other evening that in all probability, your prisoners would be executed. You cannot treat them like that, they have rights. With your approach you will destroy everything we have been working on for an equitable Justice.'

This time, Richard was ready. 'Do you realise that you and others who think like you, are probably responsible for what has happened recently in Europe. You speak of human rights, but what of the victims rights? For years you and your fellow Judges have made decisions, each more ridiculous than the one before. Practically without exception, your findings were always for the appellant and you were normally supported by weak politicians, who were only interested in their own advancement.

You do not seem to realise that Europe has under gone changes these last few days. Until such time as elections can be held, we, the European Council, will be running things. I have already stated that Military Tribunals will be the Judges of these young people, and all those found guilty, will be executed unless there are far reaching reasons for them to be reprieved. We have already re-instated the death penalty for ALL war crimes. Does that satisfy you?'

'It is criminal, I will stop you,' screamed the Judge, and Richard, non plussed said, 'How? I have just told you that things are changing and you and your so called Courts of Human Rights, have been put onto such a long back burner, that you can consider yourselves retired or unemployed. Now please excuse us as we have important work to do.'

Ringing for an aide, Richard said, 'Show this gentleman out please and, if he is interested, you may show him the forthcoming propositions for the dispensation of Justice in the New Europe.'

After he had left, Michel burst into laughter. 'Did you see his face. If only I had had a camera. I think that is possibly the first time he has been spoken to in that manner.'

'He should have stayed in his Ivory Tower,' replied Richard. 'A new broom sweeps clean and our new broom will leave things glistening.'

For Richard, time just flashed by, in a haze of meetings, arguments and excellent meals, the mealtimes also being shouting matches, as various ideas were put forward and accepted or rejected.

At 8pm. the whole of Europe was tuned in to listen to what had been decided and how those decisions would affect their lives. The opening scene showed Richard, together with his friends and colleagues seated at a raised dais in the Castle banqueting hall. Lord Hamilton was seated to Richard's right.

'Tonight,' began Richard, remaining seated, 'is the first day of a new era. Owing to circumstances out of our control, and which were thrust upon us with such speed that we were fortunate to come out vainquers, we now find ourselves in a unique situation.

Each country in the European Union has lost its Government, and Europe has lost its Ministers and deputies. Elections can be held, but they would take time to prepare and time is something we do not have in abundance. Here, therefore, is what we propose for the following six months.'

Richard paused and looked to his right. The television camera followed his gaze, and the viewers were rewarded by the sight of forty nine manacled persons, accompanied by heavily armed guards, shuffle into the hall. When they were all arraigned before the dais, Richard once again addressed the camera.

'Before you, you see the persons responsible for what took place a few days ago. All those deaths and injuries were ordered by this man,' and the camera panned onto the face of the President. 'World domination was his aim, nothing more, nothing less. I fervently hope that this is the last time you have to look upon this face, at least while the body that supports it, is still alive. What we must do is ensure that nothing like this happens again.'

Here he paused and allowed the camera to slowly pass and identify each of the Council, the television presenter filling in with a short history of each.

When this presentation was finished, Richard once again addressed the camera.

'Before these persons are returned to their cells I would like them to hear what their actions have forced upon us. Since the formation of the European Union, in spite of many and varied efforts, unity was never found, owing to various countries being unable to accept others as equals. Thanks to these persons, their actions have succeeded where all else had previously failed. Today, I can say on behalf of us all that the European Union, including Turkey, has been soldered into a single unity owing to the exceptional circumstances that were thrust upon us.

However, I hope you will excuse me if I do not thank them. Now,' he said, addressing the armed guards, 'would you please return these persons to their accomodation,' and the prisoners were led away to return to the dungeons where they were being held.

'At this point,' said Richard, 'each Country will now be addressed by one of their fellow countrymen, seated beside me. As I have stated, Europe is now bonded together by circumstances and blood, as many have suffered heavily. We hope that the future will bring us even closer together, after ratification of the few decisions we have already made.'

The television screens went blank throughout Europe, as each country prepared its own broadcast. When normal viewing was resumed, only Richard and Lord Hamilton were left seated on the dais.

'I am now addressing you, not as a Nation, but as millions of individuals, of many colours and creeds, who make up this wonderful Nation of ours. Before continuing I would like you all to bear with me a few minutes longer.'

Once again, Richard looked to his right, and the camera followed. A door opened and in walked six very smartly dressed men, of both Asian and Arab roots. They walked smartly and all stopped in front of Richard, but facing the camera.

Richard stood, descended the dais, and joined the line of six. With a voice charged with emotion he said, 'These men are six of the many who put their lives on the line for us all. I gave them each a job to do, that job being to mingle with those responsible for what has torn our families apart, in an effort to ascertain what was planned.

Unfortunately, they were unable to predict the murderous explosion which tore the heart out of our Governments, but they did, at enormous risk to themselves, manage to integrate to such a degree, that we were able to put certain measures into force and we were ready when the attack came. In spite of that, it was a mixture of good planning with a measure of good luck. I love each and everyone of them like a brother and I would like you, sitting in your homes, to applaud them. They will hear you I am sure.'

He then embraced each man in turn. After the final embrace, he once again signalled to his right and the same door opened. This time, six men of Asian or Arab descent, but dressed in prison garb and wearing manacles, were escorted into the room and made to stand facing the camera, which slowly moved along the line, showing each face in detail.

'I am sorry if anyone out there is embarrassed by the sight of a loved one amongst these six, but they were selected at random. What do you see? Examine them, compare them with my friends, and tell me what you see.'

The camera then showed the faces in comparison with the six members of Richard's workforce. 'What you see is that they are very similar in colour, age and build. What differentiates them, is inside their skulls. We are now embarking on a fantastic journey together and there will no room for people who harbour racial hatreds or who judge people by the colour of their skin. Everyone should and hopefully will be, judged on their behaviour and their actions. Try to guard this image in your minds if you can, for you will find, as I have done, that there are some really great people out there, who are just waiting for the chance to prove themselves.'

The six prisoners were led away, whilst the other six took seats alongside Lord Hamilton on the dais. Lord Hamilton rose to his feet and addressed the camera.

'I endorse wholeheartedly, the sentiments of Richard Grant. I have known him for years and had always liked and admired him, but even I am flabbergasted at what he has achieved with his fellow Police and Army colleagues throughout Europe. You are all aware of the huge, personal loss he sustained at the hands of these so-called terrorists, but I have never heard him utter a single word which could be described as racial. He has always conducted himself with honour and I am pleased to be his friend.'

Lord Hamilton paused, to wipe sweat from his face, caused by the heat of the television lights. 'I also owe him my life as I was to be forced to make a statement urging you all to offer no resistance to the terrorists, and in order to try to force me, I was very badly beaten. Fortunately, Richard arrived in time and all that is now history, but at least I have managed to tell you all what a truly great chap he is.

He has asked me to make the following address. Will all patriotic persons, having known and proven skills in commerce, banking or with International business experience, please make themselves available at the Royal Albert Hall, in London in two days time. You will be joined by senior members of the Civil Service and certain propositions will be made to you by myself and Mr. Grant.'

With that he joined Richard and the camera captured their expressions beautifully, as the programme ended.

# CHAPTER 61

At eight in the morning, two days after the television programme, Richard and Lord Hamilton arrived at the performers entrance to the Royal Albert Hall. 'I'll feel such a prat if no one turns up,' said Richard looking to his old friend for support.

Lord Hamilton, who had been in touch daily with a number of senior civil servants, allowed a small smile to play along his lips, but did not reply.

The two men walked along the corridor leading to the stage and could hear the sound of voices.

'Silence please,' called a loud voice and as Richard and Lord Hamilton arrived on the stage, a sustained burst of applause rang out from the hands of over a thousand men and women gathered there.

'Good gracious, where did all this lot come from?' exclaimed Richard, as the applause continued.

'My civil service team have been working twentyfour hours a day making up lists of patriots. This is, in their minds, the best of the applicants but I am assured there were many, many more who wanted to be here today.'

As his eyes adjusted to the lights, Richard managed to identify many of the faces beaming up at him. Captains of industry, self made billionaires, presidents of most of the major banks and finance houses, all people who rarely breathed the same air as common folk, were all jostling each other, trying to reach out and shake hands with Richard and Lord Hamilton.

Finally, after much shouting for order, the noise died down and Richard walked to a table which had been placed in the centre of the stage and took one of the two chairs, Lord Hamilton taking the other. 'Please be seated,' said Richard.

When everyone was seated, Richard rose to his feet and, on approaching the microphone, said, 'The lady seated to my right is the most important person in my working life, my secretary, Barbara.' A burst of laughter followed this remark.

'I see we are at least in agreement on what is the most important thing in a busy mans' life,' this remark bringing further laughter. 'If all subsequent agreements are as easy to follow, this should be a doddle.'

Richard waited until the laughter had died down and then addressed the audience. 'Now to the serious bits. You are all aware of the dangerous situation facing us here and indeed everyone in the European Union. No country can exist as a coherent entity, without some form of control or government. It is not possible to hold any form of election at the moment and so therefore we must find a substitute way of doing things. This is our plan and I must ask you to bear in mind that it was formulated by a bunch of police and army officers. Our plan is a unaminous one. There was much discussion, many arguments, but no blows were struck and we even managed to have a drink together afterwards. The main thing is, we are still friends and colleagues and can count on each other at all times.'

Absolute silence reigned as the persons gathered there waited to hear what was to be proposed. Richard reached into his pocket and took out a sheaf of papers which he studied, before continuing.

'In short, our idea is this. We, my friends and I, will look after all problems relating to law and order, national and international security and any day to day problems as they occur. Diplomatic problems are a different kettle of fish, but we will undoubtedly be helped by the Civil Service, present here today.

I can see you are all thinking, 'What does he want us to do?' so I shall tell you. I want you to run, not only the Country, but, with the aid of others like you throughout Europe, the whole of the European Union as an enormous commercial concern.' Immediately, discussions started all over the Hall and Richard called for silence.

'Please hear me out as I believe, as do my colleagues, that this plan is feasible, but will only work if you people can make it work. Now most of you know each other, your strengths and your weaknesses and what we would like you to do is join us in this adventure to make Europe great. You will have a free hand, within reason of course,' he added, as he noticed various people passing knowing glances, 'and naturally you will be recompensed for the work you do.

It would be easier for us if you were to work full time, but if you think you should keep your present positions as well as working for the common good, then so be it. We would like you to form yourselves into groups, those groups being made up of people with acumen in similar fields. Europe will be your oyster. Using all and every natural resource in Europe, using all available skills in every field, including manufacturing, technology and services, coupling all that with export markets as well as home consumers, we estimate that should generate great wealth for Europe.

In addition, and this will undoubtedly be a new one for all of you, consideration must and will be given to each and every individual in Europe. Therefore in your plans and calculations, you must include provisions for all types of public spending, health requirements, pensions, unemployment payments and so on and so on.

Are there any questions?'

Immediately a babble of voices was raised, and Richard seated himself. Lord Hamilton rose to his feet, and after calling for order, he said, 'This is as good a moment as any for a short break. Refreshments will be provided and we ask you to take this time to formulate any questions which you would like answering today.

As you can appreciate, this day is the first of many and the only thing I will ask of you is not to discuss with persons outside of this hall, what has been discussed today.'

With that, Richard and Lord Hamilton left the stage, going to the 'Stars' dressing room, where refreshments had been made available for them.

After sampling the tea and excellent sandwiches, Lord Hamilton said, 'What do you make of it?'

Richard did not reply as he slowly chewed on a ham and cheese sandwich.

Washing the sandwich down with a mouthful of tea, he said, 'I think we have their attention, but will they buy it? Tell me, did you notice that there are several very colourful characters out there, not at all what I would have thought as patriots,' chuckled Richard.

'Before this day is out, I am sure we are going to have a whole bag of surprises. Just goes to show you cannot judge people on their exteriors. But there again, you have already given that demonstration,' said Lord Hamilton, referring to the television broadcast two days earlier.

'Think I'll have a little snooze,' said Lord Hamilton, and Richard left him in order to visit the bathroom to freshen up for the second part of this historic day.

Forty five minutes later, the two men returned to the main hall. Waiting by their table was Sir Peter Hall, a retired diplomat and lifelong friend of Lord Hamilton. Handing a sheet of paper to Richard he said, 'Mr. Grant, here is a list of some five questions. Four of them are composites, as many questions were asked of a similar nature and I took the liberty of re-phrasing them into one pertinent question. The first question was asked, and Lord Hamilton suggested that you would probably like to deal with that one first.'

Richard glanced at the paper, scowling as he read the first question. Returning the paper to Sir Peter he said, 'Perhaps you could do the honours by reading out the questions on behalf of our audience.'

Calling for silence, Sir Peter waited until everyone was settled then said, 'The first question is, 'Are you not afraid that we may take advantage of you in order to fill our own pockets?'

A murmuring ran round the room.

Richard waited for silence, then stared out at all the faces in front of him. 'I do not know if that question was meant as a joke, but I for one, am not laughing. I would ask the person or persons responsible for that question to leave this hall, as there is no place here for you.'

With that he stood back and observed his audience looking around to see who was the guilty party. Finally, a well known City figure got to his feet and walked away, mumbling to himself. 'Now, perhaps we can get on with the very important business in hand,' said Richard, with a relieved sigh.

The questions were answered, one after the other. Richard explained in general terms what he required. 'I have been an admirer of the Google type of management,' said Richard. 'I find it appealing to have these brain storming sessions in which everyone gets to have his say. You are all very intelligent, experienced people, and I am sure that as you get to know each other better, the ideas and the information will start to flow. Imagine, if you can everyone sitting in open ended offices, with ever open doors, so that members of other groups can visit to pick brains or make suggestions.'

Here he was interrupted by a voice saying, 'Question'.

'Ask away,' replied Richard and a well known male voice said, 'There must be someone in charge. Cabinet Ministers are necessary to make the decisions and the important announcements. How do you see that happening in your system.'

Richard smiled broadly. 'Nothing easier. You are all experts in your fields and experienced to boot. You will all be of the same rank so whoever is available can do the job of Minister. However, if any group would prefer to have a spokesman, that will be for you to decide. Similarly, when it is necessary to meet with visiting Ministers, whether here or overseas, the same rules apply. What we want are results and we are convinced that with the right mental approach we can do magic together.'

Another voice called up. 'Under the old system, we were often restrained from advancing too quickly, as the politicians needed time to assimilate and in some cases, look to their proper interests, which quite often influenced final decisions.'

'That will not happen here,' said Richard firmly, 'as any person caught putting his own interests before Europes, will be dealt very short shrift. I have always been disgusted by the actions of politicians, who, after enjoying high office, leave to make fortunes by 'advising' those persons who they were fortunate to come into contact with during their service to the Country.'

'Are you saying that retired politicians should not work in other fields? That seems a bit drastic to me,' shouted yet another voice.

'Not at all,' replied Richard. Everyone has the right to work and make fortunes if they can. However, when I see persons who have held high office and have mixed with the Worlds movers and shakers, then somewhere along the line one must consider the ethics and morality. When I see, as you have all obviously seen, a person in such a position, blatantly co-operating with persons who were and still are enemies of this Country, in order to make millions for himself, then I say 'Stop.'

In all such cases I ask the same question. Who is saying what to whom and who is paying whom for what?'

Richard then ended the meeting, saying that he hoped, that before leaving the hall, those present, with the help of the Civil Service, sort themselves into working groups and make arrangements for future meetings to be held on a daily basis in order that the various groups could start working as quickly as possible.

With that he thanked them for their attendance that day, telling them all how much he was looking forward to future collaboration.

Finally, Richard found himself seated at the side of his friend on the drive back to Windsor Castle. 'Went well, I thought,' said Lord Hamilton. 'I was right about you, you have that certain thing that commands respect and I for one am thankful that you will be running Europe.'

Richard burst out laughing. 'That's a good one. There's no chance of that. I'm a lawman and that's it.'

'Oh, you poor deluded fool. You have made this bed and you will now lay in it. There are millions of Europeans who will be sleeping better this night, knowing that you are in charge. You may not have wanted it, but you've got it and I for one, am extremely pleased.'

The car arrived at Windsor Castle and both men, tired but content, took an early supper. 'Be good to get a good nights sleep' said Lord Hamilton, 'and it will do you good too. So I wish you a very good night.'

He rose to leave the room and Richard said, 'Enjoy it. I've got to give the keys back tomorrow.'

Laughing to himself, Lord Hamilton left the room, followed several seconds later by Richard.

He entered his suite of rooms and poured himself a mammoth whisky. Going across to his music centre he selected a Roy Orbison disc and settled himself in his favourite armchair, letting the music and the whisky do their magic.

Much later, slightly drunk, he stripped and tumbled into bed, the sound of 'In dreams' playing in his head. He snuggled down into the bed, feeling his eyes start to water with the famous lyrics.

'In dreams I walk with you, in dreams I talk to you, In dreams you're mine, all the time . . . . As his water filled eyes started to close he was certain he could feel Susan's arms close around him and her soft breath whispering, 'Go to sleep everything is all right.'

THE END